The Funeral Girl
stories

Don Hough

20/40 Press

Also by Don Hough

Guilty Schmilty
Cigarette Breaks

First paperback edition: July 2017
Second paperback edition: May 2023

"The Funeral Girl," "The Utility Knife," and parts of "The Devil" were originally published in *The Thirties.*

"Malia," "Melissa," "Sarah A.," "Hannah," "Lindsay," "Stephanie," and "Andrea" were originally published in *Hungry in Her World.*

These stories are 100 percent fictional. Some of them project the names of "real" public figures onto made-up characters in made-up circumstances. Where the names of corporate, media, or political figures are used here, those names are meant only to denote figures, images, the stuff of collective dreams; they do not denote, or pretend to private information about, actual 3-D persons, living, dead, or otherwise.

https://donhoughauthor.blogspot.com/

Thanks and Acknowledgment to:
Jim Driscoll
Rebecca Cross
Nick Cate
Jason Webster
Sarah Stewart Taylor and the WRJ Writer's Center
Amber Rose Crowtree

ISBN: 9781541008557

10 9 8 7 6 5 4 3 2 1

For Tony Hill

and all the real girls

CONTENTS

POOR BOY

A KNOCK ON THE DOOR. Mark gets up, happy for the distraction. He has been watching TV all evening, something he doesn't often do. He's been curious about the supposed influx of quality programming on the air these days, the best it's ever been some say. *The* storytelling medium of the hour (half-hour for sitcoms), sucking all the talent in, writers and actors and directors working with record advertising dollars to produce ultra-high-quality shows, effecting a veritable renaissance in televised entertainment, broadcast to millions every night, a steadily increasing percentage of whom are watching in high definition. Books, music, movies: they have all been usurped by TV, exposed as the time-wasters they have always been—a judgment ratified by the viewing public. Which all looks good in print, but Mark's first-hand experience has left him unimpressed. He's resorted to flipping channels, trying to find something worth giving his attention to for more than ten seconds, a predicament not dissimilar to when he last tried to watch some TV roughly two years ago. This has caused him some consternation; *Am I missing something?* he thinks. *Can thirty million Americans be wrong? (Then again, fifty million Americans are wrong every four years.)* (He likes to think parenthetically every now and then.) Each channel-change has furthered his dismay and he's been getting downright depressed as he hits the quadruple-digits, which are full of the type of programming one would be hard pressed to imagine three people watching, let alone thirty million. Super-niche shows like "Mastering the Philips Head" (The Tools & Hardware Channel) and "Following Farmhands" (24/7 Reality) and

"Perfect Strangers" (Sitcom Television Daily). Depression, dismay, disconsolation. *(A real word?* Mark wonders. *Or just a real idea?)* Then: the door knock. Just what the doctor ordered, in Mark's book.

With a sigh of relief, he bounds to the door and opens it. There's a man standing there. He looks surprised.

"Hi," the man says.

"Hi," says Mark.

Now the man looks nonplussed. "Um," he says. He takes a step back and looks at the doorway, then glances at the adjacent doors on both sides, as if trying to get his bearings. He looks at Mark apologetically. "I think I got the wrong place," he says.

"That's ok." Mark moves to close the door.

"Wait," the man says, reaching out to stop the door from shutting. Mark has that undefined expression on his face that people get right before it turns really quizzical. The man, wearing a sheepish grin, thrusts his hand out in the offering of a handshake. "I'm Lester."

Mark tentatively takes the proffered hand. "Hi Lester."

Lester takes a deliberate breath before saying, "I'm actually looking for your wife."

"Oh," says Mark. He opens the door wide and lets Lester in. "She's in the kitchen." Pointing: "Through there."

Lester nods and walks down the hallway. Mark returns to the recliner and groans when he remembers what he's been doing. The knock on the door was not diversionary enough, not by far. *Maybe,* Mark thinks, *maybe this thing is actually more entertaining shut off.* Mark presses the POWER button on the remote and stares at the blank screen for a second before turning the set back on. *Ok, that was ridiculous,* he thinks. *SOMEthing, ANYthing is better than NOthing.*

He hears a pair of voices accompanying the smells of cooking food wafting from the kitchen. He's not the type of person who eavesdrops, but the TV has landed on a live broadcast of a memorial service so everything has suddenly gotten very quiet. He hears his wife say, "You told him your *name??*" and Lester say, "Might as well babe, I'd say the jig is up."

The next channel is an international basketball game and the sounds of cheering and screaming drown out the conversation in the kitchen. This actually holds Mark's attention for a bit, more because of the ecstasy of the crowd than the actual game. *Enthusiasm is always nice to see,* he reflects, *almost regardless of what it's about.*

From his vantage point in the recliner, Mark can see through the hallway into part of the kitchen. He catches glimpses of his wife and Lester, their bodies momentarily blocking and unblocking his view of the sink and since this is more visually interesting than what is on TV right now, he concentrates his gaze toward the kitchen. They're walking back and forth, back and forth, just beyond the entrance of the kitchen, one following the other, back and forth, seemingly at a regular interval, like some entity was juggling them on the x-axis. Finally, his wife stops to wash something in the sink, affording Mark a prolonged, unobstructed view of her back. He picks apart the details in a dispassionate analytical exercise: the long chestnut hair, the slender, lithe figure, the sensible attire. She turns her head and he watches her smile at something out of view. Her smile makes him smile. That's always been the case for as long as they've known each other. He's amazed that her smile still has the power to do that, make him smile, even though they've been married for thirteen long months.

Mark wakes up in the morning, groggy and sleep-deprived. The previous night had been long; Lester just wouldn't leave. He had stayed through dinner and proceeded to raid the wine rack, all the while talking and laughing and thoroughly enjoying himself. Mark spent the night with a frozen smile on his face, determined to play polite host, a task made that much more onerous by Lester's insistence on playing impudent guest.

Mark tried to surreptitiously send signals to his wife, to wordlessly formulate a plan with her, to secretly coordinate their efforts toward the goal they both surely shared: the expulsion of an unwanted party. But her eyes rarely met his throughout the evening. She was so much better at being polite, concealing her true feelings when it was expedient. Even her smiles looked genuine. Soon, she started to drink as heavily as Lester, which Mark took as a sign of her resignation with the unfortunate situation they found themselves in. Mark, not much of a drinker, had one small glass of wine. Lester took to quaffing straight out of the bottles, passing them off to Mark's wife when they were nearly empty. Both of them found this extremely amusing. Mark stayed up for as long as he could stand it, then excused himself as apologetically and unobtrusively as he could, citing an early start to the next day. Lester nodded distractedly at him—no water off his back for he had barely said three words to Mark after their little exchange at the door. Mark went over to his wife, bent down to kiss her on the cheek, and whispered "Thank you" in her ear. She looked at him for a second and it was as if she was seeing him for the first time all night. Mark then went to the bathroom, flossed, brushed his teeth, and rinsed. On his way to the bedroom, he looked into the living room and saw his wife laughing and putting up such a good front. What a wife—what other wife would sacrifice her evening humoring an obnoxious guest so her husband could relax and not have to deal with it and get some sleep. He wrapped himself up in the comforter and clutched the pillow beneath his head. He fell asleep to the sound of his wife's laughter, with a smile on his face.

After he wakes up, the fifth thing he notices is that his wife is not beside him in bed. (This morning's initial thought process: *Ugh...who am I?(1) ... uhr ... oo ... so tired(2)...coffee(3)... mmm ... what a weird dream; being president felt so natural(4) ... hmmm ... where is she?(5))* He staggers out of bed into the living room. It's trashed, empty wine bottles everywhere. This is not a sight that Mark is used to seeing and it's been undoubtedly precipitated by that Lester guy. He is the first Lester that Mark has met in a while—if not the first ever—and Mark resolves right then to give all the Lesters he meets henceforth a wide berth. *Ok, maybe that's a little extreme,* he thinks. *It'll be enough to avoid just the one particular Lester that trashed the living room.*

Isn't that always the way, Mark continues to think. *Nights are when inhibitions are dropped and anything goes, and in the morning, retrospection (word? idea? both?) and regret kick in and we're ready to abjure everything and everyone.*

Now where's the coffee?

He goes into the kitchen and starts the brew cycle, which for him is a seven-minute prison sentence; he is unable to leave the confines of the room or do anything but sit right next to the coffee maker, a paralysis from which he is freed only when the last bit of water percolates through the filter. He can't even *think* of doing anything else until he's had that first cup—why would he want to anyway? Seemed like too much work, thinking. Before that first cup, that is.

With a cup of steaming rejuvenation securely in hand, Mark surveys the living room. Upon closer inspection, the room actually doesn't look too bad. Messy, to be sure, but lived in, strangely homey. The decor is full of squares and rectangles, including a simple, almost austere coffee table, a nightstand, a sofa, and a settee . . . a forbidding set-up all told. Everything's either gray or black, from the low-pile carpet to the antimacassars. It's as if the entire room is covered in a fuliginous patina. It's a little depressing, actually. It's always kept neat, though, which Mark knows is more the result of laziness than effort. Mark hardly uses the room and his wife only sits in here to read or watch TV—in equal measure, as if she hasn't yet decided which is less of a time-waster. They don't really host many get-togethers and when they do, everyone tends to congregate in the kitchen, drawn to the true attraction of their home. (Mark's wife is an excellent cook.) So the current disarray in the living room actually has an ameliorative effect on its usual dour atmosphere, softening the sharp edges of the decorative scheme and providing evidence of habitation, completing the room in a weird way. It's still a complete trash heap though. Mark sits on it a bit and decides to use the energy the coffee is giving him to pick up the room a little. *Much better to be clean than dirty,* he figures. And besides, every bottle he places in the garbage bag makes him smile, for each one increases the chance that his wife wasn't totally bored last night.

He leaves the apartment at the same time he usually does on a Monday, buttoning up his duster as he walks. It's cold outside but not frigidly so; there's none of the wind that slices into exposed skin, and the temperature is hovering above the point where you can't breathe in without freezing the mucus in your nose. Unseen birds are chirping away obliviously—somewhat mockingly—up in the bare trees somewhere. The sky is overcast, threatening some form of precipitation. Rain would wash away the coating of extant snow from the flurry that had ensured a somewhat anemic white Christmas; more snow would bring out the shovels and prolong everyone's search for brown earth. There's a faint burning smell, the kind that immediately evokes an image of wilderness settlements, which gives the impression that the source of the smell must be incredibly far away when, really, it just can't be that far at all.

Mark walks down the steps of the stoop and has almost cleared the parking lot when he notices their car is still in its designated spot. The sight of the car, which his wife always uses every morning to drive into work, gives him pause. He doesn't get worried—there's no reason for that. He had peripherally noticed before walking out the door that his wife's purse and keys (usually placed on a small table in the hallway) and her coat and hat (always hung up on hooks beside the door at the end of the day when she gets home) were all gone, which was customary this time of day. She *must* have gone to work. Taking that as a given, Mark is, more than anything, left confused. His mind cycles through a half-dozen explanations before settling on the most plausible: she got a ride to work. Which would certainly be out of the ordinary, but it's the best he can come up with. A stray thought of Lester actually comforts him—maybe he took her to work as some sort of recompense for draining their liquor and trashing their home. Mark doesn't bother thinking of what possible benefit his wife would get from being driven to work; in fact, it seems more an inconvenience—now she has to find a ride home. But any more pondering would make Mark late for work, so he lets it lie. The only other thing he wonders is whether he should take the usually claimed car—the only one they own—to work himself, but he dismisses the idea when he considers the possibility that his wife just went for a quick stroll and would be back before long to drive to work for a truncated shift after taking a much-deserved personal half-day for herself. And even though there are at least five scenarios more plausible than that one, the thought of the look on his wife's face when she returns from her walk (if that is in fact what she did) and finds the car missing makes Mark start walking to work without further delay.

He walks down the street—Green Street—at a brisk pace. He lives in a moderately dense residential area with modest-sized houses lining both sides of the street every few dozen feet, most of them separated by picket fences enclosing not very large lawns. A lot of the houses have some sort of Christmas decorations; when Mark walks home at night, most of his way is illuminated by blinking primary-colored lights.

After a few blocks, he takes a left and walks alongside Eric Road. The road ends after about half a mile, intersecting Sand Hill Road. At the corner of Eric and Sand Hill is a grandiose house that never fails to win the tacit neighborhood contest for Most Impressive Decorative Christmas Display. No one else comes close. This place pulls out all the stops: over-sized snow globes; life-size Santa gnome with regiment of elves; lights everywhere—most of them twinkling asynchronously and some of them programmed to spell out holiday greetings and resolve into Christmas imagery; giant wreaths about ten ft. in diameter hanging between the third story windows that make one wonder how they even got up there; the towering and usually nondescript pine trees framing the house so densely adorned with ornaments, tinsel, garland, etc. that one can only assume that the budget allotted for tree decoration is unlimited; animatronic nativity scene consisting of mobile, seemingly autonomous puppets acting out the birth of our Lord in a 10-minute sketch that gets performed every hour, on the hour, with one perfectly timed shot-off firework to symbolize the guiding star, crescendoing in a soaring choral rendition of "O Holy Night" pumping out of 24-inch speakers; a miniature Polar Express train with single seat compartments that can actually accommodate passengers provided the total load doesn't exceed something like 800 pounds, chugging its way all around the house; and even snow-generating machines that keep the tableau in Winter Wonderland splendor if the weather isn't cooperating. So yeah, it's no contest really. And the whole thing somewhat miraculously doesn't look cluttered or gaudy. The effect is truly rather majestic, which is at least partly due to the adequate space around the house to work with. Still, the owners must use private contractors or have solid backgrounds in design/architecture/engineering or something because the whole spread is just so awe-inspiring. Mark passes this house every day on his way to work.

Taking a right onto Sand Hill Road, he can never help looking wistfully across the tract of undeveloped land before him. Nine months of the year he would be walking across this patch of barren ground and quickly getting to Frost Street, which basically runs parallel to Sand Hill with this expanse of dirt and weeds between them. Then he would cross Frost Street and walk along Jackson Street, which intersects Frost at a point almost directly south of the point Eric intersects Sand Hill. After a few blocks Jackson runs into Main Street and from there his work is within sight. So normally it would be pretty much a straight shot down to Main Street after taking the left on Eric, but during the winter either an impenetrable wall of snow sprouts up on the neglected field or it turns into an impassable mud pit. Cutting across it shaves about five minutes from his walk—a significant amount of time when his home is no more than two miles from his work as the crow flies—but now he has to circumvent the shortcut-turned-impediment via Sand Hill Road.

As he walks along he sees a USPS truck parked by the curb and the mail carrier a couple houses down, walking up to someone's door. Mark usually sees the mail being delivered somewhere along Sand Hill Road on his way to work. He knows that the truck will follow the path Mark has taken from his home and be at his building in the next thirty minutes. (This is only on weekdays. On Saturday, for some reason, delivery time is variable.) Mark muses on the slight shifting of timetables that would allow him to get his mail before work. It's not possible on his end; if he waited around thirty (or more) minutes for the mail to come he'd be late for work. If, however, the delivery person set out on his route half an hour earlier, it'd all work out. Everything would be perfect.

A couple minutes later, he takes a left onto Silver Street, a short little access road to Frost. Upon reaching Frost, instead of doubling back toward Jackson, he heads in the other direction toward Dixon Lane, a couple blocks down, since Dixon intersects Main Street at a point closer to his work than the end of Jackson. He mentally extends the map a bit, without really meaning to, noting that heading east on Frost past Jackson goes toward Indian Cress Lake. Near the lake is the Indian Cress Lake Cemetery. Frost Road crosses the road outlining the lake —Indian Cress Lake Cemetery Road—bisecting it into north and south sections of the same road. So actually the eponymous cemetery borders only the south part of the road it gives its name to, and there is technically no cemetery at all to be seen on North Indian Cress Lake Cemetery Road. Mark recalls overhearing some younger co-workers a couple years ago joking about the existence of a ghost that haunted the road. It didn't haunt the lake or the cemetery, only the actual road. And only the south part of it, presumably so it could be closer to the cemetery. And while many ghosts haunted the road, this particular ghost being discussed was the most hoary and ancient of them all. And so these co-workers joked that the ghost would find innocent people walking along the road and chase them, and they would run into someone else and shout "Help! I'm being chased by the Old South Indian Cress Lake Cemetery Road Ghost!" and that person would say "You mean *the* Old South Indian Cress Lake Cemetery Road Ghost?" and they would go "Yes! I was walking down South Indian Cress Lake Cemetery Road, minding my own business, when BAM! I run smack into the one and only Old South Indian Cress—" and then the ghost would devour them both. And these co-workers said that that was how the ghost claimed so many victims, because it would take so long for someone to tell others what was going on, the ghost using its own name as a sort of paralyzing device on its victims. Mark smiles at the memory. Considering this happened a while ago and it still induces chuckles, he thinks it's safe to say that he'll always be amused by the road with the needlessly prolix name.

Finally reaching Main Street by way of Dixon, he takes a right even though his work is to the left. He's gotten into the habit of going to a small nearby deli every Monday and ordering the exact same 6-inch ham sub sandwich. He started doing this a few weeks ago. It's the first time he's altered his routine in ages, but it's for a damn good sub.

He enters the deli and sees a girl behind the counter whom he's never seen before. Usually there's a burly guy waiting on everyone.

"Can I help you?" the girl says.

Mark hesitates a moment, then outlines his order to the girl. He likes his food prepared the exact same way every time, and the burly guy has gotten his order down cold. So with this new girl he is extremely wary. He watches the girl prepare his sub and relaxes when he sees that she's making it the same way the regular guy does. As she's putting the finishing touches on his order, his mind wanders a little. *It's funny how subs have all these different names. "Sub" is of course short for "submarine sandwich." Some people also call them hero sandwiches, or heroes. You also hear them referred to as grinders or hoagies. Some people call them blimpies, supposedly.*

The girl wraps up his sandwich. "Anything else?" she asks.

"No," Mark says.

She presses a few buttons on the register. "That'll be three dollars."

Mark freezes. The girl looks expectantly at him, waiting. He clears his throat. "Um," he says, "shouldn't it be four dollars?"

"No," the girl says, drawing out the word as she presses a few more buttons. Mark waits patiently for the corrected price. The girl looks up at him. "Nope," she says resolutely. "Three dollars."

Mark balks. "It's usually four," he says, then adds: "It's *always* four, actually."

The girl remains stubborn. "The register says three," she insists. Seeing Mark struggling, she sighs. "So it's usually four, don't you want a deal?" she queries.

"Look," he finally says, "can I give you four dollars and then can you ask your boss what the correct price is and if I'm wrong you can keep the extra dollar?"

She shakes her head and rolls her eyes. "Fine," she says.

He hands her the money and exits the store, content. He crosses Main Street and heads for work. He can see a line already starting to form for the matinee show. He checks his watch. He is six minutes early. He's usually three to nine minutes early. He's never late. He likes it this way. Maneuvering between the people waiting outside, he enters the theater.

They're also called poor boys.

———

Returning home from work and entering his apartment, Mark remembers that the start of his day had been unusual, and it has become so again. He hadn't thought much about it at work, where everything remained more or less predictable. Even walking up to the building didn't set off any alarms; the car was parked outside, like it usually is. But it takes him entering the apartment to realize it probably never moved from that spot all day. Something is amiss. It takes entering the apartment and not seeing his wife to realize it—to realize that he had expected to see her when he got back, that he never considered the possibility that she wouldn't be here. It takes him coming home to an unoccupied apartment to realize that things are skirting dangerously with being wrong. It takes him realizing that the car hasn't moved an inch and seeing that his wife isn't home like she usually is and that there's a scrap of paper on the table where her purse and keys usually are—a note written in her hand. It takes seeing this note for him to Stop Everything. He hovers above the table, looking down at the note. It's full of jotted words, most of them crossed out, like a grocery list. He picks it up.

> Dear Mark
> Dearest Mark
> I have something to tell you
> By the time you read this
> Let's not make this any
> I'll see you sometime I'm sure,
> Hazel

Mark immediately looks up and finally sees his absent wife, now that he knows she's gone.

THE FUNERAL GIRL

I.

THE METEORIC RISE OF MARY FIELDS that established her as a pop culture icon was as sudden and far-reaching as it was inadvertent. It all started with a low-key and unpublicized post of a video of a funeral service on the internet. All the details of the alfresco ceremony attested to the verisimilitude of the event—the passel of attendees of various ages, the rococo flower arrangements, the burnished casket and velvet-draped bier on which it lay, the uniformly black raiment differing enough in the particulars that it was obvious that each person had picked out his or her own wardrobe and accoutrements, the dolorous ambience that suffused the scene juxtaposed with the incongruous blue sky filled with painterly tufts of cumuli, which somehow seemed right, gorgeous meteorology seeming always to be the backdrop of truly sad events (q.v. the Challenger disaster, the assassination of JFK, 9/11) (but n.b.: when it's not a pluvial mess, cf. Katrina)—so that only the most staunch skeptics could doubt that what they were seeing was an unstaged, genuine, real-life event. The camera was locked on a girl who looked to be in her early twenties standing at a lectern facing most of the bereaved. The impression most people had on their first viewing of the 55-second video was an inappropriate one considering the tableau, but still one could not help

13

thinking that s/he was looking at a very beautiful girl. Not even a "hot" one or an "attractive" one, but just a beauty that blindsides you on occasion, regardless of your preferences. It was not just because of her unblemished, softly tanned skin, and perfect face, and lustrous hair, and doe eyes. It was more than her elegant posture, which connoted an inner strength. It was that the beauty she possessed seemed inviolable. This was a beauty not subordinate to emotion, nor one that needed perfect lighting or perfect makeup or a good night's sleep or other sets of circumstances conducive to looking one's best in order to shine. Some girls are only pretty when they smile and turn ugly when any flicker of emotion distracts them from trying to look pretty, so essentially they are only beautiful when consciously posing for others. This girl was not one of those girls. This girl had a beauty that was ever-present, always there in any situation, even one as heart-wrenching as a funeral, so that even though the girl was clearly sad and had clearly been crying and feeling those basement-level feelings for at least that entire day, her indelible beauty was still present, whether she wanted it to be or not, and it was not outshining or trumping her grief but existing hand-in-hand, contemporaneously with whatever she was feeling inside, and both her beauty and grief seemed more sublime in each other's presence. Even if you couldn't articulate it quite this way, you felt *something* to this effect, or at least something that was similarly convolved and recondite. And you found yourself wondering why you didn't see more beautiful girls in internet videos, *truly* beautiful girls, as opposed to those who possessed a sort of brummagem type of beauty which required from them effort to maintain, with that effort attenuating any attractiveness they might have possessed. And coming on the heels of this wondering was the first spark of the realization that most girls who put themselves in front of cameras possess that inferior kind of beauty (if they are in possession of any at all), unlike the girl in this video you'd just stumbled upon, this effortlessly beautiful girl standing at a podium at a funeral, who was now clearing her throat, bending forward a bit, and saying into the microphone, clearly and resolutely, "I want a Latino to lick my clitoris." And suddenly you weren't thinking about much at all. You were just watching, very very intently.

II.

There is a tense pause. People are customarily pretty still during obsequies—especially in this video since most of the attendees exist (from the perspective of the camera) only as the backs of their heads, so you can't see their facial expressions or what their hands are doing—and yet still, a lot of these occiputs seem to get downright statuelike. The eyes of a priest standing off to the side narrow but don't seem to comprehend what they are taking in. The girl takes a deep breath and continues, even more firmly than before, reading from a notebook in front of her: "I want to come on a man's face. I want two men to come on my face at the same time. I want to jerk off two guys at once. I want to feel a penis slide against my toes. I want to get my ass tongue-plunged by a lesbian. I want my hot cousin Michael to corner me and ravage me against the wall." Murmurs have been building among the bewildered audience and, at this last asseveration, gasps are audible. There is a jump cut and a couple of people are now at the lectern, one of them trying to drag the girl away from the mic; she's wriggling out of his grasp and shouting "No, get away! Stop!" Another jump cut: others approaching her, beseeching her Mary please stop this craziness. Another splice in the video and she's snapping at the people around her: "I'm not finished! I'm reading the whole thing!" There's an almost hysterical tone to her voice. After a final jump cut, she's calm again, stolidly continuing to read her list of sexual desiderata, now surrounded on both sides by a bunch of people including a bearded man who glares at her viciously and a woman who's so distraught she's shaking. Her oration ends with: "And finally: I want to take part in an orgy, and be penetrated in four orifices at once." The distraught woman yelps as if struck and crumples to the ground, sobbing. The video abruptly ends.

III.

The video quickly went pandemic, becoming one of those things that are endlessly linked to, mentioned on social media, and watched millions of times, presumably by different people. There was a sudden across-the-board awareness of the thing; every type of site from celebrity gossip aggregators to sports news outlets was willing to give it exposure. Discussions proliferated on who this girl was and what in the world she could have been thinking. Armchair MDs spread out a buffet selection of diagnoses (Tourette's, amentia, vascular occlusion to the brain, typical young American girl incorrigibleness, etc.), and, in case she happened to be lurking in the v-mess boards, public forums were deluged with offers to fulfill her wishes. FUNURAL GIRL SEX RANT (along with other iterations of the same video with similarly tortured spellings) became unavoidable, taking its place alongside the most well-known internet sensations. Whatever your home page was, chances are it mentioned the video in some way. It was an in-joke one realized everyone was in on when conversation about it could be overheard while waiting in line at the supermarket. Within a week, it broke out of the internet's ambit and became actual news, getting snarky write-ups in *USA Today, Entertainment Weekly, People, Time, The New York Times,* and other print media. Soon even your grandmother was emailing you a link.

But those people were behind the curve because within twenty hours of the initial post, some guy with a moderately successful vlog—successful enough to have paying sponsors— took the apparent nympho's funeral rant and mixed it with the beats of Kool Moe Dee's "I Go To Work." Due to either the mixer's skills or sheer serendipity, they complemented each other surprisingly well. This audio track—with accompanying video featuring the cut-and-pasted girl on a makeshift platform in a dingy, squalid basement surrounded by a crowd of thugs cheering her on, i.e. all the components of the stereotypical "rap battle" setting—this what was basically a music video, in turn, went ubiquitous and by the end of the week was seen/heard more than the original video it was parodying. For a while, it spawned a whole cottage industry of amateur MCs making homemade remixes of the girl's rant set to different songs, mostly long-forgotten hits of the '80s. It also provoked the first major case of an entertainer trying to get a slice of the pecuniary pie from the parodies/mash-ups/remixes people were making and posting on the internet using what was indisputably the entertainer's property, with Kool Moe Dee suing the admin of J-Dawg's V-log for using his song on that first remix, seeking monetary compensation on the basis that the video brought his (the admin's) site more hits and therefore presumably more ad money, a case that actually went to trial (see Mohandas Dewese v. Jeremiah Dogerson, 11 ne.2d 457 (ca. MMXIX)), though the jury ultimately found Moe Dee's charges meritless and the making/posting of the video not actionable due to all the laws that protect parody in this country (not to mention that J-Dawg made a big show of openly wondering if he should pay the estates of James Brown and Lyn Collins should the verdict go against him, as well as questioning whether they had been properly compensated by Moe Dee back in the day, gleefully calculating for the press what the compound interest on royalties since 1989 would add up to).

What was interesting and bizarre was that despite universal interest in the video and subsequent epigonic parodies, no one could with any veracity shed any light on who this rabble-rousing girl at the funeral was. This was especially frustrating to those trying to reconcile the existence of such a tabula rasa girl with the extensive and continually expanding power of the internet to catalog information about pretty much everyone. Not a few people felt a low-level angst and metaphysical tension at this stonewalling, the kind of tummy-sick feeling one gets when a presumed verity of life fails to conform to expectations. And it didn't help that the ever-reliable internet, the de facto haven of solace for millions, the foundation on which so many had erected complex dependencies, the 21st century security blanket, was the cause of this angst and distress, how it was just flat out not doing what it was supposed to, the internet's whole raison d'etre for most people being its singular capacity to find info on anyone you've ever known or not known or merely just seen or just anyone at all (that and access to the world's most prodigious outlet of porn ever). People had grown used to these internet celebrities' identities being uncovered and their actions explicated satisfactorily (vide Gary Brolsma, Ghyslain Raza, Mark Hicks, Libby Hoeller, et al.), and when days passed without comment from a verifiable firsthand source—either someone at the funeral or the girl herself—the fabulists took over. Outright lies competed with one another for purchase on the bedrock of perceived truth. Depending on which site you went to, the girl was either a transsexual epileptic or a daredevil prankster pulling the ultimate stunt. A few maintained that it was all an elaborate and meticulously produced advertisement for some future movie, TV show, web venture, or iPhone app. A turning point of sorts occurred when someone claimed that the cemetery in the video was in a town in Utah and another guy declared that the priest was wearing medallions that designated affiliation with the Mormon faith. Both claims were later debunked, but not before the insinuations spread like wildfire and firmly entrenched themselves in the collective imagination to such an extent that even today a search for "mormen sex gurl" will turn up hits of the video (+ parodies). While the spurious Mormon connection didn't result in the doxing of the girl, it did have the unanticipated side effect of unleashing a spate of homemade videos featuring supposed Mormon girls doing things that didn't square with the values real Mormons espouse, things like swearing, drinking, getting into fights, vandalizing public buildings, and, on certain cloistered sites, masturbating (Adult PassKey® required). Some of the more popular "Mormons Gone Wild!"-type videos were posted on a new website called Vidiary by a girl who was totally upfront about not being Mormon but, as a lark, dressed up as a missionary and pretended to be one, accosting people and surreptitiously recording video of the interactions with one of those gēniphones with wide-angled camera lens clipped to her belt which she then posted for the enjoyment of her vidiary's subscribers. Her videos were among the most frequently viewed and/or requested for automatic download on the iPhone 12G or equivalent all-in-one Uni-Fi device every week and received the most video message ("v-mess") feedback, video messaging/production being the preferred method of communication for the under-30 set, a whole generation brought up on slickly produced films, TV shows, and web videos, and who unconsciously absorbed the rudimentary techniques and "rules" for making perspicuous videos while letting written language acuity fall by the wayside, Eisenstein and Kuleshov being these people's Strunk and White, most of these Vidiary users belonging to this video-obsessed demographic, a group that will be labeled "Geniration [sic]" (intentional sic), a whole generation of kids for whom "crossing the line" is as technically incorrect (and—in a way that the old stodgies not of their generation will fail to recognize, in the way most generations don't see eye to eye about all sorts of things—as personally expressive) as saying or inditing "I be," the first class of kids to submit more video essays than written ones with college applications, and it was this demographic who was insatiably viewing the girl's faux-missionary videos, videos that were massively popular even though no one could mistake the girl for a genuine Mormon and this wasn't just because of her nametag ("Sister Cherrypie") or her livery, which was embellished with such tasteless touches as a half-unbuttoned blouse tied up above the navel and a skirt that, while the correct shade of slate gray, was the length of a mini and

showed infinitely more leg than the long a-line skirts traditionally worn by true Latter-day Saints, or the way she would
approach old ladies or teenage boys or people eating at burger
joints or whomever and talk about how the Mormons were
"the shit yo" and refer to Jesus Christ as her "homey" and
describe the naked Jell-O fights they regularly had in Utah and
pull out fake tracts tucked inside the elastic of her underwear
that resembled more the advertisements for prostitutes than
the standard exhortations for salvation. No, it was more the girl
herself who ruined the dissembling in ways it seemed she
couldn't help, viz. the way she brought her shoulders back to
an almost comical degree in an effort to showcase her bust and
jut out her hips at such sharp and licentious angles that the
skeletal structure underneath looked permanently luxated. Not
to mention her face, which—while pretty enough—was always
heavily made-up with thick eyeliner, opaque blush, and deeply
hued lipstick, and its default expression, which could most apt-
ly be described as a kind of sneer, though one done with her
entire face so that all her features seemed to be sneering: her
eyes, her eyebrows, her nose, her cheeks, her mouth, her
chin—all sneering or like smirking, her whole face slanted and
awry as if half the muscles in her face were dead, a mien
peculiar to a certain kind of girl, typically mimicked by those
especially influenced by a social-media-saturated culture in
which one is always both spectating and spectated, the sneer
directed toward what is being seen as well as anyone who is
watching, this sort of deadening, dismaying look endemic to
certain kinds of girls 15-25, the accretive effect of this face-
wide hemiplegic sneering or smirking of this particular Vidiary
girl, aetat. around 18, not redounding well to her, aesthetically
speaking. In short: her expression was basically what made this
pretty girl ugly. This quality of hers, which resonated with
such bromides as "It's what's inside that counts" and "Beauty is
only skin-deep," also inadvertently made it Lucite-clear (to the
few people who made the connection) why so many people
were willing to buy that the funeral girl was a Mormon. Her

profanity-laced, sexually perverse hortatory address at a funeral notwithstanding, she projected a kind of earnestness that is characteristic of the religiously devout, as weird as that sounds. Her face registered a conviction, a calm rectitude, a persistence not born of a quest for personal gain. This contrasted profoundly with the sneery, canted face of the other girl. This might also explain why even though there was a fair amount of snide and sardonic comments about the funeral girl on the internet, one could detect an undercurrent of sympathy and an aroused compassion with no place to go, and how some of the armchair diagnoses seemed to be made in good faith, as if people were genuinely trying to figure out what was going on here, nobody really believing that the girl was just flat-out psychotic except for maybe a handful of girls who were most likely resentful of all the attention vectored away from them and onto another girl. Strangely, there existed a true caring about that girl at the funeral. Needless to say, nobody felt anything of the sort while watching videos of the other girl pretending to be a Mormon, or, for that matter, most of the videos on Vidiary. To be honest, most of the popularity of the sneering girl's videos probably stemmed from the notoriety her vidiary got when she went to the house of a man in his mid-50s who invited her in so she could share with him her love of Jesus and the guy ended up sitting very close to her on the couch and leering at her with unbridled lechery, which spooked even the usually dismissively carefree girl and she bolted out of the place when the man went to get her something to drink. She posted the video when she got home, having recorded every second of the encounter, and the man got wind of it and got hopping and litigiously mad. Even though he had done nothing illegal (luckily for him), he felt his reputation had been categorically smeared, which was hard to argue with. The lawsuit he brought up was notable for going after the owner and CEO of Vidiary instead of the girl, who obviously lacked the funds to cover the punitive retribution he was seeking (see Kevin Collins v. Steve Chen, 33 ne.2d 102 (nm.

MMXX)).

So anyway, a good four weeks after the initial post, pretty much everyone had seen the funeral girl video, though no one knew any more about the circumstances behind it than they did on day 1, which is why "flabbergasted" doesn't even begin to describe the reaction most people had when it was announced that the girl, the one who had described all her sexual desires from a podium in front of a mourning crowd, that that very same girl would be on Letterman, live and in the flesh, the following week.

IV.

"That night's broadcast was nothing less than the final nail in the coffin of someone most had buried long before in the bloated graveyard of pop culture irrelevancy. While Letterman's publicists insisted that it had always been his intention to retire at the end of the year, he would not have been able to come back and do his shtick with any credibility even if he had wanted to. After that show, there was nothing for him to do but plan for an ignominious exit from the late night stage, for he found himself suddenly exposed, in the most dramatic fashion, as the hopelessly out of touch dinosaur everyone suspected he had been for quite some time."

—from The History of Late Night Television: From Allen to Fallon by Handl Petrowski, ©2023 by Handl Petrowski, available for $1.99 US at HandlGerald-Petrowski.pwp in a comprehensive variety of text formats

The show was publicized by CBS as a major broadcast event, one sorely needed by a show that had been hemorrhaging viewers for a couple of years, *The Late Show* not exactly being everyone's idea of required viewing. Letterman, while still relatively spry and ambulatory, was getting undeniably senescent—into his 70s for godsakes—and it was getting hard to maintain the illusion that he was on the cutting edge of anything but geriatric RXs. This on top of an ill-conceived behavioral shift in Letterman's demeanor toward his guests starting about six months prior when he started to adopt this louche and dissipated sort of persona, especially when interviewing female guests, with whom he had always slyly flirted in the past but now his smarmy blandishments gamboled dangerously close to the threshold of good taste while being as lewd as the FCC would allow. He deployed comments about every bit of bare flesh that could be seen, comments about faces and necks and arms and legs and ankles. There was open speculation about the make and model of undergarments and long, silent ogles that verged on being prosecutable, all punctuated by heavy sighs and slurping noises. Most of these starlets played along, coquettishly swatting his shoulder or batting their eyes demurely, though there was a fairly noticeable tinge of discomfort and nervousness on the faces of some, understandably. Even Paul Shaffer appeared to get weirded out at times. Though most assumed Letterman was just losing his grip a little as he got indisputably old (World Wide Pants official statement at the time: "Dave's just getting a little frisky in his old age"), there was some speculation that this new personality (which was really just a more distilled and barebones and direct version of his old personality) was a calculated move by Letterman and his handlers to present America with a clear alternative to the harmless and endearing avuncularity embodied by Carson. Maybe some sort of maybe cherry on top in his ongoing disgruntlement with having been spurned by the *Tonight Show* overseers in the way he seemed to be completely repudiating the type of warm, cuddly personality required for that *T. Show* gig, a type of personality internalized by previous hosts Carson, Leno, and Fallon which allowed them to be welcomed into Middle Americans' homes and be as easily consumed as a smooth milkshake, Letterman seeming to decide suddenly to be really truly not that. That is, *The Late*

Show was offering a new, contrary kind of aging late night host: depraved, perverted, possibly dangerous. Uncouth, unrestrained. A patriarchal figure with sex on the brain who was totally clear of conscience. An unpredictable roué not burdened by the threat of having to live decades with whatever consequences might result from his actions. Yet still an institution, still a de rigueur stop on the promotional trail for entertainers of virtually every stripe, and so always the unceasing flow of guests.

This incarnation of Letterman posed a nasty problem for guests who didn't want to play along, especially the women. Even if a female guest wanted to take Letterman to task, the venue sort of prevented her from doing so, what with the millions of viewers watching at home and studio audience and the crew standing around; according to some guests, if they had taken vocal exception to Letterman's debauched comments during the interview it would have felt like airing out one's dirty laundry in public. So the ones who were so totally against what he was doing had to just sit there with a hopefully not too frozen smile on their face and try to defuse or manage a tension that felt like the tension that exists when there's a family gathering and the now-adult daughter has to somehow get through it despite her vivid memories of the abusive relationship she had had with her father when she was little, and every time she sees his mouth curl it sickens her and she has to put on a congenial face which she knows some of her relatives know is also a brave face because *they* know of this sad and horrible history she and her father have but no one, including herself and especially her dad, will say anything about it in public and everyone'll just keep smiling and saying the correct things while trying to keep certain dark thoughts covered under a blanket of amity.

In this way, the show became even more about Dave than it had previously been, with the audience for the most part cheering him on and the guests forced to grin and bear the come-ons and soldier through the crude comments and even become part of the routine by tossing back their own suggestive comments and thereby actively encouraging the lascivious raillery or else risk offending a legend and institution of TV who might legitimately be losing some of his mental faculties or, worse, being exposed as so hopelessly square and humorless and un-"with it" that some old fogey's practical joke/intentional farce/harmless play-acting totally befuddles them (assuming it was a joke/farce/[instance of] play-acting to begin with, which the intelligible parts of Letterman's auto-biography will eventually confirm it in fact was (so he will say, almost literally since his autobiography will be rather ob-viously dictated, although no mention of an amanuensis will be on the cover or within the flap copy or edition notice)). Hence, the guests were basically subjugated by Team Letterman—led by paterfamilias Dave—and made to assume almost otiose posi-tions of audience/playthings to Mr Letterman's antics to the point where being called a "guest" seemed like a cruel joke, not to mention that it was getting hard for these guests/victims to shoehorn in a mention of whatever they were supposed to be promoting. That CBS was allowing these shenanigans to occur was a lot less bold and edgy of them than it appeared at first glance, their acceptance of the New Dave closer to a noncha-lance or disinterestedness rooted in the realities of what a dead zone the 11:30 PM timeslot was, how it was usually impossible to fill with anything that would lure people away from their DVRs, late night becoming the default time to watch the programming one had missed during the day. Real risk-taking would have involved airing an original scripted program, which would have been drastically more expensive than the basically nothing they paid for the Worldwide Pants-produced show. And considering that Letterman's company was willing to pay incrementally more every year for leasing that late night timeslot, canceling the show would've been much more of a threat to CBS's revenue streams. So, with nothing else to air, they stuck with Dave.

"Woo, hoo, yes. Ahead of my time. Biggest star of the time, and soon to be the biggest, eventually. Both gone now though, aren't they? Yessir. Ate all the caviar too. There should be a long pause here. How do you do pauses? A bunch of spaces? How do you 'read' that? Like that one Paul? Paul's not here. Another long pause needed. Dammit, how the hell do you do them??"

> —from In Firmly Behind the Desk with Jokes: A Memoir by David Letterman, ©2027 by David Letterman, available for $15.99 (!) US at David-MichaelLetterman.pwp in PDF format only (!!) and barely more comprehensible (but much funnier) audiobook in mp3 format read by Alec Baldwin (!!!)

She wasn't the top-slotted guest that night, or even the runner-up guest. No, she was scheduled in the spot usually reserved for bands or musicians but was sometimes filled by comedians or C-list celebrities when booking options were limited. These third-tier guests were in constant danger of not making it onto the show due to time constraints; that their segments abutted and oftentimes overlapped the credits was totally not in their favor. This girl—whose real name, Mary Fields, which a lot of people were still coming to grips with, most of them only knowing her through net-created monikers, with even some CBS memos referring to her as "The Web Sensation At The Funerel" (sic), caused the programming heads to argue right up to airtime about how to introduce her, her name obviously not being adequate for most of the viewing public—she was repeatedly warned that she could very well be bumped that night, as a lot of third guests who aren't holding an instrument or howling into a mic often are, and it didn't help that she wasn't even promoting anything really, and on top of all that there was not only the prestige of headlining guest Percival Aztoben to consider but also the time-consuming, labor-intensive logistics of what they wanted to pull off for that night's extravaganza. Not to mention that, as a pièce de résistance designed to attract the maximum number of eyeballs, the whole thing was going to be broadcasted *live*, which would prevent the fine-tuning necessary to edit the show into a nice and smooth and compact thirty-two minutes of content, a process that usually took a couple hours and would have probably been a last guest's best chance for a brief appearance to be spliced into a time-crunched show. The producers resisted telling her what they really wanted to: that there was no way she was getting on that night's show, that the thought of trying to squeeze her in was causing migraines among the staff, and could she please go back to her hotel room with some comped Broadway tickets and, if she really felt up to it, come back tomorrow when the odds of getting facetime with Big Dave would be dramatically increased under the normal, much less stressful conditions of a tape-delayed show. Alas, she stayed in her dressing room, placid and unperturbed, as everyone else ran around her, engaged in all the busywork the show required.

Even Letterman, who usually made time to hang out with guests (*especially* the women) to work out generally what would be discussed on air, spent most of his pre-show preparatory time on the *Late Show* set anxiously seeking confirmation from the production crew that everything was a go, that the never-before-attempted physical manipulations of the set were not only possible but able to be executed without major snags or hiccups. Even after the production designer told him that Yes, everything had been checked and re-checked and signed off on and rehearsed to the nth degree over the weekend and all the technical bumps and wrinkles had been smoothed and ironed out, Letterman assiduously sought out similar reassurances from the art director, construction coordinator, DP, and key grip. There was no question that Letterman was a little more amped up than usual, perhaps sensing that this particular show had a unique make-or-break quality about it and that perhaps his future was hanging in the balance. Or maybe the show had grown so stagnant that anything novel immediately captured his attention. When Percival Aztoben showed up, Dave glommed onto his VIP guest and took him on a tour of the set, enthusiastically pointing out all the intricate workings of what they had planned for the show that night. Mr Aztoben was shown the stage's ingress and path to his seat. He was shown the way the stage would be laid out, the position of the band and the introductory music they would be playing, and the way Dave would greet him, the way he would get up from behind his desk with welcoming hand extended. The way the desk would be swiveled around 160°. The way both he and Mr Aztoben would be sitting in chairs whose backs were to the audience, the way they would be for all intents and purposes facing away from the audience. How the audience would only be able to see their (slightly askew) profiles, basically. The way the New York skyline typically behind the desk (now in front) would be draped with 80' of thin beige cloth, slightly slanted so as to be pretty much parallel with the desk and guest chair. How video of a studio audience—not the one actually in studio—would be rear projected by a high-powered half-million lumen video projector onto this IMAX-sized makeshift screen. How the video would output from a technician's laptop and be craftily edited on the spot so that the audience up on the screen would react to what Mr Aztoben and Dave were saying; the way this video audience would laugh, clap, and cheer at appropriate times in the interview. How the real-life studio audience would be basically watching another audience watching the interview as if they (the real-life audience) were sitting backstage. Letterman showed him the way the video screen (and so the second audience) would be off-center to the real audience and how unsettling the video audience's angle of incidence, so to speak, of approximately 20 degrees would be to the real audience. How he and Mr Aztoben would only acknowledge the projected audience, as if the actual people in the studio were not even there. And also the way the TV camera would be positioned to the dextral side of the set, equipped with a slightly fisheyed lens and taping the show laterally so as to capture all the elements in the tableau: Letterman and guest, audiences real and projected. And but also with this planned layout, the way the TV audience would see way more of Dave than Mr Aztoben, how Dave would be talking to his guest most of the time and therefore facing at least toward the general direction of the camera when doing so. The way folks at home would be pretty much hosed out of a glimpse of Mr Aztoben's countenance, how even when he would address the video audience his face would be almost completely obscured due to the angle. The way the home audience would be essentially watching an audience watch an audience watching the interview they (the home audience) thought they were tuning in to see. The way it wouldn't seem like a fourth wall being shattered so much as the home audience themselves *becoming* the fourth wall. Or rather maybe a different kind of third wall, part of a right triangle formed by the hypotenuse of both Dave's desk and projection screen, with the real audience and the TV camera's POV being the two catheti. How the real studio audience would not be apprised of the gag beforehand, and how mindbending the non-symmetricalness of it would be, especially considering the way people have come to expect a sort of order to even the bizarre things they encounter. How even more confused the viewers at home would be. The way a bird's eye view of the set would seem like a performance artist's demonstration of the Pythagorean theorem. How the whole thing would be the most warped bit of business seen on television since . . . well since the last episode of Mr Aztoben's long-running and venerated show. The way this setup would complement Mr Aztoben's show, a sort of transposition of his show's anarchic spirit to the late night interview format. How glorious it was all going to be. All of this relayed to Percival Aztoben by David Letterman. And all this chest-puffing from Big Dave without him once realizing that Aztoben's eyes were glazing over, that Mr Aztoben spent his daily professional life mired in these kinds of pseudo-clever entanglements and the last thing he wanted when clocked-out and off company time was to have some pale imitation of something he considered not all that compelling to begin with foisted on his own uninterested self. Besides, if pressed, Mr Aztoben would say that what *The Late Show* was doing that night had little to do with his hit show, which specialized more in confusing genre signals than the reflexive, nested-audience metagames Dave and crew were attempting to pull off here. But he nodded soberly at the torsions of the *Late Show* set and praised Dave's inventiveness and allowed the appearance of a complicit smirk to play across his lips—anything to keep Letterman in good humor, knowing that if his host were appeased it would make the next couple of hours a lot more bearable than they would've been otherwise.

And meanwhile Mary Fields was waiting patiently in her dressing room, sitting on the sofa next to an untouched catering spread, hands in her lap, looking toward the floor, ignoring the pendent flatscreen TV positioned overhead in the far corner of the room which was playing a loop of the greatest moments in *Late Show* history, alone in the room but little did she know not unwatched. In fact, only a few people knew that the guests' dressing rooms were outfitted with hidden hi-def cameras mounted on gimbals which allowed joystick-controlled movement with zooming capability. Installed in multiple locations within the ceiling and walls, the cameras could capture any part of the room, though their default positioning focused on the sofa. Letterman was, of course, one of the people who knew of the cameras' existence and he was the one who made the most use of them. Every guest was unknowingly recorded and Dave would oftentimes go into the closet-sized room connected to his own personal dressing room where direct feeds from the hidden cameras were patched through on 50-inch monitors. He would manipulate the cameras, panning over the oblivious guests, switching between feeds as they moved around the room. Dave would arrange for them to be left alone—instructing their handlers to make pointed though not overly suspicious mention of how the door could be deadbolted to ensure their total privacy—so he could observe those who presumed to be unobserved. Needless to say, only women received this sub rosa attention from Big Dave. Most managed not to do anything overly mortifying; most of the time nothing would happen or maybe they would just do the small bits of grooming one does when alone: there were a few cases of eyebrow tweezing, some made absurd-looking expressions in the mirror to check for particles of food wedged between their teeth, at most there would maybe be a bit of nose-picking. Or they might do the things people do to make themselves comfortable in their own skin like sing to themselves or take off their shoes (which Letterman—who obviously had a thing for women's feet—didn't mind in the least; when his personal collection of recorded hidden camera footage is eventually unearthed, most of it will seem like a promotional video for the world's most expensive pedicures). If Dave was lucky, there would be some sort of necessary wardrobe change, though this was rare and almost never happened with the A-list guests. And then there was the one very notable occasion when a young, imprudent starlet strip-ped off her clothes and masturbated. Dave probably didn't believe his luck that day, though the prevailing opinion will be that one of Dave's assistants most likely gave the starlet a substantial gratuity to put on a show for Mr Letterman, her performance—replete with guttural moans and salacious looks at the wall—being a little too over the top to convince most that she had really considered herself unobserved. The general public will be allowed to arrive at their own conclusions about the video when it is leaked to the internet along with other choice selections from Letterman's library of skeevy hidden cam footage. Regardless of popular sentiment, the woman—no longer young or a star—will sue immediately and without quarter; she will appear on TV for the first time in years with unappeasable vengeance in her eyes, armed with supernova-levels of indignation fueled by the frustration of being unable to confront the perpetrator himself, forced instead to pursue monetary compensation from his estate, as Letterman, by this time, will have been interred in Indianapolis soil for some years (eventually see Marabelle Pelling v. World Wide Pants, Inc., 23 ne.2d 84 (ny. MMXL1)).

"He seemed really busy."

—Mary Fields giving her impression of David Letterman on the night of her appearance on *The Late Show*, from <u>My Life Thus Far</u>, a vidbook by Mary Fields, ©2029 by Glen Taglio, available for $2.49 US at MaryHelenFields.pwp in mpeg-8 format

By the time Mary Fields was ready to make her first television appearance, Letterman's mood had soured considerably. The interview with Percival Aztoben hadn't gone over with the audience as well as *The Late Show* staff had hoped, and the stage's flipped around setup was more discomfiting than the producers had anticipated. Exacerbating the situation was Aztoben's lackadaisical behavior, the way he came off as bored and coolly contemptuous of the proceedings, his responses to Letterman's questions both prefaced and capped off with implicit sighs (with some real ones thrown in occasionally). His laconic and curt manner resulted in a flaccid, lifeless interview made even more soporific by being conducted backwards. Added to this, Dave couldn't defuse the tension as he had so often done in the past by looking straight at the audience with mock-incredulity on his face. Since he was unable to see the studio audience due to the gag's conceit, he instead focused that ironic expression of his on the video-projected audience before him which caused the people on the screen to laugh as the real audience normally would have, but now the people in the real audience weren't able to see the faces Dave was making so it seemed as though the people in the video audience were laughing, unprompted, at what *they* were facing, viz. the real audience. That the real audience found

could only assume to be its point. The polar-bear-costumed guy, with a showman's flair, continued to entice the lion, prancing just out of its reach while mugging for the cameras and audience, drawing the biggest laughs of the evening. Exhortations were shouted out for Dave to get in there and separate the two, the audience unable to contain its glee at the prospect of the host getting mauled on live TV. Letterman just stood fuming off to the side, glaring alternately at the shenanigans on stage and the heckling audience with equal disgust. The show's producers cut to a commercial break and needed the full four minutes to restore order to *The Late Show* set.

When they came back from the break, everyone was ready to just go home, especially Letterman. But there was still six more minutes that needed to be filled with content before the credits rolled, so Dave, with zero enthusiasm, introduced the last guest, Mary Fields, star of "some internet thing." Before she had even taken three steps onto the stage, she was scrutinized and judged by the hundreds of eyes in the studio and millions at home. Her broadcast television debut couldn't help being more muted than the splash she had made on the web, and people quickly steeled themselves for what was looking like a disheartening anticlimax. She was dressed simply, wearing jeans, sneakers, and a pale pink shirt with a silkscreened black and white image of a teenage girl on the front. She was still undeniably beautiful, even in HD, although the impression she made didn't have as much impact as it did in the funeral video. If people found her less stunning than they had expected, it was only because they were accustomed to seeing the most attractive people in the world walk out onto the late night stage and, with her reserved wardrobe, simple jewelry, and tasteful maquillage, the funeral girl was significantly less glamorous than the typical starlet guest. Those expecting to see a traditional knock-out gorgeous stunner experienced twinges of disappointment. The thing that took everyone aback, however, was that she was smiling as she walked toward Letterman, it being the first time anyone had seen her do so. This was a girl everyone had associated with funerals and it had been easy to imagine her perpetually afflicted with cafard or anger or both, so it was a revelation to many that this girl was even capable of smiling. And after the initial surprise wore off, pretty much everyone noticed that while she may not be more beautiful than big-time A-list movie stars, her smile was very different from the smiles that were usually plastered on the faces of *Late Show* guests; it was much better in some way most couldn't put their finger on in the moment. Rewatching video of her entrance a few times made the difference obvious: her smile was positively understated when compared to the kind of smile most guests walked out with. It didn't seem too big for her face, or show off precise rows of unnaturally white teeth, or get wider as people applauded her entrance as if everyone in the audience had a camera and she were saying "cheese" for each and every one of them—any or all of which qualities were symptomatic of most celebrities' smiles. Most of all, her smile didn't seem insincere in the way smiles intended to be seen by multitudes of people usually appear to be; her smile was for one person only, the person whose hand she shook before taking a seat next to him. Another scarcely noticed fact, at least during that first live viewing, was that she never acknowledged the studio audience or the TV cameras the whole time, her attention solely and exclusively on Letterman, her host.

Dave wasted no time signaling to a PA offstage, who rolled out a lectern on casters. With an arched eyebrow, he nodded to it and asked her, "Would you care to continue where you left off?"

The audience chuckled. She good-naturedly shook her head, her brow wrinkling attractively. "No thank you," she said.

"For those that don't know," Dave addressed the cameras and audience, "this young lady was recently featured in a video on the internet saying some really . . . some things of a sexual nature that we unfortunately can't repeat on this show. But check it out, on your local internet sometime." (As if everyone hadn't already seen it. Letterman himself had seen it for the first time that morning.) Dave grabbed his index cards and made a show of intensely studying them, then eyed her dubiously. "I'll start this easy," he said. "Are you married?"

"No," she said, somewhat hesitantly.

"Well, that's a surprise . . . and a relief."

There were scattered guffaws in the crowd. She just sat there, looking at Letterman pleasantly enough but uncertain of what to say.

Dave continued: "Well, was this like an open call for suitors or . . . what, you just can't get a date or something?"

"No," she said, a little edge in her voice.

"No, I wouldn't think that'd be the case. After all," straightening his tie, "you're a very attractive woman."

"Thank you," she said, though it was clear she didn't take much pleasure from the compliment.

"No, thank *you*," he countered, then went back to his cards, hunching over them slightly. He said nothing for a second, letting the awkward silence distend. A few people chortled. Her smile now had a hint of helplessness to it as she got more confused by Dave's actions. He ran his tongue over his lips and grimaced a little. Finally, he looked up and nonchalantly tossed out, "So what do the Mormons think?"

"Mormons?" she asked, now thoroughly confused.

"Yeah. Your group, your brethren, whatever. Didn't they object to the . . . speech?"

"I'm not Mormon," she said, chuckling.

"No?" he said, surprised. (His assistants had fed him some of the more pervasive rumors.) "Well, even if you don't subscribe to that particular religion, which by the way is pretty great, I think we'd all agree." He paused for sparse laughter and clapping. "Um, so even if you aren't Mormon per se, you must have some sorta moral code and whatnot. I mean, you believe in God, yeah?"

Mary was silent for a couple moments before saying, "Yes." She was no longer smiling.

"So," exhaling expansively, "you believe in . . . well, I mean what do you think God would think of, of all those things you said. In that video."

Flustered, she could only murmur, "I don't . . . I'm not sure what you mean."

"I mean," Letterman said testily, "what the hell is wrong with you anyway?"

There were audible gasps in the audience. She sat there, stone-still, caught in the headlights of something she didn't yet know the size of.

Dave swiftly pressed ahead. "Who is that?" he asked, motioning to the picture of the girl on her shirt. "Is that some lesbian lover of yours? A little young, isn't she? Some little young thing you did all that nasty stuff you were telling everyone about?"

"No," she said quietly, her eyes narrowing. "It's my sister."

"Oh, your sister," Dave said, leering at her. "Well that brings up an interesting question. So what does your family think of what you did, making a spectacle of yourself like that?" It was clear Dave was channeling all the frustration he had felt the entire show into this final acerbic interview. "Does your little sister approve of what you did up there?"

Mary allowed herself a small, sad smile. "I would think so," she said softly.

Dave shook his head, full of disdain. "Well miss, if that's the case I think you have one messed up family." There was nothing but complete silence for a few moments. Dave grunted and said, "You know what? I don't believe you. I think people would be embarrassed to be related to you. Can we call this sister of yours, maybe get her on the show so we can get it straight from her how proud she is of you?"

"No, you can't," she said.

"Oh we can't?" Dave said smugly. "And might that be because you're lying about what she thinks of you, that really she's ashamed of you?"

"No."

"Then why can't we call her?"

Mary's head dipped a little as she said, "Because she's passed."

Dave tapped his fingers on the desk. The audience was raptly watching her, practically holding their collective breath. Dave, allergic to any silence not of his own creation, filled the dead air with, "I'm sorry." Even he sensed how hollow the sentiment was. With nothing else to say, he asked, "How did it happen?"

Mary looked at him and told him about how her sister, for the first twelve years of her life, was the most wonderful, joyous sister anyone could have. How she had been amazed by the world from birth and was determined to take her place in it. How she had been loud and brash even as an infant, which, to the rest of the family, had been by turns obnoxious, then endearing, and then admirable. Her boldness was the best kind, always in service of correcting some injustice she had witnessed. How she was the kind of girl who was as likely to defend someone against a bully on the playground as she was to intelligently argue for moving her bedtime to a later hour. Her ambition matched her candor; she couldn't decide if she wanted to be a Broadway star, kindergarten teacher, or the first female president, and later decided that there was no reason she couldn't be all three. There was the day she came home from school, crying, after finding a mangled cat in the road. Between sobs, she demanded that they sell their house and open an animal hospital, and it was heartbreaking to see how serious she was. How she had once told her big sister, at the top of a Ferris wheel, how wonderful it was to breathe fall air so high up. And then came the summer when nothing should have been on her mind except how exciting it was to go to a new school, the final passage to adulthood when grades get names instead of numbers, but how a diagnosis changed all that, how they went to the hospital for a simple follow-up appointment and the doctor came in and said the words "acute myelogenous leukemia," and how afterward none of them were able to think of anything else. How she took the news as stoically as the rest of the family did, everyone planning to spare one another a display of tearful sorrow. After the initial sharp stab of pain had passed, they found that the pamphlets the doctor had given them provided no comfort. They collectively turned to the scientific journals and she was the only one who didn't throw the things at the wall in frustration at not understanding a single word. How she went immediately into intensive chemotherapy. How she spent the momentous first day of school at home in bed, pale and wiped out. How the hospital became their second home, the place where she underwent innumerable debilitating procedures. How the pain-filled days strung together, months and months of them. And how, one restless night, Mary found her jotting in a notebook, as sad as she ever allowed anyone to see her. Nothing but brave until this point, she couldn't help dissolving into tears against her sister, telling Mary that there was so much yet she wanted to do, to see, to be. She was writing it all down, vicariously living the rest of her life through the written word. She didn't tell anyone else what she was scribbling, only her big sister, whom she looked up to and admired, hardly suspecting that the feeling was mutual. How a couple of days later, she offhandedly suggested that, at her funeral, Mary announce to everyone her list of all the things she wished she could've done. Before the request could be passed off as a morbid joke, she grabbed Mary's wrist and looked at her with steel in her eyes to let her know that she was completely serious, as if her sister didn't already know that, as if she hadn't been her entire life. How the end came soon after. At the funeral, Mary took the podium to remember her sister to the congregated mourners and pulled out the notebook nobody knew existed. She told everyone what her sister, in her own words, would have wanted to do if she had had a few more decades. Some of her wishes were simple, some were grand, some made you think you'd never stop crying. But the section that riled everyone up was the list of all the sensual pleasures she regretted missing out on, inscrutable feelings she had no first-hand knowledge of, titillating adventures she could only guess at and try to piece together from what she had seen in movies, read in books, overheard in school, glimpsed on the internet—all expressed in the extravagantly overblown terms of an inexperienced but wildly imaginative girl who had only barely reached first base. Maybe she had forgotten she wrote those things, maybe she never intended that part of the notebook to be read aloud. But Mary had made a promise and decided to leave nothing to chance. A ruckus ensued and was caught on video by a cousin going to film school, who was recording the entire ceremony for a class assignment. The next day, on a whim, the cousin took the most seemingly salacious bits of her recitation and edited them into an easily digestible fifty-five seconds and posted the clip for the world to see. It became one of those videos that made up for its lack of context by being easily ridiculed.

Mary never looked away from Letterman while relaying all of this. He stopped looking at her about halfway through. After she was done, there was a long stretch of silence that seemed as if it could last forever. By complete happenstance, both Mary and Letterman broke the silence at the same time by clearing their throats. Letterman's was a fake gesture, a fake cough he used to fill silences; hers sounded like a sticky, tangled ball of grief that was lodged in her throat with no hope of ever being extracted. The two noises they made couldn't have sounded more different.

[Blue Black Red Magenta Orange Green]
    —The general consensus on what order to take which psychotropic drugs that will allow one to experience the feelings Aztoben had about his Letterman appearance, from <u>Yours Is Mine Too And There</u>, a db by Percival Aztoben composed of 39 different colored/sized spansules each containing 10-25mg of various cognition-altering substances, ©2031 by

Percival Aztoben, available for mail order w/ optional expedited shipping at PercivalJenshoAztoben.pwp

V.

A few days later, a video was posted of Mary at the funeral reading her sister's notes. This time the clip was unexpurgated and ran almost fourteen minutes. Along with the familiar excerpts, Mary relayed more of her sister's wishes such as, "I want to see Niagara Falls," and "I want to go to prom," and "I want to see my best friend Morgan become homecoming queen, because I just know she will be," and "I want to see Dad cry at my wedding when he gives me away, the big crybaby," and "I want to have four, no five kids," and "I want to be the first to congratulate my daughter when she gets accepted to Harvard and I want to be the proudest parent at her graduation," and "I want to look over at my husband on our 50th anniversary and smile to myself, knowing that I couldn't have found anyone more perfect to spend my life with," and "I want to live a full life, knowing that I loved as much as I was loved." The video was posted to multiple sites, but, for any number of reasons, not the least of which had to do with its comparably interminable running time, the aggregate number of views it got from the top five video hosting sites was about 1/1000th of the number of views the videos of the Letterman appearance had gotten. It even got fewer views than a video posted by a *Late Show* PA who had surreptitiously filmed Mary with his phone when she arrived at the studio two hours before airtime, wearing the now infamous t-shirt, as she got out of her car, gave him a tentative smile, and asked him whether this was an appropriate place to park.

MALIA

I LEARNED A LOT ABOUT LOVE while working at the local pastry shop. And, despite what he says, it was not because of John. John was an all-American boy; his dirty blond hair was cropped short, he was athletic and muscular, and he had an ego the size of Texas. But he would humor whoever would humor him and most of us at work would do so. Not because we particularly liked him but because he would always tell us the most private tidbits involving his relationships with girls and these little stories were always entertaining and helped pass the time.

There was a period when he was obsessed with deflowering virgins and he managed to do so at the rate of one or two a week. Some of his most engaging stories were told during this time. Every few days, he'd show up to work with a wide, knowing smile on his face and we'd know that during the course of the day we would get a breakdown of his exploits the night before. He would tell us of the times he'd work on a girl all night until she finally agreed to put out at six in the morning, in the back of his car. He'd find girls who hadn't even been kissed before and screw them, quickly and quietly, while her parents were asleep in the next room. Sometimes it would be some longtime friend of his, who had shielded her burning desire for him until the night they did adventurous things involving rope.

After he was done regaling us with his latest conquest, we'd chuckle and shake our heads—the girls out of shocked amazement (and probably a hidden burning lust they had more trouble concealing as each day passed), us guys out of immense envy. But it was never out of disbelief; we never had the slightest doubt that his stories were true. Maybe it was the seriousness with which he took the subject. Or the way he told his stories, stating all the events clearly and evenly in a matter-of-fact tone of voice. Or how he would never embellish what happened. There were never any tales of 14-hour lovemaking sessions or anything else that was clearly fictitious; instead, most of his stories would end with him slipping away into the night soon after the business was done. And maybe we believed him because sometimes a girl from one (or two or three) of his stories would stop in the store to see him and he would introduce her to us and we'd all smile pleasantly and think "So *this* is Katie!" while he winked at us, wearing a sly grin.

The store was flooded with human traffic every day. It was located on the main street and was frequented by a fair number of regular customers whom I eventually came to recognize. I would remember how they took their coffee or what muffin they liked and they always seemed appreciative of the gesture.

A select few of the regulars caught my attention after I saw them a few times. I found myself waiting for them during the day and greeted them with more enthusiasm than I granted the other customers. I would make a mental checklist and tick them off as they came in.

One had long, curly hair. She was petite and always seemed to be rushed or in the middle of something important. This perceived busyness was very appealing to me as I didn't have much to occupy my time after work those days and it was nice seeing someone somewhere getting something done. I indulged the fantasy that she was taking time out of her hectic schedule to get her coffee from this particular store, and it was because of me that she did so. Knowing that she was always in a hurry

"Well, I might go back to Hawaii, that's where I live, but my boyfriend's in France right now so I might visit him. And then again, my uncle's going to Australia, and he invited me along so . . . I'm really not sure yet."

"That's pretty exciting," I said, looking at the floor.

"Yeah, are you going anywhere? Oh, well, you don't really have a winter break, do you?"

"Yeah, not really. But, I mean, I'll still probably do something for Christmas or something. I might visit my friend, he's in the southern part of the state. Maybe somewhere else. In state. Pretty boring, I guess." I looked at the next table, which was covered in crumbs.

"Well," she said after a few seconds, "I better get back to these books if I want to have time to do anything tonight. What was your name again?"

"Alan."

"Alan," she repeated, almost as a final goodbye before she forgot the name forever. "Nice talking to you."

"You too," I said and moved away from her, sweeping the floor as I went. I didn't have to ask for her name again. How could I forget one of the prettiest names I'd ever heard belonging to one of the prettiest girls I'd ever seen?

Malia would come in just as often as she did before but I never approached her again. I figured we had said all that we needed to say to each other. And after that I never really took the time to listen to John's stories anymore; they no longer seemed as amusing as they once had. However, my conversation with Malia did make me feel better about never again seeing the exotic, beautiful girl who used to be a regular. I see now that it was the only way it could be and, furthermore, the way it should be.

THE UTILITY KNIFE

HE WOKE UP, even though he was exhausted, supine on his bed, and stared up at the ceiling while contemplating whether he should actually *get up* since he was awake. He hadn't slept much during the night and could've drifted back to sleep just as easily as he could've sat up, facing that inchoate moment of indecision everybody wakes up to. The sun had risen, barely, but it was enough to illuminate the room without another source of light. He thought about last night, gazing at the ceiling, then, looking over, saw her lying on the other side of the bed, her eyes closed. He stared at her face, examining her, his body inert, unchanged from the moment he woke up except for a turn of the head. He thought about reaching out, cupping her face in his hands, or reaching under the sheets, to her legs, finding her stomach maybe . . . he lay there thinking of all the tactile things he wanted to do without actually doing them. Instead, after about five minutes, he got up, walked over to his desk, grabbed a pack of cigarettes, and walked out of the room.

He opened the door to his balcony and sat on the wicker chair next to the railing. He shivered a little in the brisk dawn air. He opened the pack of cigarettes, grabbed the last remaining one, and lighted it quickly, almost hurriedly, then starting puffing on it, inhaling and exhaling as if he were experiencing walked to the door and stopped, looking back at her. She was lying on the pillow and had pulled the comforter up to her neck. She was staring out the window next to the bed. He stood there, watching her, silent. The early morning sounds of birds came into the room; she had a content smile on her face and she was faintly humming.

She finally looked toward the door and seemed surprised to see him. "Back already?" she asked.

"No." There was an unnecessary pause before he said, "I love you."

"I love you too," came the fast reply.

His heart was racing. "No, wait, listen," he said, clearly anxious but trying to keep it under control. "I *love* you."

"I love *you*," she said.

He made sure to exit the room before shaking his head.

When he came back to the room with a glass of water, she was gone. He did not immediately register her disappearance, so anxious was he to return to the room and shut the door behind him. Sealed off from the putrid fumes of spoiled dairy product and weeks-old meat, he took a deep breath, smelling vanilla scent. He walked over to the empty bed, putting down the glass of water before sitting. For several minutes, he sat there, unmoving. When he got up, he purposefully walked over to the candles and blew them out. He unconsciously reached toward his desk before realizing there were no cigarettes there. This didn't surprise him too much, and he treated their absence as something he had known and momentarily forgotten.

He walked back to the bed. He looked blankly at the rumpled sheets, wanting to slide into them and cover his head but he was also repulsed by the thought of doing so. He sat down on the bed instead, a banal compromise. The smell of extinguished wicks permeated the air, the nearly acrid smell quickly overpowering what remained of the vanilla scent. The room darkened as some clouds moved across the sun, only to be re-illuminated a few seconds later.

He was aware of his utter exhaustion, but knew that sleep was not a viable option. His mind raced unstoppably, at a rate that precluded the possibility of rest. His head was full of words and when he opened his mouth to breathe, some of them escaped his cranium involuntarily—"I. . . You. . . So much *time*. . ."—if not coherently. After the world became real to him again, he looked at the door expectantly and not without fear.

PLAIN JANE

SINCE HE WAS FACED WITH THE UNAVOIDABLE TASK of finding a new pattern to fall into and he knew this period of transition would be uncomfortable no matter how many of his old habits he reinstated, Rick decided to shake things up a bit, to do something a little different and see if it would stick and turn into a new avocation. So he went to the movies.

He hadn't gone in ages. As far as he could recall, the last time he went was when Lydia dragged him to see that big fat wedding one that everyone was going nuts about (to his gratification, she ended up hating it as much as he did). For the most part, Rick regarded movies as little more than glorified television shows and going to the theater was no different than staying home and sitting in front of an amped-up big-screen TV, only worse because you had to share an armrest with a stranger. Movies might be more glamorous and spectacular, but he could only shake his head at the money Hollywood burned through on each production and how the press would write about movie stars and the money and the stakes involved with the latest blockbuster in such a bombastic way that one would think movies were the most important thing in the world. Rick thought the whole enterprise was kind of a fraud—the studios were taking the audience's time and money and giving them something of dubious value in return. But it was something to do on a Wednesday night. So he went.

After getting out of his car and looking up at the marquee,

he realized that he didn't know anything about any of the movies currently playing. Feeling foolish and faintly embarrassed, he walked slowly up to the entrance and hesitated, trying to decide if he really wanted to do this. Finally, he pulled the door open and walked inside.

The pervasive smell of butter was the first thing he noticed. Then the décor, which was supposed to evoke the classy design of those old matinee houses that no longer exist, but it was done with a modern practicality and garish colors, creating a gaudy effect rather than a sentimental one. The lighting consisted of multiple arrays of spotlights and more than a few of them had burned out, which impaired the dramatic mood that might have otherwise obtained by making the lobby look depressingly dark. He walked over to the posters hanging on the wall and squinted at them; the credits were printed in a size and font that made him want to take the poster down and tilt it at an angle so he could actually read it. He was looking for more information about the movies that were playing but all the posters were for movies coming out "soon," some of them with release dates more than a year away.

He sighed and turned to the ticket counter. There was a girl behind the counter. She looked to be about his age, in her early twenties. She was reading a paperback. Rick looked at the names of the movies above her head and when he straightened his gaze he saw her looking at him expectantly. He sheepishly grinned and said, "Um . . . so which ones are good?"

She looked at him blankly. "Well," she said, "only one of them is starting in ten minutes. The rest don't play again for an hour."

"Oh. I'll see that one then," he said quickly. He could feel his face start to burn.

"Eight dollars please."

He handed her the money and she gave him his change and a ticket stub, along with a smile that was half amused and half sympathetic. "Enjoy the show," she said.

"Thank you," he said meekly before scampering off to the

dry," "I'm cleaning my apartment," "I'm compiling all the excuses I can use next time you ask me what I'm doing," "I'm washing my *damn hair*," etc.), forcing him to respond with the most readily available answer (viz. the truth): "No, not really."

He saw her breathe in deeply, as if she had been literally denying herself air waiting for his response. She said, "Well, there's this coffee place across the street and I was wondering if you wanted to have a cup of coffee with me." She quickly added: "They have good music and make a pretty mean cup of cappuccino."

In a more clear-headed state, he might've bantered with her: "Is this cappuccino bothering you? Cuz I can sit it down and give it a stern talking to, man-to-froth." Instead, he seized up. He couldn't believe she would have him make public an assessment of her that he hadn't even bothered to make privately to himself. He reprised the eyeballing he gave her before, this time checking her out for real, registering the previously unnoticed details of her appearance, his observations only confirming what he had suspected before the analysis: *She's nice*, he thought, *but she's so plain. Plain Jane.* He smiled involuntarily. She took this to be an encouraging sign and her eyes brightened. He quickly recomposed his features into a neutral, if not grim, physiognomy.

"Um," he said. "I actually . . . can't."

"Oh. Ok." She hung her head, as if she were being chastised. He was about to say something propitiating when she said, "Well, maybe next time."

He nodded vigorously. "Exactly," he averred.

An awkward silence descended, lasting several seconds before being broken by mumbled goodbyes. He felt relieved as he walked away.

A couple days later, he went back to the theater without any apprehension. In fact, his mood was jovial, not dampened at all by what had happened. She, too, was happy to see him. His return put her at ease; she felt as if they had jointly decided to weather this inconsequential bump in their incipient relationship. They piled on joke after joke, laughing uncontrollably. They were enjoying each other's company so much that their mirth seemed exclusionary to others.

She directed him toward a buddy comedy, which turned out to be surprisingly good—the best movie he'd seen in the past few weeks, by far. Coming out of the theater, he felt overwhelmingly content and carefree—rejuvenated, even. He strolled across the lobby toward the ticket counter with a bounce in his step, whistling softly to himself (something he almost never did). His effervescent disposition seemed to render the floor superfluous; he felt as light as air and on the verge of being lifted gently aloft by his billowing goodwill. He was overjoyed to find his happiness reflected on Jane's face and he started to say something that he hoped would convey just a tenth of what he was feeling.

Then he saw the coffee cups.

There were two of them, both sixteen ounces and fitted into cardboard sleeves, sitting side by side on the counter. He intuited their purpose almost immediately and was saddened as he realized that her every gesture, every word even, would now have to be scrutinized for hidden meaning. He was also embarrassed for her, for the way the cups were openly displayed, in plain view, as naked as her motives—she was like an inept magician who thought she had fooled her audience while the ace of spades was clearly visible, poking out of her sleeve. Despite this, he feigned ignorance.

"What are those?" he asked innocently, giving her one last chance to hide her intentions.

She picked up one of the cups and held it out to him. "Try it," she urged. When he didn't immediately take the cup, she brought it closer to his lips as if intending to pour its contents into his mouth herself.

He hastened to grab the cup, then hesitated. He knew that sampling this drink would cement his complicity in her insidious attempt to force him to partake in something for which he had already expressed a disinclination. But her eyes were glittering and expectant, so he took a sip.

"Good, isn't it?" she said cheerfully. "It's from that coffee place across the street."

"Yeah, I kinda figured that," he said shortly.

They tried to fall into their regular social rhythm, but their moods became inverses of each other, at least initially—he was as laconic as she was garrulous. Soon her words dried up and the conversation languished, devoid of the spark it usually had. By the time he brusquely excused himself, she was flustered and hurt. At the exit, he glanced back and saw her staring blankly ahead, at nothing. *Let her sit on it*, he thought. *Let her realize where she went wrong.*

When he came back to the theater five days later, Rick saw Jane manning the ticket counter, engrossed in a book as usual. He walked up to her, confident that she was regretting the stunt she had tried to pull and undoubtedly wanted nothing more than for things to return to normal—a desire he shared.

Stepping up to the counter, he grinned and, opening up with his customary greeting, said, "Hey, you live here or something?"

She didn't look up. He stood there, grinning away. A few seconds passed, though it felt longer. She turned a page of her book.

"So," he tried again, "what's that you're reading? Anything good?"

"What do you want?" she asked tersely, her eyes fixed downward.

"Well, I heard they play movies here," he said, a little more impudently than he had intended.

She sighed and rang up a ticket without consulting him. Sliding the stub toward him, she impatiently said, "Eight dollars." After snatching the money from his grasp, she resumed giving the book her undivided attention.

He stood there for a moment, waiting for her to relent and give him a proper greeting. She had not yet looked at his face—he knew this because his eyes hadn't left hers. After an amount of time that precluded a graceful and unabashed departure, he left her to her book and headed off to his movie. *She needs a couple more hours,* he thought.

The movie was quite possibly the worst one he had ever seen. It lacked imagination, wit, even a coherent plot. Through it all, he resolved to stay in his seat. If this was her idea of punishment and his required expiation, fine, though for the life of him he couldn't think of anything he had done wrong. He contented himself by picturing the good-naturedly mischievous expression sure to be on her face, awaiting him upon his release from cinematic purgatory. He looked forward to being a good sport about her little prank and laughing with her about it.

But she did not give him a playful look when he came out of the theater. In fact, she didn't look at him at all. Also, walking closer, he saw that her expression was so severely set in something very much like a scowl that laughter, if even possible at this point, might've proven painful for her.

"Wow! What an excellent movie!" he gushed with overcompensatory enthusiasm.

She glanced not so much *at* him as *through* him, blatantly dismissive.

He suddenly felt a rush of indignation. "Yes yes," he snapped, "hate to stand in the way of your book. I can see that I'm the third wheel here. So . . . bye, I guess."

She uttered a curt "Bye."

He theatrically rolled his eyes before leaving.

Over the next few days, the thought of going to the movies caused him no small amount of agitation. He wasn't sure what irritated him more: the likelihood she would still be taciturn or the possibility that he would never go back to the theater. Because why was he going to the movies in the first place? To see a movie, right? Not for her—she was a divertissement, not the main attraction. Then again, how would he know what movies to see if not for her? Of course, if she continued to spitefully recommend swill, she would not be of much use to him. But on the other hand, all the movies seemed to be awful. A randomly selected one would probably be just as good as her recommendation, and the bottom line was that he was going to the theater to see a movie, not to socialize.

But with all that said, Rick eventually had to admit that Jane was an important, if not integral, part of his moviegoing experience. He decided to go back and give her another chance to be herself again.

Five seconds after walking into the lobby, he wished he hadn't. She actually looked at him this time, but it was with an openly baleful look of resentment, held briefly before she looked down (at a book, naturally), her countenance reverting back to the saturnine expression with which he was fast becoming familiar. Undaunted, or maybe just resigned, he walked across the stretch of lobby that had once been illuminated by her welcoming smile and radiant eyes. Now the walk to the counter felt dismal and fraught with uncertainty.

He approached her slowly, cautiously, with a solemn aspect, still prepared to release the dormant happiness just under the surface, if only she would show him just a glimmer of her former bonhomie.

"Hey," he said, pleasant but hesitant.

"Hey," she said in monotone, forestalling the expression of any gaiety for either of them.

"How are you doing today?" His placid voice belied the tumult that was roiling inside him.

"What can I get for you?" she asked in the same monotone.

"A ticket to a movie would be nice."

With practiced movements, she hit a few buttons and printed up a ticket. "Eight dollars." She didn't even sound like a real person to him, let alone one capable of joy. After she shut his money in the drawer, there was a distinct sense that she considered the transaction—and, therefore, their interaction—over.

"You know what would be even nicer?" he ventured. "A smile."

She snorted, sounding incredulous. A nugget of pique swelled inside him and he abruptly ripped up his ticket. She didn't budge.

"All your movies are terrible," he stated. No reaction. "Well, then . . . bye," he said, trying to sound insouciant with limited success. She wafted her hand lifelessly in response, a cavalier gesture devoid of warmth or even respect. He turned to leave, then quickly swiveled back.

"You know, I have to say something here," he said overbearingly, like a person sitting on a particularly juicy secret he couldn't wait to divulge. "I think it's sad that you're treating me like crap just because I won't have sex with you. Because that's what you're doing—I'm not gonna mince words here." Her only reaction was a slight narrowing of eyes that were still focused away from him.

He pressed on: "All I wanted to be was friends—nothing more. I never gave you any hint that I wanted anything more. *You* were the one who had . . . desires for other things. And, frankly, why should I have to suffer for that, or be made to feel bad that I don't feel the same way or whatever. So I politely declined your advances and, and I was ready to move on. To continue being the friend I thought you to be. But no, you wouldn't have that. Instead, you're taking some perverse sort of 'all or nothing' attitude. Well, I hope you're happy you ended up with nothing. Hopefully you don't grow to resent the fact that you lost a friend just because you wanted to get laid."

He turned around and walked out of the building without looking back. He had nearly reached his car when he heard an angry "Hey!" behind him. He turned around and saw Jane stomping toward him. Her posture was aggressive, her eyes fiery, her voice dripping with venom.

"You don't want to mince words?" she spat. "*Fine*, I won't mince 'em. First of all—Friends? *Friends?* Who in the world is looking for *friends?*"

"I am," he protested.

She rolled her eyes contemptuously. "What are you, in third

grade? *Grow up.* No one our age is looking for friends. What, you're honestly gonna tell me you want another person who will borrow your money and not pay you back? Who you are obligated to help move every time they get a new apartment? Who you have to drive to the airport at five in the morning? Who will flatter you, lie to you, in service of your vanity? Who will be there for you, until it is advantageous for her not to be?" She glared at him while hot bursts of air expelled from her nostrils. "You are a man of a certain age. I am a woman of the same age. We only want one thing from each other."

"That's a pretty cynical way of looking at it," he said.

"Well hey, ok, let's say that you really did just want to be friends," she seethed, riding the next wave of hostility. "Ok, that doesn't make any sense to me either because you weren't acting very friendly toward me."

"What?!" he exclaimed. "That is a falsehood of the highest order. I was nothing *but* friendly to you."

"You were courteous, I grant you, but *friendly?* Do you even have friends? Friends do things together. They hang out at each other's houses. They touch each other when they laugh. They let themselves be seen without their shirt on. Sometimes, they even sleep with each other—"

"Oh come on."

"They drink coffee together," she insisted. "Especially when the cups are sitting *right there.*" She looked him squarely in the eye. "You didn't treat me like a friend, you treated me like a *convenience.*"

He stared at her, unsure of what to say. She leaned forward, causing him to involuntarily flinch.

"So I hope *you* remember," she said, her voice softer but still edged with malice, "when you're jerking off into a sock, pining after some girl who won't give you the time of day, I want you to recall what you could've had"—she spread her arms out, directing his attention to her body—"and I hope you drown in tears of regret."

After delivering her imprecation, she walked away in a huff.

He watched her go, still speechless. Presently, he shook his head, believing her, at that moment, to be one of the most foolish people he had ever met. He got in his car, already thinking of alternative ways to spend his Wednesday nights (as well as Friday, Saturday, Sunday, and sometimes Monday).

But, as soon as the following night, Jane and her words began to occupy his thoughts in a most importunate way. Though he was positive that he had dealt with her honorably and with the utmost civility, he really started to wonder what his intentions had been toward her, ultimately. There was no longer any sense in continuing to insist that he was going to the movies to see a movie; only a deaf blind man with an IQ less than 40 could enjoy the garbage they were projecting onto the big screen these days. No, he had to admit he was going for Jane, at least a little bit. That much was obvious, even to him. But why? *For a friendship,* he thought adamantly to himself. But her words crept furtively back into his mind and, during his more empathetic moments, he thought there was some validity in what she had said. After all, she was right: he was a boy, she was a girl, so (he found himself thinking) why not? *Because she's not a girl,* he reminded himself. *She's Plain Jane.* Ok, but so where did that leave him? He hadn't been reduced to jerking off in a sock (yet), but he had to concede that his evenings had become fairly uneventful. Wasn't ten minutes of not unpleasurable thrusting worth being able to enjoy the protracted company of someone with whom you can converse and laugh and commiserate? Someone who makes you smile and brightens your day, undeniably? As this question became less and less rhetorical, he began thinking of how he could return to the theater and tactfully suggest they try things her way, to let her know that he'd changed his mind—he wanted her, even if he had to sleep with her. But before he made it back to the theater, he met another girl. Within twenty-four hours they were having sex, and he never gave Plain Jane another thought.

MELISSA

MR. PEDERSEN was the type of teacher who actually liked us. He would take the first five, sometimes even ten minutes of every Monday morning and ask if anyone did anything interesting over the weekend. He would write the results of the NBA play-off games on the board and trade friendly barbs with students who were fans of the winning team. Instead of making us turn in research papers on prominent historical figures, he would have us dress up as the person we researched and he would come in as a late night talk show host and interview us in character. He was a great teacher, which is to say he was inspiring, knowledgeable, affable, and, most importantly, human.

So when the whole class surprised him one day with an impromptu birthday party, we had little doubt that he would indulge us. Upon walking in the door, he was greeted with a loud "Happy Birthday!" and tables arranged with soda, pizza, and chips. Someone had even brought in a boombox and a stack of CDs. And because he was the teacher he was, instead of telling us all to sit down, he smiled widely, shoved his day planner into a drawer, and grabbed a party hat. I think he realized that this was not a simple ploy to get out of doing schoolwork for the day; we genuinely wanted to celebrate the birthday of someone we greatly respected.

Everyone grabbed some food and talked and laughed. We cleared a giant space in the center of the room and turned on some dance music. One of the guys acted as the DJ, switching

CDs every so often, and Mr. Pedersen told him to turn it down only once. Occasionally, other students and teachers would peek in the room to see what the commotion was and they would leave with faces full of deep envy, which pleased us to no end. We wanted the whole school to know that Mr. Pedersen's classroom was liberated while every other class was chained to the unyielding monotony of rules and routines.

About thirty minutes into the party, someone flicked off the lights and a couple guys carried in a big birthday cake, replete with thirty-three candles. There was enough illumination to see all our smiling faces as we sang Happy Birthday. Mr. Pedersen paused dramatically, then blew them out in one try. We erupted in applause.

The cake was big enough for everyone to get a piece. I took mine back to the spot I had monopolized for nearly the entire day, content to watch the proceedings alongside a couple other guys. While my adoration of Mr. Pedersen equaled or exceeded that of my classmates, I did not have the clout to convince the others to help organize something like this. As a result, I found out about the party only shortly before Mr. Pedersen had. Those of us left in the dark had of course quickly endorsed the plan and were pleased with the initiative that had been taken by our more enterprising peers.

At some point, I realized that a slow song had begun to play. The class couples met in the center of the room and swayed in each other's arms to the sentimental music. There was Bryan and Kelly, by far the most popular students in the class and probably the organizers of the party. Their best friends, Dave and Sarah, danced beside them. Girls and guys not currently involved in a relationship walked across the room and asked classmates for a dance. Mr. Pedersen encouragingly prodded several people toward each other. A few, like myself, stayed on the periphery and watched.

I saw Ann walking toward the group I was standing with, dragging her reluctant friend Melissa along. After exchanging nervous pleasantries, Ann asked if one of us wanted to dance with Melissa. I looked at Melissa; she timidly looked away, her chestnut head of hair flowing down her back, her cheeks growing redder. I continued to look at her, suddenly mesmerized. My gaze wandered down and I noticed the summery tint of her bare arms and the slenderness and glow of her legs. When I reached her black strappy shoes, I looked back up and met her large eyes, her timidness momentarily replaced by something else entirely. My heart started to race and I wished the slow song would end already.

One of the guys turned down the offer. Another just looked away and didn't say a word. Ann turned to me.

"Well?" she said. "How about you?" Melissa continued to look at me. I smiled nervously.

"I don't dance," I said with attempted conviction.

"You don't dance?" Ann said incredulously. Melissa smiled at me and, despite myself, I smiled back and shrugged my shoulders.

"Stop being ridiculous," Ann said. "Dance with her."

A couple of the other guys, sensing their emancipation from this ordeal was near, encouraged me with increasing persistence to do what Ann said. I concentrated on the drink in my hand, feigning nonchalance. When I looked up, everyone was staring at me, expectantly.

"Isn't there anyone else?" I suggested. Ann clicked her tongue and the smile on Melissa's face faded. She looked stricken, wounded. "I don't dance," I said as apologetically as I could.

Ann grabbed her friend's arm and led her back across the room. I finished the rest of my drink and absently ate a few crackers as my heartbeat slowly fell back into a normal pattern. By the time I saw Melissa dancing with Nathan near the corner of the room, I realized, too late, that I had crossed the line between cute diffidence and complete obnoxiousness.

One of the guys saw them and told me I should've danced with her. With an edge to my voice I repeated that I didn't dance. And it was true, I didn't. Not at that place, not at that time. . . .

SARAH A.

ANDREW ORDERED a latte, sat down at one of the tables, and watched Sarah from across the cafe. She had a notebook computer on her table and was periodically hitting keys while lazily sipping her chai. Andrew pulled some index cards from his pocket and spread them out carefully in front of him. He meticulously scanned each card, committing the words written on them to memory. He paid particular attention to the cards with a star in the corner—those were the key points in his speech and he'd be damned if he was going to allow himself to forget them.

Feeling nearly ready, he looked up at Sarah. Damn. She was looking right at him, her lips turned slightly upward in a knowing smile. Andrew acknowledged her with a short nod and gathered his cards together. Now that he had been spotted, there was no sense in staying where he was. He stood up, buttoned his overcoat and straightened his tie, and walked as casually as he could over to where Sarah was sitting.

He watched her the whole way, picking apart the details. The brown hair, the brown eyes, the brown legs. Her perfect genes worked in perfect unison with her daily regimen of exercise and tanning. The result was nothing short of stunning; she was beautiful. This last-minute assessment made Andrew more resolved than ever in his task. *How could anyone want to hurt something so beautiful?* he thought. *How?*

She turned her attention away from the laptop just long enough to motion for him to sit down, then resumed her typing. He took the seat across from her, watching her face scrunch up in intense concentration, her brow furrowed. He mentally rehearsed his index cards. After a few moments, she stopped typing and with a final click-click, she shut the notebook computer off. After a contented sigh, she smiled warmly across the table.

"Hello Andy," she said.

"Hello Sarah," he said. "How are you?"

"Good. How are you?"

"Fine."

"What brings you here? Business or pleasure?"

"A little of both, I suppose." Andrew looked around as if seeing the cafe for the first time. "Nice little place. You come here often?"

"Sure; yeah, I do," she shrugged. "Nice atmosphere, good place to get stuff done, you know—bring the work here, no distractions."

"Yeah." He took a sip of his drink. "I saw you, figured I'd come over."

"More like I saw you and you decided to come over," she laughed.

"Well, you looked busy," he said defensively. "I didn't want to disturb you."

"Aw, always thinking of someone else, always the gentleman."

"Someone has to do it, right?"

"That's why you're tops in my book Andy."

"Thanks."

Andrew finished off his drink and, without anything else to distract him, nervously fiddled with his watch. Sarah regarded him, tilting her head slightly, curious. She shifted in her seat and nonchalantly tossed out "Something on your mind Andy?"

Andrew glanced at her, then looked back at his hands. "Yes

actually," he said slowly and deliberately. "I need to talk to you."

"Ok," she said, sitting back in her chair. "We're talking; what are we talking about?"

Andrew cleared his throat and forced himself to look directly into Sarah's eyes like he had planned. He imperceptibly steeled himself before saying "I've been thinking about what you said yesterday."

She didn't move and continued to look at Andrew looking at her. "And?" she said in a neutral voice.

Andrew took a deep breath and, before he had time to think about it anymore, he blurted out "Do you love him?"

Sarah betrayed no emotion one way or another as she calmly said "Why?"

"Well . . . I . . . that is to say . . ." Andrew looked down at his hands again, unnerved by Sarah's unyielding gaze. He had wanted her complete attention and now that he had it, he wasn't sure if he was up to the challenge. "Well, if you don't . . . then . . . that's just not right. You know?" He looked at her with pleading eyes, seeking some kind of affirmation but meeting a stoic indifference instead. He realized then that he was resigned to continue, no matter how much of a fool he made of himself. "That's . . . it's not fair to you . . . ok? I . . ." He sighed. "Listen, do you love him or not?"

Sarah leaned forward and was amused by the way Andrew flinched when she did so. She propped her head with one hand and drummed the table with her other fingers. She finally looked away from Andrew (for which he was greatly relieved) and stared out the window. "Do I love him?" she mused aloud. Andrew suffered through many seconds of monotonous tapping before she turned to him and said "I don't know" with a shrug of her shoulders.

"Well," Andrew said quickly, then stopped, unsure of how to continue. Hopeless, he could only sputter "Shouldn't you?" with a tinge of desperation in his voice.

Sarah looked at him with a blank stare, then turned to the

window again. Andrew decided to push ahead. "Look," he said, regaining some of his resolve, "I want you to know that I'm here for you, ok? I'm saying that I'll help you get through this and if this guy runs away from this situation, that I . . . see, you . . ." He started to lose his focus again and tried in vain to remember exactly what was written on his index cards, specifically the ones with a star in the corner. "You are . . ." he began again. "See, you are one of the most amazing people I've ever met and I'm willing to make a commitment, if needed, because you deserve it, my respect, see? And you don't deserve what this other guy is . . . doing . . . Man, this sounded a lot better on paper . . ." He trailed off. He hoped Sarah was getting at least some of what he had been meaning to convey.

But when he looked at her face, there was no hint of the respect he had hoped for. Instead there was skepticism mixed with an alarming sense of indifference. "What are you saying Andy? That if Brian dumps me, you'll help me with the kid?" she asked incredulously.

"If it came to that," Andrew said in a surprisingly strong voice.

Sarah re-crossed her legs as she considered this. "So you'd raise a kid that wasn't yours?" she said, keeping her disbelieving tone. "What would people say? How would that look?"

"Hey I think we're beyond the stage where we're concerned about appearances," Andrew snapped. "This is serious."

His sudden flash of anger seemed to sober Sarah up, and she appeared to shrink in her seat, growing smaller before his eyes. Traces of weariness and melancholy worked over her face. "I know," she said heavily. "I know this is serious." She looked at him and for the first time she seemed vulnerable and in need of reassurance. "Are you serious?"

"I am," he said resolutely. "I've never been more serious."

She closed her eyes as his love and adoration flowed over her. She sighed deeply. "I need a cigarette," she said distractedly.

"You should quit," Andrew said as she put her coat on. He

picked up the pack of cigarettes lying next to her computer. "I'll buy these from you, five dollars . . ." He stopped and shrugged. "That won't work, you'll just buy two more packs," he said forlornly.

She grabbed the pack out of his hands and he followed her outside.

They stood in silence as she took a long drag off one of her Parliament Lights. "I'll stop," she said in between puffs, "if it turns out I'm actually pregnant. Of course I will."

"And what will you do if this guy never calls you again?" he asked without looking at her.

"I don't know," she said simply.

He watched her smoking and holding the weight of the world on her shoulders. "Give me one of those," he said suddenly.

She obligingly held out the pack and he pried a cigarette loose. She handed him a lighter. He lit the cigarette and took a couple of short puffs. He inhaled deeply and instantly started coughing. He bent over, still gagging, and she sympathetically patted him on the back. It took him a few moments to recover; when he was able to breathe again, he stood up and disgustedly flicked away what remained of the cigarette. He put his hands in his pockets and turned to Sarah. "Think about what I said, ok?" he said.

"I will," she said. He reached over and squeezed her arm, then walked away. She watched him go, took one last drag of her cigarette, then went back into the cafe. By the time Andrew looked back for one last glimpse of her, she was already inside.

their own world, a world at once opaque and transparent, filled with naked motives and unencumbered emotions that dictate their actions with maddening simplicity. It was downright confounding to anyone with a diploma. It didn't matter if you were three years or three months removed from that insular world—each new crop had their own code of conduct incomprehensible to everyone else.

"Exactly. That's exactly what it is—ignorance and *ingratitude*. They really are completely unaware of how *good* they have it. Someone does their laundry, the bathroom cabinet is always stocked, they have a warm house to go home to in the winter—"

"Home-cooked meals." Roy takes off his maroon vest.

"Ah, how I miss home-cooked meals." Guy's eyes go wistful for a second. "These ungrateful brats have it all. But my point of contention with them today is the boredom. I just don't understand it, how can they be bored? Have they not discovered sex? Do all their girlfriends give lousy head and all their boyfriends last thirty seconds? They should all be constantly screwing in their pulled-over cars. A license isn't a permit to drive, it's a permit to screw. How can they be so bored when they should be having the best sex of their lives?"

"The best?"

"Sure. Not only is it new and exciting, but since they're carefree and all their quotidian needs are taken care of, they're in a position to completely enjoy it. None of us can say that."

"I still find it pretty invigorating."

"No doubt. But the fact is, we are laden with certain matters, with certain responsibilities, let's say, most of them pecuniary in nature, that preclude the total enjoyment of sex. We are no longer naifs running around without a care in the world, able to construe sexual pleasure as the crux, the very point of human existence. No, we are no longer that innocent, we have been besmirched, despoiled. And, worse, we get a monthly reminder of our ignominy in the form of credit card statements. Our fall from grace is as unceasing as the electric bill.

Because I tell ya, the true loss of innocence happens when you fork over the money for your first month's rent and security deposit. At that point, your primary concerns irrevocably shift to the mundane. From then on, you are a marked, vaguely troubled man, a shell of your former self. You could be having the greatest sex in the world, and yet there'll still be that nagging thought in the back of your mind: How am I gonna pay next month's rent? You'll wish you'd had more sex or, hell, even enjoyed life, *really*, before you had to deal with all this crap like rent and automatic deductions and late fees . . . but by then, it'll be too late. Freakin' ungrateful, bored teenagers. Won't know what hit them."

Roy regards his soda can for a few seconds, then looks up. "All that, plus when else can you go through five girls a week without raising anyone's eyebrows."

A reflective pause. "Ya damn right. *Damn* right."

They both sit there, finishing their drinks.

A Memory from Roy's late adolescence:

Junior year. Roy was hanging out with—let's face it—the nerd crowd. Socially inept, they would laugh at things nobody else found especially funny.

On this day, sitting in physics lab, they amused themselves by mispronouncing "impedance" to sound like "impotence." One would say to another, "Your circuits have more *impotence* than mine" and they would crack up like only a group of virgins could. Except for Roy, who only smiled vaguely before finally asking, "Ok, am I missing something? What's so funny?"

"What's funny," one of them said, "is that this lab is all about impotence." They snickered. Roy looked at them blankly.

"Uh, you know what impotence is, right?" somebody asked him.

Roy shook his head. This made them laugh even harder. Nothing gave them greater pleasure than being able to tell somebody something he didn't know, and here was a chance to enlighten one of their ignorant peers on a *sexual* matter, no less, thereby emasculating him in front of everyone—an opportunity rarely presented to a nerd, making this moment particularly sweet.

"Impotence," one of them said in a condescending voice, loud enough to be heard by the group of cool pretty girls the next table over, "is the inability to maintain an *erection* for the purposes of sexual *intercourse*."

"Duh!" someone else added, setting off another round of guffaws.

Roy saw the cool pretty girls look at each other, trying not to laugh. He shrugged. "Why would I know anything about that?" he said simply.

That shut them right up. Roy glanced over at the girls and, riding a wave of confidence, slyly winked at the coolest and prettiest of them. She blushed and smiled, biting her lower lip flirtatiously, as if she knew then that she would be the one to take his virginity, which is what happened a month later, at which time they both discovered that he hadn't been lying.

—. . . *you are a highway, I wanna ride you all night long!*
—Haha!
—*If we do it my way, we'll do it doggy All-Night-Long!*
—Haha!
—Heh.
—Ok, ok, what about: *Hey now, you're a porn star, get your hard-on, get laid!*
—Haha!
—*All that . . . sucks my cock is gold . . . or something . . .*
—Wait wait wait, ok: *So you're Dirk Diggler. That don't impress me much. So you got a 13-inch cock but do you got the touch?*
—Haha!
—*Don't get me wrong, your shlong's pretty long, but will it keep me warm in the middle of the night?*

—Haha!

—Heh heh heh.

—God that's good.

Roy and Guy commiserate about their respective girl problems:

"Carrie says I talk out of my ass," Guy is saying. "All the time, she says this. I can't say anything sometimes, one word— 'That is such bullshit' and 'There you go, talkin out your ass again.' Well, if that's the case, then she's being a real carie in my ass."

Roy barely grunts. He's in no mood for witticisms. He's much closer to falling in the dark pit of depression than Guy is. Guy can afford to be blithely epigrammatical because his girl problem is a problem with an actual girl whereas Roy's girl problem is of the nonexistent variety—the girl, not the problem. That's what Roy feels at least; he's in between girlfriends and he's getting restless.

"My problem is meeting them," Roy says, bringing the conversation back to his struggles where he feels it never should have left. "I don't know if you've noticed but it's pretty hard to meet promising candidates out there right now. If you go out alone, on the prowl as they say, forget it, you're dead in the water. I'm currently trying to accrue some girl acquaintances so they can introduce me to their hot friends. I've heard that most couples meet each other through a third party."

"Well there's your problem," Guy says decisively. "You're usually going to just one party a night."

Roy ignores him. "But that's proving to be an arduous task in and of itself, making friends with girls. I tell ya, sometimes it seems just as hard, if not *harder*, to get a girl in a coffee shop as it is to get her in the sack."

"I hate coffee," Guy says not quite but pretty much almost non-sequiturishly.

Roy just nods. *You smug bastard*, he thinks, looking at Guy. *You smug, lucky bastard. You're all set, a warm body to curl up next to, you're probably having sex every night. Make-up sex no less, from the sounds of it. God, you lucky son of a . . .*

Guy's face suddenly changes. The wrinkles around the vague smirk he's been wearing disappear and remanifest themselves as creases of concern around his eyes. "But seriously . . ." he says in a lower-pitched voice befitting the more serious expression on his face. Roy immediately gets attentive; he knows that Guy can be (and usually is) like a stand-up comedian who doesn't know when to get off the stage, but when he gets serious about something he can be as analytical and insightful as those guys that caught Nixon out on whatever it was Nixon did. Guy continues, "I think the problem lies in how you approach these potential 'coffee shop' girls."

"How so?" asks Roy with interest.

"Well, what's on your mind when you walk up to these girls? Probably how you take your coffee or whether you're gonna get anything to eat with your coffee or the coffee place itself. . . ."

"I'm usually thinking of how many lattes I'll have to buy her before she brings one of her hot friends along."

"Yeah, that's perfect." Guy gives him an encouraging smile. "Now, what's on your mind when you see a girl you want to get in the sack? Most likely stuff like bedrooms, Marvin Gaye playing in the background, different positions you want to try. . . ."

"Vegetables." Guy gives him a bemused look. Roy shrugs. "What? I like to introduce food into the proceedings fairly early."

". . . ok, whatever." Guy presses on: "The point I'm trying to illustrate is that you have two different mindsets here. And the girl you want to bag, you know she's not gonna let you sleep with her just like that—especially if you want to use vegetables. You know that saying 'Easy as pie?' Well you can be sure that the pie they were talking about wasn't pussy."

"Right," Roy nods in agreement.

"So you know if you wanna do your broccoli-thing with her

or whatever, you're gonna hafta utilize some of your *charm*, pull out that suave shit every guy's got in his arsenal. Whereas with these other girls," he gesticulates with his hands to indicate the shift to a whole separate thing, "these coffee shop girls, you're not doing any of that. I mean, you're being cordial, sure, but mainly you're impatient with how she's dragging her feet. Like why all the hesitation? It's just a damn coffee shop after all, it's not like you asked her to marry you."

"Exactly!" Roy almost shouts.

"Well I'm telling you right now that you have to treat these two different types of girls more similarly." Seeing Roy's confused look, he elaborates: "See, girls want to feel wanted by guys. They want to feel desired, even if that desire is to stick a carrot up their ass."

"Um, actually—"

"I don't even want to know," Guy interrupts. "So these girls sense your craving for them and they get excited, or at least intrigued. Now these other girls, these unfortunately-but-now-permanently named 'coffee shop girls,' all they sense from you is a vague resentment and impatience and then they start to get the feeling of being used. And, believe it or not, girls don't like feeling used. So." He levels his eyes at Roy, letting him know that this is the important part. "What I'm suggesting you do is start treating the coffee shop girls like you want *them*, not their friends, and the whole coffee shop experience as an end in itself, not a means to an end. You have to get *excited*."

"Excited?" Roy says. "For *coffee?*"

"There are plenty of things in there to stimulate the imagination," Guys insists, "what with the steaming, the grinding, the percolating . . . think of it as going to the coffee bean boudoir or the cappuccino Caribbean. Think of the froth, man."

"Ok. . . ." Roy says skeptically.

"Ok, you know what?" Guy says, drawing back a little. "Let's just keep things simple. Just act like you want to sleep with the coffee shop girls, ok?"

"But some, if not most—if not *all* of them—are pretty much homely," Roy whines.

"You don't have to have sex with them," Guy sighs. "Just *pretend* you want to. I guarantee that'll get them in the coffee shop, where, according to their now official title, they apparently belong. What you decide to do at that point—wait around for their hot friends or whatever—is up to you. That reminds me, have I ever told you my theory about average-looking girls, how they're up shit creek sexual activity-wise, especially compared to average-looking men?"

Roy is still sitting on Guy's advice, giving it a fair amount of thought. "Let's try it," he says. "Next girl that walks through the doors."

"Yeah, a trial run, good," Guy nods. "I'll supervise."

They both watch the entrance to the lobby in charged anticipation. After about a minute, a middle-aged woman walks in. She's draped in a muumuu-ish type of thing with a faded floral design and shoes that look sort of like clogs, only more unfashionable. Her ensemble is topped off by an old-fashioned hat with what might or might not be a real six-petaled daisy sticking straight out of it. Her face reflects the placidity of a proper citizen who uses her vegetables exclusively for food. The dowdy woman sees the two guys and starts to waddle over. "Perfect," Roy says, smiling.

"Oh god no," Guy says, completely horrified. "Please, for the love of—"

"Hi boys," the woman says, standing in front of them.

"Hi Mrs. Ambrose," Roy says pleasantly. "How are you today?"

"Oh, I'm good," says Guy's mother. "We're just having some gorgeous weather right now."

"That we are, that we are," Roy says in his most agreeable voice.

"How you doing sweetie?" she asks her son. Guy mumbles something inaudible in return.

"I must say," Roy comments, "that is one fetching hat you're wearing."

"Why thank you," she beams. "I pulled it out today, hadn't worn it in a while. . . ."

"Yeah, since 1933," mutters Guy.

"What was that dear?"

"Nothing," he says.

"Well I think it looks A-mazing," Roy says. "I can't take my eyes off it . . . or you for that matter."

"Thank you," she says, slightly blushing.

"Say," Roy says, offhandedly, "I'm about to go on lunch break pretty soon. Would you like to join me for some coffee across the street? They have an outdoor patio where we can enjoy this heavenly weather."

"Why sure. That would be fun," she says amiably. Roy reaches out and gives her hand a short squeeze. "Wonderful," he says, his smile all teeth.

Guy suddenly bolts into the bathroom. The sound of retching is heard a few moments later and it's not at all clear if it is genuine or merely feigned.

—Why do Jim Borgman's political cartoons suck so much?

—Suck hardcore.

—They're so simplistic. They break everything down to the simplest elements, like nothing's more complicated than the most basic interpretation of an idea. He draws like big SUVs and parents getting a big college bill and wants us to laugh.

—Borgman's stuff is about as penetrating as two inches of limp dick.

—I feel stupider just looking at his stuff.

—Tom Toles kicks Borgman's ass.

—Toles is the *man*. His stuff's got more layers than a Roman orgy. He's awesome.

—No doubt.

— . . .

—You ever notice, like around 1950, Flannery O'Connor

situation, the guy would bang her not only because she'd have the only orifice(s) around but also because there'd be no one to make fun of him afterward. That's the way it is, these are the social norms. This is not a world of sex acts consummated with physical, emotional, and social impunity. So if average-looking girls would just stay in their league and stop lusting after insanely attractive guys, it would save them from embarrassment, heartbreak, and a sexless future, and spare everyone else the same queasy feeling they used to get watching Michael Jordan trying to play baseball.

And but even if an average-looking girl decides to stop pining after super hot guys and start acting sensibly when she realizes she hasn't had sex in like 32 months (most likely a regrettable drunken liaison that is becoming less and less lamentable with each passing sexless day) and she resolves to give average-looking guys her full attention, if not outright jump the next one she sees, and resigns herself to average-looking dick because it's either that or no dick—if she decides to do what is right and give average-looking guys their due, she may be in for a surprise, an unpleasant discovery that'll make her want to rip out her possibly dyed but still average-looking hair and abjure sex forever on the grounds that nothing about it makes any sense, least of all the so-called "rules of engagement." What she might perplexedly find is that a fair percentage of average-looking guys are already getting their nuts drained . . . by insanely attractive girls. That's right. To an average-looking girl, it must seem like a cruel joke, completely inexplicable, a sign of impending apocalypse, etc. But the fact remains: super hot girls are open to the idea of sex with average-looking members of the opposite sex, enormously more receptive to the idea than hot guys are, anyway. The question probably burning a hole through every average-looking girl's (and guy's—though they're not asking it as pressingly because why question a good—no, *great*—thing?) head right now is: why would a hot girl who could have her pick of bed partners choose to straddle an average-looking specimen? Well, for one of a couple-three reasons, or maybe a multifaceted reason combining aspects of all the possible reasons and but still the three main reasons are—

One—and most uncomplexly—for their money. This one's pretty understandable. Money still influences, if not outright effects, transactions of all stripes, including sex, and nothing mixes business and pleasure like legal tender. For an insanely attractive girl who has never applied herself to anything that could be construed as useful to society, surrounded as she is by admirers but also beset by opportunists looking to exploit her appreciable assets in lurid and filmable ways, or even for those insanely attractive girls with heads on their shoulders but not unmindful of a good opportunity when they see one—whatever kind of insanely attractive girl they are, whether they're out on their ass or just looking to get ahead, it's not too hard to see how they would regard a roll in the hay every now and then with an average-looking guy as a minuscule price to pay for security from destitution and an AMEX card with virtually unlimited credit. This wouldn't be a formal, notarized agreement or anything (most of the time), more like a tacit understanding, and the girl isn't really using the guy (again, in most cases) because there's like total complicity here and the guy's cool with the arrangement and really he couldn't be happier because he's screwing an insanely attractive girl every couple days. Now, it goes without saying that this can work flip-side-of-the-coinishly, that insanely attractive men can be just as venal and money-hungry and be totally up for rocking a rich girl's world for her bank account. The reason you don't see that as much is due to the difficulty of finding a rich, single, average-looking girl, the last criterion almost being the hardest one to fulfill since most rich girls earn their fabulous wealth by being outrageously beautiful in front of a camera lens, and most men would have sex with them even if they didn't have a penny to their name. Plain-looking rich spinsters almost always inherit their wealth from their parents—specifically, in almost all cases, from their father (which is where they also inherit their plain looks, sometimes). And while hot women who grow up with inherited wealth have no reason to screw average-looking men for their money, they end up, like a lot of other women, screwing them anyway in a lot of cases for reasons unrelated to money, including—

Two—to satisfy a need to nurture, to comfort, to take care of someone. They see an average-looking guy who's a bit lost, helpless, down-and-out, and what they feel for this forlorn figure isn't exactly pity, more like the feeling of finding a dirty and bedraggled (but probably pretty cute if it could just be cleaned up a little) stray kitten at your doorstep and knowing that you would be the best thing that's happened in its life if you would take it in and it would flourish in your care and it would be so appreciative and people would remark about how cute it is after you're done bathing it and feeding it and primping it. It's basically the feeling of seeing a suffering creature and knowing you have exactly the right tools, disposition, etc. to make its life immeasurably better and it wouldn't even take that much effort from you or be that strenuous or inconvenient so how could you not? And no one is better equipped to help out an average-looking man than an insanely attractive woman because a down on his luck, slightly depressed average-looking man's friends and barroom commiserators are probably right when they say he just needs to get laid. An insanely attractive woman can most certainly do that and chances are she'd be allowed to by almost any average-looking man, especially one in need of day-brightening. No other type of man will be as thoroughly transformed and sated by a lay. Nobody will be as appreciative either. It'll hit just the spot, guaranteed to emancipate him from any sort of doldrums with optimum celerity. It's exhilarating for her to watch him grow before her eyes, become a more complete person in her warm embrace, and she gets an odd sense of pride for both him and herself, knowing she can take full responsibility for his turnaround and future successes. In fact, the attendant feelings she experiences are not without similarities to the ones that spring from a maternal instinct, something childless single women are particularly susceptible to, having had no real-life opportunities to employ them, i.e. the nurturing feelings. This possibly explains why a maternal woman will cleave to a man with low self-esteem, dote on him with a vigilant eye toward his improvement, basically refashion him into a surrogate child (though out of consideration for our gag reflexes, we might not want to consider the implications of this too thoroughly). N.b.: Men, insanely attractive or not, do *not* possess this nurturing instinct. Average-looking women cannot count on getting laid by appealing to a man's sense of rectitude or sympathy or compassion because these things do not exist in men. From a man's POV, anybody who attempts to engender these feelings is perceived as weak, and, in accordance with years of inculcation and ingrained reasoning, weak things are meant to be crushed, or at least ridiculed. That's why those Ultimate Fighting shows are so popular with the agnate set and not Ultimate Take In A Stray Kitten. Destruction is much more interesting to men than recovery; they would rather see something torn down than built up any day of the week. Resuscitation is the province of nurses, and nurses are girls, unless they're gay. Any man that might have had an inclination toward tender beneficence was most likely castigated, traduced, called a "pussy" so many times that he willingly eradicated any of his "girly" tendencies to avoid further torment by "manly" men. Added to this, men are unreservedly self-centered and solipsistic to the extreme. Notice how men— and this is an all-encompassing generalization which, in all fairness, should be preceded with a "most"—how most men have zero aptitude for cooking, conversing, and making love— but demonstrate preternatural talents for ordering takeout, soliloquizing, and masturbating since these things do not require the consideration of another person's gratification (they also require less effort—men are also really lazy). So you just don't envy these average-looking girls who are trying to get done doggy-style by these cruel, vain, lazy, borderline autistic, insanely attractive guys who will show no sympathy and cut them no slack for unimpressive qualities and are only concerned about themselves. And the more an average-looking girl puts herself out there trying to attract a hot man, the more her averageness will be scrutinized by a crowd used to waking up next to someone with perfect features, a perfect body, a perfect smile, etc. and she (the average-looking girl) faces the likely prospect of being laughed at, at best, and all this must be very discouraging, to say the least. As for an average-looking man, even if he were willing to be more forgiving and less judgmental about a girl's less than stellar traits, chances are he lacks the caregiving instincts that would impel him to take on the responsibility of an average-looking girl and give her what she needs most (viz. a roll in the hay, same as an average-looking man's overriding need), assuming he's not already being coddled and administered to by an insanely attractive woman, in which case he would have no time to attend an average-looking girl, as his nights would be filled with prolonged and involved lascivious activity, his days spent recovering from the previous night and anticipating the next.

And then there's the third, and possibly oddest reason hot women have sex with average-looking guys: Because they (the hot women) don't want sex anymore. Actually, it's not as blatantly contradictory as that; it's more a matter of their just being tremendously bored with it. Insanely attractive women know better than anyone how boring and tedious and chorelike sex can be, even with insanely attractive guys. It gets to the point where they realize that sex isn't everything—an insight only cognizable to insanely attractive girls (in the same way that only billionaires can say with a straight face, "Money isn't everything"), who, by the time they can legally buy alcohol, have had more and better sex than most people will have in their entire lives. They've had their fill and are looking for a change of pace so they turn to this whole subdivision of prospective boyfriends they had never once considered and it's like their favorite restaurant has all of a sudden doubled the number of items on their menu. They eventually (this could take years) get around to sampling from this new, unchristened pool of guys, secure in the knowledge they can always go back to the "standard" arrangement of sleeping with hot guys and there's no danger of being ragged on or treated like a pariah since other girls know there are myriad respectable reasons for having sex with an average-looking guy and hot guys will never not want to sleep with a hot girl and a hot girl doesn't become less hot by screwing an average-looking guy. At most people might raise their eyebrows, but other things will rise as well and an insanely attractive girl can rest assured that there'll be no shortage of erections wherever she decides to roam.

And so she can start dating average-looking men, see what these guys have to offer exactly. She will expect differences and have strong assumptions about what will be different and by how much, but, this being completely new and unfamiliar to her, dating an average-looking guy, she will still be surprised by any number of things, including something she would've staked anything on being impossible before dipping her toe in these uncharted, average-looking waters. The most surprising thing—shocking, really—is when she realizes that not only does she like dating average-looking men, in most ways, or in an overall way maybe, she *prefers* them to insanely attractive guys. In these cases, the girl is pleasantly—almost ecstatically—surprised at the average average-looking guy's willingness to accompany her to places the insanely attractives would refuse to step foot in, e.g. clothing stores, perfumeries, TJ Maxx—basically places that seem exclusively for her. He's also whole-heartedly amenable to chick flicks, walks in the park, visits to her friends—all without ever trying to weasel out to watch a supposedly unmissable televised sporting event. Additionally, his spontaneous giving of flowers and gifts, attentiveness during conversations, and obsequiousness bordering on idolatry make it kind of a no-brainer; why wouldn't a girl favor someone who gives her queen-like treatment over a guy who treats her like an accessory, something to establish his rank and worth with? On one level, the contrasting dispositions of average- and good-looking men shouldn't be all that surprising—since it's kind of a cliché that the more attractive guys are jerks and the uglier guys are like wicked smart and have great personalities and stuff and it's always a balancing act for girls when they have to choose either a hottie that'll treat them like shit or a homely guy with a heart of gold—but the reality is that average-looking guys aren't inherently nicer than everyone else, they're just nicer to girls who'll have sex with them. And they do have sex, these insanely attractive girls seen out and about with average-looking guys—even though the girl's kind of over it (sex) and the guy's looks don't inspire raging lustful desires and he lacks the bedroom proficiency, the skills in the sack she's used to (even if he is an eager pupil) and she'd rather just go to the movies and go out dancing and laugh and shop with him and cut out the sex stuff altogether—they have sex because it's SOP for a girl and a guy who go to the movies and go out dancing and laugh and shop together to also have sex with each other. And nobody regards what on the surface appears to be this mass acquiescence to her whims—all this hanging out in girly places and talking about girly things and basically being his girlfriend's girlfriend, only with a deeper voice—nobody thinks of all these non-sexual activities as like a bribe or remuneration for sex, least of all the guy. He would be flabbergasted and more than a little horrified at the accusation that all this bending to her will was a deliberately calculated, subtly coercive way of getting her to put out more often. To him, it all just seems like the obvious and apodictic way of treating a girl one is dating. There's no trickery involved, no one is exploiting the other; this is just the way things are done, like working a job and getting a paycheck every week, just incontestable. He also sees the heap of sense it makes to treat a girlfriend, someone who presumably embodies all these princess-like qualities, like—big surprise!—a princess. Granted, his sources for these suppositions—old movies and sitcoms, mostly—tend not to conform to reality but what else is he going to do? Chances are, he's as unfamiliar with dating her as she is with him; with pairings-off of average-looking guys and insanely attractive girls, while clearly happening with increasing frequency, being not exactly commonplace yet, there's not a lot of real world experience he can draw upon, so he doesn't know that you can treat a girl like day-old dog shit and still get laid, which, even if he did know, might not be a tenable option for him, possibly being a course of action open only to the insanely attractives.

But he's doing fine with what he does know; he's getting laid plenty. This is crucial because sex is the most important thing to him in a relationship. A lot of girls may find this surprising, that he values sex over the other things they do that are way more fun like watching sunsets on the porchswing with a mug of hot cocoa or going to the Gap. But average-looking guys are a dissipated bunch, tumid with carnal desires, their days filled with incessant arousing thoughts, their nights drenched in wet dreams, and they want sex, crave sex, *need* sex as much as insanely attractive men do, probably more. The only thing that separates average-looking and insanely attractive guys—besides their physicalities and sexual abilities—is the tolerance one group has for all the non-sex stuff girls want to do. And just because average-looking guys have a tolerance for those girl-centric activities doesn't mean they are disposed to doing them unprompted. If the girl stopped having sex with him, she would find out just how little interest he really had in going to the mall; he may even refuse to go from then on, which might strike a discordant note with that supposedly tacit understanding that the guy wasn't doing all the girly things for sex. And he wasn't, but a termination of sexual activity strongly implies the dissolution of the boyfriend/girlfriend relationship and now there's the matter of appropriateness. E.g. it would be just as inappropriate for a girl to have sex with a guy who isn't her boyfriend as it would be for a guy to shop all day with a girl who isn't his girlfriend, spending hours looking for the perfect nail polish with her, then going to her house and painting the toenails of this girl. All this is shoulders-shrug-gingly obvious to an average-looking guy. And if a girl says to a guy in an attempt to ensure that their energy gets expended on what she finds most fulfilling about his company that, ok, she wants to be his girlfriend but she doesn't want to have sex, she will find herself on the receiving end of the blankest stare she will ever see because, in the guy's mind, her words are non-sensical; to him it's like she said "I want a pet dog so I'm gonna buy a rhinoceros." If an average-looking guy's thoughts on sex—how he considers it integral to a relationship, better than anything else, worth thinking incessantly about, and more along those lines—if everything was laid out plainly for the insanely attractive girl dating him, her response would prob-ably take the form of insouciance. She'd probably consider his preoccupation with sex a bit silly but ultimately deem it his prerogative if he wants to regard sex as the highlight of the relationship even though the trade-off (not that there is a trade-off, of course) is hardly commensurate, with her getting far more out of it, in her opinion, since sex comprises what, maybe 1% of the relationship (if a relationship consists of the waking hours of the day, roughly 16 hours, and assuming a daily sex session of 10 minutes (a generous estimate with average-looking men), 10 mins / 16 hrs = 1.04%), leaving 99% of their daily time together (almost 16 hours!) to shop, go to chick flicks, etc. So, yeah, she's fine with the arrangement, and so is he, as a matter of fact, because for 10 ineffable minutes a day he gets to experience heaven. The happiest couples in the world may very well be insanely attractive girl/average-look-ing guy pairings.

So anyway, that's what an average-looking girl could poten-tially run up against in her quest to get laid: An average-looking man in a perfectly content sexual relationship with an insanely attractive girl. And, taking into account the way average-looking men deify the sex act, it shouldn't be much of a surprise that he resents the average-looking girl a little for always being in a position to allow him the indescribable pleasure of ejaculating into a vagina, for being in fact the most logical type of person to afford him this pleasure, and yet perpetually denying him, withholding from him transcendent joys, joys which (he eventually came to discover) exceeded his already grand expectations. She forbade even the simplest of delights, the suckling of a nipple or the tonguing of her petal-like folds—a borderline malicious interdiction, like a particularly stingy miser denying a beggar alms of even a penny. She denied him the ecstatic, propulsive means to leave this drab earth and know a radiant splendor, prevented his accent into a redeeming paradise. She denied him, denied both of them really, selfishly, arrogantly, rapaciously, illogically; it's like he had all the ingredients for a delicious spaghetti dinner—fresh vegetables, delectable sauces, the most piquant varieties of cheese—a meal he was willing to share; all he needed from her was the water to boil the pasta, that's all, and she refused. So yeah, even if he's available, he's a little miffed at her. Maybe not enough to unconditionally refuse to sleep with her, but the longer she waits to seek out an average-looking guy, the greater the odds are he'll get laid by an insanely attractive girl, or even dozens of them. And if she likes a guy, any guy, who's slept with a hot girl before, she's shit out of luck because why would he want to compromise his status as a man who can bag an insanely attractive girl by screwing an average-looking one?

—Did you watch the show last night?

—Yeah.

—Pretty good huh?

—It's not bad.

—See I told you, it's pretty good. Do you get the title? The joke in the title?

—Yeah. Actually it reminded me in a weird way about this idea for a show I once had.

—Last week's episode was better, but last night's was still pretty good. Last week it turned into a cooking show at the twenty-minute mark, I shit you not. Aztoben is hi*larious*.

—It'd be a show called *Crazy Ex-Boyfriend*. It'd be about a guy who's obsessed with his ex. You know, he's not over the relationship, he's still in love with her and everything, and so he keeps tabs on her and basically stalks her and stuff. And every episode she'd have a new boyfriend and this guy would do crazy things to break up the relationship, like get the guy thrown in jail somehow or finagle it so the guy accidentally got on a plane to Djibouti or something. All without the former girlfriend knowing he was the one doing these things behind the scenes. And she'd end up always calling him up, kind of commiserating with him about how she can't find a good guy, and all the while this is part of his master plan for him to get back together with her. It's like a half-hour sitcom sort of thing. What do you think?

—Yeah, pretty good. But do you get the title, though? "Police Modern"? Po—

—Yeah yeah, I get the title, christ.

AN EXCERPT OF THE UNPRODUCED PILOT SCRIPT FOR THE TELEVISUAL ADAPTATION OF (S)EXECREBLE JOKES, THE FIRST PLAY IN A CYCLE OF TWENTY (WHICH PLAY N.B. CLOSED AFTER THREE PERFORMANCES IN ITS INITIAL AND ONLY RUN AT AN AVANT-GARDE THEA-TER IN SOME SLEEPY NEW ENGLAND TOWN, SHUT DOWN DUE TO "COMMUNITY OUTRAGE" (MAINLY IN THE FORM OF AN UNSUSPECTING SEPTUAGENARIAN WHO BASICALLY WALKED IN OFF THE STREET AND WAS HORRIFIED BY WHAT SHE WITNESSED AT HER FIRST—AND LAST—SHOW AT *THE LOCUS*, A VENUE WHOSE SHOWS ARE NOT FOR EVERYONE, NEEDLESS TO SAY (THOUGH SOMEONE REALLY SHOULD HAVE TOLD THAT OLD LADY WHAT SHE WAS GETTING HERSELF INTO), AND BUT SO THIS WOMAN WAS A RESPECTED MULTI-GENERATIONAL ELEMENTARY SCHOOL TEACH-

ER WITH SOME PULL WITH VARIOUS TOWN BOARD MEMBERS AND SELECTMEN WHO ALL GOT TOGETHER AND MADE IT CLEAR TO THE PROPRIETOR OF THE THEATER THAT IT'D BE IN HIS BEST INTEREST TO CLOSE THIS PARTICULAR PLAY, A SUGGESTION THE PROPRIETOR WAS SHOULDERS-SHRUGGINGLY RECEPTIVE TO SINCE, UNBEKNOWNST TO EVERYONE ELSE, THE PRINCIPAL ACTORS WERE LEAVING IN A WEEK ANYWAY, THIS BEING AN EXTREMELY LIMITED ENGAGEMENT, AND ALSO HE KNEW THAT ONCE THE COMMOTION DIED DOWN HE COULD JUST RE-OPEN THE PLAY IN SIX MONTHS USING A DIFFERENT TITLE LIKE <u>DETESTICLE COMEDY</u> OR SOMETHING AND BY THEN NOBODY WOULD BE PAYING ATTENTION OR CARE WHAT KIND OF SHOWS THE RINKY-DINK EXPERIMENTAL THEATER WAS PRESENTING AND HE COULD RUN THE PLAY FOR AS LONG AS HE WANTED)), THIS PILOT WRITTEN BY J.A. SURSTEN, THE AUTHOR OF THE PLAY, RETITLED <u>BAD SEX JOKES</u> FOR TV, THE SHOW NOT EVEN GETTING TO THE CASTING AND CAMERA RENTAL STAGE BECAUSE THE SCRIPT GOT NO FURTHER THAN THE DESK OF AN ABC PROGRAMMING EXECUTIVE (READERS AT FOX AND NBC SENT BACK THE UNSOLICITED MANUSCRIPT UNREAD) WHO NEARLY BURNED IT IN DISGUST AND ENDED UP FIRING TWO OF HIS ASSISTANTS FOR ALLOWING SUCH DISPICABLE GARBAGE TO ENTER HIS KEN

Man #1: I know. They always do. This one especially. She was all over me man, telling me how interesting I was, how she wanted to get to know me better, all that stuff. And let me tell you, she was the hottest girl in the whole place. There was this guy sitting on the other side of her, someone who thought he was so cool, and he was telling her he would buy her drinks for the rest of the month if she'd just talk to him for five minutes, just one of those guys who thinks he's so cool and so slick. And she didn't even *glance* at the guy. She doesn't take her eyes off me, she's hanging on every word I say, she's laughing, touching my arm, everything she does tells me she *wants* me. And I'm just trying to get enough drinks in her that she'll let me have my way with her. And after two drinks she whispers in my ear "Let's get out of here" and this is after two little bitty drinks and I swear I sent a little prayer up to the Big Guy, just saying "Thank you God. God bless the lightweights." [chuckles] So we stumble out of that dive and we get in her car and I tell ya, this girl was Hot to Trot. She was not gonna wait to get back to my place, she was gonna get it started right in the car. First she pulls out a tape recorder and I figure she's one of these chicks that likes to record herself having sex and like masturbate to it afterwards so I'm like "That's cool." And then she says she's gonna screw me and I say that that is *definitely* cool. Then she pulls out some handcuffs and I'm like whoa this girl is hardcore but hey, I'm really into that stuff too so I let her cuff my hands together and all the while she's talking dirty to me, daring me not to make a sound, saying I can totally screw some girlfriend of hers named Anna, that this girl she's talking about belongs to me or something, like I control her and all that. A bunch more freaky stuff. Then she's driving us away, I figure to her place where we'll be making like bunnies, just humping like crazy. And we pull up to her place and next thing I know I'm being thrown around by these big guys and I'm not really so cool with that but I go with it, just figure it's more rough stuff. Then they throw me in a cell and I figure she's just trying to soften me up, get me ready for her and what she's gonna do to me. And y'know, I see some cameras in the room outside the cell so I figure she's also gonna video us, make a sex tape or something so I decide to give her a little show beforehand and I start masturbating, spuming all over the walls of that cell, figuring she's watching me in the next room, playing with herself. Now, I was in that cell a *long time*, and all I thought was *Jay-sis*, this girl is *Hard-core* with a capital H. Eventually I'm dragged out of the cell and into a courtroom with all these people around and a judge and everything and I'm thinking "Damn, she's taking her S&M pretty far." And I see her in the crowd and I like wink at her and after a while she walks closer to me and I say "Hey babe, when you gonna introduce me to your friend, a Miss Terney I think you said." And she just ignores me and I figure Uh oh, I been a naughty boy and this girl's *punishing* me. So I just smile and blow her a kiss to let her know I'm still into it and everything. I mean I still am dying to fuck this girl, I've got this raging boner this entire time. Anyways, hours later, it's starting to dawn on me that this might not be a sex game. I mean this trial just keeps going on and on and they're talking about stuff I never told the girl, stuff I didn't *want* her to know just in case she wasn't into it. They were bringing out pictures of ex-girlfriends I'd broken up, relationships I just buried, you know? I mean, I went back with some of them a couple times just for laughs and stuff, nothing serious. Anyways, this stuff just keeps going and going and it finally hits me: This is for real. And I'm like "Damn." And the thing wraps up and the jury, apparently real, finds me guilty of all sorts of stuff and the judge sentences me to death and they start dragging me away and I see that chick and I'm like "What the hell girl? I thought you liked me!" And she gets up and starts walking away and I'm like "Didn't you like me? Don't walk away from me bitch! You were into me and you know it! You told me I was interesting!" And she stops and slowly walks back and gets right in my face and she's got this murderous look in her eyes and she says "I didn't say you were *interesting*, I said you were a *person of interest*, you sick idiot."

Man #2, lying in the bottom bunk with his head propped up, has been listening avidly.

Man #2: Wow.

Man #1: Yeah, I know. Cold, innit?

Man #1 walks across the jail cell and gets in the top bunk. He stares at the ceiling with his hands behind his head.

Man #1: I tell ya kid, that's the last time I try to fuck something that's alive.

Fade out.

HANNAH

EVERYONE LOVED HANNAH, and I couldn't blame them. She was the most lovely and beautiful girl I'd ever seen. I met her at work when she showed me the ropes on my first day and three hours later I was in love. Long auburn hair, unusual eyes, average height but extraordinary legs . . . though that was something I wouldn't know until later. To explain: She was *conservative*. I find it hard to imagine her indulging in excesses of any kind, and that extends to her clothing. She was always wearing sweaters with long sleeves or unrevealing shirts that left everything to the imagination. But about those legs . . . I'll stop my baiting and just reveal that we didn't have a passionate tryst on the beach one warm summer night. Rather, she stopped in the store one time on her way to a party and was wearing a dress that actually ended above the knee; she left quickly and it was the day of our dreams.

Hannah was kind, considerate, compassionate. I bet she'd be so even if she weren't Mormon, which she was, very much so. As far as I could tell, that only deepened her appeal to her admirers. Bagging an unmarried Mormon is an act of Holy Grail-like proportions—like fucking the virgin prom queen in the backseat of your car.

Hannah had more than a few admirers, she had veritable droves of them. They would use any excuse to come into the store: they were in the area, they were on their way home, they forgot what the math homework was, they were struck with a sudden need to know the capitol of Bolivia and were wondering if, perchance, she knew it. They would come into the store and say "Hey, is Hannah he—" and I'd interrupt them with "The library is also in the area, you know; we're at the end of a cul-de-sac so unless you were on your way into the river . . . ; problems 12-26; and La Paz, you maggoty pissant."

It was bad. It was pathetic. The way they scampered in, quickly scanning the store with their beady little eyes. If they wanted to see her so much, they should've done it in a respectable manner. Assholes, get a job here like I did!

Hannah was nice to all these suitors in disguise, which in my opinion only encouraged them. Some of them she even indulged further by spending time with them after work ("Friends," she called them). They would have ice cream parties at her house and watch PG-rated movies. I didn't believe it at first but after I spent enough time picking her apart, I came to the conclusion that she was utterly unlike every other 17-year-old in existence. I even forced her to admit that the ice cream was *lowfat* and sometimes they even watched G-rated cartoons.

Hannah didn't have a boyfriend. I found a way to casually bring up this subject at work ("Yeah I like dogs more than cats. Hey, do you have a boyfriend?") and she admitted that she was unattached. More than that, she *wanted* to be single. I respected that. Here was a beautiful girl, a girl who could make any guy beat his mother with a Louisville Slugger if she would only give him a dewy look and an innocent smile. This girl could have any one of the literally bajillion guys who proposed to her daily . . . and she had waited for me to enter her life. I was touched, but the most disappointing thing about it was that I entered her life and she decided to wait some more.

She's the type of girl where you think about the guy she'll end up with and reflect: "Now there's a lucky guy." The thing is, we couldn't envision anything other than the copious amount of envy we'd feel toward him because, for all we knew, he didn't exist. After all, he apparently was not in a 30-mile radius or she would've found him. (Or rather, he would've found Hannah. Everyone was sure to make their presence known to her; the list of names she's forgotten must be immeasurably long.) With no prototype, we couldn't imagine this theoretical guy, no more than we could imagine how she was in bed.

I pressed her about this one day, as nonchalantly as I could ("Yeah, I like sunsets too. So, like, what do you look for in a guy?") and she smiled and looked away and demurely purred "Oh, I don't know." For the thousandth time, I thought how fortunate it was that she was living in these compassionate times, where enlightened and civilized people appreciated the lithe, modest, natural, and generous (not to mention *hot!*) beauty that Hannah possessed. Had she lived during darker days—when restraint was smothered by the id and raping and pillaging were as natural as breathing and eating—I don't think the local heathens would've been able to appreciate Hannah's subtler qualities. Whether she knew it or not, she treated her beauty like it was a great piece of art she had created; the beauty belonged to her, but it was for everyone to share. That's something she didn't have to do; she could've easily locked it away like Salinger's old letters. These pieces of herself that she gave out weren't enough for some people (the ones, for example, who aren't content just looking at Da Vinci's sketches, they must *possess* them) but it sure as hell was enough for me and I loved her more because of it.

Eventually, she'd admit the desire to find "a nice Mormon guy." I was never that familiar with the practices of the Mormon religion and before I met Hannah all I knew was that they infested Utah and published ridiculous pamphlets on the sin of masturbation, which I took as a personal slight of one of my hobbies. Hannah told me all about their traditions and idiosyncrasies: they're as straight edge as you get, couples are married at the Cathedral of the Madeleine in Salt Lake City, and Utah consumes more Jell-O than any other state in the country. (She didn't elaborate and I didn't ask.) She told me about Mormon sex, how there was none before marriage. (How this organization thrives is beyond me.) Utah must be more sheltered from the rest of the world than a well-burrowed mole.

Suddenly, a "nice Mormon guy" just didn't clarify things. Imagining a teenage guy who doesn't drink and force himself on girls is more difficult than picturing the fifth dimension of a circle. What'd she expect, this guy to come swooping down from the sky riding a unicorn and carrying a viable solution to world hunger? I would've wished her good fucking luck in finding this guy . . . not that she needed it or, for that matter, wanted it. She was content with her ice cream parties and adoring fanbase. ("They're friends," she continued to insist. Hey, I have friends too but they don't stare at me with the fiery look of lust, ready to drop their pants at the slightest sign of weakness.) When I asked her about past paramours, she offhandedly mentioned something that didn't work out, her expression remaining neutral but her body stiffening just a bit; she politely refused to discuss it further. Oh, the stories she must have.

There *were* Mormon guys around, part of the small but devoted following that had set up base in town. I'm sure that their membership went up 500 percent after all the local boys got an eyeful of Hannah. I got her to reveal that one boy, Pete—who made a particular point to make daily visits to the store—had been a carefree, scruffy-looking ruffian whose most remarkable quality before joining the Mormon ranks was his BB gun. He traded his raggedy, unkempt hair for a clean-cut look, washed his hands and scrubbed his face free of dirt and grime, and gave his BB gun to his former pals, a distressed posse of rabble-rousers who stood there in their torn jeans with strings and frogs in their pockets, as they watched dejectedly as their former leader strutted away, responding to a higher calling than stink bombs and infantile pranks. His conversion's close conjunction with his first sight of Hannah was of course passed off as coincidence by the girl he secretly pined for. Now, three years after making that plunge, he stood in line with a dozen others, struggling to stay near the front, fighting for every bit of Hannah's attention he felt he rightly deserved for espousing her sensibilities. How disheartened he must have felt when he saw a score of others at that first meeting he went to, running into other guys who even a week ago had slingshots in their hands and firecrackers under their bed . . . all this traded for a Bible and a haircut. The fact that he was still around was testament to his ability to take a challenge and run with it, although his persistence was bearing little fruit.

But Pete wasn't the most helpless case of Hannah's devotees. That title belonged solely to Jack. He was a guy who probably started praying and reading the Bible because of Hannah, but to his credit, he didn't have to change a damn thing about himself. This kid was squeaky clean. His shit probably sang joyous show tunes as they were happily flushed down the toilet. Here's a kid who was told "Ok, you want to be Mormon, you have to do community service" and said "What's the catch?" He wasn't hiding behind a facade like the others; he was a genuinely nice person. At the time, he was helping his mother through terminal cancer. The other greasy slimeballs seeking Hannah's approval would've probably also helped their mothers through a terminal disease . . . but I wouldn't have been surprised if they had also infected their mothers with a permanent ailment for the opportunity to appear good-hearted.

Jack was also intelligent, which made him a truly tragic figure. He should've realized more than any of them what he was getting into, which would've made him the only sheep who knew he was being led to slaughter. And maybe he did, but I doubt it. The blindfold he donned for protection from Hannah's radiance became a permanent fixture over his eyes . . . he was blind to everything going on around him, all the time. If not for that, he would've been able to see the farce that took place right in front of me nearly every day when he came in to talk to her. It was a hard thing to watch: Him—eyes full of love and longing, optimistic to a fault, his every movement meant to convey an enduring adoration for Hannah and Hannah only. Her—eyes downcast, largely disinterested, her actions and words chosen carefully for maximal politeness. Jack would leave after a while and I imagined him going home, sick to his stomach, trying to navigate through his personal sturm and drang.

I usually had no patience for Hannah's admirers, yet I felt sorry for Jack. It certainly wasn't because of his persistence since that was equaled by many others. It was his purity, his lack of hidden deviance that I respected. There was little doubt that most of these guys would want to use Hannah as a humping post for a couple weeks, grunting and squirming on some filth-encrusted floor, and then discard her by the side of the road, broken and bruised, crushed of all life. It's the impulse one gets when he sees something beautiful and immediately wants to destroy it. Many of the young people in town had this impulse, which seemed frighteningly natural to them. But not Jack. If Hannah would just give him her hand, he would whisk her away to some exotic land, to days filled with frolicking on the beach; evenings of exquisite dining and fruitful conversation; nights of lovemaking. He could give her so much—his time, his resources, his love—and in the end it just meant that he could give her so many things she didn't want. And he was struck helpless by this.

Knowing that, I was glad when he came in one day and announced that he was going on his mission in a month. It was to some far away country in Africa, where correspondence by mail would be difficult, which I thought was for the best. This rite of passage would take him away for two years, an adequate amount of time to forget this mess he'd made for himself here. Maybe he'd meet a nice Mozambican girl, build a modest straw hut on a patch of fairly level ground, and live out the rest of his days in contentment, the memory of lost love fading away in the African sunset.

I snapped out of my reverie of African safaris and tribal rituals when Jack, in a very earnest and serious tone, told Hannah that he needed to talk to her . . . alone. She looked at him for a second, then got up and they went to the backroom. I shook my head and sighed; he was so close to getting out of this ordeal relatively unscathed. I should've known that he was masochistic, a quality that's part and parcel of being a hopeless romantic.

Jack came out of the room a few minutes later and walked stiffly and quickly out of the store, his brow furrowed and eyes dark. Hannah strolled to the counter and slowly eased back into her seat. Her face looked no different than it had before Jack came in, and when she saw me looking at her, she gave me a short smile, then looked away. I didn't ask her what happened. A couple weeks later, I found out through friends of friends of friends that Jack asked Hannah to wait for him until he got back and, when he returned, they could build a life together. Hannah didn't see much sense in this plan and, more importantly, she didn't want to wait for anyone. No one ever knew of her plans for the future because she'd always obligingly allowed people to babble on about their own.

Whenever I saw Jack after that incident, he was always stewing and sulking, his eyes perpetually narrowed, his features more angular, his body always tense; he was turning into a cynic right before our eyes. Then, four weeks later, he got on a plane to Africa and we all put him out of our minds.

Soon, it was time to leave on my mission . . . just kidding. But, truthfully, the area had worn out its possibilities and I decided it was time to move on. I gave the store my two weeks' notice which allowed all the regulars to wish me well. I can't say that I wouldn't miss seeing Hannah nearly every day; there are far worse sights one can encounter. Plus, I think we had an unspoken understanding: if I didn't make a fool of myself, she'd let me in a little more than she had the others. We established a kind of rapport with each other, one that was mutually agreeable and genuinely enjoyed by both of us.

On the day that was to be the last I'd see her, I casually tossed her an envelope. She smiled widely but her eyes betrayed her concern: Was I joining the ranks of commoners? Was I going to ruin this slight, though pleasant time in her company? The diffuse clouds in her eyes quickly dissipated as she saw that the card was an innocuously worded farewell, written with just the right amount of wit, mostly given over to wishing her good luck with an upcoming school play. I even managed to avoid insidiously placing the word "Love" in front of my name, as people often do. Instead it read "I Bid You Farewell, J."

She let out a sigh (of relief, I'm sure) and said that she'd miss me. She meant it a certain way, and in that context, she was telling the truth.

Later that day, Pete came in and he was incensed. He went up to Hannah and launched into a whiny diatribe about how she went to the beach with a bunch of friends when they were supposed to hang out, effectively stranding him. Hannah apologized profusely and swore to make it up to him at a later date. The strain of pretending to be someone he was not must have been weighing heavily on Pete that day because, for a couple minutes at least, he would have none of Hannah's explanations. He went on and on about the clear distinction she made between friends she preferred and those she didn't, and how she gave no thought to the latter group, which comprised people she had known for years. Hannah protested and after a few more promises of taking future time out of her schedule for him, Pete calmed down. Now that he had said what he meant to say, his shoulders slumped and he trudged out of the store, looking thoroughly defeated. It was obvious that he had not made any gains by this outburst and what little he'd had may have been lost forever.

I politely carried on like nothing had happened but glanced at Hannah out of the corner of my eye. She was slumped on the table, her face hidden, buried in her arms. When she sat up, her face was red and her eyes were wet. After a few moments, she got up and went out back.

It was probably not Pete's rebuke that sent her over the edge (although Pete would've been ecstatic to think that he had provoked this reaction in her), but the combination of Pete, Jack, and countless others . . . it probably felt like the sky was falling down around her. It was then that I realized that not only did *I* not really know her, there were probably few people who did. What must go through her mind, the mind of a person who everyone wants a piece of? What's she going through? What does she think of other people when she is perfectly willing to give as much as she can to them and it's still not enough? How will this change what she does from now on? Almost unfairly, the burden of other people's dreams, their hopes, their very expectations of the world had been placed on her slim shoulders. She had risen admirably to the task, but now. . . .

I guess I'll never know, for I left soon thereafter. And when all is said and done, what am I left with? A piece of her. And I'm happy with the piece I got and she would probably be grateful to me for being content with that. In the end, she is the most beautiful girl I've ever seen . . . but not the most beautiful I've ever known.

Liquid Almond Eyes

Walking down Main Street on his lunch break, Gabe runs into the coffee kiosk girl for the first time since word got out that he's hit the jackpot. Her greeting is customary: a big, generous, two-armed hug. What's new is the shriek of excitement and enthusiastic squeeze of his upper arm afterward. She's "Coffee Girl" for short; this antonomasia is well established: say to anyone (especially a guy) "I saw Coffee Girl at the video store today" and he will know whom you're talking about. She's a mainstay, a cornerstone of Main Street, dispensing java and good cheer in equal measure for close to a decade now. Gabe does not know a downtown without her. She's been a fixture ever since he established his daily routine, dutifully manning her enclosed post between City Hall and the pharmacy. Rain or shine, snow or sun, she's there, usually with a smile and a disposition no less affable than cheerful bonhomie.

For a one-girl operation, business is booming. Wait times almost require reading material. There's little doubt that her pleasing temperament attracts more business than it turns away, but it's hard to pinpoint that as the only reason her sales are brisk because her coffee is actually good. Some go as far as deeming it superlative and refuse to drink anything but her unique, personally-concocted blend. Gabe considers that judgment a bit hyperbolic, though her brew definitely falls within his acceptable limits for coffee. She's also located within walking distance of several businesses, a distance easily traversed during a lunch- or cigarette-break, if one were inclined. And you can always count on her being there. She's one of those people who seem to consider their presence at what they consider to be their job mandatory, another of her puzzling affects along with what appears to be unforced happiness.

Plus she's hot. The fact that a significant percentage of her customer base consists of men with dilated pupils cannot be passed off as coincidence. Some women do frequent the kiosk (another indicator of above-average coffee) but it's obvious what the main attraction is for the males, which annoys a lot of the females. Even though there isn't any appreciable difference in her treatments of men and women, she is confronted by a far greater number of irate women customers, termagants who cavil in shrill, unhinged voices about the most venial things ranging from coffee temperature to cup size with an indignation that couldn't possibly be rooted in the vast insignificance of their complaint. At times, there is the unmistakable whiff of jealousy in the tones of some of these belligerent women (most of whom could be equitably described as "less hot") and their attacks swing wildly on the verge of being ad hominem. Yet even when excoriated in front of other patrons, Coffee Girl never loses her cool or lashes out with reciprocal vitriol. She turns the other cheek in the face of raving customers, evincing almost inhuman forbearance and equanimity, helpful and willing to correct any perceived wrong, but with also a firmness to her voice that indicates a line where crossing is prohibited. The pugnacious women who push her that far understand then that they are not dealing with a pushover or emotional weakling who will burst into tears at the slightest reprimand, and, upon this realization, they invariably slink off to private embarrassment. Gabe has been witness to a few dust-ups and can testify that the crowd's sympathies always lie with the girl in the kiosk and that the aggressors had generally been regarded as unpleasant and unattractive bitches before proving it publicly. In the face of Coffee Girl's understated dignity these catty women seem to exemplify the worst in petty American righteousness, the kind of people who honestly buy into that oft-repeated sophistry: The Customer Is Always Right. Though no one intervenes on Coffee Girl's behalf while she's being upbraided (since it's a situation in which she's clearly in control), the next customer almost always feels compelled to apologize: for the departing shrew, for himself, for the national identity. She always laughs, dismissive, already over the incident, truly water off the duck's back.

Her inability to brood or be perpetually slightly pissed off would mark her as Not From Around Here if her dark-complected features didn't already give the game away. Her birth country is the subject of light speculation. No one really has any clue. A blind throw of a dart at the world map from twenty feet is better than anyone's best guess. People can't agree on a hemisphere, let alone a continent. Baseless conjecture covers every possibility from Central to South America, through Europe to the ends of Asia. To be sure, she's from some place on Earth, miraculously. Beyond that, no one feels a pressing need to know any more than they already do: all the foreign, rarely-seen things about her have combined in a way that is extremely pleasing to the eye.

What she is not is conventionally beautiful. Tête-à-têtes have included the observation that she would never be in a Victoria's Secret catalogue or even a K-Mart flyer for that matter. She lacks the Amazonian quality, the hourglass figure, the plastic sameness of American sylphs. She is short, with an overall shape more like a bowling pin or a pear. She is cursed with a foreign-born nose, hers flat and a little wide, covering a bit more real estate on her face than most people in town are used to seeing. Her crooked teeth bespeak parents who, during her adolescence, lacked the dental fastidiousness (or the funds) that most parents in the good ole U.S. of A. seem to possess. None of this detracts from the final judgment. All her putative flaws are barely motes in her eye when compared to the defects of truly homely women. Her peculiarities add charm when they don't outright stun. Her imbricate teeth are otherwise perfect—clean, upkept, and an integral part of a searingly disarming smile. Her physicality suggests an over-sized stuffed animal that you want to snuggle, squeeze, and mount like a dog. Her facial features are unbearably adorable; they seem to have sprung from the end of a children's film's animator's pen—from the lovably wide nose to the chipmunk-like cheeks and buttony dimples to the liquid almond eyes of an Arabian princess: everything designed and arranged for maximal winsomeness. This borderline-zaftig woman's semi-rounded figure is not a turn-off. On the contrary, her shape gives the impression that her body is all curves, full of the kind of precipitous slopes any man would kill to traverse with hand, tongue, or congruently writhing body. The air around her is thick with the suggestion that underneath her swathe of clothes lies the true meaning of the word "voluptuousness." Her jet-black hair, in itself a wondrous oddity, purls down her back in wavy tendrils, that is when it's not clipped up and falling across her face in perfect cute strands. There's hardly a man alive who has seen her from the back and has not wondered what her luscious ass would look like stripped bare and, after she turns around, what her equally tantalizing breasts would feel like if cupped and caressed. It's hard to imagine someone not taking her "as is."

And then there's her voice. Hearing her talk is an aural joy. Her enunciation is delightfully unique, full of languorous vowels and consonants devoid of sharp edges. Her syllables swirl into each other, creating a pleasing hum. Through her lips, unremarkable digraphs become sensual diphthongs, and you don't even mind the cacoepy. Her syncopated rhythms quickly turn from novelty into something beautiful that you want to hear again. She's like a composer, placing each phoneme on a staff, forming delightful movements of words, words the rest of us can think of only as prose. Her sound is unencumbered, soothing to anyone who hears it. The noises she makes meld into a 19th-century impressionist masterpiece; by contrast, white Americans' voices have all the nuance of a Sunday comic strip. She, a foreigner, has managed to tease the delitescent musicality out of the English language.

Plus there's her refreshingly direct way of speaking. Her phraseology is stripped of the conversational tics, pop culture references, and eu-/dysphemisms that litter your typical U.S. citizen's chatter. The thrust of what she's saying is never muddled by colloquialisms, opaque metaphors, regional idioms, pleonastic phrases, or sesquipedalians. All this probably goes hand-in-hand with learning a second language, but still. Her diction is almost disconcertingly but actually really pleasingly simple. Not that she's unintelligent, just really to the point. Like, for example, when you ask her how she's doing, she'll say something like "I'm trying to be good" and this will be said without any coyness, irony, sarcasm, jocosity, disingenuousness, or the like because what she truly means is just what she has said: she is going through her day *literally* trying to be good. And in one pithy statement she has gotten to the heart of the sentiment we all probably mean to convey when we respond to the question of how we're doing with things like "Not bad" or "Can't complain" or that weird parroted nonresponse "What's up?" or any number of other listless stock answers, and one quickly sees that her response is a superior one if for no other reason than it actually *means* something and actual communication has taken place, which—not to put too fine a point on it—makes everyone involved in the exchange feel more human. Any speaker of English can attest that achieving clarity is no mean feat—too often the words get in the way—which makes her facility with the language nothing short of astonishing, especially considering that her lexicon is probably no larger than an average elementary school student's. It might be strange to cite a person like her for precision, but the undeniable truth remains: she picks the exact right words to say, which, again, most likely stems from her learning the language as an adult. As a corollary, her limited vocabulary and verbal punctiliousness virtually eliminates pretense and dissimulation. There's no B.S. with her, no prevarication. She doesn't resort to logorrhea when confronted with silence. With her, what you see is what you get, pretty much. Not totally because everyone, no matter how much integrity they have, recalibrates their persona with each person they encounter—saying things to men they would never say to women, treating the old differently from the young, things like that. But with Coffee Girl, you get the sense that all the play-acting is kept to a minimum. And this realization might take a while because when you see a nice, generous, cheery girl with adorable phrasing, you naturally assume it's an act. But she like inculcates you to the inescapable veracity of her innate traits and after never seeing her any other way, you have to admit that that's probably the kind of person she really is. Which is a pleasant surprise. Compared to her, most people seem to be spouting the kind of manipulative periphrastic jargon practiced by used car salesmen.

To the delight of men everywhere, she is also an openly tactile girl. She has no compunction or squeamishness about venturing into someone's so-called "personal space." Hence: the hugs. They're not deployed totally indiscriminately of course, but it's not too hard to become one of the huggables. If you're a regular at her kiosk and see her out and about in a store, chances are you'll get a salutatory hug. She is also not averse to reaching out to gently guide one's arm as she points out directions, or grasping one's forearm to convey emphasis or excitement, or playfully swatting one's shoulder after they tell a ribald joke, or rubbing someone's upper arm (or even back, if she's in a position to do so) while the person relates some lamentable misfortune. In an age when physical reservedness between non-blood relations is the norm, her barrage of hugs, touches, and rubs initially comes across as somewhat outré, but through repetition becomes accepted, then appreciated and even looked forward to, since being hugged by an attractive woman turns out to be an instant mood-booster.

She separates herself from the herd of cookie-cutter girls that populates every small town in the U.S. by just being herself. She's an exotic flower sprouting up from the cracks on Main Street. She's different, a change of pace, new, exciting. More than a few octogenarians have referred to her as the knees and pajamas of bees and cats, respectively. She's a breath of fresh air from who knows where. All this and a wonderfully vaginal name: Favia. It's no surprise that she has inadvertently fostered a number of secret crushes. Full-blown, adolescent-era crushes that turn men into gabbling bad joke generators. The kind of debilitating infatuation that renders a man near useless in the presence of his object of affection. Who knows how many harbor carnal fantasies; their number could be legion. This is despite her semi-advanced age (her years are in as much question as her provenance) and her kids in high school (a daughter and son) and, not to mention, her husband and the at least ten years of matrimony under her belt. These things are common knowledge, even though they sound like convenient discouragements fabricated by jealous female rivals. No one's really seen her dependents or the guy she shares her bed with, making their existences easily pretermitted, which is necessary to facilitate any one-on-one fantasies. The hard facts are attenuated by dulcet rumors: her husband is an overweight American schlub; she's unhappily married, has been for years; her daughter is almost legal and even hotter. Truths and untruths swirl around her, calumnies mix with wishful thinking, surrounding her in an aura of unreality, making her seem more exalted, truly sui generis. No wonder everyone acts as if they're in their cups around her. What's great is that she seems oblivious to all the tumult she causes.

Gabe had been impervious to falling in with the like-minded, googly-eyed crowd at her feet. He has thought her cute in the past and has far from minded her generous hugs, but he had somehow resisted falling in something between love and lust. He had not succumbed to her unintentional charms and she'd been largely off his radar . . . until now. All it takes (he reflects later, somewhat perturbedly) is an arm-squeeze—a shorthand for intimacy, a representational gesture devoid of sexual meaning since no lover has ever squeezed another's arm in this way, with quick collegial applications of pressure, like checking a plum for ripeness. It's an ersatz statement of affection, an autotelic touching that lacks the desire for further exploration. A hand that stays decorously above the waist. It's an illusion, invisible to all but the most credulous. But it does the trick. Gabe's heart starts beating out a corybantic rhythm, beyond his understanding. Sweat films his clothed crevices. He feels faint; God help him, even his knees feel weak. He steals a look toward her lustrous eyes, whose emanating warmth rules out a returned steady gaze. He feels her hand on his arm; each squeeze inspissates his friable attention, vectors his awareness to the locus of her touch and the excruciating proximity of her fingers, their skin denied access to each other by the thin fabric of his exasperating shirt. It feels as if she's testing the girth of his biceps; some unctuous part of his brain tells him he should flex, but his nervous system is on the fritz. (The designation never seemed more apt—"nervous" system indeed!) All he can do is stand there frozen while his insides go haywire. She starts talking and he finds himself entranced by the poetry issuing from her mouth. His side of the conversation feels stilted, disjunctive even, and he quickly errs on the side of purposeful laconicism—every one of his words and gestures calculated to elicit a response from her. All he wants is to keep the music playing.

She mentions the money, of course, but only in the abstract, as a triviality subordinate to the more pressing concern: his happiness. "You must be so happy," she gushes. He sees that she is happy for his good fortune, specifically for how it has (presumably) made him happy. This unadulterated, unqualified happiness she's exuding causes his heart to be filled with something like happiness, if not the genuine article—something that produces the same elation, at least. "I am," he assents and, for a minute, her joy is the whole point of his windfall. He gets caught in the full candent blast of her smile and it feels like a benediction. He does not want to be anywhere else, doing anything other than talking to this exquisite woman.

After too short a while, the conversation winds down despite his best efforts to perpetuate it. Even though her amicable expression never changes, he feels a twinge of sadness as they start tossing contentless, conversation-enervating monosyllabic interjections back and forth. But she summarily extirpates his disappointment with a farewell that mirrors her greeting. He dares to hold her for a half-second longer than the first hug, because he hardly dares not to. She reaches out and latches onto his arm, thrilling him with one last squeeze— made more exciting and important simply by being next in the series—before turning to the line of disgruntled interlopers that has formed behind him.

He walks away, dazed, discombobulated. Every step feels like coming up for air. Sights and sounds fail to register for the better part of an hour. When he finally gets his equilibrium back midway through his shift, the first thing he notices is that he can still smell her. Discreetly crooking his neck downward, he verifies that it's not just his imagination—his shirt has absorbed the fragrances of all her perfumes and cosmetics. It's a sweet smell, a piquant medley of flowery scents that immediately conjures up pleasing memories of that afternoon's embrace. His shirt becomes a kind of olfactory time machine, granting him access to an event he is eager to relive, if only in his mind. He finds himself stealing whiffs by pretending to inspect his shirt's collar. Roy walks in on him in the bathroom when he's holding his shirt up to his face with both hands, looking as if he's trying to inhale it. After an awkward pause, Roy heads toward one of the stalls. Neither of them says anything. Gabe slinks out, trailing his tattered dignity. For the rest of the workday, he manages not to draw any further attention to what appears to be either a new shirt-sniffing fetish or an OCD-level compulsion to check for what can only be rank B.O. This does not stop his co-workers from casting furtive glances in his direction and surrounding him in susurrous indictment.

By the time he gets home, only a faint trace of her evocative scent remains. Before he can properly lament the evanescence of a redolence that has kept him stimulated all the live-long day, Jessica brings him back down to earth, re-acclimating him to the comforts of home by using the most effective decompression method at her disposal: a blowjob. He is barely through the door when he finds himself thrust in a situation that reifies the inchoate whimsy floating in his head—there is no need to fantasize anymore since his member sliding in and out of Jessica's mouth is a physical truth. All errant thoughts exit his mind, for the spectacle before him is an avaricious one and attention must be paid. The BJ proves to be a prolegomenon to a long treatise on sexual pleasure that takes all night to explore the ins and outs of. Somewhere along the way, he completely forgets about anything to do with Coffee Girl.

His oblivescence persists until five minutes before his lunch break the next day, when the possibility of another encounter with a girl he is finding it easier with each remembrance to think of as some sort of goddess fills him with excruciating anticipation. Walking down the street, he feels his palpitant heart straining against its suddenly inadequate confines. When she comes into view, emerging renascent as he rounds the corner, he feels the inexorable curling of the corners of his mouth. He gets into the line already five-men-deep and just stands there, grinning, unable to avoid looking like the simpleton he knows he must appear to be. Better that, however, than the bashful schoolboy he feels like deep down inside. Oblivious to everything else, he watches her with an uncritical eye, reveling in every graceful movement. His countenance is a gift to her, whether he intends it or not. Does a smile exist if no one sees it? In the brief interstice between orders, she espies him waiting and his heart skips a beat when her expression kicks it up a few notches. The pleasant, amicable affect she was formerly going with doesn't really change by an order of magnitude so much as it simply becomes an entirely different thing altogether. She's truly smiling now, a smile that exposes what she was previously doing as a factitious contortion of her lips into a congenial but perfunctory breve, short and un-stressed, denoting nothing more than telemarketer-level politeness. Her newly widened smile narrows the aperture of her eyes, allowing her to focus on the source of her newfound joy. They're both smiling at each other now, blurring the dis-tinction between cause and effect. Gabe senses the glower and annoyed vibe directed toward him by the man who just got his coffee. This guy has probably waited months and made scores of witty remarks and observations to see this gorgeous woman do what Gabe is making her do just by standing there. He has managed to extract the immanent sugar from the cane under everyone's noses. Gabe feels like lifting his hands obligingly to the others and swiveling them around. *Look, no hands.* And, with a leer: *Imagine what I could make her do* with *them.*

When he gets to the front of the line, she seems to become even more delighted, as if she's been storing her excitement for when it could be shared with the right person. After an ejaculatory greeting, she moves around the counter and peremptorily spreads her arms. There is no way to refuse her. Not that he had been thinking of abnegating the pleasure of her embrace—in fact, he'd been looking forward to it. He takes a chance and presses his whole body flush against hers, en-gaging her in a more intimate clasping than the prim, slightly kyphotic politeness they've deployed in the past. He also resolves to hold her until she makes a motion to move away and thrills when a suitably decorous duration (considering the line of spectators) comes and goes. They hold each other, her face level with and buried in his chest. He rubs her back a little. Feeling their bodies conform to each other, he can't help the titillating thought: *we fit.* After a few eternities, lasting many seconds each, she pulls away with a sigh so content he feels his face start to flush. She looks up at him and, proving their symmetry extends beyond the somatic, voices one of the foremost thoughts in his head: "Mm, you smell good." He nearly starts at her eerie entry into his psychic space, then recovers enough to say the obvious: "Thanks. You do too." With consummate aplomb, she leans in for another smell while he involuntarily holds his breath. She looks up at him, smiling. "I like, I like." The unconventional construction of her affirmation sets off waves of pleasure through his body. Even an awkward phrase, through her lips, becomes an aphrodisiac. The elided object of her compliment could be any number of auspicious possibilities: she likes his scent, she likes that she likes his scent, she likes *him*. For now, it's enough that "she likes" in his presence. They stand there, taking each other in, seeing their happy expressions mirrored on the other's face. Would a third party see a lopsided vase between them or possibly a different type of optical—sparks maybe? Perhaps between them lies a fireworks display of a magnificence not seen since Kelly and Grant hit the south of France. Gabe is too rapturous to say for sure.

Upon returning to work, he holes up in the employee room, which is little more than a small cramped storage area with last year's calendar on the wall and a single metal folding chair for anyone needing seclusion at the expense of comfort. He spends the last ten minutes of his lunch break absorbed in his shirt. With both hands he lifts it to his face and takes deep, nourishing breaths, as if he were recovering from a traumatic event. The smell of her perfume prevails. He tries to nail down the constituent elements of the fragrance, but finds his aromal discernment frustratingly lacking. Every time he thinks he has a handle on it, the next inhalation wipes him out anew. The scent never changes, yet he can't get enough. There'd be no reason to get all analytical about it if he could just smell her all day, every day. But not having this option, and with only a few more minutes of intensive panting left before he has to return to a social setting where excessive huffing and puffing is stigmatized, he desperately tries to activate the latent olfactometer that surely must reside in him somewhere. No go. Every exhalation is a reawakening that causes him to completely forget the preceding sapid imagery in his head, if there was any at all. He just can't seem to nail the scent down.

Intensity isn't the problem. This is not a subtle perfume as delicate as a butterfly kiss. This one leaves no doubt you are smelling something meant to be noticed. It starts out strong, bracing, and sends you on an invigorating ride, seeming, like sex, to build to a climax that leaves you just as insensate as you are immediately after orgasm. It practically screams its ingredients at you but mental decoction is extremely difficult, like trying to take down all the notes of Rachmaninoff's Piano Concerto No. 4 in real time while it's blasting at 150 decibels. It's starting to look like an insurmountable task. He's in need of a serious cheat sheet, and only the perfume's box will do.

Running out of time, he tries a different tack. Instead of letting the fragrance overwhelm him and then trying to parse in the confusion, he takes several short breaths, hoping to grasp some initial data point before the scent's strength goes exponential. He imagines he smells something flowery, and he isn't sure whether this being cliché discounts it from being possibly true. Flowers smell nice, why not perfume? There's more than flowers in there, obviously, not to mention a botanist's library worth of knowledge that would narrow down his broad generalization—but for now, "flowery" does its shorthand job at limning one of the textures for a scent-deficient layman.

There's a vinous tinge in there too, he would almost swear. Something fruity, refined into something intoxicating—the formula strikes him in its simplicity. He absentmindedly finishes a long breath and, before the full wave crashes into him, he gets the revelatory impression that a large part of what he smells is *her*. She must be providing the extra kick herself, her natural musk, the ur-stimulant, wafting off her skin, transuding out her pores, her sweat mingling with the perfume to form an entirely new concoction. The perfume box wouldn't help after all—nothing has ever smelled like the residue she's left on his shirt and, after she's gone, nothing will ever smell this way again.

This new insight stimulates him all over and, as he reverts back to long, deep, heaving breaths, he can feel stirrings beneath his waist. In his mind's eye, he sees a luxurious and sensual scene, a tableau whose opulence fixes it in an ancient epoch, biblical, Greek. Marble statues abound in a palatial atrium, enclosed by Corinthian columns. Baroque fountains spray iridescence into a central wading pool. A tribute to the gods is taking place. Servant girls offer fruits and liniments to the revelers who are prescribed a dress code of loincloths and robes by divine mandate, which fosters a lubricious atmosphere. The proceedings tend quickly toward the orgiastic. Then the gods themselves arrive, manifest in corporeal forms upon which Man's gaze can alight without fear of sensory overload. This is an homage to the gods attended by the gods. They're all here: Aphrodite, Priapas, Eros, Hymen, Uranus. Peitho pushes the surprisingly taciturn Dionysus toward Antheia, who is doing such a good job of taking on the aspect of a wallflower one would think the plant really exists. Within minutes they have broken the ice and begun copulating. Everyone follows their lead. The stench of wine, flowers, and bodily secretions is overwhelming. The coition gets more frenzied; the orgy turns dithyrambic.

In the middle of all this, Coffee Girl emerges: numinous, inviolate, oneiric. And like in a dream, she inexplicably becomes the object of this unrestrained fete. Everyone, be they supplicant or idol, vouchsafes their attention to the newly arriving figure. There she is, a vision to be savored, looking no less compelling for being the only one wearing clothes and the short-billed cap she sometimes dons. They all genuflect and screw each other in her honor. Gabe approaches her. Never has her smile looked more encouraging. He kneels before her and she positions her crotch in front of his face and loosens her belt, a clear indication of where he should focus his worship.

He snaps out of the eidetic fantasy when he hears the door

to the backroom open and a voice call out, requesting his presence for the start of the next show. Flustered, he manages to stammer out assurances of an imminent return and as he hears the door close he tries to envision images antipodal to the ones that so deliciously paraded through his mind ten seconds ago. He thinks of vivisected amphibians, excrement, friends in thongs—anything to ablate his massive and conspicuous hard-on.

After getting home, the first thing he does is sit in the easy chair in the living room, close his eyes, and drift back to the fantasy world he had started to create at work. Her scent has once again dissipated from his shirt but he no longer needs a material reminder of the evocative fragrance. Thanks to the intense wheezing he did at work, her smell is imprinted in his memory. All he has to do is close his eyes and he can "see" it, along with all the sumptuous pictures it creates. Later that evening, as he finishes his ablutions in the bathroom, he sees the nearly empty bottle of cologne in the cabinet. He uncaps it and positions the atomizer under his nostrils. This must have been what Favia smelled when she issued her encomium. He always squirts himself a couple times before going to work, more out of habit than a desire for favorable notice. He's been using the same brand for years. Carol had always given him an exact copy (even down to the bottle size) every Christmas— again, more out of perennial tradition than actual preference. He can't even remember if she had ever commented on it qua cologne—whether she liked the scent, enjoyed smelling it on him, etc. In all fairness, even he had ceased thinking about it and he was the one wearing it. He had vaguely registered that the bottle would soon be empty and had briefly wondered why Carol didn't restock his supply this past Christmas until he'd realized that her thwarting of expectation was more portentous than it had seemed at the time. In any case, Coffee Girl has alerted him to a permanence all but forgotten. He smells the scent through her (somewhat large) nose and arrives at the same conclusion—it is quite nice. He'll have to pick up another bottle sometime.

As soon as he sees Coffee Girl the next day, he can smell her, even though she's still forty feet away. The two-way synesthetic reaction is complete—the sight of her evokes her scent and vice versa. She's delighted to see him, of course, and today he is the lucky recipient of an embarrassment of riches. He gets not only a smile and new-and-improved hug, but also a few minutes of alone time with no other customers in sight, the world working in his favor by saddling everyone else with exigent matters requiring their full and immediate attention. He milks the opportunity to be in her presence (if not her person), to get to know her a little better (if not in the biblical sense). As he watches her lips move, he wonders what exactly is going through her head. He knows that behind his own phatic words lies a torrent of vulgarity separated from the open air and her delicate ears by the glacis of his vocal cords and breezy countenance. He can feel his true thoughts demanding a voice. The more he opens his mouth, the more he says, the closer he gets to revealing all, to referring to the unspoken. He considers the words he would die to say, words that would kill him if uttered, and then the words she could use to resurrect him, to deliver him to paradise. The thought immoderately thrills: that she—who has so far proved to be his exotic counterpart, an emotionally-aligned mirror image, she and he two birds of a feather—could be harboring thoughts and desires symmetrical to his own. Maybe not exactly the same but complementary; he has what she needs what he has. Perhaps they fit in multiple configurations, not only in body but mind, too. And there could lie the key to accessing these cravings that fester on one side of a dichotomy of the sundered entity that is a human being. These ineffable desires of the body seem to be known, expressed, and accessible only *through* the body. The willingness of the spirit to be unwilling: a sentiment that can only be penetrated by weak flesh, flesh that can get stronger, harder, that can swell, clench, indurate to the point of bursting. The idea excites Gabe—that he could share with Favia more than just what's on the surface. But for now, even he can see that a meaningful exchange—spiritual or otherwise—would be impossible right then with this respecter of persons. There are still no customers but there is the prevailing sense that taking up any more of her time would be an impertinence. Still, he lingers, protracting his valediction as much as possible, a choice made easier by her unwavering smile.

Finally, after a final forced iteration of goodbyes, he starts to take his leave of her. Frustration wells up inside him as he turns away. Every departure is becoming a torment. His digestive system feels like it's malfunctioning. His stomach feels both hollow and oedematous, as if swelling to accommodate the emptiness expanding within him. He already cannot wait until he sees her again. The hope that their next meeting will be very soon is the only thing that attenuates the fear that their interactions may have just concluded *sine die*.

Before taking two more steps, and before any tempering deliberation, he swivels around to face her again while at the same time extending his hand. When he thinks about it in an unvexed setting later that day, he will be certain, crazy as it sounds and ruinous as it would have been had his hand reached its intended target, that he had been reaching for her left breast. As his arm shoots forth, his mind is a blank. Repercussions are not a factor. The future becomes as inconsequential as the past, and all that matters is touching her in a way that matters. His eyes are practically closed as he makes his blind grasp. He doesn't dare bear witness to what could prove to be a catastrophic transgression—the "look, don't touch" caveat of gentleman's clubs seems to obtain in the public arena —so he is surprised when he feels her hand slip into his. At first he's ashamed that she very reasonably felt the need to intervene, to intercalate the closest thing at hand between him and his hunger for impropriety. He timorously looks up at her face, fully expecting an expression of reproof and disdain. Instead he glimpses a new sparkle in her eyes. She is pleased and for a second he has no idea why. Then the realization hits: she thinks he was going for her hand the whole time. And his gesture, the very same one that had had such crass intent, is being perceived as entirely appropriate. An apposite display of the connection they feel. Physical manifestation of their emotional propinquity. Further symmetry—they are like two paper dolls, cut from one design, joined like Siamese twins. They are now comme il faut. It nearly takes his breath away, especially when he beholds his consolation prize.

It's not a breast, but it's a lot more prehensile. Her hand continues to surprise beyond the wonder of its presence. He's taken aback by the unexpected coarseness of her skin. Her calluses testify to a hidden lifestyle of hard work, either at home or her rumored second job at a cleaning service. Her unsoft hands endear her to him more, instilling in him protective urges alongside the previously existing amatory ones. This initial grasp is tentative, the movements of his hand rigid. His phalanges are fused together as his jammed brain frantically tries to revive basic motor skills. His extremities degrade against his will, regress into incipient ur-versions of hands, transform into basically what amounts to flippers. Still, desperate, he enfolds what's there over her offering. He gently squeezes and feels her apply pressure of her own. Her complicity makes him deliriously happy. She is his partner, willing to follow his lead in a dance he is improvising by the seat of his pants. By *something* in his pants, at least. After a few gravid moments, they separate, having to extricate themselves physically now, and he finally departs only after they silently agree to incorporate what they've just done into their method of communication. It's an exciting addition to their idioglossia, which comprises significant looks, meaningful smiles, and now actual dermal contact.

He begins to wonder if she's on any sort of birth control.

Subsequent latchings-on to her hand prove to be less awkward than the initial (accidental) foray. Hugs easily transition into hand-holding, his hands seeking hers and clasping even before they pull away and face each other. He always goes for both hands, discovering that his contentment is directly proportional to the total surface area of his skin in contact with her. She is always accommodating—it sometimes seems as if she's racing him to initiate contact—and she continues to hold his hands for the duration of his visits. The only thing that can prematurely sever the link is the appearance of a stranger. The reasons for this are unspoken and obvious.

This new plateau in their interactions does not make him as anxious as he would've thought. Holding the hand of someone you haven't slept with but want to proves to have an assuasive effect. What should be a sudorific nerve-racker instead turns out to be a calmative. His arm is a cable, his hand an anchor that moors him to the safe haven of her grasp, sheltering him from the turbulent storm of his emotions. After regaining control of his fingers, he finds it useful to channel the nervous fidgety energy that builds during their encounters through his touch so that their hand-holding is never staid. Together, they create myriad variations on an eternal theme. He palpates the back of her hand. He plaits his fingers with hers in various reticulate formations. They play cat's cradle without string. His thumb effleurages hers. Swinging the skein of digits between them, he gets an intimation of what it would feel like if they were giddy childhood sweethearts. He tries to convey meaning with every movement, express what he feels about her with the heat from the friction of their skin. He hopes the apothegm holds true, that his body won't lie. Maybe physical contact can become for them a kind of lingua franca wherein he can achieve the clarity and directness she accomplishes verbally. *We're doing exactly what I want*, he would say. *Now if only we could go a bit* further. . . .

Ironically, if not cruelly, what he desires from Favia he is getting no shortage of at home in his bed with Jessica. It had never been this way with Carol, or perhaps ever. Sex with Jessica is constant, spontaneous, so much so that he often finds himself embedded in lubricity within a half-hour of his last glance of Coffee Girl. Unceasing copulation is not unusual for him but what is new is the recurring impulse to mentally transpose the grunting, sweating, naked bundle of sexuality beneath him with a girl he hasn't even seen discalced yet and whose foremost quality is platonic altruism and yet who nevertheless arouses in him a frenzied lust. It is an act of pure invention to imagine what Coffee Girl would be like in bed, and, in this respect, Gabe is only too glad to play fabulist. But his attempts to proceed from a foundation of verity are continually thwarted: Jessica frustrates his efforts to recreate the only sensation approaching a sexual nature he knows with any certainty with Favia—the feeling of her hand in his—by keeping her hands constantly roving. At any given time during intercourse she is running her nails down his back, or pulling on his thighs to add force to his thrusts, or stimulating herself to orgasm, but she never leaves her hands quiescent, which prevents him from attempting anything as prosaic as a handhold. No matter; if that action alone were enough to get him off, he'd have to bring in a change of underwear every day to work.

Jessica takes amazingly good care of his body's needs, allowing his mind to filter the experience through his consciousness the way he sees fit. Her enthusiasms help when they don't hinder. Every moan, every pelvic abrasion, every arch of her back is vetted for comparison with the fabricated idea of Favia's sexual behavior—her reactions and sounds and involuntary movements—and are either rejected or deemed plausible and used as fuel for his indelible fantasies. There are enough similarities—real or imagined—between the girls for this fanciful substitution to hold water: Jessica has a similarly curvaceous body, comparable midnight hair, and largish breasts the mirror image of which Gabe has only a noumenal sense of.

The illusion is of course easier to maintain from the back. Not even necessarily doggy-style, where one is compelled to watch, to gaze upon, to analyze what is usually more unclothed flesh normally seen from a lover—especially a diffident one (not a problem with Jessica)—or at least those parts of the body (viz. her back, her buttocks) not easily appraised for a length of time without coming across as slightly deviant, and one can do all this staring without being observed oneself, making dorsal spectation during doggy-style humping practically irresistible, and but n.b. that all this pointed and focused staring severely hampers one's ability to picture anyone but the person one is screwing, what with all the particular details of the topography of her body (e.g. moles, collops, spinal alignment, tattoos, etc.) accreting to form an incontrovertible image of what can possibly be only one person in the world, and that's if one is inclined to want to think about making mental substitutions for sexual gratification in the first place because (A.) all this analysis can get dispassionate and a bit unerotic (the same way repeating a word over and over until it is pure sound strips it of any meaning, staring intently at discrete body parts drains them of sexual connotation and all that is seen is flesh covering musculature and bones) and (B.) the position itself is physically tiring to maintain, and one ends up either concentrating on keeping up the steady thrusting or adopting the grim blankness of thought that seems to help people get through repetitive physical exertion. For Gabe, the position maximally conducive to envisioning an alternate lover is side-by-side spooning. This position requires less effort and keeps her occiput front and center, the reminder of her face firmly out of view. Missionary also works but only when he buries his face in the pillow beside her head and even then it doesn't work as well. Spooning allows him easy access to her breasts and affords him enough arousing visuals so he doesn't have to completely imagine the sights that will get him to the point when he shuts his eyes and nothing else in the world matters.

The look of Jessica's skin supports the illusion almost as much as the feel of it. The coloration is similar to Favia's, although obviously darker. Chroma and hue are close enough, only the value has to be adjusted. Contrary to all laws of ocular perception, the only way to lighten Jessica's skin is to remove the light sources in the room. Only in the semi-darkness can the value-correction take place, and then only in his mind. He convinces himself that he's seeing Favia's skin, closing his eyes sometimes to get over the hump of reality and maintain what he imagines to be there. He ignores the truth of darkness, counters the decreasing value of every color in the room by making the naked body before him more valuable for it, more useful to him for being something different. A bit lighter, coarse around the hands, smooth as silk everywhere else.

One day, a late season ice storm descends on the area. After a night of gelid conditions, every traversable spot outside is turned into a hockey rink. Gabe ventures out during his lunch break into light sleet and frigid desolation. The climate has sucked all the urgency out of outdoor activities and sent every-one to shelter. So it's no surprise that Coffee Girl is where she always is, though her kiosk is icily corticated and she's getting a respite from the scourge of long lines that usually harry her. They rejoice at the sight of each other, friendly faces glad-dening their wearers' spirits, united in solidarity against the inclement weather. He knows he's been drawn out by the necessity of seeing her and she is only there, in a way, to see him, the only person in sight, a prospective customer, poten-tially more. She quickly expresses horror that he's willingly submitted himself to the elements and, proving her tut-tutting is rooted more in genuine concern than feigned compassion, she unlatches the side panel of the kiosk and invites him in. He stoops down and enters as she pulls down the jointed slats that cover the counter opening, enclosing them in, shielding them from the rest of the world.

He's excited to find himself truly alone with her for the first time, immured in an unobservable space away from the in-quisitive glances of the overly solicitous. He momentarily has the impression, no doubt abetted by the feeling of isolation prevailing this day, that they are an old impecunious couple, nestled together in this hovel, relying on each other for need and want and no less happy for it. One of the first things he notices is a feeling of warmth—not the heat radiating through his insides but the warmth of his surroundings, enveloping him in a shroud of comfort. The emanating source of this comfort, he sees, is a space heater in the corner which has no doubt made the day easier to bear for Coffee Girl. It has also allowed her to be decked out in such incongruous raiment as hunter green capris with adorable ties on the bottom, affording him a provocative glimpse of crural skin, and glittery sandals, which show off the impressively upkept peach-colored polish on her toes. She looks breathtaking, as always. He grabs her hands and her expression positively shines. She directs him to a stool and pulls another one close so that their fingers can continue to play. His excitement is beyond measure at this opportunity to interact with her sans the intervening chaperone of a counter or someone looking over his shoulder, hanging on their words. The small talk turns from weather to the rigors of maintaining the kiosk, which include but are not limited to the ungodly hour she's expected to be open for business and, of course, the unappeasable customers. She doesn't whine her litany of grievances; instead she unfurls them in a slightly eager way, as if she lacked for confidantes, betraying her need for understanding, her gratefulness for a sympathetic ear. Gabe squeezes her hand and rubs her arm consolingly. Before the mood can become doleful, she smiles at him and they veer off onto more congenial topics. They discuss his job, mutual likes and dislikes, favorite music (his: anything, hers: slow romantic songs). He manages to pry out of her that she takes belly dancing lessons and makes her promise to show him her moves sometime, a promise that lacks the specificity to be taken seriously but is potent enough in its potential form. Their conversation takes on the easy unimpeded rhythm of two people enjoying each other's company.

While she talks, Favia slips her feet out of her sandals and places them alternately on the rungs of the stool and on the seat, folded up against the inside of her thigh. It's a familiar move copied by girls everywhere. Gabe wonders how deliberate it is, if they know how crazy men are driven by the gesture. Like all girls, Favia does not overtly draw attention to what she's doing; her movements are easy, airy, as naturally executed as a smile. The foot apparently persists as the only body part that can be denuded without sexual import. Can girls really be oblivious to the suggestive power of this habit? Perhaps it is truly an unconscious movement for them, as unremarkable as placing their hands in their pockets, a custom made meaningless through countless reiteration, a reflexive motion the purpose of which has long been forgotten, like the covering of one's mouth when yawning. Nevertheless, intentional or not, Gabe is stimulated by the sight. After a few seconds, he decides that something must be done lest he wonder for the rest of his life what *could've* been done. Attempting to match her nonchalance, he casually reaches out and takes hold of her foot. "Here," he says, willing his voice not to crack, "you've been working hard lately. Let me give you a foot massage." She gives him a short chuckle and looks momentarily taken aback, lending further credence to the possibility that she had no idea what she was doing. However, she quickly responds to the offer, out of either desire or an amenable spirit, stretching her feet onto his lap in gratifying acquiescence. She becomes for him suddenly effaced above the ankle, no longer even appurtenant to the newly discovered body part, though her feet more than adequately attest to her overall loveliness. His hands rove freely, claiming territory on her insteps. He discerns her metatarsals and ungual phalanges, a budding podiatrist alone with ten live little piggies. He grazes the underside of her toes. Her feet are as coarse as her hands and he rubs her calluses as if hoping to intenerate them. Upon reaching her arches, his fingers linger on the soft virginal flesh they find there, a cavernous and illicit place which sends suggestive thoughts racing pell-mell through his mind. He subtly shifts position and he honestly doesn't know if it's to get her feet closer or farther away from the newly formed protrusion in his pants.

During this ostensible massage, their conversation continues unabated. The talk turns to personal matters, as all conversations invariably do. In ten minutes, he learns more about her than he has in ten years as she opens like a book in front of him. It's as if everything they had ever said to each other up to this point had been part of a pour parler before the big colloquy. For starters, she hails from Brazil. She arrived in country about fourteen years ago, rooming with four other Brazilian girls. A crazy, exciting time she relates, her eyes wistful at the memory. Gabe can only imagine, his mind filled with gamboling sex-starved beauties and their nights of tequila-fueled experimentation. She's fluent in Portuguese, which is her home country's official language, a fact that may throw for a loop those who were leaning toward Europe as the place of her birth. She claims she's thirty-four years old and, in the face of his skepticism, insists on the accuracy of this number, though she stops short of pulling out her driver's license to prove it. Not that Gabe really doubts her, he just finds it propitious to express shock, ingenuous or not, whenever a woman says a number over thirty. Although, when she reveals that her daughter is a junior in high school, she prompts more questions than she answers and her assertion barely manages to hang on a thin thread of plausibility. Still, Gabe can't deny that the math leads down some intriguing roads—pretty hot ones actually.

Just as all talk tends to the personal, all personal talk eventually arrives at sex. The subject is eased into via a few words about Gabe's recently terminated relationship. Coffee Girl, like everyone else, knows about the big split with Carol and, through inference or access to someone with inside information or just plain old gossip, she knows about the brusque and peremptory way he was informed of the break-up. Actually, there is no way for Coffee Girl to know the exact details, but she interpolates the anguish he must have felt, the unnecessary heartbreak that has befallen him, and the derogation he has undeservedly been subjected to. If there exists a mold of compassion, she conforms to it utterly, right before his eyes: brow scrunched up in concern; eyes free of judgment, completely unwavering and filled to the brim with caring. The empathetic slight downward curve of her mouth. Her whole body leaning forward, ready to be his fulcrum, both physically and emotionally. The comforting way she rubs his arm, her touch of solace. All of this forces him to adopt a downtrodden aspect so as not to waste her display of consolation. She reassures him of his favorable prospects for finding someone else, someone he deserves. She appears to know nothing about Jessica, and he sees no reason to apprise her of his current relationship status. Secretly, he exults in the fulsome attention she's giving him.

An offering of seemingly invested solicitude confers on the recipient of the sympathy a responsibility to comfort the now-distressed comforter; it is incumbent on Gabe, as the cause of her worry, to smooth out the wrinkles of concern on her face. He assures her that his dignity had not been comminuted beyond reconstruction, that he has emerged from the evirating ordeal with his self-respect intact, and besides. . . . Here he breaks off. A slightly waggish grin plays on his lips. He knows that this aposiopesis is all but irresistibly compelling. Sure enough, she senses that he's on the cusp of revealing some scabrous tidbit and urges him to continue. After a suitably dramatic pause, he confides that he's really not sweating the break-up because it's not like Carol was that great in the sack. This is false, a flight of fancy. He had been nothing but satisfied with Carol's bedroom performance. Whether out of a desire to steer the discussion in a stimulating direction or to slyly hint at unfulfilled needs that can be met by a willing party, he has preempted the truth with a lie and must now run with it. Coffee Girl emits even more sympathetic mewls; she considers the revelation just one more piteous thing on top of the rest. A good, mutually nurturing sex life is important, she avers, and proceeds to elucidate the differences between Brazilian and American women with respect to sexual praxis while Gabe, to whom all this is news, listens avidly.

Apparently, Brazilian gals are a more halcyon bunch when it comes to sex. Not only are they free of the priggishness and hesitancies that seem to be part and parcel of the U.S.'s most truly desirable girls (which include the girl-next-door types, the southern belles, the three-sport goddesses—basically the non-skanks), but they're this way from the moment they step onto the scene. During courtship in her hometown of Mariana, sex comes early and often. It's a non-issue in the dating ritual, unremarkable in its occurrence, as intrinsic and expected as a first kiss. You like someone, you have sex, she shrugs. It's ingrained in the culture—everyone is screwing without inhibition, even the "nice girls," and they can do so without the specter of elders with stern faces fixed in expressions of disapproval or the puerile gossip from their peers. Without the need to feel coy or abashed, lovers in Brazil are free to make sex the sweaty, fulfilling enterprise it was always meant to be.

She relays all this to Gabe equably, as calm and matter-of-fact when talking about the act as she claims to be when engaging in it. In fact, Gabe has never seen her look more composed—this is her bailiwick, she's in her comfort zone, she's got a pitch in her wheelhouse and is knocking it out of the park. Her words have the confident flow of a teacher imparting brand-new knowledge to an eager student, the kind of knowledge the teacher knows is no less interesting once learned. Coffee Girl even manages to multitask while she talks (a real indicator of a stressless comfort level), getting up to make him a cup of coffee on the house. He comments on how wonderful international sex sounds, and muses that if Carol had been a Brazilian girl they would probably still be together. He tells her that Carol was too reserved, too austere in the sack: another made-up bit come up with on the fly, once again proving that truth is the quintessential liquid commodity, always exchangeable for a more interesting lie. He looks at her

conspiratorially and says he was willing to do anything—
anything—Carol wanted him to do, but she lacked the sexual
wherewithal to capitalize on his submissiveness. "I still am," he
adds, "willing to do anything." He grins at her. "With another
woman, of course." Suggestive, hopeful, lecherous.

He takes a sip of coffee, lets out a contented sigh, and once
again beseeches her to divulge her secret ingredients. This is a
familiar method of joshing her, and she submits to it gleefully,
teasing him right back. "No, no," she says. "I'll never tell." He
lunges at her, wrapping his arms around her as she squeals and
laughs. He is in the dark about his intent, but since his hands
are on her, he squeezes and tickles and rubs. They giggle
uncontrollably, like two youths—one Brazilian, one willing to
learn to be. They disentangle from each other after a few minutes, out of breath and flushed. They look at each other ador-
ingly. He reaches out and soberly takes her hand, no longer
playful, and gives it an optative squeeze. "Out of all the coffee
places in town," he says, "you're my fave." He gives her a
meaningful look and repeats it: "You're my fave." It's more
than a simple paronomasia on her name. It's a perfect mimesis
of the sort of affectionate diminutive used by long-time lovers,
a personal cognomen indicating carnal familiarity. Coffee Girl
seems to grasp the implications. Her cheeks bloom red. The
effect is like a cherry cordial with its attendant juices showing
through a veneer of dark chocolate. She is exquisitely esculent,
the dessert one indulgently orders for the entrée. At this
moment, she is the meal he would most like to order off a
menu comprising roughly three billion choices, a meal, it
would seem, he is also prohibited from having—a forbidden
fruit.

As he watches her reconcile his affection with her perception of the truth, he considers, not for the first time, whether
there's a way to tell her that he thinks of her when he comes—
both alone and with Jessica. That that's what puts him over the
edge: the image of her in his mind. He wonders whether she
would take it how he intends it to be taken—as a supreme

compliment; she is the angel who guides him to the only heaven he knows. He tries to conceive of circumstances—baring impending eschaton—in which such an expression could be voiced and received properly, with no equivocation by the speaker and no misunderstanding by the listener. Perhaps no such setting exists, or perhaps what's missing is the courage to tell her the truth. Is he being untruthful to her, letting lies taint the relationship before it has a chance to take flight? By acting as if she's not a part of his most intimate acts, is he nothing but an abhorrent whited sepulcher? Even if this is the case, he is mindful of the potential ruination that could result from such a proclamation and instead tells her something safe and almost trite, though no less true: "You look really beautiful today."

For a moment, his comment seems to affect her adversely; she freezes and looks stunned—this despite what has been, by all indication, her endless capacity for praise. This time he has waylaid her with a judgment she never expected to hear from his lips, maybe from anyone's. The idea that she isn't told what she so clearly deserves to hear on a daily basis is piteous to Gabe. The way he has so simply induced a flabbergasted aphonia in her, the way her mouth lies open in a rictus of momentary incomprehension, it breaks his heart. He tries to savor her unguarded reaction, knowing that he'll never see it in all its glory again, as she's bound to become inured to this particular combination of words, which he intends to repeat to her ad nauseam. A strange pang of regret and nostalgia jabs him even as she reaches out and pulls him close. She blubbers her appreciation, her thanks, discomfiting Gabe in return, who isn't sure how to respond. Her actions seem born of a need for momentum, for her to do something besides just stand there, to be a gracious recipient of his kindness and offer some reciprocity of commensurate value. After some hugs and clutches and grasps, with need still lying between them unfulfilled, she improvises and gives him a kiss on the cheek. Her lips on his skin feel unreal. He automatically goes to kiss her opposite cheek before she can pull away. She has regained enough presence of mind to expect it, turning her head to offer him a receptive target. The skin of her face is smooth; the surface of his lips feels calcified in comparison and he doesn't press in too firmly for fear of leaving an indentation.

As she starts to pull away, he is not ready to give her up. He maintains contact as she brings herself back upright, his hands sliding across her back, around her sides, arriving at the long-sought destinations residing about chest high. Unable to help himself, he grazes the sides of her breasts, letting his hands drift across their bulbous mass. She's wearing an unpadded bra, a wisp of fabric that does little to conceal the softness underneath. His fingers trace these globular twins along their equators, achieving liftoff just before reaching the nipple, the passing into another hemisphere for a return trip deemed too flagrant even in his mindlessly excited state. He takes his hands away reluctantly, slowly, as if resisting a strong gravitational pull. He looks to her face immediately, an apology sitting in the back of his throat ready to be deployed at the slightest trace of objurgation in her eyes. Instead, he sees her familiar pleasant expression containing no hint of acknowledgement of the liberties he has just taken, no castigating look, no wry smile or bemused pause, no nod to the event at all. Her continuing insouciance to all forms of physical contact strikes Gabe as auspicious.

A moment after straightening herself, she announces her need to use the powder room. Would he mind staying here and watching the kiosk while she goes to the gas station down the street for a few minutes? She asks as though there is any chance at all he would refuse. Her unassuming nature charms him and he wants to tell her of all the things he would be willing to do for her that would involve much more discomfort, pain, and hardship than he will incur by the bagatelle of simply watching her workstation. Not to mention the intensely pleasurable things he could do *to* her as well, given the chance. She puts on some socks and slips her feet into boots, then bends down to grab a coat lying in the corner. She's facing away from him, putting her backside on display. The bottom of her camisole and the waistband of her capris slide away from each other, parting to reveal thong underwear. It's black and appears to be made of a shiny spandex-like material, pulled taut across the top of her buttocks into a "T" that threatens to disappear if stretched any further. Standing up, she puts on her coat and conceals the sight, to his eternal disappointment. After switching her cap for a wool hat, she smiles at him in a slightly embarrassed way and says she'll be right back and exits the kiosk, shutting the panel behind her.

He is alone. After a second of deliberation, he picks up the baker boy cap she's left behind and holds it to his face. He smells what he usually smells when they hug, when her head is nestled right underneath his nose. Only now, smothering himself with her hat, the smell is more concentrated than ever. Her perfume mixes with shampoo, beauty product, and dried sebum. Handling an item of her personal effects—something that has touched her skin, pressed against her, something that retains the secrets it knows of her by being so close, something she has exposed herself to, and now that something enveloping his face as he drinks in the sensations—makes him tremble with gratitude. He wouldn't be more aroused if it were her thong occluding his nostrils. In this cramped space, surrounded by the mundane everyday accoutrements of a dedicated coffee slinger, with nothing more inspiring than a still-warm hat to work with, all he can think of is release. He would tame the angry python, even in this constricting space, but his concerns are more temporal than spatial. What if she came back and found him in a compromised position: using her hat to burke himself but trying for all the world to come before biting the big one? Then again, so what if she did? He allows himself to imagine the unimaginable: that she would come upon him in a similarly frustrated state. She would mask her delight by pretending to be shocked, though there would be little question whether she took offense after she reaches out to take over his own hand's task. The hand he was jerking off with would be free to slip underneath her shirt, though his other hand would still be clamping the hat to his face so as not to interrupt the fantasy. There would be time for conventional lovemaking later; now is the time for fetishistic indulgence. The hat would be incorporated in their future playing; he would come home to find her sprawled out on the bed wearing nothing but. With a carefree laugh and confident flick of her wrist, she would fling the hat across the room, toward his pelvis, trying to score a ringer. He would catch it, hold it to his face, and whatever problems he had faced that day—none involving her—would wash away in the remembrance of his initial furtive desire.

He hears the latch of the kiosk release and, without thinking—or perhaps with a stunning amount of compressed calculation—he stuffs the hat inside his jacket. As Coffee Girl reenters the kiosk, he greets her effusively, willing her attention not to wander, barely concealing his need for flight. After some energetic but vacuous conversational sallies which are all he is capable of in his current nervous state, he stutters that he must really be leaving now. She calms his anxiety by holding him close and he feels how at ease she is, how free from worry. She stands on her toes and, with a stillness, whispers in his ear, "You're so good. I'm lucky to have you in my life right now." He looks down at her, amazed by this thing in his arms, and presses against her, exerting pressure on her whole body with the willful intention of making her change her position, of making her step back against the counter for leverage so she can withstand what he irrationally plans for them both to engage in, right here, right now. She misreads his signals, holds him tighter, leans against him harder, an indomitable object as true and secure as the statements she has made to him. When she releases him, he brushes a stray strand of hair off her face and lightly kisses her fingers. Eventually he leaves, because he has to, all the while feeling the lump in his jacket he can't wait to extract, something he knows he will find benign, delightful even. He will live, and in so doing will find his release, many,

many times over.

Lying in bed that night, alone, Jessica away on a two-day conference, he goes over his options. There is no question that he wants Coffee Girl in the only meaningful way one can: as an inamorata, and there is no chicaning himself to believe otherwise. The possibility seems close at hand, so close that he has little trouble imagining the deed already done. The jump from woman to lover is so small, the actions needed to fulfill the requirements of the change in title so inconsequential, that it's easy at times to bask in the gorgeous prolepsis of every girl he sees being his lover, just ones who haven't taken the ten seconds or so and participated in the pro forma act of copulation with him. And after all the formalities are dispensed with, before you know it, a quondam lover becomes a partner, a metamorphosis that leaves her no less hungry for sex (Gabe has little doubt in Favia's case) but affords a different, quotidian set of pleasures, and, since he has spent ample time thinking about the more immediate gratifications she could offer, Gabe speculates on long-term delights, the various things that could be in store for him years down the road. Coffee Girl's sleep-encrusted eyes being the first thing he sees in the morning. Knowing all her stories, every opinion she has and ever will have. Taking the sight of her naked body for granted, as just the wallpaper of his life. Lust must be as blind as love, because it all sounds great to Gabe. He begins careful consideration of how these things can come to pass. He thinks of inviting her over, maybe not for a cup of coffee exactly, but in a sort of neighborly spirit. Then, through some contrivance most likely tied to the decorative scheme of his home, leading her through the apartment. The key is getting her in the bedroom; behind closed doors, anything's possible. The decision to make the plunge isn't decided by quorum and consent need not be given the next day or even the next *minute* for something to happen *now*. He needs to corner her into a situation where a "yes" would be so much more easily uttered than a "no" and then let biology take over. Position her in the exact time and space, align her carefully along four dimensions, and the decision is no longer hers; something implacable takes over, something the non-perspicacious are disposed to call "fate," not knowing that doing so absolves those guilty of orchestrating the machinations that hide from the ignorant every path but one. How lucky she is, Gabe reflects, that the person behind the scenes is working toward her direct and unambiguous pleasure.

The major impediment would seem to be the ring of platinum cinctured around her finger. She never references the person it represents, yet the ring is always present, serving as a reminder to all in sight. Gabe has traced his finger around it a few times, pinched it between his forefinger and thumb as if testing its integrity. He ponders the unknowable: how often do they have sex? Did she have a strong religious upbringing, adequate to instill in her enough fear that she takes the vows of matrimony seriously? Most important, does he make her happy? Because if this unknown guy is uxorious, he has almost no chance with Coffee Wife. But what of her other suitors? He just cannot be the first to throw his hat into the ring; she sticks out like Everest, both prominent and irresistible, something people will inevitably try to climb and conquer. How did those other hapless glory(hole) seekers fare? Crashed and burned, no doubt, ending up with the rest who got no further with her than having their change handed back. But what if that's not the case? Gabe has fancied himself as treading on uncharted territory—to a destination visited a few times, sure, but blazing a new trail, arriving there in a wholly new way. But now he considers the possibility that he is only following in the footsteps of many who have gone before him. He may even meet a few of these intrepid folk when he reaches the summit, on their way down after exhausting the pleasures of the peak. With one guy, a weary king of the hill, presumably overseeing all the comings and goings. This perspective casts the husband in a new light as a possible wittol, more of a help than a hindrance. Maybe he's even encouraging his wife to find guys for troilism, which Gabe has no interest in at all. No, easier to think of the guy as an uninspiring shlub, married only in a legal sense to someone better than he deserves, to someone who is looking to abdicate whatever obligations she foolishly agreed to, the two of them living under one roof but hardly together in any sort of meaningful union, biding their time in a stultifying modus vivendi, locked into a regrettable mesalliance. Gabe has to show her that marriage vows are more honored in the breach than the observance—something he can personally attest to. Only then can they. . . . He thinks of her elliptical thighs and soft belly and inviting hips and reaches over for her hat sitting on the nightstand, fully intending on putting it to use one more time before turning in.

The next day, sloshing through the runnels on the sidewalk created by melting ice, he anxiously debates the best way to give the hat back to its rightful owner. It bears no trace of the use and abuse it was subjected to the previous night, but the actual handing it back could be awkward since there is no plausible reason for him to have it. He considers stealthy legerdemain—distracting her then throwing it into a corner of the kiosk. He thinks of keeping it and disavowing its existence, even if confronted with direct questioning. In the end he decides to claim a different sort of ignorance, handing the hat back sheepishly, apologizing for taking it inadvertently and finding it when he got home bundled in a coat he's not even sure he took off—a literally incredible explanation. With no better option, that's what he goes with, and what's more incredible is her easy acceptance of it, her thanking him, assuring him that these things happen, putting the hat off to the side and moving on. As he stands there dumbfounded, she reaches out toward his neck and starts fiddling with his shirt. It takes him a second to realize that, in a swivet about the hat, he has rushed out of the house in a minor state of dishabille, with a half-tucked-in collar on open display. He submits to her sartorial ministrations and she takes her time making sedulous adjustments. The moment distends. Gabe feels as though he is taking part in a domestic scene: the big-hearted wife seeing her husband off, preparing him for a hard day's work—they play the roles exactly, a preview of things to come, a dress rehearsal before they do it for real. Her movements have an underwater feel to them; she's absorbed in fixing his shirt, as if she's doing it by habit but is surprised at how much she's enjoying it. He feels safe and comforted and contented. She sighs, indicating she may feel some of the same. Finished with straightening him out, she pats him on the chest and says, "You're so good." Her eyes turn sorrowful. "I wish I could do things for you. I wish I could."

Before he can respond, maybe to let her know that what she wishes is possible, her head goes down and she noticeably slumps as she drops the big news on him. Her mother, living back in Brazil, is unwell. Favia is unable to articulate the specifics of the malady, but Gabe gets the impression that it has happened suddenly and is unexpected and more than a little worrisome. The grasping of her hand is automatic; he's always looking for the flimsiest pretext to touch her, though this time it's for honorable reasons, his caresses meant to be more soothing than stimulating. He wonders if she perceives the difference on her end or if his hands are even moving any differently at all. While his face is scrunched up in concern and sorrowful hums rumble from the back of his throat, there is only so much invested empathy on display until she says the thing that truly disturbs him: she's leaving very soon to go be with her. His hands reflexively clamp on hers, as if she intends to bolt immediately. With his mouth suddenly desiccated, he mechanically gets the answers from her he knows he will want to know later, when he has regained the ability to think straight. Yes, of course she's coming back; she'll be gone for a month. Yes, she's going alone; the husband and kids are remaining stateside. No, the illness does not appear to be life-threatening, for now. The overwhelming sadness of the situation is evident by her blank expression and even tone of voice; it's the kind of serious news that drains the emotion from a person. Still, she tries to maintain the compassionate optimism that defines her. She clenches his hands just as hard in return, asking him to pray for her, and he promises he will, convincing even himself. She wills a wan smile, citing encouraging facts such as the fast detection and her mother's relatively young age, which seems to substantiate her truism about the accelerated nature of sex in Brazil; Gabe's attention is momentarily derailed as he thinks of three generations of dark-skinned beauties—from teenager to grandmother—separated from being contemporaries by the slimmest of margins. She misreads his silence and attempts to cheer him up by saying she'll miss him. He emphatically returns the sentiment. He expresses mock concern that she'll find a suave, good-looking guy over there, a lusophone chevalier who will win her heart and he'll never see her again. He's half joking, half feeling out her receptiveness to the idea. The hypothetical causes a genuine grin, and she assures him that it isn't even a remote possibility, that she has no intention of repatriation. Despite her demurral, he has his doubts.

Their time together no longer feels like a refreshing break from the world, more like sand slipping through his fingers. He's running out of time to do something, though he's not sure what. He's in a dream, ill-prepared for the mysterious task before him. When they say goodbye, she once again presses her lips to the side of his face, a movement he mimics, and somewhere he finds the determination to do something else, to push things forward while he still can. He goes in for another kiss, deluding himself that he's going for the center of her lips, ending up exactly where he had really intended: the corner of her mouth. His lips touch pliable matter, something that moves, something labile, alive. He feels as if he's touching something clean, pure, something rubbed smooth or missing the layer of protective integument that covers the rest of her body. He feels closer to her, closer to exposed nerve endings and hot humid cavernous enclosures—passageways to her soul. He pulls away, no longer overly concerned about her reaction, which appears to be favorable; there is laughter in her eyes. A customer comes up and he tells her he'll see her later and walks away. He feels a coolness as the trace of her saliva evaporates off his skin. He runs his tongue over his lips, licking the rest of her away, hoping for a residual taste but getting nothing. He looks back and she's still watching him with a child's arch delight. He resolves right then to prepare a dramatic gesture for her, one that will show her every facet of his desire.

That night, he paces around his apartment, expending the pent-up nervous energy that has built up throughout the day. He visualizes what he wants to see happen the next day, all the best possibilities, a panoply of favorable scenarios that result in his sweeping Coffee Girl off her feet. An event they can both look back on fondly as a turning point, a daring escalation, the time he bravely consigned the consequences to hell. He says her name again and again. "Favia. Favia. Favia." He paces back and forth, ranging all over the apartment. He repeats the dactyl over and over—"Fa-via, Fa-via, Fa-via"—as if introducing the concept of her to the apartment before she makes an appearance. He eventually exhausts himself, allowing the previously unthinkable notion of getting some shut-eye to creep into his bones, and wearily gets into bed. The gears of his mind grind away at his anxiety, and slowly his nervous anticipation gets sublimated into a dispersing flock of gold-tipped, well-intentioned butterflies fluttering gently in his stomach. He closes his eyes and lets his mind and hands wander. "Oh, Favia."

He isn't completely sure he will go through with his plan until he rises the next morning to shut off the alarm, which starts blaring at 4:45—needlessly, since he has been lying awake in bed for the last twenty minutes. He gets up quickly, and stumbles into the bathroom. After relieving himself and brushing his teeth and washing his face and combing his hair, he turns off the bathroom light and wanders into the kitchen, glancing at the digital display of the time in the kitchen. He stands at the table, drumming his fingers on the tabletop, staring into a bouquet of flowers placed in a makeshift vase (a glass pitcher he found in the cupboard), twelve long-stemmed roses purchased yesterday at the florist on Dixon after getting out of work, the glass container filled about three-fourths of the way with water, the flowers wrapped in pellucid red-tinted cellophane and prettily arranged with baby's breath, the water slightly murky, the pitcher positioned at almost the exact center of the table. He stands transfixed, going over a plan that is dangerously close to being enacted, the linchpin of the plan right there in front of him, in full bloom. He is so lost in thought that a few minutes pass before he realizes he should've already left, and only then does he register that he's still in his nightclothes.

A few minutes later, he rushes out of the apartment, dressed, surrounded by an invisible cloud of (newly purchased) cologne, keys in one hand, flowers in the other, and strides to the parking lot with a sense of urgency. He gets in his car and carefully places the flowers in the passenger seat. He looks at them again, recalling the precise calculation with which they were chosen, the consideration taken to ensure an optimally perspicuous representation of his intent. Even the color choice was deliberate. Twelve red roses—the meaning is unmistakable in any language. It's a semion of romantic love, which implies intimacy, which is synonymous with sexual intercourse, which is a euphemism for anal action. He wants her ass, and his message could not be more clear.

He drives into the enshrouding solvent of darkness. The morning light has yet to break and the sky is a deep indigo color Gabe is unused to seeing. It irrationally seems unnatural, the color of a painter's failed experiment. Under flickering streetlights, Gabe slowly passes quiet houses as he drives down deserted streets. It is still a touch too early for widespread activity, which unnerves Gabe. Though it is as dark as the dead of night, there is the feeling that the day should be starting, that the darkness has lasted about as long as it can and is starting to ripen, that night is over and what he is seeing is a facade, an untruth—day dissembling as night. The sense that things are not as they appear gives everything a slightly sinister edge. He feels assaulted by waves of suspicion from unseen eyes in umbral alcoves. A still small voice within him says he should not be out here, and he would normally have no reason to be, but he feels the pull of a beacon heralding him from Main Street and the rapidly closing window he has to answer its call; Coffee Girl will be leaving soon and Jessica will be back from her trip later today and be next to him in bed at this time tomorrow and would surely have questions—which could not be answered plausibly—about his sneaking out with a bunch of roses at the crack of dawn. Thinking of Jessica dampens his spirits, and not because of the vehement objections he knows she would have to this morning's activities. What saddens Gabe is that among the many reasons not to be doing what he is doing, Jessica's a priori disapproval—and the very probable hurt she would feel if she could see him now—does not affect him more and is not reason enough to turn around.

Coming onto Main Street, he sees Favia opening the kiosk and he is simultaneously proud and thankful of his perfect timing. He pulls up to the curb and gets out, carefully hiding the flowers behind his back. She is still fiddling with the lock as he strolls up. He impulsively reaches out to rub her back. He fights the urge to drop the flowers and wrap his arms around her, stroke the belly he is owed sight of, hold her close with the overly familiar ease he feels they've already achieved. Before he throws caution to the wind and just does it, she turns around and starts, opens her mouth slightly, and makes a startled sound; she seems more surprised by the sight of him than she is by his touch. She quickly recovers though and beams at him, giving him her hand, which he raises to his mouth and kisses. She always bows her head and smiles too widely when he does this, a young schoolgirl's smile, one that is both abashed and thrilled. She asks him what he is doing out so early and he casually says that he just happened to be up and thought he would swing by and say good morning. "So," he says, "good morning." She smiles warmly and says it's good to see him. He asks how she's doing and she says she's doing O.K. and asks how he's doing. In his nervousness, he responds with the rote geniality "Good, how are you?" absurdly volleying the question back to her. He immediately feels the heat of embarrassment on his face, but she mercifully overlooks his slip-up, though she does pull away. She turns to the kiosk and scowls, muttering something, half in another language, about forgetting her keys. He clicks his tongue and sympathetically groans, arranging his face into an expression of shared frustration, unnecessarily since her attention is squarely in the other direction. He is still holding the flowers behind his back. He has been waiting for her curiosity to kick in; there is no reason it shouldn't since he obviously has something for her, posed as he is in the instantly recognizable semaphore denoting the possession of a concealed gift: standing straight, awkwardly balanced, arm bent out of view, a game of guess-which-hand with only one choice. Still, she doesn't seem to notice. And suddenly he gets very nervous about the fact that she hasn't noticed him standing there clearly wanting to give her something. It doesn't seem to be a simple oversight, and she also doesn't appear to be intentionally ignoring what can so plainly be seen. An aperçu flashes through him like a bolt from the sky, hollowing out his insides in the process. She neither craves nor dreads what he has behind his back because, for her, there is nothing there to feel one way or another about. It's more than a lack of observation. It's that what's behind his back is a void, a big fat null set that precludes consideration. His mouth goes dry. She is literally devoid of anticipation. For her, there is nothing behind his back; she is not able to envision anything behind his back, and never will. Despite blood being pumped rapidly through his body, he feels cold. She does not expect what he has come to unleash, to spring on her. To surprise her with. Her obliviousness is symptomatic, more effect than cause. It's not that she has missed the portents or failed to recognize that the consecution of their interactions would naturally lead to him standing where he is right now, with flowers in tow. It's worse: she's indifferent. Now she's looking up but still away from him, down the street, and even though it is now bright enough for the day not to be mistaken for night, he does not need to follow her gaze to know she is looking at nothing. She has not thought enough about him to even begin to fear he would pull this stunt. He is beneath consideration, always has been. She has no interest in him. He himself might as well be behind his back. If presented with the option, she would not want to sleep with him and would not be able to say why; he is such a blank to her, she has not even registered his flaws. He feels his deodorant failing. He wants out, he wants home, he wants away. To thrust flowers at her now would be out of the question. She would be stricken, dazed, shocked. Forced to have excruciating reactions. Put in a bind. Faced with a catch-22. Caught between a rock and a hard place. Caught with her pants down, up. He looks at the sky and holds his breath. Even though it is getting brighter every minute, the light is still coming from an invisible source, as if God is incrementally turning the dimmer knob. He ruefully thinks that he should have made his move that storm-ridden day in the kiosk, after the foot massage. Now the appropriate time has passed, and now it is past the 11th hour . . . there is no turning back. More than his dignity is at stake, and mortification is not the sole consequence he faces. She does not know him. She thinks she does; she does *not*. Only he knows that he stands as a stranger in front of her. He is now forced to reveal himself to her, the real him, and in doing so destroy the person she thought she knew. Literally wipe out that persona—him, but not him. Something about the precarious nature of what exactly would be effaced if he were to present her with his gift makes him wobble a little on enervated legs. He feels a total annihilation waiting behind a fragile partition, a bomb about to explode. Even if he isn't the target, he is fearful of being caught in a decimating blast. It's that close and that nebulous. Both everything and nothing would change. He hears her sigh and looks up. She is still looking away, her lips drawn tight in a thin line. "So. How is your life?" she asks. He automatically tells her it's good and asks how hers is. She responds, "O.K." She wraps her arms around herself, tugging at the sleeves of her coat, and says "I have to tell you something." He is locked into position. He manages to croak "What's that?" She finally turns to him. "I'm getting a—" She freezes, staring at him. It's obvious that, for the first time today, she sees him, really sees him standing there. Lines appear on her forehead, her eyes are blank. Her mouth stays open on her words. He tenses, ready to reveal everything at her slightest move. The sound of a car door shutting breaks the silence. She looks to the side, turning her head into profile. She closes her mouth. He sees a square of light in her right eye. He watches her. His hands clench. The cellophane crumples and forms sharp edges that cut into his hand. He feels seized up, glued to the spot. Immobile. The helpless feelings of childhood. He sucks on dry skin. The ground feels both there and not. Everything is impossibly close. She's still looking away. He lolls his head to the side, sees two legs approaching, and is not able to lift his gaze above the man's swinging hands and the ring of keys he's holding, the keys jangling, making a slightly abrasive sound as they lightly hit against each other, a sound like crystal shards being ground up, and he can't turn away and he stands there and he watches and all he can hear is wind hitting his ears and all he can feel is that his insides are reaching a point he doesn't know if he can take and then that point passes and he is still there.

LINDSAY

I DIDN'T CARE TOO MUCH FOR LINDSAY before she said "Why do we have to go all the way to Michigan?" After she said that, I decided that I hated her. It was how she said it, like Michigan was a frivolous addition to the plan and hadn't always been part of the experience for the last four years.

I blinked. I conceded a "Huh?"

"Michigan," she said, absently grabbing a book she was never going to read off the shelves and looking at the back cover. "Why do we have to go there?"

"It's where we go every year," I said, hoping to end the conversation with cold, hard veracity.

"It's so far away," she complained. "Why can't we go someplace closer? Like Shelbyville?"

"The fish are much better in Huron," I explained. "And it's what we do every year."

"I think it's too far away," she said with the conviction of somebody who honestly thought her opinion mattered. "Plus, it'd be more expensive." She put the book back and looked at me. "I don't think I'd go if we were going to Michigan."

I said nothing. I picked *The Sun Also Rises* off the shelf and flipped through it. Tact, I thought. That's the best way to approach an emotional creature. With loads and loads of tact. Did I want to get into a fight with someone who had the mental age of a second-grader? Certainly not, not if I could help it. But truthfully, her gall had taken me aback a bit. Her presumptuousness knew no bounds and it had claimed another few meters of territory with these brass remarks.

"In fact, I'm sure of it," she continued. "Michigan is out of the question." She was on a roll, and while it may be fun for an outside observer to see these types of people get on a roll, it's not a pleasant experience to be a participant in a one-way battle of wits that one side thinks it's winning when the reverse is true. It's comparable to the difference of witnessing a nine-car pileup and being car number four in said pileup.

Facts.

Truth.

Logic.

Reason.

These things mean nothing to an emotional creature, so I didn't bother with the obvious "Don't go; you weren't invited anyway." No, she was not going to bait me that easily. So I said nothing and continued to look through Hemingway's collected works.

She was perturbed by my silence, my unwillingness to contradict her confrontational assessment of the situation. "You know, Joseph won't go if I don't go," she said in clipped notes. She had anticipated my response and was calling my bluff, in a way. But I was not so easily fooled.

"He said that?" I said diplomatically.

"He mentioned the possibility," she said. "You know how much he likes fishing."

I sat on this a moment. "Well," I said carefully, "it's not all about the fishing. It's about being together. As a group."

"So if it's about being together, it doesn't have to be in Michigan," she said, whining her coup de grâce with the aplomb of someone being impatient with a nine-year-old. And since she was seven (mentally speaking), I treated her how a nine-year-old would treat an impertinent seven-year-old. "We go to Michigan every year," I said. "This is the fifth year we're doing this. It's really not open to debate this year, nor has it been any other year." I started this explanation in a deliberate and even manner, but toward the end my statements were sharpened with an edge that let her know my patience was being rapidly depleted. It was my hope that she would see that this wasn't simple rhetoric—this was tradition among friends.

Her look changed from incredulousness, to indifference, to anger. In the end, she decided to ignore what she was being told. "It doesn't have to be in Michigan," she lashed out. "All the people going on this trip live in Illinois, it'd be easier for everyone if it's in the state we live in. Not to mention it'd be a lot less expensive, and everyone can use their paychecks for something more useful than traveling an unnecessary distance." She sighed in a way that embarrassed and shocked everyone who heard it—for while this sigh may have understandably passed through the lips of a starving and dying child in a poor African country, it was entirely inappropriate for a young twenty-something carrying about thirty pounds of expendable weight. It was a sigh that would've put Atlas to shame. It was the most selfish sigh in the world. "You just don't think, do you?"

To hell with civility. "Look you . . ." I couldn't finish as Joseph came out of the bathroom then.

"Ready to go?" he said.

"Yes sweetie," she said, linking her arm in his and dragging him forward. I straggled behind them as we exited the bookstore.

Lindsay never brought it up again, for what I assumed to be fear—fear of contradiction by Joseph. She stuck to safely banal topics such as the weather and the color of the shoes she just had to have (so much so that she didn't buy them). I refused to converse about irrelevant matters and for the rest of the day I got to quietly observe the train wreck of a relationship that was in front of me. There's no greater mismatch than the pairing of a loud person with a quiet one and Lindsay was one of the loudest people on earth while Joseph was one of the quietest. Another bad combination is an intelligent person and a dullard. Now Joseph wasn't the smartest guy around and Lindsay wasn't quite the stupidest. It was still a bad match.

We ended up at a restaurant of Lindsay's choosing for lunch. She said it came highly recommended by one of her friends who told her the food was superb. It was garishly decorated with various oddities and trinkets meant to evoke nostalgia in the uneducated. To no one's great surprise, Lindsay squealed with delight at the sight of a seemingly old lantern that she swore her grandfather once owned. "One just like that exactly," proclaimed our new expert on antique lantern designers.

However, it did not take long for Lindsay to decide that she ultimately did not like the restaurant. When we were seated and started to look through the menu, she "tsk"ed and clicked her tongue numerous times. "The prices here are hideous," she moaned. Joseph and I spent the next couple minutes reassuring her that not only were the prices comparable to other such eating establishments in the area, in many cases they were actually quite reasonable. That did not stop her from fretting, and each turn of a page in the menu brought a new set of complaints. Joseph suggested that we might try to find another place, but Lindsay continually turned down the suggestion, finally saying "We're here, aren't we." We certainly were.

I ordered a steak, medium, with the vegetable of the day, corn. Joseph ordered fettuccine alfredo with a side salad. Lindsay was going to order a grilled chicken sandwich but ended up getting a seared shrimp platter with an eggplant casserole side dish. She was talked into it by our waiter, who mentioned it in a rushed way (he was probably new) as "Today's Special" before he asked us what we wanted for our drinks. After he left to get us two cokes and a sparkling water with "just a bit" of lemon, she announced that "Today's Special" sounded delicious. I barely caught what our waiter had said but Lindsay focused right in on it like an eagle who had spotted a mouse—

about to be elevated to the status of "prey"—running through an open field. She asked our opinion on it; I shrugged my shoulders and Joseph said he didn't really like seafood too much, an opinion that she refused to let dampen her interest in the dish.

When our waiter returned with our drinks, she assaulted him with "What kind of shrimp are in Today's Special?"

"Uh, baby shrimp, I think," came his reply.

"Hm, ok. Made with rice correct?" She made this sound like a threat.

"Yes, that's right."

"Brown or white?"

He paused before saying "White."

"Sticky or not?"

"Excuse me?"

"The rice. Is it sticky? Or are all the grains fairly well separated?"

"Um . . . they're . . . apart . . . yes." He was definitely new.

"Is it made with any garlic sauce? I hate any form of garlic," she shot back.

"I'm not sure . . ." he hesitated.

"Can you check?" she said with such harsh inflections I wondered why she didn't just say "Go check now."

While our waiter was off to verify more information than anyone had ever requested on a "Today's Special" anywhere at any time, Lindsay took the opportunity to make a snide remark about the quality of food service workers ("Aren't they supposed to know this stuff?") and I took the opportunity to look at the bar, the party of five that had just come in, a painting on the wall—anything but her.

Our waiter returned and told us that there was, in fact, no garlic in Today's Special. Still, she waffled. "It's just so expensive," she said, returning to her original complaint. We all waited while she wrestled with this apparently difficult decision, the same decision that Joseph and I spent about two minutes total to make for ourselves. She finally turned to our waiter and asked "Have you heard anything about it from other customers?"

"Uh," he said, "uh . . . they seem to like it . . . ok." He waited to see if that would be sufficient and when Lindsay offered him nothing but an impassive stare, he exhaled slightly and said "I'll go see what the guys out back have heard . . ."

"Oh no," she interrupted, "that won't be necessary." She smiled at him, a smile without joy. "I'll just take it."

"Ok," our waiter said, scooping up the menus before we could change our minds. He walked toward the kitchen and I watched him leave. Then I looked at Lindsay and for a moment I wished I was someone she didn't know, someone who she didn't think she was better than, so I could convince her to go to Michigan.

She started to talk again and my eyes wandered past the replica tandem bicycle and artificially aged photo of New York circa 1928 hanging on the wall and ended up looking out the window. I focused on a rather large woman walking her rather small dog, an aesthetically pleasing juxtaposition. The spry dog was leading its owner (who was at least five hundred times stronger than it) this way and that, toward any slightest bit of movement it spotted. The woman was having the darnedest time simultaneously trying to keep her hat from falling off her head and steering her manic pet in at least the general direction she wanted to go. It was really quite humorous. When they went around the corner and out of my sight, the reality of our table filtered back into my consciousness.

". . . and then I got the bill," Lindsay was saying, "and it turns out that they did charge me for the call. But under the agreement, my roaming charges should have been free for that area. So I called them and issued a complaint."

"Uh huh," Joseph said, looking at Lindsay but glancing out the window as I was with increasing frequency.

I wondered how many times a day Joseph had to conceal the fact that the only thing he hated worse than cellphones was talking about cellphones. I caught his eye every so often and although there was no perceptible change in our expressions, we wordlessly communicated as only people who have known each other many years can do. He and Lindsay were not at that level yet and maybe that's why she was always blathering.

Seemingly oblivious to the disconcerting nature of a non sequitur devoid of irony, she interrupted her discourse on cellphone bills with "Look at that license plate on the wall. It's from Montana. I've never been to Montana before." A horrible realization dawned on me: This is how she converses with people. By telling them random things. And she expects the courtesy to be reciprocated back to her. I remembered that Lindsay and Joseph had been dating for a couple months now, and I suddenly felt very sorry for my friend.

I briefly considered bringing up the trip and turning this friendly, if dreary, little gathering into a brawl that would result in bruised egos and hurt feelings. Mostly I wanted to prove Lindsay wrong. I wanted her to hear from her boyfriend that he and I were on the same page, that Michigan was, is, and has always been the plan and damn anyone who disagreed. Proving people like Lindsay wrong is almost always a simple task—and as dangerous as cornering a grizzly bear. As she was going down, she would lash out and try to take as many people with her as she could. My confidence was high though and I probably would've gotten the ball rolling if our food hadn't arrived at that moment.

The sight of my steak reminded me how hungry I was and I reached over and grabbed the steak sauce. Joseph dabbed a bit of cheese topping on his pasta. Lindsay looked at her food, picked at it a little, watched us dive into our meals, and finally took a tentative bite. Her face scrunched up and she made a show of swallowing what little she had put into her mouth. "I don't like this," she declared. Who was I kidding? I didn't want to convince her to go to Michigan. I didn't want her to go at all.

STEPHANIE

HM? NO, IT'S ALRIGHT. Pull up a seat, you're not disturbing anything but my thoughts.

. . . Sorry. That came out a little crass, please come back. It's right that you should sit down with me, it's perfect actually. Sit down and I'll tell you why.

There. Firstly: Thank you. For sitting down with me. It *does* make perfect sense though, yes, it does and I'll tell you . . . please, don't brush this off as drunken rambling because, truthfully, I am not drinking. This here, is one half-finished glass, the same glass I had three hours ago with the same drink it contained at that time. Minus half, of course.

Now, why you should be sitting with me right now: Because you are here. You're here instead of over there. Clever, eh? Come now, let us be like the others for a second; smile, laugh, and be merry. A toast!

You see how I manage my drink? A sip only, to make it last although God knows why I'd want to do that. You, with just that swig you took, are drunker than I am! I joke, I jest, for isn't this a time to be joyous? So you can forgive me my little quips, right?

. . . But you do not want to be joyous. And neither do I. If we did, we'd be over *there*. With the revelers, the lovers and friends without a care in the world. But I find you wandering over here . . . you see what I mean? Yes, that is why it is right for us to be sitting together, at this moment, *here* not *there.*

I don't know what is on your mind friend, but if you'll humor me, I'll tell you what's on mine. Are you settled? Do you want a cigarette? Another drink? Then I'll begin.

It was about a year or so ago. Some diner somewhere. Afternoonish, sometime between two and four. And I saw her. She was bringing me the reuben sandwich I had ordered and I watched her come out of the kitchen, with my sandwich, and I thought "Not Bad." That was my snap-judgment thought.

I pretended to be fully engrossed in my newspaper as she approached my table. I looked up, she smiled, I smiled back. She set my sandwich down, asked if I needed anything else, I shook my head, and she left. And still I thought "Not Bad."

I finished my sandwich and was reading the last part of the sports section when the other waitress, the one who had been my server for most of lunch, came up to me. This one, incidentally, was "Not Acceptable." She smiled pleasantly, asked me if everything was satisfactory, took my money, and left. I left soon after.

I was standing outside, searching my pockets for cigarettes, when she came up to me. Her eyes were bright and her smile was warm and her hands were inside gloves covered with holiday-themed embroidery and I still thought "Not Bad."

She asked if I was a regular and I said "yes." I asked if she was new and she said "yes." She talked about her work and how everyone was being so nice and how it was the most homey diner she'd ever worked in, all while I nodded, finally finding the pocket my cigarettes were in. I pulled out the pack and offered her one. She refused and I lit up and inhaled deeply while she watched. After a few seconds of nothing but the sounds of me inhaling and exhaling, I told her that I had to leave and she nodded. I bid her good day and walked toward my car.

I had barely opened the driver's side door when I felt a tap on my shoulder. It was her and she was stumbling over her words but managed to semi-coherently ask if I wanted to do anything sometime. I looked at her, having to tilt my head down on account of her being about three inches shorter than me. I looked at her eyes, which were looking at anything but mine. My gaze continued down and then back up again. I asked if she was free the next day and her face betrayed a look of relief mixed with delight before it scrunched into thought as she recalled her schedule. After a fair share of *um*'s and *let me see*'s and *I'm trying to think*'s (during which time I took a few more drags of my cigarette), she determined that she got off work at five and could do something tomorrow night. She told me where she lived and I agreed to pick her up at around six. As an afterthought (correcting an oversight that she was greatly amused by), she told me her name was Stephanie. I watched her run back into the diner, skipping over ice patches, skirt swishing in the frigid breeze and I flicked my cigarette away, thinking "Not Bad."

I arrived at her place ten minutes past six. I finished off the last bit of my cigarette before entering the building. Her apartment was on the fifth floor and the elevator was out of order so I opened the stairwell door and started to climb. The physical activity kept me warm, as the stairwell was only a few degrees warmer than it was outside. After a couple minutes, I opened a door and walked onto the fifth floor.

I tracked the apartment numbers down the hall, past peeling wallpaper, over threadbare and heavily stained carpeting, and under flickering lights. Ahead of me, a small child, maybe five or six years old, entered one of the apartments. He stared at me as I came closer and I saw that he was holding a plastic sled that was cracked and chipped in many places. He didn't move as I passed and, as I turned the corner, he was still frozen in place.

After walking past a few more doors, I came upon Stephanie's apartment. I rapped on the door two times in quick succession. It was quickly opened by a young lady who did not have gray-blue eyes like Stephanie and had jet-black hair, very much unlike Stephanie's dirty blond. In short, she was not Stephanie, but she was still "Not Bad."

She identified herself as Kelly, Stephanie's roommate, and let me in. She told me that Stephanie was still getting ready. I nodded and she invited me to sit down in the living room. She offered me a drink and I refused. We sat across from each other, her in a divan on one side of the coffee table and me in the sofa on the other side; she looked at her hands, fidgeting, obviously uncomfortable with simple chit-chat but not knowing what else to do. I didn't mind, content to look at her as she absentmindedly played with her hair. She caught my gaze, gave me a short smile, then excused herself.

Without something to hold my attention, I looked around the room. There had been an obvious effort to make the apartment feel warm and comforting—pictures adhered to the fridge with quaint magnets, framed prints of landscape paintings on the wall, a bowl of fruit on the table. I picked an apple from the bowl and rubbed it on my shirt before discovering that it was fake.

At that moment, Stephanie entered the room. She apologized profusely for making me wait, and I assured her that it was fine. I made some comment about the layout of her home, asked her who her designer was, and she laughed, a bit too loudly. She attempted a witty rejoinder that fell flat and an awkward moment was relieved by her roommate reentering the room. They talked a little about the noise the neighboring tenants were making and the rent bill that month, things that did not engage my interest so I busied myself by looking at the knickknacks on a bureau. The roommate, Kelly, asked her where we were going and she looked at me expectantly. Truthfully, I hadn't really given it much thought but decided right then to take her to an eating establishment I often frequented for dinner. I told her this and she seemed overly delighted at the idea, and I got the impression she would've been just as excited if I said we were going to the dump to catch rats.

We bid goodbye to her roommate and left the apartment. As we walked to my car, she stayed in step beside me, her eyes pointed at the ground, her movements shy and unsure. When we got in my car, I asked her if she was ready and she nodded, looking out the window. As we pulled out into the street, I saw that she was fiddling with her hands and I wondered if she had picked up this habit from her roommate or vice versa. I made some perfunctory comments about the weather which she jumped on and used as the impetus to meanderingly ramble about all kinds of thoughts that came to her mind; it was like a full container of water with a hole punched in the bottom, water flowing out, the stream slowly dwindling until the jug was empty. Eventually she fell silent and I decided to do the same, thinking she would calm down after we were seated in the restaurant.

After the waitress had taken our orders, I sat back in my seat and pulled out a pack of cigarettes. I questioningly held it out for her, but she shook her head. As I lit a cigarette, she explained that she didn't smoke and for the next five minutes I was briefed on the history of cancer in her family. I nodded while puffing away; she unconsciously waved the smoke away until she caught herself, at which point she profusely apologized in a sincere manner . . . at this I merely nodded again and stubbed out the cigarette in the ashtray.

I looked across the table at this girl, whose unassuming manner created the illusion that she was shrinking, growing smaller and smaller before my very eyes. She had a helpless quality about her. She'd skittishly avert her eyes after catching my gaze. It was as if she sought my approval but was too scared or lacked the self-confidence to get it. I started to play games. I said things, baiting her, almost daring her to agree with me. They were outrageous opinions but I said them in a steady tone, carelessly throwing out words like I had given them much thought and anything I said was already a foregone certainty. She furrowed her brow, honestly considering my arguments on their own merits, and never failed to agree with my conclusions. It was as easy as convincing a three-year-old that Santa Claus existed. I was growing tired of this game by the time our food arrived and we ate our meals in mostly silence.

After dinner, I came up with some excuse to get out of the evening early. She protested, surprising me with her first clear inclination all evening to do one thing over another. She suggested that we go to "one of [her] favorite spots in the world" and after a few seconds of deliberation, I decided to indulge her, thinking that, at the very least, I was encouraging her to have original thoughts.

She refused to tell me exactly where we were going. She gave me directions to our destination, telling me to turn left, right, or go straight, her voice filled with anticipation. I looked over at her and suggested a cigarette would calm her nerves; she laughed shrilly. I concentrated on the world, her incessant nervousness making me more uncomfortable by the minute.

After a ten-minute drive, she made me pull over to the side of the road. We had been driving on backroads for most of the way there and were now surrounded by woodland. The sun had set a while ago and it was dark; if it wasn't for the full moon on this cloudless night, we would've been shrouded in total darkness. She opened her door and hopped out of the car; I stepped out more trepidatiously.

I could see her face from the moonlight and she was smiling at me. I asked her what she had brought me to see and she pointed across a field to a wall of trees. I looked at her skeptically and she assured me that it wasn't far. I mulled this over as she pleadingly made her case. I could see in her eyes that she was afraid we'd leave and her opportunity to show me whatever it was she wanted to show me would be lost forever (she was right to think so). I eventually consented, and her eyes lit up again and she gave me a wide, glowing smile and for the first time since the previous day, I saw the girl I thought was "Not Bad." She walked a few steps toward the woods and then looked back at me expectantly. I shivered a little as a brisk breeze passed through me; I lit a cigarette in the hope of warming up a little and we walked side by side toward her must-see attraction.

To her credit, it wasn't a long walk at all. Just past the trees we came into a clearing and were treated to the sight of a modest-sized lake. We took a few seconds to look it over. She looked at me and I knew she was gauging my opinion of the location. I gave her a short smile and nodded. She walked us over to some benches near the lake, while I finished my cigarette. She told me I should quit and I nodded. I felt her hand grab mine and hold it tight. I looked at her face, the moonlight reflecting off the lake illuminating her features. She was looking into my eyes and I was momentarily startled by the look in hers; her eyes betrayed a parasitic need, like a tapeworm in frantic search of an intestine. She grasped my hand like her life depended on it. Her face came closer and closer to mine.

I stood up suddenly and backed away. Her eager look was replaced with one of confusion. I said "Look," and proceeded to launch into an inane explanation of why I had to end the night here. I must have rambled on for a good ten or fifteen minutes, maybe even longer. I didn't mean to prolong the ordeal but I wanted to be sure that she understood. I also inadvertently became grotesquely fascinated by the change in her demeanor. Confusion turned into disappointment which then turned into knowing acceptance. Looking back on that night, all her actions seemed to be informed by a feeling of inevitability, like she knew what was going to happen and there was no way to avoid it. I stopped speaking well past the point where my points had been adequately made; she slowly nodded, unable to hide her sadness, and we walked back to the car.

Well, friend, that's my story. I'm sure you have a similar one, maybe not one that involves diners and cigarettes or even girls . . . but a similar one nonetheless. Who said there were only a couple stories in the world . . .? Or was it only just the one story? I don't know; it doesn't matter. Here's the thing though, here's what I've been thinking about all night, while the party carries on next door—I mean, isn't it . . . It's just . . . Dammit.

Can I dispense with . . . whatever? Be simple-minded, just for a second? Ignore the tones of gray of reality? Declare the obvious, spout off things people have been spouting off by rote for centuries? Are you drunk enough to put up with it? Ok then, here it is: There's so much hate in this world, right? There's hate, there's greed, there's . . . all that and more, yes? And we're living in uncertain times, friend. The future has never been more nebulous, yes, and that's . . . well, make of *that* what you will. The year's ending, a new one begins . . . a new *uncertain* one; we don't know what's going to happen, who's to say? We could all get blown sky high tomorrow or later tonight or next week . . . who knows? Right . . . so . . . taking all this together, here's the thing: If someone wants to love, who are we to say No, You Can't? There's so little of it out there, right? I'm sorry . . . this is so simple. . . .

. . . Here's what we'll do, friend. Let's forget what I just said, forget what's out there, forget everything for a second. Let's just go into the next room and join the party. It'll be good to forget everything, if only for a second. Come, let's go.

A HISTORY

THERE WAS ONCE A TIME when Fred really fixated on sex, especially sex with girls he was sleeping with. This was when he was around college-aged, even though he never went to college, which might have contributed to some of the problems he ran into. He was probably no more consumed by carnal desires than your average college undergrad, but lacked access to the pool of girls with commensurate horniness one invariably finds at colleges across the country. The number of prospective sexual partners decreases dramatically for near-/drinking-aged guys not enrolled in a university, especially if they don't live near a college town, and even then there are a few hurdles to negotiate due to the entirely different social spheres college people reside in and the non-matriculants' inability to talk knowledgeably about midterms or which professors suck or homecoming, i.e. things college girls think about when they're not thinking about sex, which, admittedly, doesn't take up a big chunk of their time or anything, but still.

With girls literally everywhere on a college campus—flowing from every doorway, pumping their well-defined gams on exercise bikes, jiggling their breasts as they jump up and down for no reason any guy can fathom but for which he is eternally grateful—there are prevalent opportunities for every guy to fulfill all his sexual desiderata, no matter how esoteric. For every chick that doesn't give head, there are fifty that do.

If a girl doesn't do anal, chances are her roommate does. Your girl won't let you cum on her face? Dump her for the girl in your philosophy class who *insists* on it. There's a girl up for everything in the book: ass-licking, vertical doggy, ménage à trois, you name it. Even the simple need of getting enough is taken care of; if one girl isn't sufficient, go visit five or six more on the side. Not only is promiscuity accepted, it's *expected*. It's like the female community is there solely for the males' gratification, with each girl doing her small part. That's the best part: taken as a (w)hole, the female student body (pun intended) is a hot-to-trot, fairly sluttish thing, willing to do everything and more, while each individual girl gets to maintain her integrity by drawing the line at activities she considers degrading—a line that is, of course, gloriously variable from girl to girl. (N.b.: This all goes vice versa, i.e. guys seem like they're only there to be the girls' sex slaves, are willing to satisfy all their desires, etc. That's what we call gender equality, and that's also why college is so damn wonderful.)

College is also one of those places where what goes down there stays there. It's a bubble world, college, with its own rules and regulations, the air thick with airborne shit that wouldn't fly in the "real world." Regarding college as an isolated island isn't exactly right; it's more accurate to say college is a vast archipelago with each dorm room being its own segregated island nation with its own notions of acceptable sexual behavior, which, more often than not, err on the side of unfettered concupiscence. Along with the rampant promiscuity, the things going on behind dorm room doors are, not to put too fine a point on it, downright *deviant*. We're talking prolonged, intricate, messy rituals of something that starts out as sex but then takes the form of something unrecognizable, something no one over the age of thirty has the *time* to do, let alone the *stamina*. Incessant rutting, contortions and configurations right out of an Escher drawing, overlapping operas of orgasms—all part of what the college student would call "normal," or perhaps even "kick-ass." If all womankind can be looked at as Queen Trollop and all men King Priapism, college can be regarded as a 24/7/as-long-as-class-is-in-session orgy. It's a place everyone needs to go at least once, just to get it out of their systems and move on with their lives.

But Fred never had the chance to take advantage of the opportunities of college life so his girlfriend at any given time had to shoulder a responsibility normally divvied up among a bevy of coeds: the responsibility (chore, really) of keeping a virile young man satisfied and content. None were very successful. At times, Fred would get a little annoyed at a girlfriend's inability (or unwillingness, he sometimes suspected) to match his voracious sexual appetite. It was distressing and kind of antithetical to his gut feeling of what a young woman's sex drive should be capable of (he would've been right about this had he gone to college and been surrounded by the cumulative friskiness of all the girls on campus). He was just a normal man asking her to be a normal woman. A straight shooting, red-blooded man looking to assert himself in a world where there no longer exists a need for hunting or gathering, where displays of physical prowess have been replaced with explosions at the press of a button, where the actual sowing of one's seed has been thwarted by prophylactics, abortions, and societal disapproval. Not that he was thinking explicitly of these things; all he knew is he wanted to get laid more. From his first girlfriend on, he was unable to come up with a cogent argument as to why they should be having more sex that didn't sound crass, so he ended up just sticking his hands down her pants instead. Sometimes this worked, sometimes it didn't. Sometimes she was turned on, sometimes she got really irritated. When this direct tactic seriously backfired, sex would be off the table for the next twenty-four hours and there was the distinct possibility he would get lectured.

"I love when Polly puts her hands down my pants. It's the first thing she does to really kick things off and I love it. I get such a thrill every time she does it, I literally start trembling. Not just in anticipation of what is to follow but because it feels really really good. I love the way she does it too. Her hands start on my back (we're usually hugging) and they ease down and slide inside my pants and under my briefs and then she's like cupping my ass (which also feels great). Then she slides her hands around my sides, brushing over my hips, never leaving the inside of my underwear (I love that), then she reaches the front and she's there. And it feels amazing. I'm not really sure what she does exactly. I know the stroking starts almost immediately but I'm pretty sure she uses only one hand. I wonder what the other hand is doing. Is it touching the tip? Alongside the other hand for support? Tending to my balls? I don't even know because as soon as she starts doing it my head starts spinning. It's like falling, in a good way. I really love the tactile journey her hands make. It really illustrates how being touched there is unlike being touched anywhere else. There's nothing like it. God I love it. She loves doing it too. Her last boyfriend didn't allow her to touch it that much because he was uncircumcised and it was extra sensitive. The fool. Erin would play around with my penis a bit but it's not like she actively sought it out unless she was giving me a blowjob. So the new attention it's been getting is pretty exciting. I also like putting my hands down *her* pants. She lets me too. Erin never really let me. I was forbidden from going anywhere near her vagina with my hands. The one thing she wouldn't abide, sexually speaking. Not even while we were doing from-the-behind positions, which I thought was standard operating pro-cedure, fingering a girl while doing her from behind. I know its main purpose is to help a woman cum and Erin had zero problem cumming (I'd barely penetrate her and the spasms would start sometimes), but still. It would have been nice to allow it every once in a while. Oh well. Her and her over-sensitive clit . . . kinda like that poor schmuck's uncut dick I suppose. I'm just glad Polly lets me play with her as often as I want. I had forgotten what it was like to slip my fingers into a girl down there, so it's all new and exciting again. I feel like a teenager who's reached second base for the first time. I know how lucky I am—at twenty-nine, to have an aspect of sex seem new and exciting is a major blessing. I just love it. I'm not even really sure why I love it. I think I have penis envy. Wait, that's something else. What it is is I'm envious of my penis. When it gets all engorged, it really does feel like its own entity, a separate living organism that's no longer a part of me. Sometimes, during sex, I don't really feel involved, like something else is doing the penetrating and thrusting and I'm just along for the ride. Sex always feels great of course but sometimes my penis feels like a buffer, an obstruction between me and real pleasure, and if I could just get more of myself in there I'd start having a truly mind-blowing time. After sex it's obvious my penis had a good time, the way it's glistening and pulsating. And it's not fair because I'm the one who got it there in the first place and it's hogging all the fun. Worst part is when I try to get some satisfaction afterwards and Mr. Selfish decides he's had enough, stays limp and ruins everyone else's fun. Man. Wish I could get a leg in there or an elbow or something. But I can't because I'm too big. You hear that penis? You're not too big, *I'm* the one that's too big. Look at you, all flaccid, no bigger than an Almond Joy. Even erect you're not that big, you know that, right? What you are is just the right size and that's just the luck of the draw. And some biology stuff, I guess. Screw biology. Actually, penis, *you* screw biology and I'll screw the girls. With my fingers. My hands never feel disconnected from me, they always do my bidding, they are a true extension of myself. My fingers and I are in league with each other. Together we will receive the ecstasy that has been denied us by you, the impudent penis. The fingers know how to share, too. They make room for the tongue if it wants in on the action. I definitely feel more attuned to sensations processed through the tongue, probably due to its utilization of two senses and its proximity to the brain. The tongue's great for lapping up the juices the fingers create. You don't have a taste for the juices, do you Almond Joy? Sure, they help with lubrication and all but after the show is over you don't like absorb the juices or anything. You just sit there, waiting to be wiped off. Such a waste of sweet nectar. My fingers, tongue, and I all crave those luscious secretions and we will make use of every last drop. With the help of my more cooperative body parts, I'll fulfill my capacity for sensual pleasure like never before. I'll get my face right down there, I'll see the exquisite opening, the incipient wetness, smell the aromatic scents issuing from the damp fissure, caress each moist fold . . . oh, are you perking up now Almond Joy? Turning into a Baby Ruth? (King-sized maybe, but still.) Well too bad. I'm benching you. When Polly gets back, the fingers and tongue are taking over. We're gonna show you how it's done. We're gonna get those juices *gushing*. We're gonna take her to heights you can't even fathom. We can stimulate her g-spot while sucking on her clit, let's see you do *that* on your best day. We'll give her more orgasms in one hour than you've been responsible for in two weeks. You won't even be missed. Any minute now she'll walk through that door and you'll be safely tucked away and we'll go right to work. Starting on her back like she does with me and slowly, luxuriously making our way to the front . . . although I do wish it were easier to finger a girl from the front, when you're face-to-face, either standing up or lying down. Easier in terms of the physical logistics of it. It seems so awkward, like you're practicing to be a contortionist or something. Such an unnatural position for your hands to be in: palms up, facing directly away from you, set below the waist— when else are your hands going to be in that position? I suppose baseball players have to put their hands like that to field ground balls. Plus the finger-motion is atypical, though Spider-man does it to activate those web-shooter things. I bet Ozzie Smith and Spider-man are amazing fingerbangers. The rest of us need wrists that swivel 360 degrees or elbows and knuckles that can bend both ways, like a pet door or those doors in restaurants that lead into the kitchen. That'd put less strain on the joints. It's much easier to finger a girl when her back's to you and it's like your arms are her arms while she's masturbating. From the front it can be a very strenuous enterprise. Girls have it easy when it comes to working on us. For them it's like polishing a trophy that's right in front of them. We have to deal with empty space and sometimes confusing— even changing—topographies down there. But somehow we manage. Heh. Man I'm horny. When Polly gets here I'm going to absolutely ravage her. With my fingers. And tongue. Nectar. Mmm . . ."

One of Fred's girl friends called—i.e. a friend who happened to be a girl—just to talk, chat, catch up, shoot the breeze. And since he had nothing better to do he fell comfortably into the role of interlocutor. They exchanged pleasantries, latest personal news, amusing anecdotes, credulity-stretching second-hand stories, future plans, and just stuff. Chit-chat. Palaver. Gab. Gossip. Yadda yadda. He experienced that frisson of pleasure that invariably accompanies the recognition of the voice of someone you haven't heard from in a while, as long as it doesn't interrupt you when you're in the middle of something or on your way out or otherwise have a very limited time to talk. And for a while this little confab was pleasant enough, listening to someone whose enunciation and phrasing were not quite like anyone else he knew.

He was thinking of *his* enunciation and phrasing, of course.

Sentences—whole *paragraphs*, at times—he had said to other people almost word-for-word sounded new and fresh and interesting when recounted for her virgin ears. When a phone conversation is going well the receiver seems to be custom-molded to fit your hand and/or recess of your neck, optimizing comfort to such a degree that it feels like it's always been a part of you, connected via a mandatory surgery you don't remember, and you can't imagine ever parting with it, this phone. So, yeah, they had a pleasant little chat.

But then, after a bit of time during which he had seemingly been taking part in a very real and interesting and meaningful social interaction that he would swear up and down he had been deriving loads of pleasure from and enjoying *thoroughly*, the conversation crossed some inscrutable boundary or outlasted its prescribed duration or something and he all of a sudden wanted nothing more than to terminate the call. Just hang up, mid-sentence. But words kept streaming out of the receiver. He started saying "uh huh" and "Mmhm" every time she paused for breath in blander and blander tones. He totally lost the thread of whatever she was talking about. He no longer heard words, only vocal pitch and cadence. The phone had inexplicably turned into an ambient noise generator. He started playing with the bric-a-brac on his coffee table. He thought of more interesting things to do, things that if he were doing them when she had called, he would not have been able to start talking to her in the first place. He managed to fit an "oh yeah?" into one of her em dashes. His neck hurt. He couldn't think of a tact-/graceful way to say goodbye. See ya. Take care. Later. Tired of talking. More tired of listening. Click. He tried to remember if people were more curt back in the days of phones with spirally cords connected to a base attached to the wall, essentially chaining people to the phone, confining them to a three-square-foot prison in their own home. It's horrifying when a conversation passes its expiration date and all you want to do is put the whole putrid thing behind you. Or worse, when you're the only one who realizes there's a festering, lifeless thing in front of you and she's either oblivious to its terminal condition or keeps trying to zap it (i.e. the conversation) back to life with bon mots or stories or informational bits of an OhmigodIalmostforgottotellyou-type caliber and she absolutely refuses to call the time of death on this sucker (to extend the conversation-as-living-entity metaphor, possibly past acceptable limits) so you're just left waiting for her to realize you haven't absorbed anything she's said in the last ten minutes. Or even worse, *you* are the one that has misjudged the lifespan of the conversation and by the time you want to tell her something—a something you intentionally withheld for later because etiquette requires you not to open a conversation with something as complex, convoluted, and quite possibly anxiety-producing as the thing you are about to relay to her after all this time, after all the preliminaries have been dispensed with, the *hi*'s and *how are you*'s and *I'm fine*'s, and since you've had so much more time to think about what you're about to relay, the event or story or situation or whatever it is has become disproportionately important to you, like you're probably emotionally and personally connected to it now, even if it doesn't involve you directly, but you've added so many mental threads (as it were) to it that it's become not only a Jupiter-sized emotionally-fraught yarnball (so to speak) but *your* monster of a yarnball comprising all the thoughts, feelings, and ideas you've had in the ungodly amount of time you've spent rolling the thing around in your mind. Suffice it to say, you've cathected the thing into The Most Important Thing At This Moment In Time—and so by the time you are finally ready to impart what seems so vital to you, what you've been waiting all conversation to deploy like an atomic bomb, she's on the other end picking at a hole in her sock while half-watching TV and uttering monotone *uh huh*'s every so often. And maybe even worse: maybe you know she can't wait to hang up and get on with her life and you realize you're being rude and importunate and self-centered, but you just have to tell her this One Last Thing even in the face of very probable indifference. And your inability to refrain from telling her this thing or saving it for the next conversation feels like real weakness on your part and you end up thinking less of yourself and get a little depressed.

———

The weather's all wonky. It's the middle of January and it's shorts weather. No joke. There is no trace of any snow on the ground from the incapacitating storm that caused municipal cancellations across the board last week. The newspaper is reporting record high temperatures and is full of testimonials with the common refrain that it "feels like spring." Fred disagrees. He thinks it feels more like fall. There's this feeling that it's going to get colder before it gets warmer, which is a feeling associated with fall, not spring. As he walks home, sloshing through puddles that were, until very recently, blocks of ice, he is struck with the urge to take stock of the year so far, enumerate his various successes and failures, bemoan how little he's accomplished, and make plans to salvage what time remains—all traditionally autumnal ruminations. And then he remembers the actual date, and the clash between those melancholic thoughts and the unbridled enthusiasm one is supposed to feel at the onset of a new year disorients him. A funny feeling forms in his gut and percolates throughout his body, causing him to feel displaced, as if he were walking home in a memory instead of tangibly in the here and now.

He wonders if he should break up with Polly. He wonders if it's time. He has no idea of what is necessary for it to be "time," what confluence of events and emotions must occur to precipitate a break-up. He doesn't know if the decision is based on a specific configuration of thoughts expressed, feelings hidden, passionless lovemaking sessions, and spats both trivial and caustic over a predetermined amount of time—a rigid equation that accurately determines the duration of a relationship. If, however, breaking up is more of an intuitive decision, Fred's never been as ready to end the relationship as he is today.

As he approaches the house he sees Polly's face framed in the window. Even though he's too far away to distinguish her facial features, he can sense her engaging smile. She disappears and is immediately replaced by the curtains. He knows she will greet him at the door. The door will swing open as he's reaching for the knob, in fact. Her eyes will be iridescent, her smile will be stretching the limits of what facial muscles can allow, her eagerness will be infectious; he will be inside her within sixty seconds and terminating this wondrous union will be the last thing on his mind. Afterward, looking at her glistening body, her joyous, grateful, and complaisant face, her ever-present smile, he will know she makes him happy. He just wishes she felt more like spring.

Fred sips from a cup of coffee. He looks over at Rachel. She's holding the newspaper wide open, scanning the finance section while wearing her thin reading glasses. He gazes at her serious, intent expression and reflects on his ability to loosen the knots that constrict her face into a look that spells business—the cutthroat kind, at that. He smiles. He knows nothing about business or finance, nothing about stocks and bonds and expense ratios on mutual funds, but that doesn't matter. Only he has the ability to make her ease her guard, an ability her competitors and rivals on the other side of the negotiating tables at which she sits would dearly love to possess. She's dressed in razor-sharp attire: trim skirt, pressed blouse, dangerous heels. She's play-acting the role of a professional woman, which is the side of her the world sees, when she's even-keeled and temperate and in control. She turns a page and squints her eyes a little in an incipient scowl, a frown playing at her lips. He smiles wider. He can't help feeling he knows the real her, the vulnerable side only he gets to see, when she's helpless before the overwhelming pleasure only he can induce, when she's totally defenseless. Only he sees her at her most uninhibited, when her naked body reveals those business clothes as nothing but unnecessary, restrictive things, the sweat on her body a refutation of the supposed importance of her job.

He suddenly wants very much for her to see him smiling at her. He makes a sound like a cough. Her focus stays unwaveringly on the newspaper. He "coughs" again, this time with obvious affectation. She flips to the stock quotes—executed by anyone else, it might seem like a defiant or coy gesture, but with Rachel its purpose is purely functional; she really *is* reading the newspaper, a newspaper which, along with her arms, is creating a physical barrier between them, a hermetic area where her thoughts can swirl around undisturbed. He reaches for the sugar, banging the spoon against the bowl. He makes use of the other spoon, creating as much clangor as he can with the utensils at hand, his movements pure artifice at this point. Her attention remains implacably with the *Times*. He tips his cup over, spilling coffee in her direction. The coffee absorbs its way through the tablecloth toward her. She registers the dampness in the periphery of her vision and finally looks up at him. Her assessment of the distraction has already been made—an element of admonition resides in her look. His smile is still fixedly attached to his face, less genuine than it was a minute ago when the impetus to get her attention wasn't tempered by his annoyance at the effort it took to wrest her gaze from the newspaper, but he hopes his smile is still a sly, knowing one and not suggestive of culpability and abashment. She returns to the newspaper but after a second looks back at him, not, as far as he can see, out of restlessness but rather a genuine curiosity, all but confirming the presence of at least a vestigial coquettishness that must still be an intrinsic component of his smile.

"What?" she asks.

"What?" he non-answers.

"What are you looking at me like that for?"—a needless clarification.

"Like what?" a bit daftly.

"Like . . . I dunno. Like you're looking and smiling at something." She is on the cusp of deciding not to be a cooperating participant in this morning's badinage; her eyes flick back to the newspaper in a willful challenge to interest her.

He gets out in a sudden rush, "I was just thinking about this morning," before she no longer cares.

"What about it?" Her curiosity is back, though she tries to

hide it.

"Well, just how you seemed to enjoy yourself." She looks at him and this time he's wearing the confident, slightly leering smile he'd meant for her to see from the beginning. She deploys her own smile, one constructed for single-use only, one that deflates as soon as it crests, one that's gone almost immediately.

"Yeah, it was fun," she says with a definitiveness that strongly implies that elaboration will not be forthcoming.

He tries to keep her on-track: "But you did enjoy yourself, more than usual, I mean."

"Well, I wouldn't say *more* than usual. About the same, maybe."

"But what about when you told me not to stop?" He's not quite whining, but he does say this with a healthy amount of incredulity.

"Yeah, so?" she says plainly. "We were running late and if you hadn't finished soon, we'd've been crazily behind schedule. In fact, before I give my boss a reason to fire me, I better get going." She picks her purse off the table and lopes to the door.

He follows languidly, in somewhat of a daze. "So you were just trying to expedite things this morning?" he asks skeptically.

"Mmhm," she murmurs as she slips on her strappy heels.

"Ok, but wait, seriously," he says, still disbelieving. "Toward the end, when—

He was getting close. On the verge. The thrusting had reached a nice, steady rhythm: in, out, in, out. The sensations were not so much intensifying as becoming more real, being truly felt, as though for the first time. God, he was close to cumming. His head was buried in the pillow, beside her head; his eyes were squeezed shut. Her pelvis thrusted up to meet him, the pressure she exerted on the head of his penis was accompanied by moist, plopping sounds. Her scent filled the air. He felt drenched down there; even his pubic hair felt soaked by her wetness. In, out, in, out. The pleasure was mounting. He had to slow up a bit if not pause completely if he wanted to prolong this ecstasy. He shifted to face her, trying to mask the interruption with a kiss. She tore away from his lips and breathlessly gasped 'Don't stop!' Her voice was hungry, nakedly pleading, begging him to continue delivering her to passionate heights previously unreachable. It was a moan of lusty desire. He almost came right then. Instead, he grabbed her shoulders and bore down, quickly reestablishing the indescribably pleasurable rhythm: in, out, in, out. She was writhing against him erratically now, but still he persisted, never deviating from the constant, steady penetrations. In, out, in, out. He was slipping into her now; her natural lubrication had built up to such a degree that it felt like his penis was being plunged into a pool of warm secretions. The nearly unbearable sensations were returning and the head of his penis swelled and felt about to burst but he refused to stop pumping it into the increasingly moist vagina in front of it in the same arousing rhythm. In, out, in, out, squish, squish. He could feel himself passing the point of no return. Her incessant moaning and gasps were lost in the roar building up in his ears and he felt an electric sensation build up in his loins and start spreading to the rest of his body. He grabbed any part of her he could use for leverage and rode out those last few moments of now involuntary thrusting, sliding closer toward culmination, an undeniable feeling of impending explosion. In, out, in, out, closer, closer, closer . . . !

—when that happened, you felt nothing different, just pretty standard, normal sex?" He crosses his arms expectantly, almost challengingly.

She finishes applying her blush and closes the compact she had been holding. "Yep, that's right," she says offhandedly, and therefore convincingly. She gives him a quick peck on the cheek and says, "See you after work honey," before gliding out the door, leaving him dumbfounded and questioning the veracity of all the perceptions he's ever had during sex.

Fred sat in his car, eyeing the store warily. In the last five minutes he had seen three men—two shifty-looking fellows and an old guy with a cane—come out holding plain brown paper bags. *I can't believe it's come to this*, he thought dejectedly. Not that he found the store, called Dis-Robe, unsavory; he had been inside once before to buy a box of premium cigars (they sold a little of everything) and found the store to be like any other—neat, organized, and well-lit. The depressing thing was that this store with the slightly salacious-sounding name was so clearly frequented by the hopeless and impotent, which, if he were honest, was exactly how he felt.

He hadn't been overly concerned about Nicole's lack of orgasms when they first started having sex, even after she told him she had never had one. He'd been a little taken aback to be sure, but she had cited recent studies she found on the internet that apparently confirmed the existence of a not insignificant portion of the female population that had never climaxed, a group she had resigned herself to. (He had her print out these studies and, after reading them, he had to admit there were a lot more orgasm-less women out there than he had ever suspected, if the statistics were accurate.) After a little investigative probing of his own, he concluded that the cause of her predicament lay primarily with the inadequacies of her previous lovers. She told him about this one guy she dated who never lasted more than thirty seconds. Every time, thirty seconds max. And she slept with him for over a year! He shuddered at this gross imbalance of orgasms. And it got even worse, unbelievably. Sometimes her lovers combined a non-existent sexual technique with an utter disregard of her needs, like the guy who played Tetris on his Game Boy while they had sex or the guy whose idea of foreplay was looking at his watch and nudging his head toward the bedroom and sing-songing, "I've got five minutes!" or the guy who invariably insisted on a handjob every night when they got in bed, after which he would roll over and fall asleep by the time she got back from washing her hands. Just horror story after horror story of relationships with crude, feckless, inconsiderate slimeballs. Fred knew he was no Casanova, but felt soaringly confident in his ability to exceed the lowly standard set by the pathetic specimen of men she was used to. And he secretly thrilled at the prospect of guiding her up a plateau of pleasure she had never known before. This was already an inevitability in his mind.

The added build-up and pressure notwithstanding, he had actually been heartened by their first sex session. After getting through the initial timidity, she turned out to be an enthusiastic participant. She emitted sharp little cries of pleasure, her face scrunched up in sensual concentration, her body undulated forcefully and eagerly, her back glistened with sweat and she was dripping wet in other places as well. In his view, she did everything *except* cum. Before succumbing to his own orgasm, he thought, *Well, we're off to a good start, a VERY good start, mm, ah, ah, ah . . . !*

Afterward, as he lay beside her, running his hands through her damp hair while their panting subsided, he idly speculated on her imminent first orgasm. He wondered how it would affect her, whether she would handle it quietly or hysterically. Something he discovered over the past few months was that every woman came differently. Polly was a loud one. Her orgasms were built up to with increasingly loud grunts and punctuated with a loud screech when her pleasure peaked. Rachel came like she didn't want to; as her climax approached, she wore a permanent scowl and made whining, plangent sounds, as if something inside her were being extracted against her will. Her orgasm brought a series of sobs, calling into question whether she felt any pleasure at all (she assured him it was amazing). Erin usually wouldn't make much noise at all. Her orgasms were characterized by a stillness, followed immediately by several short intakes of breath. Only the tiny beads of sweat that would form on her forehead gave any indication of her mounting ecstasy. Sometimes, when her pleasure built to unbearable levels, a sudden moan would issue from her lips and turn into a desperate-sounding "Oh god!" which would cause him to cum without fail. Afterward, looking thoroughly sated, she would give him an enigmatic smile, as if cluing him in on the exhilarating sensations flowing through her, her secret trove of boundless delight inaccessible to everyone else, including him.

In the afterglow of their first time together, he clasped Nicole's hand and nuzzled the top of her head with his nose. When he made her cum, he would be in possession of a unique key—not a duplicate owned by numerous guys before him, but one fashioned by him for her specific dimensions. This would give him a sense of proprietorship about the whole thing. He would not only find a way to access her orgasm, he would be creating it from scratch, and therefore be able to calibrate its intensity to any level he saw fit. He envisioned Nicole's orgasm as an eruption, the bursting of a dam holding back twenty years of sexual frustration. There would be erumpent gushing and hysterical flailing. It would be glorious and he looked forward to it with a sense of gratitude; he was grateful to be in a position to witness what was sure to be one of the most thrilling sexual events he would ever see, outside of rented porn. And this would be better than rented porn because he would be involved, right in the thick of things. He couldn't wait. Thinking about it brought his erection back and she responded to its reappearance with glee, so they immediately made another go of it.

But by the end of the week, the progress he thought they were making had stagnated and she seemed no closer to climaxing than she had that first time, which is to say she was practically there (from his perspective). He was pretty sure she got particularly close on a couple of occasions and he berated himself for not lasting longer and giving her more time to finish, even though he usually held out for a length of time that wasn't exactly brief and had been of ample duration to give plenty of girls the full ride in the past. He was nine orgasms up on her before he took drastic measures to ensure that their next bout of sex would go the full fifteen rounds, so to speak. One day, anticipating the sex they would be having that night, he masturbated four times before dusk. By the time they retired to bed, any impulse he had to cum had been obliterated. That night, they had sex for much longer than they ever had before, which turned out to be more desirable in concept than in execution. After about forty-five minutes of pumping away, she pried herself loose, citing exhaustion and soreness. He noticed she didn't get any closer to orgasm the longer they went—in fact, at around the 25-minute mark, her usual enthusiasm took on a strained quality, as though she were struggling to maintain her customary level of arousal. The sounds she made were ones of exertion instead of desire, the sweat that coated her skin the result of what amounted to a vigorous workout, nothing more. After that night, he could officially cross off prolonged sex as a means to achieving his goal.

His next tack involved concentrating on what was actually being done to her, anatomically speaking. He had never before considered the mechanics of what he did during sex; since he had never failed to produce favorable results for both parties, there had been no need for in-depth analysis. But it was apparent that he had to abandon what had previously worked in favor of the "correct" way of doing this stuff. Even the purported sure-fire way to induce orgasms by the truckload, viz. cunnilingus, turned out to be anything but a straightforward affair, as he discovered when he hunched down and found himself confronted with something he had presumed to have intimate knowledge of but in actuality was bewilderingly unfamiliar to him up close. He knew basically how things were situated down there, anatomy-wise, but his general style when it came to eating girls out was, to be honest, a bit haphazard, characterized by a sort of spastic lapping, a here/there/everywhere approach that, again, always did the trick with former partners but proved to be woefully inadequate with Nicole. Compounding his frustration, she was unable to tell him what to do, having as little idea of what would arouse her as he did. He had her print out a precise diagram of female genitalia from a medical website, but it ultimately proved useless when he saw that her various intricacies didn't match up exactly to the anatomical schematic; upside-down V's turned out to be up-side-down Y's and her parts weren't as clearly delineated as they were in the picture. (This did not overly surprise him; after all, all the pictures of penises he'd seen in anatomy books never looked like what he had in his pants, either.) So he resorted to giving her erratic tongue lashings and firm nuzzlings, hoping to fortuitously hit a bundle of pleasure-giving nerves. After a while, she insisted he stop, feeling a point of diminishing returns had been reached, an assessment he had to agree with if her vagina felt anything like his jaw, which ended up sore and aching for two days.

Next on the agenda was experimentation with different positions. He concentrated on the "from-behind" positions—doggy style, spoon, reverse cowgirl—on the basis of their supposeed effectiveness in stimulating certain areas—certain *pleasurable* areas—not usually stimulated in more traditional positions. She was game for almost anything he wanted to try, as long as they did them at night with the lights off because a lot of these conjoinings made her feel either too exposed or utterly ridiculous. (What *he* found most ridiculous was her insistence that missionary was her favorite position even though it clearly wasn't getting the job done.) Anyway, it turned out not to matter because mixing up their coital configurations was a complete bust; she would get exhausted and weary and want to stop even sooner than she usually did.

He then started to think it was a question of atmosphere. A lot of fairly scientific-looking articles he found on the internet (he spent a lot of time at the library scouring the web for anything that looked even vaguely relevant to female sexuality) stated that the psychological aspect had an unusually lot to do with achieving orgasm. The woman really did have to be in the mood, the articles said. If she wasn't, no amount of physical manipulation would have her crawling up the walls. The surest way to get her in the mood, the articles went on to say, was to *set* the mood, to have an active awareness of not only the bed but the surroundings as well. Think flowers, they said. Think candles, think music. Think of sights, smells, whispered declarations of love. Think of it like stimulation for her eyes, ears, and nose before the actual sex took care of the sensations involving touch and taste.

Fred collated the suggestions of all these articles and re-solved to give Nicole the surprise of her life. One night, she came home to three dozen roses—red, pink, and white—wrapped in shimmery tissue paper. He took her hand and kissed it lightly and they followed a trail of flickering votive candles to the bedroom. The door opened to a rich, candle-lit glow. There was a plethora of candles: tea lights arranged in heart patterns, subtly suggestive pillar candles, strongly fra-grant jar candles that enveloped the room in the redolent scent of lilacs and lilies. The room was brimming with dozens of tiny flames on bureaus, windowsills, and highly reflective salvers, so many that the addition of one more candle would've surely burned the house down. The smooth crooning of Marvin Gaye—followed by Otis Redding and Lionel Ritchie—eman-ated softly from the stereo speakers. The bed was covered with rose petals and newly purchased lacy throw pillows. A bottle of zinfandel sat in the middle of the bed beside two delicate wine glasses. The overall effect was out of this world, heavenly. The mood had definitely been set. He saw the ardor in her eyes; their caresses took on a charged urgency. Her kisses were long and languorous expressions of a newfound passion. She pulled him on top of her, hungrily, wantonly, and for a second he had the distinct impression she was trying to devour him, and he was momentarily frightened. But her eager hands—working to unclasp his belt—and her impatient grunts made it clear she was dying for the ride, or to be ridden, whatever, as long as it involved him being inside her. Like a cowardly amusement park attendee going on a rollercoaster for the first time, he closed his eyes and hoped for the best. And, of course, it didn't work at all. The only paroxysms he felt were within himself instead of the ones he so desperately wished to feel against his body. Her thrusting was calculated and almost cruelly voluntary. He started to think she considered sex an endeavor with clearly defined limits: "Sex is that in which you don't cum." He finally had to admit that he had reached an impasse and required some sort of aid, perhaps an implement of some kind. And that's why he was now scoping out Dis-Robe, mustering the courage to go in and find the help he needed.

It's 9:38 and even though she is obliged to call him back, Fred picks up the phone and dials her number. She hasn't called since the first commercial break, which was around 9:05, and he's sure there's been at least one interruption by advertisers since then. Most likely there's been a couple, maybe even three or four. He's already slightly annoyed that she's currently being transfixed by a show she purports to be indifferent to; even if this week's episode was one she could "take" rather than "leave," surely the sound of his voice is preferable to this week's commercials . . . right??

"Hello?" she answers.

"Hi," he says.

"Hi," she says, pleasantly enough.

"How are you doing?" he asks, like they have all the time in the world.

"Good," she says, drawing out the vowels as if she's unsure.

"Good," he says, definitively.

A short pause follows, which he does not allow to lengthen: "Is it cold over there?" he asks.

"Yeah, but I'm under the electric blanket." She sounds distracted.

"Yeah, it's not too cold over here," he says, "maybe around

63-ish." As soon as the words leave his mouth, he realizes he could not have said anything more boring. The silence on the other end seems to confirm this. He's about to say something else about the temperature but stumbles when he can't think of anything more to say about it. The silence stretches out many seconds; any momentum to the conversation that might have existed is now lost. He's losing her. Desperate, he addresses the elephant in the room: "How's your show?"

"Good," she says as if he had asked her how she was doing.

"Yeah?" he says, unable to hide his skepticism. But he has no choice but to babble on: "Yeah, I actually read an article in the paper about it the other day, how Aztoben almost left the show last year, and they were saying how it's been getting better recently, how it was definitely better than last season but nowhere near as good as it was during the first season and it probably never will be again, that its time has passed, but it's at least watchable now. Do you find this to be the case?"

". . . I'm gonna let you go," she says.

"Oh, ok."

"Bye."

CLICK. He disconnects his end of the line and, after a moment's consideration, begins to sulk. He knows he shouldn't read into every little thing she says or does, but he's finding it hard not to in this instance. The way he sees it, she is making a clear-cut choice, a choice that leaves him out in the cold (or rather, leaves him inside his kinda chilly apartment because— let's admit it—63-ish is kinda chilly). He analyzes the conversation and tries to determine where he went wrong. Talking about the show, he sees now, was a bad move; she had it there in front of her, why would she want to talk about it now? But, ultimately, he decides there's nothing he could've used as a verbal crowbar to pry her away from the TV. Nothing at all. He could've said he had the cure for cancer, which would probably have ended the conversation sooner: "Oh, that sounds complicated, why don't I call you back after the show and you can tell me all about it." There was nothing he could do but wait for her to call back.

The phone doesn't ring until 10:04. He's anxious to get the momentum back in his favor, to not let the advanced age of the evening discourage him.

"Hi!" he says enthusiastically.

"Hi." He hears the sound of her yawning. "Brr! It's cold!"

"Yeah," he says, impatient. He knows he brought up the temperature first, but christ, is there really nothing else to talk about?

"Brrr, it's *really* cold in here!" She sounds genuinely taken aback. *I really shouldn't feel so bad*, he thinks. After all, television—the Great Attention Vacuum—had divested her of all but two senses, leaving her in a state in which frostbite would've gone unnoticed. Picturing her like that, he understands what an intrusion his voice had been, or, rather, *would* have been, had she tolerated it.

"Glad I got my kitty here," she continues. "He's so warm."

"Yeah, he's a good boy," he says.

"Yes he is," she says, pitching her voice higher. "He's my precious, oh, aren't you, my precious boy? Yes, yes you are, handsome boy. Mmm, thank you for the kisses, thank you, thank you. You've got awful cat breath but I still love you." Reverting back to her plain, human-talk voice (which isn't nearly as playful), she says, "Tuffy is so cute, isn't he?"

"The cutest," he agrees.

"Too bad you don't have him over there, he could keep you warm, but you can't take this one because he's all mine, *aren't you?*" (The last part in higher-octive cat-speak.) "You better bundle up tonight. They said it could dip into the twenties."

His heart starts racing as pangs of worry shoot through him. The conversation definitely has momentum now but he doesn't like where it's heading. "Ur, um," he stammers, "do you, I mean, do you want me to come over?"

"Uh . . . if you want." There's confusion in her voice. *Ingenuous* confusion, which is the worst kind. "But I'm going to bed. I was just calling to say goodnight. I'm wicked tired." She starts to yawn before finishing her sentence, as if to accentuate the point. Could've even been a real yawn too, for all he knows, but, honestly, he doesn't know what he thinks about almost everything right now. All he knows is that his plans for the evening have gone awry and he's not sure how it happened.

Mind a-jumble, he struggles to find the words to express his anxiety, disappointment, frustration, sadness, and anger, finally arriving at: "Oh." Not even a complete thought, let alone a sentence, and yet it kind of says it all, doesn't it?

"So . . . I'll call you in the morning, ok?" she says.

"Ok."

"Goodnight."

"Goodnight."

CLICK. And just like that, before he can even think of any potentially resuscitative comments, the night is ostensibly over. A total wash. Dead. They're calling it: Time of death, 10:09 PM. Might as well set the clocks to midnight now, for all the time he's going to waste staring at the wall, wondering if things could've turned out differently. Right now, he would gladly trade all the remaining pre-dawn hours for a quick sunrise; it would deprive him of a night's sleep, but he knows he's in for a long night anyway, marked by sporadic, fitful dozings—if he falls asleep at all. He gets into bed and glares defiantly into the darkness—like it's some corporeal mother-like entity entreating him to go to sleep already—and he begins a train of thought full of reenactments and speculations that will ultimately lead him back to the conclusion that there was nothing he could do and that tomorrow, as they say, is another day.

Despite his best grumpy intentions, his body's needs take over shortly after one in the morning and his eyes close and he starts to drift off. *Maybe if I could stand to watch TV with her*, he thinks, drowsily, his last thought of the day.

And, with that, his brain shuts off, only to presently be turned on again, subjecting him to an experience not dissimilar to watching the boob tube, only more vivid and participatory.

But not before a fanciful message from the network: *With our sincerest regret, tonight's scheduled round of zestful sex will be preempted by a middling episode of a soon-to-be-canceled one-hour post-post-modern dramedy. And now we bring you Bears on Ice, followed by a former co-worker you haven't seen in seven years talking with your mom in K-Mart about contraceptives, and then the evening will cap off with that recurring one with the ax-wielding psycho you can escape from only by jumping off a 40-story building. Enjoy. . . .*

THE ASSIGNMENT

SAY THERE WAS THIS GIRL. And say she was in high school, a
sophomore. She wasn't among the most popular girls in the
school but she wasn't an outcast either; she was well-regarded
by the people who knew her and even the people who didn't
know her thought she was cool, or at least ok. And say she did
well in school, got A's and B's, and she was clearly going places
but she was not a geek or nerd or valedictorian material or
even in the top five percent of her class but what she was was
better than a nerd because what she had was something no
nerd ever has, which is style. The kind of effortless style that
even most of the popular kids lacked and which caused her to
be subjected to a fair amount of envy (from the girls) and
crushes (from the boys, and one lonely girl actually). Luckily
most of these kinds of sentiments were kept hidden from her,
harbored by those in whom they originated, so that she was
able to glide through her secondary schooling without worrying her not unpretty head about the opinions of her, both
favorable and not, bubbling inside her classmates. (If she had
been privy to these private thoughts, she would've been concerned, if only for a scant ten minutes—but hey there are a lot
of people who would be way less concerned for sure.) Say she
was peachy keen, A-ok, and leave it at that.

And let's say she (along with the rest of her class) was given this homework assignment in one of those classes called like Anthropological Survey 204 but which most people just call Social Studies right up to the point when they get married or get rich or get religion and stop referring to school courses altogether. And say this assignment was like every other assignment she had ever been given—that is to say it was dull, boring, and further evidence of the sadism that lies within every high school teacher—and that the students were going to handle it in their usual way, which is to say indolently, dismissively, sarcastically if possible. This went for the girl, too, though she would do it indolently, dismissively, etc. with flair, because she had style, a surfeit of it. If only she could've bottled it or distilled its essence so it could be easily taught to the style-deprived, she could've founded a Fortune 500 company before she graduated. (She did not think these things by the way; they were thought of for her, in typical geek-like fashion, by a geek who'd had a crush on her since the 8th grade.) But anyway, say this assignment was this: How would you describe what life on earth is like to an alien being who has no concept of what it's like to be human or even alive? ("You will be required to support your answer with a ten-minute oral presentation consisting of verifiable data (statistics, primary source accounts, research papers, etc.) that also has at least one multimedia element (slides, video, Powerpoint, overhead projector, etc.)") Needless to say, the teacher described this project with great relish, his candent eyes betraying his sadistic glee, and many students claimed afterward that his smile got bigger when he heard the chorus of groans (which is eminently believable if you know the guy) and some even claimed he cackled and rubbed his hands together after class let out, thanking whatever academic deity gave him the idea for such a malicious assignment (only slightly less believable).

And say this girl didn't have the disdain that her peers had for teachers in general—and but still, she found this assignment to be frustratingly abstruse and open-ended, preventing an obvious solution or approach from immediately presenting itself. In fact, let's say that thinking about it gave her a head-ache, which means she was thinking about it a lot harder than everyone else was. So, it goes without saying, that she put it out of her mind, procrastinated—the only thing a high school-er, generally speaking, seems willing to do early and often. And still, let's consider how it pained her to do this, to put the assignment off like some slacker, for she was not one to shirk a responsibility or cast aside an obligation due to expected difficulty; she was usually more stalwart, possessed by a game spirit which would serve her well in her post-secondary school endeavors especially since, to put it bluntly, her grades just didn't match those of the elite students.

But anyway, moving on, we can safely assume her anxiety increased each day, being keenly aware as she was of this albatross of a project and its due date, or, more specifically, the ineluctable gravitational pull of the due date, dragging her across the calendar in accordance with the temporal laws of our universe, which are as unyielding as the physical ones. This ever-present burden of worry steadily intensified until she couldn't take the stress anymore and resolved to start working that day, a good two and a half weeks before the due date, which made her the first person in the class to begin working on the assignment.

And let's say, on that day, after turning off the TV at around 4 PM after watching her customary music request show on MTV, when she definitively sat down to get to it, to buckle down and get started on the real work, that as soon as she finally decided to start working in earnest, she found that she had no idea where to begin. She stared idly at the blank screen of her TV and scribbled some doodles on her notepad. Nothing came to her. *No seriously,* she thought to herself. She forced herself to jot down some ideas, mentally squeezing her brain as if it were in a juicer and letting the runoff trickle down her arm, through the pen in her hand, and onto the paper. The results were unusable, just a bunch of irrelevant ruminations. She berated herself, it must be said, really getting frustrated as a debilitating helplessness skittered along the outer fringes of her usual confidence, threatening to overwhelm it and her. A tough, steely girl she was though, and persistent, too. She took a deep breath and calmed down. She determined that her typical methods for approaching schoolwork were ineffectual in this case; it was an unconventional assignment that required from her unconventional ideas. *Think outside the box,* she thought. She closed her eyes, counted to ten, picked up her pen and began to write: "I wonder"—*yes, yes* she thought, patient and encouraging with her creativity, *go on*—"what is"—*uh huh, yes?* she excitedly prompted herself, certain that the ponderable question she was inscribing would reveal the formerly ungraspable solutions—". . . what is . . ."—she was faltering, her heart raced, her certainty ebbed—". . . for dinner." Heaving an exasperated sigh, she slumped back into the couch as if it had taken everything she had to come up with this trifling thought. A foreign sensation came over her that instant: a feeling of inadequacy. This project was insurmountable, the question it posed too huge—planetary in scope even—for a teenage girl who had never been farther than sixty miles from the hospital at which she was born. She called it quits right there and then, for the rest of the day at least.

Let's say she walked to the window then, slowly, languidly, feeling depleted and a little rankled she had no work to show for the exhaustion she felt. And say she absently drew the curtains aside, saw in the drab surroundings and overcast skies a reflection of her state of mind, pried her cellphone out of her jeans' pocket, flipped it open and took a picture composed of 1.2 megapixels. She briefly glanced at the picture, as if to confirm the lifelessness in front of her, then wandered away to finish her evening elsewhere.

And let's suppose she attempted another kick at the can the following day with similarly unproductive results. There just didn't seem to be an entrance in—the spark of inspiration eluded her and the secrets of this godforsaken project remained hidden. We can assume that it probably didn't help that she was reluctant to even think about it anymore. Knowing the hardships she kept encountering even in this most nascent of stages, she whiled away the post-school hours, watching TV show after TV show which put her in a lazy mood worsened by her indifference to the boring guests on that day's talk shows. By the time she shut off the TV, she felt truly brain-dead.

And say she walked to the window again, and, out of a caprice that had more and more the hint of calculation, snapped another picture of the scene outside the window. And let's say that she didn't give it a second thought; dinner was again imminent and she would always let her stomach do the thinking this time of day. It wasn't until later that evening, while texting a friend and idly flipping through the pictures on her phone—images of the pep rally, some friends hanging out in the parking lot, a locker filled to capacity with what looked like actual garbage, etc.—that she noticed the striking similarity of the two pictures she took of what was outside the living room window. The composition was of course the same, but, amazingly, so were a lot of things in the frame: a USPS truck parked by the side of the road, a Golden Retriever leashed to a runner in someone's yard, full trash barrels outside a neighbor's house, an old man with glassy eyes slouched in a folding chair on his porch, and, most interestingly, a man wearing a duster with its collar upturned, facing away, walking toward the end of the street. The peculiar thing was the man's almost identical position on both days. Oscillating between the two pictures only displaced him a step or two, as if they were consecutive pages of one of those crude but serviceable flip-books that simulate movement. The open defiance of the laws of probability tickled her. *What are the chances,* she thought, *that I take a picture on two different days and get the same image?* But let's say the more she thought about it, the less miraculous it seemed. And it was this amended perspective that gave her an idea of how to proceed with her school assignment. She went to bed that night hoping for—counting on, really—a repeat performance the next day by the people and animals she was already thinking of as her "subjects."

Let's suppose, the next afternoon, she dutifully stood by the window, even turning off the TV fifteen minutes earlier than usual to ensure that she wouldn't miss anything. Just imagine her nervously enumerating all the peripheral elements already in place—the ever-present dog, the quiescent elderly man, the near-daily mail truck—impatient for the perambulating piece of the puzzle that would complete the tableau she sought. And what if the man didn't show, what would she have done then? Well, let's interdict any further speculation along those lines and just say that the man showed up right on schedule, to the young girl's delight. She waited until he was roughly in the same spot he was in in the other two pictures and pressed the capture button on her phone. Let's assume she sighed with relief at that point, then wandered into the kitchen, looking to pilfer what she could from the nearly prepared dinner before it was properly served.

Let's say that that's how it went for the next 2.5 weeks as she strived to record as many identical moments as she could. Granted, the pictures unavoidably differed from one another in all sorts of small ways. The weather was different, for instance; some days the sun shone and on others rain came down. And the figurants in her manufactured still life were never exactly in the same pose. The dog, interestingly, proved to be the most protean; it would constantly be facing different directions, sometimes moving so fast it was nothing more than an auburn blur in the picture, and on drizzly days it would lie in its doghouse, out of view. The people, by comparison, were like docile cows, herded together once a day, amenable and prompt, making the dog seem like the only one in possession of free will and, on rainy days, common sense. The mailman was absent one day a week, of course, but everyone else stayed remarkably in place. She was worried when the duster-clad man failed to show up one day, but her worries were assuaged when she deduced that he, like she, probably operated on a five-day-a-week schedule. Besides, it's not like she was especially assiduous with her picture-taking—lapses included days when she went to the mall for the afternoon and other times when lengthy phone conversations took precedence, resulting in data-less days, which were easily remedied by some shrewd digital manipulation of the previous day's picture, using Photoshop to reimagine the scene as it may very well have looked 24 hours later.

Let's also say that due to the angle from which they were taken the pictures revealed no more of the man than his back (the back of his duster, more precisely), but that she was privy to more aspects of his appearance than she recorded, for as he walked down the street he passed close to her house and she was able to see his face for a few seconds. It was always blank, unremarkable, the perfect reflection of serenity, calm, peacefulness. Not so much a dull phiz as a content one. He was just an actor, placidly taking his position on the stage existing only in her mind. She continued to take pictures, CLICK SNAP.

On the day of her presentation, she projected her pictures onto a screen in front of the classroom. She'd also made a giant neon-green cardstock poster with smaller versions of the pictures placed side-by-side in ordered columns and rows that accentuated the repetitive effect they had, especially when viewed at a distance of more than three feet. She told the class of her troubles in wrapping her mind around the project, how the scope seemed too momentous to easily or handily grasp, how she struggled until finally arriving at the solution: instead of broadening her imagination to an unmanageable degree, she would expound on the minute, focus on the only world she could decisively and accurately describe: the street outside her window. By documenting life at a specific time and place (every picture was labeled 4:14 PM even though she took the pictures at slightly different times, waiting for all the elements to align felicitously; as any intelligent student would, she finessed the data for clarity's sake) she hoped any insight into human life gleaned by the reiterating vista could be applied on a larger scale to existence in general. In short, she presented what she hoped was a microcosm of the world, figures and elements repeating without surcease, implacable, dependably relentless. Here today, here tomorrow, here the next day, here to stay.

Her presentation evoked a tepid response from the class, not surprising since most of their faces seemed carved into permanently stolid expressions, or perhaps covered in layer upon sludgy layer of what was once boredom and apathy, now desiccated by dry wit and withering humor, leaving them corticated in a hardened shell of indifference. Even the teacher looked bored and weary. He was tired of suffering students who thought they were clever—almost as tired as he was of the ones that were irredeemably stupid—and he began to regard this week of presentations as karmic punishment for giving the assignment in the first place. He'd already jotted down a "B+" in his gradebook next to the girl's name and was resisting the temptation to fill in the rest of the columns with random grades and call it a semester.

And say the girl was perfectly content with the grade she got. She was just happy that the ordeal was over and she could go back to homework that had unequivocal answers which could be confirmed or even copied from the back of the textbook. She really couldn't care less what her classmates thought of her report, if they even thought anything at all. She viewed her oral presentation as nothing more than an opportunity to work on her elocution, shrewdly figuring that having public-speaking skills would be an asset in her future, a future in which the prospect of an Ivy League school burned brightly. So say she rambled on, coming up with new opinions and conclusions on the spot, smiling to herself as she listened to the pleasant hum of her own voice.

And let's say, sitting obediently at their desks, her friends and the boys who liked her listened to her increasingly unfocused discourse with admiration in their eyes, and, reversing the principle of a well-known public speaking trick, pictured her in various stages of undress—on the beach in (most of) the girls' minds and in their bedrooms in the boys'—while the classmates who considered her snobby or unpretty or bitchy focused their attention elsewhere. Let's say one of these kids, a bored, restless boy in the process of burgeoning into a bored, restless young man, was staring out the window, out of indifference for not so much the girl or her presentation but the world, generally speaking, and, you know, *existence*, glassily staring out the window as if he had abandoned any hope of finding in the classroom the answers he sought for questions he couldn't articulate—but was also clearly not heartened by what he saw outside either—and so was just staring lifelessly out the window when the hand-out the girl had instructed be passed around the class reached his desk. He almost passed it back without a glance but instead he flipped through it, turning the pages in the same rhythm that the listless employ in changing channels on their TVs. The hand-out was a pamphlet containing all of the girl's pictures, one per page. Let's suppose it took a few seconds for the magnitude of the pictures to hit him, but when it did, he was penetrated utterly. He froze, his heart kicked into a higher gear, his pupils dilated in a desperate attempt to procure more visual information, his neurons fired like an endless barrage of fireworks as he attempted to comprehend what was in front of him. What threw him for a loop was the realization that the pictures were the same and yet clearly *different*—but, as realization became revelation, he knew they were even more clearly *the same* in a deeper sense, on an intrinsic level, that rendered any perceivable differences among them both superficial and moot. What might have been overlooked by viewing the pictures singly became obvious when they were presented seriatim in the pamphlet and the boy felt like a puzzle had been assembled before him, one made up of nonsensical pieces conjoining to reveal a true vision that was both terrible and beautiful. Mirroring the paradoxical nature of his discovery, his spirits seemed to soar and sink simultaneously.

As the class filtered out of the room, say this usually bored boy approached the girl, tremulously, holding her pamphlet in his hand. And say he nervously asked her if he could borrow the pamphlet until the end of the day and say she dismissively told him he could keep it before waltzing out of the room to her next class.

Now let's say the boy, during study hall, went to the library and worked diligently with pen and paper for a good twenty-five minutes, then set about making dozens and dozens of photocopies of what he gleefully considered his own little samizdat. For within the girl's pamphlet, the boy saw the means to, with a little tweaking, convey to everyone else his whole take on life, existence as *he* saw it—a point of view he was unable to adequately express in his own presentation when he sat in front of the class and literally and truly picked his nose while behind him a television played a video of random segments of news reports, game shows, movies, and static spliced together. (The teacher gave him a "C-".) He desperately hoped this new attempt at communication would open eyes and that those eyes would be filled with awe and enlightenment instead of the disgust he usually provoked and was becoming accustomed to seeing.

The next day, in the morning before the first bell, when everyone was still packing into the cafeteria, the usually-bored-but-now-surprisingly-industrious boy sneaked into the hallways and swiftly opened one of the unlocked lockers lining the hall, threw in a copy of his publication, and shut the locker door. He made his way down the hall, feeling like a revolutionist postman, delivering treatises meant to foment a rise to action in a disgruntled populace, finding more unsecured lockers to harbor his pamphlet—an easy task since most lockers proved to be lock-less, which bespoke either the students' blind trust in their classmates or the worthlessness of the items contained within. By the time he reached the end of the hall all his pamphlets were gone, embedded in personal effects, lying in wait, ready to waylay the unsuspecting masses, to be that strong, unyielding beam of probity that would disperse the clouds of their ignorance. Or at least that's what he hoped.

The first bell rang and his heart thump-thump-thumped in anticipation. The students who discovered their lockers had been clandestinely breached—the "lucky ones" in the breacher's estimation—were confronted with a document composed of a dozen or so pages of eight-and-a-half by eleven inch copy paper folded in half and stapled together, the top and bottom of each page forming the sides of a primitive but serviceable pamphlet whose cover displayed one of the pictures from the girl's presentation—the dog, mail truck, and duster-wearing man being familiar sights to those students in the girl's class who were paying enough attention to retain the memory of the picture or any number of its strikingly similar near-duplicates; to most of the student body, however, its meaning or referent was initially unclear—under which was the primly handwritten title: "Reasonings for an Exodus." Inside, each page featured another picture from another day—let's say the whole thing was a lot like the girl's hand-out really, the salient differences being the captions written underneath the pictures, in the same formal handwriting, which attempted, page by page, one word at a time, to fulfill the promise of the pamphlet's title. Say the boy expected the response would be as immediate as it would be cataclysmic; he assumed that by the end of the day, the class size would be halved due to the number of students suddenly deciding to liberate themselves from the shackles of high school by dropping out. Those too young to exercise the right to terminate their education would turn to suicide. Their parents would be in an uproar; it could get ugly fast, best to leave as soon as possible. Those who decided to leave could perhaps charter a bus to transport them all to some agreed upon waypoint. After reaching a temporary safe haven, they would each make individual plans and then, maybe after a communal orgy to celebrate the limitless possibilities that lay ahead, the diaspora would officially begin, with each person

himself had appropriated someone else's work with only the barest of blessings. Still, he would've deemed the GGY an inferior and even meretricious publication—what with the comments implying that the dog and the mailman were having secret assignations, among the other vulgarities that constituted the revised text—an epigone of "Reasonings . . ." that couldn't hold a candle to the elegance of the original. Then again, he would also know, at this point having a couple years' experience in worldly matters, that both booklets were specious, that the points they were trying to make were misleading, even the ones not concerning the dog's deviant sexual activity. After high school it didn't take long for him to realize that one generated the excitement in one's own life, that waiting around for your surroundings to give you joy would result in a wasted life. The truth was that an orgy was just as likely to happen in a small town as a big city and one boring-ass place was the same as the next (unless you lived in like Chicago or something, but who wanted to do that?). And but also he would've discovered that moments of personal glory were few and far between in this world, so if the new generation of kids wanted to perpetuate something he'd had a hand in creating, he would've been glad to take a disproportionate amount of pride in that.

As for the girl, let's say that she would be completely baffled at the turn of events following her presentation. It was just a homework assignment, after all. She would be amazed that a random picture she took with her phone had ramifications for so many people years later. If she were forced to read the GGY she might've smiled at a couple of the jokes, but on the whole would consider the humor to be of the adolescent variety she had outgrown not long after graduation. As for the central idea it promulgated, let's say she would've disagreed with the conclusions everyone seemed to be reaching. She didn't really know what her overriding point was when she gave her presentation—again, it was just a silly school project, not a call to put in actual thought—but her intention most certainly was not to make everyone want to leave town, if not the state or even, in some cases, the country. She never had any problem with the place she called home all through her childhood. For her part, when she looked at the pictures she didn't see a bleak monotony that portended a dull existence for the town's residents. On the contrary, the pictures filled her with reassurance; she was comforted by the recurring events, they were something she could count on—like a favorite TV show that was on at the same time every week—and she already had intimations of the delights of constancy in a labile world—an appreciation rarely found in one so young (it's no surprise that she is already married at the relatively inexperienced age of twenty-four and thinking even now of having multiple kids). One of the things she would've recalled if shown the GGY— the *only* thing that stuck with her actually, which understandably would've heavily influenced her interpretations had she been forced to glean the meaning or point of her pictures— was the look on the face of the man who always wore the duster. His unwaveringly calm expression seemed to be the front of a double-gilt mirror with the obverse side reflecting true happiness. She never got tired of seeing that face, the same way some people never tire of watching babies sleep. Let's say she would've suspected that if others had been granted sight of the man from the front instead of perpetually from the back, they would retract their dire inferences. The man was not to be pitied but envied, for he was fully content in a turbulent world where the struggle for equanimity seemed an ongoing battle for all, probably never to be won by a depressingly large portion of the population. But maybe that was the point; maybe she had captured not just any life but a *good* life; maybe the meaning of it all was contained within the pictures, not outside the borders like all those kids assumed.

Say those would've been her thoughts on the subject before her focus returned to the troubles of her own life. Say she currently has problems that pertain only to her and having them makes her similar to every girl who has ever lived.

Say there were many girls. . . .

ANDREA

MY MOTHER'S FRIEND'S HOUSE was an enigma to me as a young boy. Whenever my mother announced that we'd be going there to make a visit, I fought her with conflicting emotions. My immediate impulse was to protest and back then my mouth was much faster than my brain so I'd quickly start complaining in a whiny, childish voice (I was about ten or eleven at the time). My mother would put up with this for a couple of minutes, but if I persisted with my dissension, she would get angry and I'd have to grumble to myself, lest she threaten to stay there through dinner. We'd get in the car and I'd have twenty-five minutes to think about the wasted afternoon, spent at a house with only about a dozen television stations and no videogame system, while my mother chattered endlessly with her friend for five or more hours.

To be fair, my mother's friend was nice enough. She'd always greet me warmly and ask if I wanted a drink or some food. She'd lead me to the living room and find the TV remote for me. After all my needs had been taken care of, she and my mother would retreat into the dining room and an incessant stream of conversation would waft through the house, occasionally broken up by ebullient laughter. I'd kill time, flipping through the small amount of channels. If I was lucky, I'd stumble upon some tennis match or re-run of an old sitcom I didn't detest.

Sometimes, even when I had kept quiet and out of her way, my mother would announce that we were staying for dinner after all. As all hope of salvaging the rest of the day vanished, I would rail against the injustice of the situation, raising my voice, crossing my arms, and sometimes even going as far as stamping my foot. My mother would turn crimson and yell at me in return. I would never learn that all the foot-stamping and vocal outbursts did little but anger my mother; when she decided that we would stay, we stayed.

Amazingly, my mother's friend never took these tantrums of mine personally. She didn't seem embarrassed or ashamed (maybe a tad uncomfortable, but that's understandable really) and she certainly never got angry. In fact, oftentimes she would help assuage my mother's anger, reminding her that my resistance to the plan was only due to my being surprised by it and she'd reassure me that not only would dinner be delicious, it would also (for my benefit) be as short as possible. Her patience made staying for dinner a little more bearable and probably saved me from punishment when I returned home.

By the end of the night, I would be hurriedly putting my shoes on and scrambling out the door while my mother rolled her eyes and attributed my behavior and lack of respect to youthful tendencies. They would laugh, my mother and her friend, and I always thought it was at my expense (not that I minded; I was happy to play whatever role got me back home the fastest), but now I see that I was mistaken. My mother's friend's laugh was not malicious; rather, it was understanding.

My mother would drag me to her friend's house about once every two weeks. And every time, her friend would greet us warmly and offer me some treat, then I would be left in the living room. I eventually came to expect these visits, not that I liked them any better the more we went.

On the worst occasions, the cruelty of being away from my

room and neighborhood friends was almost too much to bear. On one of these visits, I couldn't find anything good on television so I disgustedly shut the set off. I lay back on the couch and looked out the window. It seemed nature had conspired with my mother to ruin my day—torrential downpour fell from the sky and darkness blanketed the surrounding area even though it was only mid-afternoon. I couldn't even take a walk.

Bored and restless, I wandered over to the bookshelf. On top of the shelves sat pictures of various people I didn't know. I recognized my mother's friend in a couple of them and her 11-month old daughter and the daughter's father, a man I knew was no longer living in the house.

My attention flittered to the books below. One of my fingers traced the spines from left to right as I read the titles. Most of them were children's books, presumably for when her daughter grew up. I pulled out a fairy tale book and glanced briefly at the cover, which featured a bear riding a bicycle. I moved to put it back on the shelf when I noticed a thin pamphlet lying diagonally across the empty space where the book had been. It must have been wedged between the book I was holding and a children's guide to cars. I picked it off the shelf and, when I saw what it was, immediately put it back. I turned my head toward the hallway and heard the ever-present sound of my mother and her friend nattering away. Reassured of their position in the house, I slowly pulled the small booklet off the shelf and opened it.

It was a catalog for women's lingerie. On one page was a woman in her mid-to-late twenties wearing a red satin bra and low-rise thong. On the next page was a slightly younger, well-tanned Hispanic girl; her dark skin juxtaposed with the stark white cotton briefs and push-up bra created an exquisite effect. The catalog also contained women in swimwear (one piece suits and bikini sets) and flowing, translucent nightgowns. It took me a few moments to fully digest what was on each page and I was barely halfway through the catalog when I heard footsteps in the hallway and hurriedly put the catalog back on the shelf. I may not have known much about that sort of thing at the time, but I knew that it would not be appropriate to be perusing it when my mother walked into the room.

A couple weeks later, I walked into my mother's friend's bedroom, where my mother and her friend were talking. As soon as I entered, I averted my eyes toward the far wall, uncomfortable with the fact that my mother's friend was breast-feeding her daughter. I tossed glances back and forth between them and the wall as I told my mother I was going for a walk and I'd be back in a little bit. My mother's friend asked me a question, something I can't even recall, and I was in the awkward position of addressing her as I spoke. As a senseless mumble dribbled from my lips, I saw that not only was my mother's friend's nipple hidden safely out of sight, her baby actually concealed more of her breast than some of her clothes did. This fact afforded me the opportunity to look at her with minimal embarrassment, an offer I accepted for a good five seconds before scampering out of the room, heart racing.

During another visit, my mother called to me from the dining room, saying that supper was ready. I was glad because I was actually hungry and the smells floating through the house were appealing. A good dinner coupled with the discovery of a televised tennis match made me acutely aware that I did not mind this visit as much as I usually did.

I ran down the hall and turned the doorknob to the bathroom and entered. I caught the briefest glimpse of my mother's friend sitting on the toilet before emitting an exclamation of surprise and apology, while at the same time stepping backwards through the doorway. Before I could shut the door, my mother's friend called for me to re-enter, which I did automatically, conditioned to simple-mindedly follow commands from people who were older than me. I stood just inside the room as my mother's friend explained that she was just about finished and the bathroom facilities would be free in a moment. Unable to see her on account of the unusual architectural scheme of the room (the toilet was in an alcove of sorts and could not be seen unless one took a few steps in), I stumblingly explained that I just wanted to wash my hands for dinner. She clicked her tongue in a way that was the verbal equivalent of shrugging her shoulders and told me to go ahead. I hesitantly walked to the faucet and turned the water on. I concentrated on my hands. I knew that from my position I could look in the mirror and see her behind me, but I continued to look down toward the sink. After a few seconds, the toilet flushed and she walked up next to me. I felt her presence instead of looking at her, still unable to lift my eyes toward her even then, when she was fully clothed. I quickly wiped my hands on the towel and moved toward the door. Right before leaving the room, I managed to bring myself to toss a glance her way, taking a quick mental snapshot. When I thought back to it days later, she was doing nothing more than checking her hair in the mirror.

One Friday night, my mother trapped me. I initially didn't mind the visit to my mother's friend's house; in fact, it had been rather pleasant, owing to my mother buying me a few packs of baseball cards that day and the presence of a new videogame system my mother's friend had borrowed in anticipation of our visit. As dinner came and went and the day grew longer and longer, I asked what time we were leaving. My mother informed me that she and her friend were going out that night and I was to stay here overnight and we'd go back home in the morning.

My subsequent outburst rivaled the intensity of any of my prior bouts of yelling and complaining. Before my mother could fly into a rage, her friend reminded me that I could play video games all night. I told her, rather snottily, that while the video game system was a nice diversion for an afternoon, it was no consolation for not being able to sleep in my own bed. As was always her wont, she didn't take this personally as a subtle barb, mainly because she knew I was incapable of expressing anything subtly. I wasn't insensitive, only self-centered and naive.

I made a few more futile complaints, but my mother ignored me as she busily made herself up, preparing for her night. My mother's friend was doing the same, applying make-up to her face. She would occasionally try to console me by inviting me to drink as much soda or eat as much ice cream as I wished. By the time she reminded me that I could go to bed as late as I wanted, I was resigned to my fate and comforted by a baseball game I found on TV.

They were nearly ready to leave when there was a knock at the door. My mother's friend left the room and returned a few moments later with a young girl. I recognized her from times when my mother's friend would bring my mother and me to one of *her* friend's house (this didn't happen too often but I really despised those times nonetheless); this girl was the daughter of one of those friends. They informed me that she was here to baby-sit the eleven-month old, whom I had forgotten was just down the hall. My mother's friend re-introduced us, which reminded me that her name was Andrea. She obviously remembered me more than I remembered her since she immediately started gushing about how much I had grown since last we saw each other. She talked about what I was like when I was younger, staying off in the corner by myself whenever I came over her house. My mother and her friend laughed at this, although I found it slightly annoying. It might have been true, but the last time we saw each other wasn't that long ago (a year at most) and while Andrea may have been a good four inches taller than me, she was only a couple years older.

A few minutes later, my mother and her friend were finally

ready to leave. I looked up from the TV and watched them grab their purses and look themselves over in the mirror one more time. Andrea gushed over how good they looked while I tried not to stare at my mother's friend's mesh shirt, where flashes of what was underneath could be seen every time she moved. After checking that everything was in its right place for what seemed like the fiftieth time, they said good night and left.

After the car drove away, Andrea walked out of the room. Half an hour later, I was wondering where she had gone when she reappeared and plopped down on the couch. She explained that she was taking care of the baby and I nodded. We watched the last three innings of the ball game in near silence. The game had already been decided at that point, but I didn't know what else to do so I left it on. Restless, my eyes would flit over to Andrea, who had pulled out a magazine and was looking intently through it. She had small eyes that made her look tired (except when she smiled) and shoulder-length, tawny hair. She was tall for her age and lanky.

The game ended and I went to the kitchen for a soda. When I returned, she put her magazine on the table and asked me what I wanted to watch next. I told her that if it was all right, I'd like to play some video games. She asked if there were any two-player games and I pointed out that it was moot considering we had only one controller. I suggested we play a one-player game and pass the controller back and forth and she agreed.

It was quickly apparent that I was the better player and I usurped most of the playing time. She complimented me on my gaming skills and I tried helping her out with the trickier parts of each level. We grew tired of the game after about an hour and she went off to check on the baby again.

I slumped in the recliner and turned the TV to a music video channel. Andrea came back ten minutes later and announced that the baby was sound asleep. My gaze lingered on her as she sat on the sofa across from me. She had changed into a cotton

That was the last night I spent over my mother's friend's house. We would still go there, but only for an afternoon or early evening. I saw Andrea a couple more times after that night and it was always in passing with a few banal pleasantries exchanged, nothing more. After another year, my mother stopped dragging me to her friend's house, deciding that I was old enough to look after myself at our own home. It was then that I lost all hope of ever spending the night at my mother's friend's house again, something I was secretly hoping would happen, under the same conditions as before, with the videogame system, the baseball game, and Andrea with her big, ticklish feet.

Sarah R.

I.

THE SUN—hovering halfway to the horizon like an exhausted balloon at the end of a birthday party—cast late afternoon light on the pacing figure outside the jewelry store. The little boy had been a conspicuous presence for the last fifteen minutes, ever since school let out. He was seen gliding through the parking lot not long after the final bell and scampering across the street, chased by car horns and what were, if you asked him, overdramatic tire squeals. The store—or, rather, the roof of the store—had been tantalizingly visible during his last class of the day, as it had been all semester, from his seat near the window. His view of the store had been largely obstructed by the small knoll in front of the school—on which perched the flagpole and message board for students and passersby—but even this compromised vantage of what he had for many weeks thought of as his "objective" was enough to inflame the little boy's impatience in the same way that the last flip of a wall calendar brings Christmas into all but attainable view. Now that the much anticipated day had finally arrived, he had hastened to the store at the earliest opportunity without giving a damn how it looked to others.

Once outside the store, the relief he felt at being so close to realizing his long-gestating goal was quickly replaced by the anxiety of moving on to the next phase of his plan. No amount of advance preparation could calm the urgent rhythm his heart insisted on broadcasting throughout his body. He was a natural conductor of nervous energy; fretting and worrying came easily to him. He had the kind of skittish temperament that presaged a young adulthood that would be absolutely lousy with tics and distasteful habits. He paced, for just one example, with the vigor of someone who would assuredly develop a pack-a-day smoking habit in his early twenties and even insist on a particular brand (which would be widely available, mercifully).

He busied himself criss-crossing the slats of pale sunlight shining through the trees, kicking aside any fair-sized stone or bit of sediment that happened to be in his way until the ground in front of the store's entrance looked swept. He made the mistake of briefly looking up and caught the proprietor of the store giving him the eye through the window, and from then on he alternated his gaze between the ground and the school. He watched the procession of buses—including the one that would normally convey him home—pull out into the street and drive away. Unlike most of his peers, he did not have a car; he hadn't even taken driver's ed yet.

After an interminable ten minutes, the little boy finally saw his friend, Sean, approach from the direction of the school. Sean waited on the other side of the road as a procession of cars flew by. One of them finally slowed down and stopped for him. When he saw there was nothing coming from the other direction, he took long, purposeful strides across the road. As he approached the front of the idling car, his steps shortened and he searched out the driver's face for assurance that the car wouldn't suddenly and tragically lurch forward, turning him into a lurid footnote in the history of West Main Street. This was more for the driver's benefit than his own. It wasn't a display of true hesitancy, more a nod to hesitancy—an acknowledgment that it existed in the world, if not something with which he was on intimate terms. Really it was nothing more than a courteous gesture, executed in a self-assured way that embarrassed neither party. Sean had a way of mixing confidence and politeness that seemed beyond his years. It was a characteristic that made him attractive to a fair number of people, the little boy included. It was one of the reasons the little boy had approached Sean for help instead of going to his other friends. On top of his other estimable qualities, Sean also possessed a certain kind of discretion the little boy considered paramount in matters such as this. It wasn't so much that Sean could keep a secret—a burden no person in history has been able to lug around successfully—rather that he knew under what circumstances a secret should be revealed. His other friends would've had no idea how to handle what he was about to divulge to Sean, and it was not hard to imagine the disastrous consequences that would've followed had he confided in the wrong person.

As Sean walked up to him, the little boy held out his hand without thinking. After a short but perceptible moment, Sean took it, an amused grin on his face as he nimbly embraced this sudden spirit of formality.

"So," he said.

"Thanks for doing this," said the little boy as he took his hand back. He was a little startled by how firm Sean's handshake had been, but it also set him at ease as he now fully believed he had chosen the right person to confide in.

"Sure. No problem. Let's do this."

A small bell chimed when they opened the door, and again when the door closed behind them. It was a small building, and all the wares were packed into one room about half the size of a classroom. Glass display cases encaged the room, lining the three walls not connected to the door. The cashier, a middle-aged lady whose name graced the store's sign (she was also the owner), looked up and regarded them with the cautious—not to say skeptical—aspect all storeowners give customers whose youthful age calls their purchasing power into question.

"Hi," Sean called out. The lady nodded.

The two boys stood in the middle of the room, shifting their weight from foot to foot on the lacquered hardwood as they looked around with exaggeratedly casual interest.

"So," Sean prompted. "Have you decided what you're going with?"

"What do you mean?" asked the little boy.

"Well, like a bracelet or a necklace or earrings or what?"

"I think a necklace," the little boy said. "But I might be open to something else."

"Well. Let's take a look."

He nudged the little boy toward one of the displays, and the little boy approached it with the trepidation of someone walking across a frozen lake on an unseasonably warm day. They looked down at the glittering array of jewelry in the case before them, heaps of gold, silver, and other precious matter, attractively displayed.

To the little boy it was the sort of thing that he had only known in fantasy books, the kind of treasure that dragons hoard and men die trying to procure. The thought that some of this lucre, however small, would soon be in his possession—if only momentarily, long enough to admire before giving it to its rightful owner—gave him a thrill that was new to him.

"You start on that psych paper yet?" Sean said.

"No," said the little boy.

"I should start it. I should really do it this weekend, actually. When Monday rolls around, I know I'll wish I had started it."

"Yeah. Me too. I mean, I should start it too."

"So," Sean said. "Are you married to the idea of a necklace? Sure you don't want to do a bracelet or ring or earrings or something?"

Sean picked a hefty silver bracelet off a display on the counter and held it up to the light. The little boy hesitated for the briefest moment before replying, "No, I think I want to do a necklace."

He had no real idea why it had to be a necklace. It was the first thing he had thought of when the plan materialized in his mind, and since this whole endeavor was propelled largely on a mix of impulse and intuition, he had decided not to question this initial inclination all that much.

The sound of a clearing throat diverted their attention across the store. The cashier was giving them a look that, while pointed, was softening as she saw they weren't just hanging out, completely devoid of purpose. "The necklaces are over here. In this case," she said primly.

Sean put the bracelet down and strolled over to where the cashier had indicated. The little boy followed. Sean's gaze quickly passed over the necklaces in the display and he looked up at the cashier, his head slightly cocked.

"Thanks," he said pleasantly.

The cashier nodded.

He turned to the little boy and expansively fanned his arm over the display. The little boy missed the humor in his friend's gesture, so entranced was he by the sights before him. Necklace after necklace, arrangements of precious chains, each more perfect than the last. The tiny linkages constituting each one seemed to him as elegant in construction and design as anything he had ever seen in his life. It was difficult, in the moment, to believe that they were man-made—made by and for people. They seemed instead to have appeared out of nowhere, flawless and mystical and wondrous. The way the little boy saw it, they were ideals that imperfect people should have to conform to, perfect objects that would be complemented by whoever wore them instead of the other way around.

To his credit, Sean was similarly awed, albeit in his characteristically understated way. "Some of these look nice," he admitted. "I might come back and get one for Heather."

The little boy was amused at his friend's understatement, though he was slightly annoyed that Sean seemed for a moment to forget why they were there. He turned his attention to the gold chains, bypassing the silver and platinum ones. Gold had been another non-negotiable part of the plan; it was inconceivable that he would choose another foundational material—again, for reasons he couldn't fully articulate. All he knew is that he needed the message he intended to convey with the necklace to be as clear as possible, and gold seemed to have exactly the unambiguous significance he was looking for.

"I can take out anything you want to see," the cashier said helpfully.

"Sure," the little boy said automatically. While he was pretty sure his decision could be made just by looking at them, her offer seemed to him one that any respectable and conscientious consumer would accept. "I'd like to see that one," he said, choosing almost at random.

The cashier unlocked the case with a satisfying click and carefully reached in and took out the chain. She handed it to the little boy, who took it from her gingerly. He was taken aback by how delicate it was. It barely touched his skin, a weightless golden rivulet flowing down his hand, purling over his palm and down his wrist. He couldn't quite overcome the feeling that there was nothing there to hold at all. It worried the little boy, to be honest. Up close, the necklace, while lovely, didn't have the substantiality that matched the magnitude of his intentions, he felt.

"Does it, like, come with a jewel or something," the little boy said, his throat a trifle dry.

"You can buy them separately," the cashier patiently explained. "We have a wide selection in this case here."

The little boy carefully handed back the chain and turned his attention to the case, looking intently at the pendants as he waited for his embarrassment to subside. It was something he should've known, the two-part nature of this transaction. He had done as much research as he could before this moment, of course, but scavenging the daily junk mail for catalogs and collecting free circulars around town hadn't provided as much information as he had hoped. (He hadn't even considered entering the store before today and making inquiries.) There was still a lot about these things that remained mysterious to him.

But this was to be expected, he had to remind himself. He was, after all, taking the first step across some invisible threshold, one that he knew—or hoped—would open up whole new areas of knowledge and experience.

The little boy's eyes scanned row after row of pendants. Multi-colored gems set in prongs of gold and silver, every facet catching and throwing back the light in very deliberate ways. Here was chaos bound, tamed. It was through these prisms that the little boy felt his somewhat scattered feelings could be refracted and honed into a message both clear in purpose and beautiful in expression. He just needed to find the exact one that would express what he was feeling inside, things he could not yet verbalize. He quickly apprehended how important this decision was, and it both thrilled and frightened him.

"Can I see that one," the little boy said, pointing to an emerald pendant he was almost sure was not the right one.

The cashier obligingly got it out of the case and handed it to him. He looked it over, turning it around in the palm of his hand, and showed it to Sean. "What do you think?"

"It's nice. What color are her eyes?"

"Her eyes?"

"Yeah, your aunt's. What color are they?"

"Uh . . . I'm not sure. Why?"

"Well, you'll want something that'll go with her eyes, probably. Something that complements them or sets them off or something." Sean shrugged, giving the impression that he didn't much care whether his suggestion was taken or not. But it was enough to paralyze the little boy for a good ten seconds.

"I think they're brown," he finally said. He silently berated himself for not knowing for sure. "I'll have to pay attention the next time I see her. What goes with brown eyes?"

Sean shrugged again. "Anything?" he said.

The cashier sighed, softly but audibly. The little boy went back to scanning the rows of pendants. Of course, what he was really looking at were the prices, which were handwritten on little tags attached to each one, the number followed by a definitive-looking dash that seemed to say "This is the final price, take it or leave it." He had noted the cost of the necklace chains and even if he bought the least expensive one, it left him with only fifty dollars or so to spend on a pendant.

Taking a quick inventory of what was in his price range, he zeroed in on one that caught his eye. "Can I see that one," he said, pointing.

The cashier opened the case and retrieved a pendant whose gem was deep crimson in color. He held it up with his thumb and forefinger and turned it over, inspecting it from all angles.

"Is this real gold?" he asked the cashier.

"It's a 14k setting, yes," the cashier said.

He showed it to Sean, who nodded in approval. "Looks good to me," he said. The little boy could tell Sean was getting restless, and any endorsement he bestowed at this point would come easily and mean little. But it didn't matter because the little boy had already made up his mind.

"I think I'll take this one," he told the cashier.

"Excellent choice," she said.

"I just need one of these necklaces now," he said, looking them over again.

"What kind of stone is that?" Sean asked, willing to be a little more loquacious as he sensed the end of the transaction was near.

"It's a garnet," the cashier told him.

The little boy was pretending to inspect the necklaces, though the price of the garnet pendant cut down his options severely—down to one, in fact: a 14-inch chain that cost a little less than the pendant.

He pointed to it and asked, "Is that real gold?"

The cashier nodded. "That one is also 14k."

The little boy gave her a short nod. He had no idea what that meant, "14k," but it sounded official to his ears. "I'll take it," he said.

The cashier fished the chain out of the case, took the pendant from the little boy, and put them both in an elegantly minimalist box. They walked over to the register and the cashier rang him up.

"That'll be one hundred dollars even," she said. "Will that be cash or credit today?"

"Cash," the little boy said, pulling out a wad of bills. He carefully counted out six ten-dollar bills, four fives, and twenty ones—the entire stack. He breathed a sigh of relief and handed over every cent he had on him.

The cashier re-counted the money and put it in the register. "Thank you boys very much," she said, handing him the receipt.

"Thank you," said the little boy.

"Thanks," Sean said.

They walked out of the store and crossed the street, heading back toward the school. The little boy was in a daze. It took him a mere sixty seconds after handing over his money for doubt to start setting in.

"I hope the necklace isn't too small," he mused aloud. "Fourteen inches. . . . Do you think it's too small?"

"Naw," Sean said.

"I don't know, now I'm worried that it's too small."

"Why? Does she have a fat neck?"

"No!" the little boy protested.

"Then you have nothing to worry about."

As they approached the school, the little boy knew that Sean was about to say he had to go to his meeting now, and that he'd see him tomorrow. He had put off telling Sean the whole truth of the matter—perhaps longer than he should have—and the time had come to reveal everything. It was his last chance.

"So hey," the little boy said. He stopped walking. "I have something, I have to tell you something."

Sean looked back at him. "Yeah?"

"This necklace. It's not for my aunt." He swallowed.

"Ok . . . who's it for?"

He swallowed again. "It's for Sarah."

Sean looked at him blankly. "Sarah who?"

The little boy told him and Sean's eyes went wide. He repeated her full name, giving her last name such incredulous spin that the whole thing toppled over as soon as it left his mouth.

"Quiet," the little boy hissed, afraid that the person in question could suddenly be conjured up solely by giving voice to her name. Or, somewhat more likely, that she would materialize from around the corner, sitcom-like, and catch them in the midst of their conspiring, and, in so doing, know the unvarnished truth at the absolute worst possible moment.

Sean, meanwhile, was scrambling to fit what he had been told into a configuration of the world that made some sort of sense to him. "So wait, you *like* her?" he said.

"Well . . . yeah," said the little boy.

"Since *when?*"

"I don't know. Six months or so?" The little boy gave him a wry smile.

"Does she know you like her?" he said. "I mean, does she know?"

"No," the little boy said. "I mean, not yet." He lifted up the box containing the necklace.

"That's how you're going to tell her?" Sean looked as if someone he trusted implicitly had just told him he had been eating the wrong way his entire life, that you were supposed to put the food in your ears instead of your mouth.

"I . . . yeah. I just, you know," the little boy said, struggling to explain himself. It wasn't helping that Sean was looking at him like that. "I thought this would be the best way," he finally said.

"Let's see it again," Sean said, motioning to the box.

The little boy opened it and they both looked at the necklace tastefully arranged in the white box.

"You should've told me before," Sean said. "I thought we were getting this for your *aunt.*"

The little boy was overcome by a sinking feeling in his stomach. "Wait, this isn't like a necklace for old people, is it?"

he said. "Like the style or whatever isn't for an old person, right?"

"No no," Sean said. "I could see Sarah wearing it. I just wish I *knew* what it was we were *doing* in there, is all."

"I haven't told anyone," the little boy said, closing the box. "You're the only one who knows."

Sean nodded and it was hard to tell how he felt about being in possession of this privileged information. "Everyone is going to find out though," he warned.

"Maybe," the little boy said ambiguously.

"When are you going to give it to her?"

"Well, I'm not. That is, I'm not going to actually *hand* it to her." Sean looked at him quizzically and he took a deep breath. "I'm going to leave it in her locker."

Sean processed this for a second. "Ok. . . ." he said. "How are you going to get in her locker?"

"She doesn't lock it. I checked."

"Ok. So . . . what, you're going to leave it with a note or something?"

"No, no note. Just the necklace."

"Well how is she going to know it was from you?"

"I'll talk to her tomorrow. But I was thinking it'd be this nice surprise, that she doesn't know who it's from, at least initally."

Sean's skeptical expression said all that needed to be said about what he thought of this plan.

"It's like a grand romantic gesture sort of thing," the little boy insisted. "Like something out of a movie or something."

Sean remained unconvinced. "You're not even going to put a little note with your name on it or something?"

"I don't know, should I?" the little boy waffled.

"Hey, however you want to do it. This is all you."

The little boy thought for a moment. "No, I don't want to leave a note or anything," he said.

"Your decision." Sean looked at the little boy and chuckled. "Well, I guess good luck with everything."

"Thanks, but wait there's something else." The little boy bit his lip and dragged his foot on the ground in front of him.

"What?"

"I was wondering if. . . ." The little boy looked up. The day suddenly seemed late. Their stretched shadows almost reached a nearby copse of pines. "I was wondering if maybe you could put it in her locker for me."

"You want *me* to?" Sean said. "Why?"

"Just so there's no chance anyone will see me do it. I mean, there's no chance anyone would see *you* do it, either. But . . . I don't know. Could you?"

"Really? I mean it's just as easy for you to do it. Why do you want me to?"

"Could you please? I just think it'd be better if you did it, like you'd be better at making sure no one was around and stuff. Plus, if anyone happened to see you they wouldn't think anything of it because you have that meeting and all, whereas if they saw me, they might think something was up." He looked at Sean. "The truth is I'm too nervous to, ok? There, I said it. Can you just help me out here?"

Sean shook his head and looked away. After a moment he said, "Ok, fine. Give it to me."

The little boy handed him the box. "Thank you, thank you for this," he effused, appearing grateful but also knowing there was never any real danger of Sean refusing his request.

"What's her locker number," Sean said.

The little boy told him and he nodded. They stood there as the moment distended. They were both smiling, but to themselves, not at each other. It really was a beautiful day, the little boy noticed.

"Ok, I gotta go to my meeting, I'm already late," Sean said. "Last chance, are you sure you want to do this?"

"Of course, yes, definitely," the little boy said. "Go. I'll call you tonight to make sure it went ok and to maybe explain myself better. And thank you again."

Sean nodded and walked toward the school. The little boy watched him go, marveling at his friend's casual stride. It was the stride of someone not particularly hungry walking across the room to retrieve an apple out of a bowl of fruit.

Sean disappeared into the school. The little boy's gaze lingered on the building. The bricks were a color he had never noticed before, and it preoccupied him for a moment.

When at last he turned around and walked away, he was again overwhelmed with a feeling he had never experienced before. It was an all-enveloping and nourishing sensation, something that suffused his entire being. It didn't seem as ephemeral as excitement or even happiness. It felt more significant, and it was something he hoped would largely define him from then on.

But he would soon discover that, like all sentiments, it would pass, and he would feel this way only a handful of times in his life. The next time it came over him would be a little over a year later when, hanging out with friends, he bought a paperback upon which the movie they were about to see was based and, at the restaurant they went to, left his waitress—a plain-looking fledgling at least six years his senior who he imagined to be just out of college and starting her life—a tip of eight dollars on a fifteen-dollar check.

II.

He had no idea when he planned to tell her, but regardless of what he had in mind, he realized pretty quickly that he had to talk to her as soon as possible. They had only two classes together this semester: first period physics and Algebra II later in the afternoon. He didn't know where she would be in between those two classes, so he couldn't count on running into her at some point during the day. Besides, trying to talk to her in the hallway surrounded by crowds of people was hardly ideal. It was hard to think of a time or a situation when they would be able to talk one on one. He was disappointed in himself for not anticipating this problem beforehand.

He knew she had found the necklace the day before. She'd had some kind of afterschool activity yesterday—a team practice, or maybe something else—and before heading home she went to her locker and discovered the necklace. That was all he knew, because that was all Sean was able to figure out and tell him that morning before the first bell.

The thought of her having the necklace in her possession for the last fifteen hours unnerved him for some reason. He realized then that he'd had vague notions of revealing everything to her minutes after she had found the necklace, but he had clearly not worked out the logistics of how that would happen exactly. Now here he was, sitting in first period, waiting for her to enter the classroom. *Then what?* he thought. He couldn't very well walk across the room to where she usually sat and proceed to have a highly private conversation with her. The thought of talking to her surrounded by mostly anonymous people was nerve-racking enough; to do it in front of familiar classmates and friends was completely out of the question.

As he was pondering this dilemma, she walked into the room. He tightened up; his heart raced. She looked nice, as usual. She was wearing a purple-shaded polyester sundress with thick black straps that sat on her shoulders, leaving her bare arms exposed. He tried to see if she was wearing the necklace but she was too far away to tell.

She joined her circle of roistering friends. He pretended not to stare while making note of every gesture she made, every time she laughed, every smile she unleashed. He waited to see if she would make some sort of clandestine acknowledgement of him across the room, some sign that she knew it was he who put the necklace in her locker, but she gave no indication of being aware that he was sitting twenty feet away, silently dying.

Everyone settled in as the first bell was about to ring. He steeled himself for an even longer physics class than usual. He understood little about the concepts that were being taught, and the girl sitting across the room was just one more thing that baffled him.

Then, miraculously, she got up and he watched her walk over to the teacher's desk and ask if she could go use the restroom. The teacher nodded and she left the room.

He waited a few seconds and then got up and went over to the teacher's desk himself. He asked for permission to go to the bathroom and it was freely granted.

He walked down the barren hall, everyone already in their first period classrooms. The bathrooms were at the very end of the hallway, next to the stairwell. The boys' room was situated before the girls'. He took a few steps into the L-shaped passageway leading into the doorless restroom. He crossed his arms and leaned against the painted stone wall, out of the hallway but able to see into it.

He didn't have to wait long for her to walk past, heading back to physics class. The part of him that seized up when he saw her was quickly overridden by the part of him full of purpose.

"Hey. Sarah," he said.

She turned around, startled.

"Hi," she said.

"Hi," he said. "Um, can I talk to you a second?"

"Sure," she said.

"Ok, so. . . ." He steadied himself, realizing he didn't have a lot of time to get it all out. "Ok. I don't know if you know, but it was me who left the necklace in your locker yesterday."

"Oh. I was wondering who did that!" The way she said it made him suspect she already knew somehow.

"Yeah, it was me." He tried to smile. "Guilty as charged."

"Well. I'm not sure what to say." This was already more words than she had ever said to him. "I was very . . . surprised."

They stood there awkwardly, each waiting for the other to give some indication of how to proceed.

"Did you like it?" he managed to ask.

"Yeah, it was nice." Before he could smile, she cleared her

with ~~without being actual friends~~ (most of his actual friends were in the advanced math classes). For the most part, he kept to himself. The push and pull of his conflicting emotions gently rocked him into a ~~passive mood~~ passivity that one might easily mistake for ~~reflectiveness~~ contemplation. ~~But nobody~~ Of course, ~~anyone who~~ no one currently in the room would ~~make~~ have this mistaken ~~observation~~ impression. ~~It's always your lifelong friends~~ ~~The first thing lifelong friends do is mistake you~~ After all, these were not his friends, and the first step in establishing a friendship is ~~mistaking~~ seeing in someone's mundane qualities ~~for~~ something ~~better~~ breathtaking.

She was across the room, and he barely looked over at her. This was very calculated on his part. He felt he just had to get through this day—and then the rest of his life—without ~~seeing~~ catching sight of her, and then he'd be fine.

~~The last year of high school would always be remembered for the unnecessary inner turmoil he felt. (That is, of course, until it wasn't, adolescent angst melting away as easily as winter snow and similarly forgotten when one is looking up at the blue sky on a temperate July day.) The turmoil continued throughout this final day.~~

In truth, he didn't have to look at her to feel thoroughly depressed. His memory was cruel and it had saved ~~various painful~~ plenty of abrasive snapshots throughout the year ~~recalling them unbidden and fanning them out in tortuous open display~~ with which he used to torture himself.

Conversations between the two of them had been scarce, which made them easier to recall and dissect. ~~There had been a couple times he~~ On a couple of occasions he used the pretext of schoolwork to call her, asking her some inane question about the homework or a project neither of them had started yet. There had been awkward segues into more conversational topics. One time she took mercy on him and they ~~talked about~~ discussed their lives in an ostensible attempt to see whether they shared any interests or global perspectives. A ~~cursory enumeration~~ quick summary of their likes and dislikes showed

~~little common ground they were at odds in~~ that their tastes in music, movies, and food were hopelessly at odds with one another. Their hobbies also clashed discordantly; activities considered fun by one of them sounded horrendous to the other. There was, however, common ground in their respective future plans, predictably, since the future is always the thing young people think about the least and then only in the most diffuse and general terms. But it was enough to fill the dead air between them. They talked about the colleges they were going to attend, both in New England, and what they hoped to study there. They were both eyeing professions in the medical field —he was looking to specialize in neurology maybe, while she was set on becoming a dermatologist. ~~He never completely realized~~ It never really ~~hit~~ dawned on him that their conversations flowed more smoothly when they were talking about ~~themselves as people they hadn't turned into yet~~ the people they hoped to ~~turn into~~ become instead of who they ~~were currently~~ actually were.

These inauspicious talks should've discouraged him from thinking about her, let alone pursuing her, but for whatever reason they didn't. ~~He had decided on his object of affection, his idée fixe, and nothing would sway him from his choice. It was something he decided he needed—a high school crush, before he no longer had the opportunity—and she was the best available candidate. He had picked her arbitrarily, having no real interest in her the first three years he had known her, so why would something as arbitrary as opposing personalities~~ Having little else to ~~think about~~ occupy his mind, he thought of her often during senior year and kept his eyes and ears open, hoping to ~~glean any little bit of~~ catch any little bit of biographical detail about her he didn't already know~~, which proved to be~~. It was a lesson in masochism. Among other things, he got to hear about whomever she was dating at the time. He never learned her boyfriend's name (he didn't go to their high school) but found out he was apparently from Delaware, and so took to referring to him, with as much derision as he could muster, as "Delaware Boy" to himself and aloud to Sean. He heard her one day tell Jen, her best friend, that she was "decked out in her man," and he was bitterly crestfallen for the rest of the day. Then, finally, she must have broken up with Delaware Boy because he eventually heard a snippet of her conversation from across a room that included her saying, "He asked if I had a boyfriend and I said no. . . ." ~~At that point he *still* did not know that a girl's response to this question is all but meaningless—they are telling the truth unless they aren't—but this break-up seemed to be corroborated days later when he heard Avidy tell her "You went pretty far with him" as he passed them in the hall.~~

He considered asking her out again after he knew she was single. ~~Of course he did.~~ But before he could work up the nerve, he caught wind that she was dating someone else. This time she was seeing someone who had already graduated and was living in his own apartment. It took a lot of willpower on his part not to think poorly of her at this point. Some days he ~~just didn't have it~~ lost the ability to be level-headed~~, though,~~ and on those days he would phone Sean and go on lengthy tirades. He would bemoan the unfairness of it all for the millionth time, and criticisms of her would seep into his diatribes. He would criticize her imperfect complexion and slightly doughy figure, trying to convince himself that she wasn't worth chasing after. Sean didn't encourage these ~~kinds of remarks~~ insults, but he ~~remained quiet as~~ let his friend ~~give voice~~ rant away, probably recognizing the therapeutic ~~quality~~ aspect benefit of these outbursts. He always toned it down by the end of their conversation anyway, and by the time they hung up he was usually back to thinking of ways to win her heart.

One of the last things he tried was three weeks before the last day of school. He asked her out to dinner and a movie. This was ~~a~~ positively understated ~~attempt to win her affection~~ compared to ~~what~~ how he had tried to entice her ~~with~~ in the past. And with the movie being the much-anticipated sequel to Jurassic Park, he allowed himself to be fairly optimistic about

~~his chances~~ the possibility that she'd say yes. An added benefit was that it didn't take long to save up the money that would be required for this date, unlike when he had bought her the necklace and had to ~~not eat~~ starve for two months, squirreling away the lunch money his mother gave him every week. Ditto for the hundred dollars in mall gift certificates he got her for Christmas. He actually got pretty excited as the day approached when he planned to ask her out. He made little silent pacts with whatever higher powers might be out there, telling them he would stop being mad about the Celtics losing the number one draft pick if she just agreed to go on this one date. But in the end his optimism turned out to be completely unfounded as she quickly and politely rejected him again. Nothing about his offer appealed to her—not even the movie, which she didn't even know was coming out. (He found *that* to be the most unbelievable part of her rejection, and his ~~incredulity~~ disbelief only ~~increased~~ intensified when Lost World smashed every box office record in its opening weekend.)

Yearbook supplements were being passed around the room for people to sign. He handed most of them back as soon as they reached him; in a couple of them he scribbled some banality along with his name on a random page.

After one of them landed on his desk he realized it was hers. He knew this was likely to happen, so he remained composed, at least on the outside. He briefly considered going back on his plan and opening to a large blank page and writing a fulsome note to her. Some grand statement of adoration. But he refrained and passed it on without prolonged hesitation.

With about fifteen minutes left until the bell, he heard someone say his name. He looked up and saw her. She was a couple of rows over, talking over the head of someone who was sitting down. She was smiling, the happiest she had ever been while looking at him. He waved unnecessarily. She asked him if he wanted one of her photos. She was giving out wallet-sizes of her senior picture. Did he want one?

He shook his head. He told her no thank you. He saw her expression freeze and he turned away. His face flushed as he pretended to look at the book on his desk. He heard titters around him, as well as some amused whispering. He knew she was probably making whatever expressions and gestures she needed to in order to save herself from further embarrassment and that they were probably at his expense, but he didn't care. Almost immediately, he wished he hadn't refused her. It was too late to laugh it off though. He was not quick on his feet like the socially adept were. Improvisation would never be his strong suit, and once he made a decision he usually followed through, for better or worse.

While he rarely felt the intoxication of success, the hollow feeling of regret was something he was fast becoming familiar with. He spent the last ten minutes of class in the worst kind of self-imposed purgatory, sick to his stomach.

When at last the final bell rang, he stood up. Before he could walk over to her, he saw her approaching. She walked right up to him and gave him a slightly abashed look, her eyes soft and gentle. She told him that she would really like him to have her picture. He told her that he was going to go over to her right after the bell and tell her he would actually really love to have her picture. As he said this he was aware of the people standing around them, but he didn't care.

She looked eminently relieved and handed him a picture. He took it and put it in his pocket. She stood there and gave a subtle indication that she was waiting for him, so that they could walk out together and talk some more.

He had to really focus to get his limbs to move and voice to work as they walked side by side down the hall, heading to their lockers one last time. They gave each other shy, genuine smiles. He said that he hoped she wasn't offended or got the wrong idea about his refusal. She said she spent the rest of the class wondering what she had done wrong. Aghast, he assured her that she had done nothing wrong, that if anyone had behaved wrongly it was him. She said she was glad things were ok between them. He said he was too. They talked a little about their summer plans. They wished each other good luck with their freshmen years of college. He made a quick joke about meeting in four years to help each other study for the MCATs. She gave him a slightly dimmer smile than the one she had been wearing before, and he knew that he shouldn't have said that. But in terms of transgressions it was a minor one that was easily overlooked. They talked a little more about how glad they were that high school was over. It was the most pleasant interaction they had ever had, and it was almost like she had never told Eric that she thought he was insane and that his phone calls were cute at first but were starting to scare her a little.

His locker was before hers, so when he stopped to get his things she took the opportunity to say goodbye. He told her goodbye and to take care. She thanked him and said the same. He was a physically reserved person, over three years away from his first kiss, so he didn't reach out for a hug. Either she was also physically reserved or just didn't want to hug him, so they parted only on their words.

He watched her go down the hallway until she disappeared from view. He would see her again during the graduation ceremony, though this would be the second to last time he saw her in regular clothes.

He walked to the stairwell and went back down to the ground floor. The school was quickly being abandoned, everyone filtering out as fast as possible, eager to begin their summer in earnest. When he was sure he had put enough distance between them that she wouldn't suddenly appear, he pulled out her picture. He stopped dead and stared at her monochromatic visage for a long time. He turned it over and carefully read the incredibly nice note she had written on the back. He flipped it around and looked at the picture again, his vision suddenly blurry.

IV.

He woke up that morning groggily, shaking off the sleep that seemed to accrete into big, burdensome things during the night, weighing him down and instantly enervating him. The sky was overcast and it was muggy out.

establish mood: dark, depressing, an extension of the desolate dreams he had been having

He woke up fitfully, his body seeking to reclaim the sleep it sorely needed after a few restless nights in a row. Sweat filmed his arms even this early in the day, which only fueled his reluctance to get up and start the day.

possibly describe dreams? compare/contrast with various real-life dreams: daydreams, "living in a dream," etc.

As if waking up wasn't hardship enough, he was not prepared for how difficult it was to slough off the disturbing imagery that populated his dreamscape during the night. The oppressive heat had only exacerbated the restlessness with which he had been lately afflicted.

find some way to create a pall over the surroundings in an observable way, the equivalent of overcast skies indoors

He woke up into a day that still seemed like night. The window shades were up, but the outside world had been draped with an impenetrable overcast sky, and hardly any light filtered into the room.

unchanging routines, the same thing every day

He brought his oatmeal over to his computer and turned it on.

He turned his computer on and retrieved the bowl of oatmeal from the kitchen.

He sat down in front of his computer with his oatmeal.

how to convey that this is years later? reference to 9/11 seems inevitable

He opened his email. His eyes quickly passed over the increasing amount of junk mail he got, the digital equivalents of flyers and circulars. Embedded in his inbox was yet another message he deigned to read, scornfully, from someone he had resolved never to respond to.

accentuate the clunkiness of the technology? dial-up sounds?

is adult life a series of extravagant gestures or banal ones? show the difference between how it seemed when young and what it is now—through emails?

work in—but don't directly address—the various rifts that had formed between friends and family—esp. parents, let reader figure it out

I'm tired of prettifying murky memories

"Her picture was long gone, torn up long ago in a fit of pique"

never found out why they called her turtle

finding "the one" is a much longer shot than being a dermatologist (9,600 in the USA)—factor meeting thirty people who could be "the one" in lifetime, each of those thirty people will grant access to 18 people on average (qv. Guardian survey) = 540 chances; 540<9600; and yet and yet and yet people say not to worry about finding someone that it'll just happen, why? hardships never discussed

checkers' death, time passing

Words to use: Weltschmerz   dysphoria   inanition   lentor
tristitia   cafard   lassitude   malaise   torpor   melancholia

possibly bring up synchronicity between future married name and pendant (Garnett/garnet) or is it just way too cute and/or unbelievable? (And how about KG eventually getting the C's the ring that had been promised by the expected—though ultimately thwarted—arrival of Duncan?)

any way to mention sean's diagnosis without trivializing it or have it seem like a shameless plea for pathos? how to/why even do it, when it occurs many years after?

all the unwritten stories about the unmentioned girls? possibly finish some to round out the collection?

He opened the email and read its contents in a cold, detached way. The words on the screen were ones that he had used before, but their configuration seemed to profane their individual meanings. He hated that they were used as instruments to hurt him, and in what he regarded as such a passive-aggressive way.

Their latest attempt to get him to call would not work, no matter what piece of mail they dangled in front of him. He had similarly not been swayed by the imminent passing of the family pet six months earlier.

He wished they would stop trying to use his past against him. Only he was allowed to do that.

all the ones I never got around to giving the full fictional treatment—a monogamy of limerence, no overlap, each one defining an era:

Jill – can still see her at recess in my mind, distraught, crying, ruined me for crying girls

had a crush on Elizabeth in 8th grade but who didn't?

Allison – the one who was going to take my virginity until I told her I respected comics as a medium much more than straight prose on our first "date"—almost too much irony here (note: any way to track down such a common last name with nothing in the granite yearbook for '01 or subsequent years?)

Kelly – I want that night back when our hands brushed against each other in the dark, me on the floor, you on the bed

Ms. Kaufman – makes sense, most engaging professor I ever had and treated me like an equal; ages get smoothed over a couple decades later anyway

The Levi's crew – Jennifer, hottest boss I've ever had; Nicole, when she told me that Van Morrison wrote "Brown Eyed Girl" for her; Kimmy (Kimmie?), exotropic strabismus only adding to her consummate cuteness (another one with seemingly zero net presence); Christina, a Modigliani beauty, cool, dignified, the perfect embodiment of the word "lithe" or perhaps even "statuesque"; Sarah, another tall stunner, probably also would've taken my virginity if I had realized the implications of "What are you doing tonight?"—would give anything to have that moment back (how many Sarahs am I going to fall for, how many sphinxes in calico dresses? Add in the ridiculously cute nurse (doctor? who knows) from DHMC, with her weekly dark roast)

Zuzana – dancing to a cover of I Feel Fine, carefree and happy, as I sit on the ground and watch (will I ever just dance already?)

Meghan – I said we weren't going to talk about my sex life not out of propriety but because it was non-existent at the time

Courtney – I knew enough at that point never to call her Punk Rock Girl . . . Laura? Lauren? Forget her name. (Also forget if plain jane is about her.) Meta-mention of hoping she would like my stuff half as much as master and margarita?

China girl – still waiting for you to come back so we can watch Cars 2 together

Stacey – the best intercourse I ever had (*verbal* intercourse, of course) I miss our calls, I miss reassuring you that there was no way the Sox could come back from an 0-3 deficit, I miss our letters and tapes . . . I really messed up with you

Diane – I could listen to you talk about this book all day long; you're funny, witty, beautiful

The ones I should really revisit:

Stephanie – the story was unfair to her, that's not how it went, the truth reflects more badly on me than that

Michelle – For years I carried around a mix tape on which there was nothing more than a slightly-edited version of "If You See Her, Say Hello" to give to Ellie to give to you . . . You deserve more than a mediocre short novel, the time you came in to hang out was one of my favorite days of my life

ending should strike a note of . . . what?

still wonder what was in the xmas card she sent, probably just a short genial note at best, but still but still but still

THE DEVIL

THE DEVIL DOESN'T KNOW WHERE TO BEGIN. It probably doesn't matter because he is going to say all there is to say. He is going to tell her everything. So maybe the order isn't important.

The Devil is sad and tired and exhausted and depressed. And angry. For all the reasons one would think. If he explained the situation to an impartial third party, that person would say that The Devil is justified in feeling all those things. Just because he doesn't show it, it doesn't mean he's not feeling this way. Or maybe he does show it. Maybe it's all too obvious that The Devil is sad and depressed, but they choose to ignore it, in the hopes that these feelings will eventually go away or lessen. Is it obvious that The Devil is depressed? He has no idea. It's pretty clear when he's mad, The Devil knows that. Pretty clear to both of them.

The Devil asked for so little from her. So little that he didn't even really ask for the things he needed from her. Maybe he should've made it more explicit, to make sure she knew the bare minimum he required from her. He honestly doesn't think it'd have made a difference if he had told her, though. But maybe he still should have, to make absolutely sure she was aware. The Devil needed to see or hear from her every day. Actually see her, preferably.

The Devil can't stand what he perceives as the look of indifference she gives him, when he sees her now. The Devil knows she is a naturally reserved person, but it still gets to him. He knows it's all a show for other people, the way she acts when she's around him, but, like the person who sees nothing but shadows on the wall, he no longer knows what's *real* anymore. Is she just acting cold toward him or does she really feel that way? He no longer knows. No one knows what she is thinking at any given time, let alone him. He should know, one would think, taking into consideration the hours and hours they've spent talking, telling each other every little thing on their minds. But The Devil very, very rarely does, know what she's thinking.

Unless he has a reason not to, The Devil will kill himself in 2025.

She probably wonders why The Devil stopped coming into her work, even though that was really the only time they got to see each other on a given day. The Devil wonders if maybe she feels a little bit, just a tiny bit, how he felt when she stopped coming over. Actually, he imagines if she feels anything at all, it *is* just a small fraction of the crushing disappointment he felt when he realized she wasn't going to come over anymore.

The Devil thinks she was secretly glad she got to use the stalker as an excuse not to come over anymore. She had stopped coming over anyway, for some reason. But now there was a concrete reason she could express to The Devil, one that he had to accept. Ultimately it's no less crushing than the actual reason she stopped coming, whatever that was, because they both result in her not coming over.

She is no longer the most important thing in The Devil's life. And second for him is a big drop off.

The Devil is going to break it down for her: He loves her, but he's no longer in love with her, and he's not even sure he likes her. He feels like he doesn't know her anymore, so how can he form an opinion of whether he likes her or not? He's tired of fighting through people to get her attention. So far this year, she's probably given him about two hours of her un-divided attention, total. He wants to tell her: Get back to him when they can do traditional bf/gf stuff: going out on dates, being able to hold hands whenever they want, etc.

There's not someone else, but there might as well be. She might ask what has changed. The Devil would say not much in the past three or four years, sadly. The difference is he has something in his life that gives him the strength to stop being stomped on.

The Devil hasn't slept with anyone else. But don't think his hands haven't brushed another's, kickstarting his heart and hardening his groin. Don't think he hasn't kissed someone else, and found the sensation remarkably similar to what he experiences with her.

The Devil hasn't gotten a good night's sleep in years. When he finds himself still awake at four AM, punching his pillow and yelling out, he knows things must change.

Maybe his mood swings, his sudden animosity toward her, seem to come out of nowhere, prompted by no reason at all. At times he must seem bipolar to her. But she doesn't realize that every glimpse of anger from him is a crack in a dam holding back a deluge of grievances. And now the dam has burst and he is free to be mad about everything. And he will be, from now on. Every little thing he has a *right* to be mad about, he will be.

After over a decade of settling for scraps, The Devil now wants everything. He will no longer accept anything else. All she's deigned to give him has been whittled down over the years. He's been left to accept less and less. And he has done so, willingly. But no longer. She went too far. She gave him too little; for years she has given him almost nothing. And he is furious now. Now he refuses to make concessions. Now he wants *everything*. He has a list of what is now required from her. She must fulfill *all* these requirements if she wants the relationship to continue:

—She must come over in the morning at least four days a week. Probably Mondays and then Wednesdays through Fridays, but they can be any four days. On the days she doesn't come over, she must call. He wants to know what she is doing on the days he doesn't see her. This is how he will be able to feel like he still knows who she is.

—She must tell the stalker to *fuck off.* She can use whatever additional words necessary to make him understand, but she must use the words "fuck off" somewhere in telling him to leave her alone and that she never wants to see or speak to him ever again. The Devil must be there when she does this.

—She must come up with a solid plan for them to live together by no later than fall 2020. That is the absolute latest date he will abide them not cohabitating.

If he got hit by a bus today, The Devil wonders what she would wish she had done differently. He wonders if she'd wish she had come over more often, if he was suddenly gone. All the opportunities she had to come over, when there was nothing standing in her way, and she just didn't. When coming over was totally up to her and she decided not to, or was distracted by some inconsequential thing or another. Maybe she'd wish she had come over a lot more. Or maybe she wouldn't. The Devil is not sure which response would be more painful to know, now, while he's still here. Maybe she was sick of coming over. Based on her actions, that was a distinct possibility.

The Devil wonders what she would wish she had said to him, if he suddenly died. Whenever someone passes unexpectedly, people always think about things they wished they had told the person. Things they didn't tell them when they were here, or things they didn't tell them enough. Things they wished the person knew. Maybe she'd tell him she loved him. That she did, really. If she were suddenly gone, The Devil would wish he told her that a part of him, a significant part of him, hated her. Blamed her for everything that was wrong and shitty in his life. She might not have known that, that he hated her, with the force of someone who used to care about her more than anything.

There's a part of The Devil that says he should be grateful. She gave him eight good years . . . maybe it's selfish to ask for more than that. Maybe it was a burden for her to give him even that much, and after eight years the weight just became too much. Some people don't get any good years. The Devil had eight really, really good ones. How much should that matter? Some days he thinks it matters quite a lot. Eight years of pure happiness is nothing to take lightly. On other days it means less so. What is the past but a particularly vivid memory? It doesn't do him any good now, in his day-to-day life. It's nothing more than a vivid dream, meaningful and momentous when one first wakes up but hazier and less important as time elapses. Soon it can be like it never happened. The Devil has had very vivid dreams and thought that they might as well have happened, that there was no difference between the dream and reality in his mind. Once he had a vivid dream of having sex with Randa. The physical sensations he felt in the dream were no different from those he'd experienced in real life. Everything that happened in the dream conformed to the physical laws of the universe. So couldn't a case be made that, for all intents and purposes, it really happened? True, nobody else would believe it to be true, but to him it would be part of what he thinks of as "reality." The only thing preventing him from believing that it happened is the rational part of his brain telling him that it didn't. But really, there is no difference between his memory of that dream and those eight great years. And that leads him to a different conclusion: Those eight great years might as well never have happened. There is no way to "prove" they happened. All The Devil has for proof are memories that are of the same consistency as those memories he has of having sex with Randa. Both seem equally real to him, sometimes. It's not too much of a stretch to believe that he'd be happier now, today, without any of those memories lodged in his head.

And maybe their relationship was like a dream. After all, there is no physical evidence in the real world that it even existed, save a few notes and some stray pictures (way fewer than one might think). There's no proof they were ever together, which was at least partly intentional. He thinks that it worked for both of them, that they were both having their cake and eating it too, to some extent. On his end he never needed any of the customary assurances that what they had together was "real." One has to remember that The Devil deals with "unreal" things all the time, "fictional" worlds and whatnot. Characters in books "exist" for him, etc. Decades of immersing oneself in movies, books, and music makes one accustomed to treating "second worlds" as real, meaningful. But then something happened, The Devil thinks. He found himself needing "real world" assurance because he no longer believed in the "other world" they had created together. He was no longer certain of her loyalty or interest or intentions. Or maybe he didn't want their time to be like those times in books, movies, etc. Maybe he finally succumbed to being seduced by the earthly and tangible. Maybe he wanted them, him and her together, to be Real with a capital R. It might be similar to a thought experiment he always went back to: that love probably needs to be expressed in an actual, observable way for it to be real. The concept that you can love someone silently and have that mean anything in the end is a fictional construction, maybe. It's like if, at the end of your life, Miranda Kerr comes up to you and says she has always loved you. That's nice, but what possible good would that do you now, and what possible good would that have done you in the past? Is it an "accomplishment" that makes you feel ok about dying? Conversely, if someone doesn't love you but acts as if they do with every action that they take, does it really matter that they technically don't love you inside? If they're laughing with you and looking at you with adoring eyes and fucking you and letting you fuck them, does it really matter that they technically don't feel "love" for you inside? So The Devil would ask her who she thinks gets the short end of the stick: the one she really loves or the one who just thinks she does?

There's a case to be made that The Devil should be grateful even now. He should be happy with the scraps she is giving him. At least they are scraps; without them, he would have nothing. Would he rather have nothing? Are these outbursts nothing more than selfishness, ungratefulness? Is he despicable for demanding more from her? Here's the thing: The Devil thinks it's impossible to be in a perpetual state of gratitude. Sooner or later, whatever you are grateful for just becomes standard and weaves itself into your life, becomes your life, and is thought about no more than the air you breathe. This is unavoidable. People can become inured to anything, especially success. Think of how lucky you are to be alive. You could very easily just never have been born. Then think about how lucky you are to be alive during this moment in history, surrounded by unparalleled prosperity. You could have been born in the middle ages, before electricity and cars and hand-held devices. And then think about how lucky it is to be American in this time period. We are the most prosperous people in a world of prosperity. Does all this mean we have to be constantly grateful and thankful? Does this mean we can't complain about comparatively insignificant things, like when the line we're in is too long or we've been passed over for a promotion? Do we have to be in a constant state of awed and humble gratitude? No, The Devil doesn't think so. Eventually you become acclimated to what is occurring and find something to be aggrieved about. And The Devil doesn't think that just because you've been incredibly lucky it minimizes those grievances. Everyone has their own problems, and no one's problems are more pressing or urgent than another's. We all have a point when we complain. We all have a case to be made. We are all afflicted. This is what The Devil thinks, and it's unfortunate for her. It's unfortunate that she's involved with someone who is incapable of either being grateful all the time or worrying about "bigger problems." There is no bigger problem to him than her right now, so that's what he fixates on. And, in the same way people think of other monumental problems, The Devil believes that when he solves this problem, everything will be all right in his life. Everything will be fine again, he will be able to rest, he will be content. His life will be right once he solves her.

The Devil once made a mix CD for her that he never actually gave to her. The track listing is as follows:
"True Love Waits" by Radiohead
"The One That Got Away" (acoustic) by Katy Perry
"I'm Looking Through You" by The Beatles
"Quit Playing Games (With My Heart)" by Backstreet Boys
"The Story of Us" by Taylor Swift
"Where Do We Go From Here" by Alicia Keys
"Ex-Factor" by Lauryn Hill
"Doin' Just Fine" by Boyz II Men
"Lost Cause" by Beck
"Fake Plastic Trees" by Radiohead
"All Too Well" by Taylor Swift
"Most of the Time" by Bob Dylan
"I Will Remember You" by Amy Grant
"Motion Picture Soundtrack" (demo) by Radiohead
"Motion Picture Soundtrack" by Radiohead

All the things The Devil liked about her turned out to be awful in the end. Like her niceness. She will probably be the nicest person The Devil will ever meet. She does things for strangers without seeking reward or recognition. She is very traditionally nice. But in the end it just means that, out of all the people in her life, she treats The Devil the worst. She treats strangers better than she treats him. He gets to watch this, too. He sees her treat everyone around her better than she treats him. He is a second- or third-class person to her. And she might try to absolve herself by saying "Well, that's not how I feel inside." Well, what good does that do The Devil, that she feels a certain way inside? He'd rather she didn't feel quite so much compassion for him inside and instead demonstrate real caring for him out here, in the real world. That would do him a lot more good than some feelings she may or may not have on the matter.

It would be disingenuous to say her niceness hasn't worked to The Devil's advantage, at times. For example, she was always willing to forgive his blowups. Actually, "forgive" is not even the right word. She just acted like they didn't happen. Like truly forgot they ever happened. She did not harbor resentments or treat him differently or anything. The sun would rise the next day and she would greet him with a cheery smile and genial expression. There was never any hint that she was thinking of the previous day's blowup. Most of the time he was grateful she did this.

It's a testament to how much she made The Devil feel loved and central to her life that he never had a nightmare about her in the first eight years. Not one. Now he has them all the time. He just had one last night. Another restless night. "Restless" isn't even a strong enough word. They are soul-crushing nights that hollow him out. When he wakes up he doesn't even feel like he's alive. The nightmares are usually simple, just scenes of her and *him*. Not even doing anything particularly tender. Just her and *him,* together, in plain, even boring domestic situations. It kills The Devil. It kills him in the same way it'd probably kill him to see a video of her average day, from the time she gets up in the morning to the time she goes to bed at night. She sometimes goes out of her way to assure The Devil that "nothing happens," and he chooses to believe her, most of the time. But doesn't she know that that isn't the only thing that would kill him to know? She doesn't realize that any little acknowledgment of *him*—an understanding nod, a half-smirk at some stupid joke, an offered word devoid of recrimination, a pleasant greeting when *he* enters the room, her naturally soft voice stripped of acrimony—it'd all be so many stabs through The Devil's heart. Each of her benign gestures toward *him,* of which The Devil has no doubt there are many on a daily basis, would draw blood. He would die from a thousand cuts. She did such a good job of blinding him to this certainty those first eight years—by talking to him all the time, by coming over, by being a *present* figure in his life. And now that she's gone, he is haunted by nightmares, both night and day.

He has become haunted by the thought that it's possible she's being nice to him now. He has always thought that her niceness and non-confrontational manner and overall instinct to appease have all contributed to *him* having no idea she is going to leave someday soon. But maybe she is being nice to The Devil, allowing him to think that they will eventually end up together, when really she has no intention of leaving *him.* Maybe she does not want to live with The Devil. Maybe she's just being nice.

She never learned how to treat people, both the people she likes and the people she doesn't. She treats them both the same, essentially.

There was an imbalance in their respective opportunities to see each other. She could basically see him any time she wanted. He didn't have that luxury. So what does that tell him when she can see him any time she wants and she lets whole days pass without seeing him? The Devil can only think she doesn't want to see him. And she might make some excuse about how she couldn't see him or how she was very busy with some activity or another. To which The Devil says: Bullshit. Is she not the same person who snuck out while they were all bowling and drove miles to see him for a few minutes? The same person who pulled him into a public restroom in the middle of a busy day with crowds of people milling around? The same person who drove to his house in the middle of the night, drunk? She's even spent the night for crissakes. She could see him any time she wanted, and she did. She never let obstacles even he assumed were insurmountable stop her. She bent reality itself to see him. That night she drove over while drunk? She was even stopped by a cop. (He let her off without a ticket, of course.)

She does not play fair. Even after saying all these things, The Devil knows that the next time he sees her, she will smile and things will be ok again. Or, if not ok, then at least close enough. She will instill in him a sense of calm. He will forget most of what he was mad about, at least momentarily. Even when he resolves not to look at her, to ensure that her trickster smile doesn't even get a chance to work, she does not play fair. She brings animals into the mix. He can't be in a foul mood around animals he likes. She knows this, he thinks, and deploys her pets like a secret weapon. Also, some of the people in her life. Close family. The Devil is constitutionally unable to be dour around very young people or very old people. He can't do it because one group is at the beginning of their lives (and therefore have yet to know hardships and sadness, so he doesn't want to alarm them prematurely) and the other is at the end (and so haven't they dealt with enough). She knows this too, he thinks. And so she brings them along, surrounds herself with human and animal shields. He can't be nasty to her in their presence. But if it was just her and him, maybe he'd be bitter all the time and sneer at her all the time. Maybe he'd be mad all the time. Then again, if it were just the two of them, there might not be a problem at all. If they could see each other all the time, spend the whole day together, wake up and fall asleep in each other's arms, maybe then it would be all right. The problem, he always thought, is the world. And she lets too much of the world in, while he is seeking to erase it, to be in a situation where it's just him and someone else, and together they would *take on* the world. He's always existed in opposition to the world and all he's been searching for is someone to join him in that fight. She likes the world too much to abandon it as he has. She has too many connections to it to discard it completely. On his end, The Devil thinks she might be his last connection to the world. It feels that way sometimes. It's another reason to resent her.

Were there good things to remember? Of course. If The Devil were to give their story the same treatment he gave the others, what would he choose to immortalize? He doesn't know. There are good memories, but there are just as many indelible memories that don't flatter their relationship. He sometimes thinks he remembers these off-putting memories more vividly than the good ones because they contain an unshakable kernel of the sort of truth that worries him. He is harried by some of these truths. Like when they had just started talking on the phone regularly and she called up and breathlessly told him that the radio station had begun to play Christmas music. It was the day after Thanksgiving, and The Devil had heard it on his way to work. He was about to agree with her that it was unbelievable and assumed they'd start to commiserate about the torture of having to hear the same jingles for a solid month. But he had missed the excitement in her voice, and she proceeded to express her delight in hearing songs that brought her immeasurable joy. He quickly readjusted and said that he, too, was happy to hear the songs, even though the truth was the exact opposite. Even this early in their relationship, an undesirable amount of pretense was injected into their interactions. This did not bode well for the future disclosure of honesties.

Sometimes she would say she was glad that he was "himself" again, that he was acting "like himself" again. She would tell him this on days when he made a conscious effort to pretend that he was happy and content, when what he felt inside was the exact opposite. He pretends to be happy for her. It was easier to pretend those first eight years—in fact, it wasn't even pretending; he *did* feel happy during that time. But now he has to wear a big plastic smile whenever he's around her so she won't be less favorably inclined toward him than she already is.

He remembers the time he tried to get his writing accepted by the Vermont Stage for their annual Winter Tales performances. It was only the first or second year they had been doing it, so all the "big-name" (i.e., published) writers hadn't come in and crowded out all the amateurs yet. He remembers reading about the contest a couple days before the submission deadline. They were putting out an open call for New England stories that took place in winter. They wanted something fewer than 2500 words that was vaguely monologue-ish (so that it could be "performed" onstage) and also something that was preferably heartwarming to all who heard it. This was something The Devil thought he could do that would also stand a decent chance at getting accepted (unlike the many, many things he was rejected for that year, a year he still thinks of as the Year of Rejection). Most of all, he wanted to impress her and show her he could be successful at something. He worked all night on a nice, warmly-written short story. He was excited to show it to her the next day. She had her customary reaction to his work, offering the same unwavering support she always gave him, with multiple assurances that she thought it was good. After some light editing, he sent it off just hours before the deadline. A couple weeks later, he got an email from the director of the Vermont Stage saying The Devil had neglected to include his mailing address with his submission. The Devil took this as an incredibly auspicious sign and sent along his address, managing to restrain himself from asking for any further details, figuring he was in for some good news. He happened to be on the phone with her when the much-anticipated letter came in from the Vermont Stage. He tore it open, ready to share his success with her—the first that had ever involved his writing. He couldn't wait to prove to her that he wasn't wasting his time with these words flowing out of his head. It took about three seconds for him to realize it was a rejection. She became aware of the bad news through his silence. She insisted he read it to her. It had the cadence and syntax of all rejection letters—"We're honored you took the time . . . it was a difficult decision . . . this is one organization's opinion and should by no means be taken as a universal evaluation of the work, blah, blah, blah." But the worst thing was they actually said how many submissions they received. Out of 107 submissions, they said, they chose seven to dramatize for their evening of theater. When The Devil read that figure, he felt sick. He couldn't even distinguish himself in a field of just over a hundred amateur dabblers. And they chose seven, one out of fifteen, and he still couldn't get in. When he read her that part of the rejection, she let out a snort before she could help it. She was thinking the same thing he was, only more along the lines of "Wow, he really isn't that good, is he?" This was all but confirmed when they were talking about it later and he was complaining that he didn't get picked when there were so few entries and during a break in his rant she quietly slipped in, "Well, maybe you should have spent more time on it instead of just doing it in one night." Maybe she was right, but then again, maybe she was just demonstrating a misunderstanding of how this stuff works. When it comes to writing, if there were a correlation between the amount of time spent on the work and the results, writing would be the easiest thing in the world. Just because something is done quickly doesn't mean it's without worth and sometimes a lousy piece of writing can be worked on endlessly. The Devil rather likes the story, and their rejection of it still baffles him over ten years later. Though, looking at it again, he thinks maybe they rejected it on the grounds that it was more an autumn story than a winter one, especially since it was going to be performed just before Christmas. Whatever its faults, it's a story that The Devil still clings to, and it's even been published somewhere under the pseudonym "Jerome Davids." Here it is, in its entirety:

Thanksgiving break had been surprisingly peaceful and devoid of the calamitous incidents that tended to characterize any of our family gatherings, regardless of size. The absence of Justin, my brother and wayward nihilist or intrepid adventurer (depending on whom you talked to), though undeniably regrettable, surely helped matters by removing a skittishness his presence invariably engenders in some of the less-informed members residing in the more-removed branches of our family tree. But even knowing he would not be there well in advance—he told me during a phone conversation sometime in October; I might've been the first person he informed—I was still not quite convinced that my peace of mind wouldn't be better served wandering the streets of Detroit than sojourning at my parents' house in Vermont for the holiday, surrounded by a combustible mixture of dozens of relatives. Even excluding my brother, potentially contentious elements abounded: owed favors, unreturned lawn equipment, Aunt Jody's unconscionable new boyfriend (or so I'd heard), Uncle Jerry's ribald humor, any number of obstreperous nephews and nieces running unbridled from room to room, unrelenting as river rapids . . . all of which would be positively *heavenly* if everyone could find the necessary mercifulness within themselves to not bring up the damn *inheritance* issue again. A vain hope, I know, as some sadistic soul will always find the audacity to bring up this . . . *situation* . . . I can't even discuss further in my currently sober state.

But, as I said, the vacation had been an honest-to-god reprieve from Professor Jennings's creative writing course and all the other stress inducers one pays a college to provide. The biggest commotion came when one of the aforementioned hellions stumbled upon a cache of unwrapped Christmas gifts in my parents' closet and proceeded to distribute them to his fellow cousins. As a lifelong procrastinator, I could only shake my head and look at my mom with a smug smile as shrieking children, delightfully pelting each other with foam balls fired out of plastic guns, transformed the living room into a Christmas Morning scene, a whole month early. My look was a silent, playful admonition of my mother—*Shouldn't you take care of one holiday before worrying about the next?* (The narrow-eyed, don't-push-your-luck look she shot back quickly put an end to my gloating.) But other than that joyful chaos, a relaxing peace obtained for the first couple of days. In retrospect, I suppose I should've recognized the pleasant, diversionary nature of the first part of my vacation for what it was: the calm before the storm.

On Thanksgiving morning, I awoke early and crept outside, starting my day with a customary cigarette. It had been unseasonably warm and rainy. I stood on the porch, securely watching the drizzle, wearing a thin flannel shirt, as yet having no need for the neatly folded sweaters that had greeted me upon my return, conscientiously placed on my bed by my mother. Lifting the cigarette to my mouth, I paused when I saw a truck coming up the dirt driveway toward the house. I hadn't put in my contact lenses yet, but my glasses were adequate to identify the vehicle as my father's. I also noticed a bulky mass in its bed, covered with a tarp, which made my heart start racing in the manner all hearts tend to do when there is anticipation of imminent trouble. As the truck pulled up to the house, I thought of exactly two things—two seemingly disparate things—that were hurtling toward each other, and, imagining the resultant explosion when they collided, I involuntarily flinched.

The first thing I thought of was my father, or, more specifically, my father's annual Thanksgiving morning ritual. Every last Thursday of November, my father would invariably strike out while everybody was still nestled in their beds, load his truck with the necessary accessories, drive out to the edge of some woods, venture forth, and hunt deer. If asked why he did this, he would become noncommittal, at most proffering such trifles as "I'll catch 'em by surprise. That's the day they'll all think we only have *turkey* on the brain, and let their guard down. Then: BAMO!" (That last part was reserved for any children in the audience, who would squeal with delight at the unexpected outburst from someone most people, particularly non-family members, perceived to be a resolutely stoic, not to say *dour*, example of a man.) This tradition was apparently established decades ago, before I was born, before he had even met mom, the protracted history effectively turning what, in all probability, began as superstition into sacrosanct ritual. Even if he was too busy to utilize his license every other day of the hunting season, on Thanksgiving morning he made sure he was out there, trying to get his deer. Now, regrettably, I must add that my father, the lifelong hunter, has never gotten his deer. It may seem unfair, but there it is. His slavish dedication had yielded no tangible results   . . . until, perhaps, this morning. But instead of feeling elation for my father, my mind swiftly turned to something else—that second train on a collision course, if you will.

My second thought was of my little sister, Aubrey. She was the baby of the family at eight years old. I must confess to some difficulty arriving at the proper words to describe her . . . the words other people use—words like "precocious," "compassionate," and "smart-as-a-whip"—don't seem so much inapt as they do banal. Or maybe those descriptions don't hit the nail quite as squarely on the head as I'd like. That she is intelligent and compassionate, there is no question. But those traits, inhabiting my wonderful sister, are a bit deeper, more multi-faceted, than those words uncomplicatedly imply. I'll now try to paint a more elaborate picture of specific parts of her nature—the ones most pertinent to this story, I hope—more elaborate, at least, than a big red crayola heart drawn on pink construction paper. (Which, I admit, isn't entirely inappropriate and, on certain days, I'm sure would strike me as a perfect encapsulation of my sister.)

One thing I've always found enchanting about Aubrey is that she is both an optimist and a realist, simultaneously, which is a little like jumping and sitting down at the same time. I'm not sure how she pulls it off, but she does so gloriously. Also—some people (you know the type) take lemons and make them into lemonade. Aubrey takes lemons and makes them into the biggest, hugest Fortune 500 lemonade company that's ever existed, complete with Olympic sponsorship and a commercial jingle you can't get out of your head. Hopefully this gives you a ballpark idea of what I'm talking about when I say she's quite the unique individual.

Which leads me to the (possible) point of contention. Aubrey had always demonstrated a special compassion for animals in a way that perhaps only a little girl who owned an excessive amount of stuffed bears and dogs and dolphins can possess. Trips to the pet store became onerous; Aubrey found the term "window-shopping" incomprehensible in such an environment and would demand that nearly every animal be immediately purchased and brought home. The fact that she loved all the animals, not just the obviously cute ones, nearly broke down everyone's defenses (I know it did mine) and I suspect that she was closer to owning a zoo of domesticated animals than she realized.

When her particular affection for deer began is the subject of some debate in our family—with my mother having an outlandish theory that the constant use of the word "dear" for her children somehow, through phonetic association, inculcated Aubrey with a misdirected fondness for the animal—but, in my opinion, it can be pretty obviously pinpointed to a seemingly innocuous incident that took place a little over three years ago in our very living room. The room was ominously filled to the brim with a large mix of acquaintances, most of them family. (I'm telling you, these family gatherings always spell T-R-O-U-B-L-E.) Uncle Alan, a jovial and loquacious fellow possessing more than a fair-sized sense of theatricality, was holding forth, regaling a rapt (and, among the adults at least, fairly drunk) audience with an anecdote involving a nighttime drive back to his house after a fruitless day of hunting, an incident in the road involving a smashed headlight and a suddenly crippled deer, and pointblank gunshots to dying flesh. It was a story that amused almost everyone—especially lifelong hunters who've never gotten their deer. Aubrey was, perhaps understandably, horrified.

On Thanksgiving Eve, she requested to say the prayer before dinner. It went smoothly until she got to the part about "And please, God, please please *please* let all the deer get away from Daddy tomorrow. Amen." My father wasn't much of a talker at the dinner table but, even so, he seemed especially quiet throughout that evening.

Later that night, as I was lying in bed, I heard some raised voices coming from down the hall. I slipped out of bed and tiptoed right outside my parents' room, just in time to hear my mother say, "Keep your voice down."

"I can't help it," I heard my father say. He sounded like he was seething. "Do you know how long I've been at this? Am I *ever* going to get one? I'm running out of time, you know. I've got enough odds stacked against me without my daughter praying for *divine intervention!*"

When dad came home empty-handed the next day, Aubrey was nice enough to wait until he had left the room before she smiled. Ever since then, dad has had his annual ritual and Aubrey has had hers, repeating the prayer every Thanksgiving Eve.

And now, three years later, my dad parked the truck, got out, and walked toward me. I watched his face, which, as usual, gave nothing away. He reached the porch, making no motion toward the steps, and stood there, looking up at me in my elevated position. He gave me a slight nod and I walked down the steps and silently followed him to the truck, disposing of my cigarette on the way. We walked directly to the back of the truck, as if it had some uncontrollable pull on us. Dad paused for just a second, then lifted the tarp, revealing the 150-pound, 9-point buck underneath. It was an impressive and beautiful thing. Words seemed moot. I looked up at him admiringly, gave him a grin and a congratulatory nod. He nodded back, but his face didn't reflect the exultation I expected to see at his hard-earned and long-fought success. Instead, there was something akin to depression on his face.

"So," I said, breaking the silence. "I assume this wasn't an accident."

"You think it would make a difference to her if it was?" he asked mournfully.

We stood there for a few moments, silent. "What are you going to do?" I asked.

He had probably been thinking of little else because he immediately said, "I'll take it over to Reggie's. He'll be ecstatic to have something to mount in his garage."

He suddenly looked down the road, as if he couldn't bear to face his prize anymore. "Just wanted someone to see it," he continued. "So I wouldn't be the only one who *knew*."

I nodded. He sighed and slowly got back into the truck. I stood beside him as he started the engine. "Are you sure you want to do this?" I asked him.

He looked helpless for a second, then his features softened as his mouth curled into a wry grin. "Sure I'm sure," he said. "I'll just have to visit Reg more often."

I gave him a pat on the back before he drove off.

Aubrey didn't ask him how his morning went. She just took it as a matter of course that no shots were fired and she didn't want to rub it in. Exhibiting incredible restraint, Dad said nothing to make her think otherwise and Thanksgiving Day passed with the typical amount of conviviality.

When early evening rolled around, Aubrey looked up from her coloring book and fixed Dad with a questioning stare. "Aren't you going out?" she asked.

"Going out where?" he said languidly, even though he knew exactly what she was talking about. He always made a point to "give it another go" before the sun went down, always with the same results he got in the morning.

"You *know*," she said, almost impatiently. "To get your *deer*."

"Nah," he said. "Not this year."

She looked at him for a full minute while he sat there, clearly uncomfortable with being analyzed, unable to meet her eyes. Finally she said in a voice barely above a whisper, "Where is it?"

"What's that sweatpea?" he asked.

"Where *is* it?" she repeated.

"Where's what ladybug?" he said.

"Don't *ladybug* me!" she said with force. "Where's the *deer* you got this morning?"

God, she was quick. I looked up from my book and saw a defiant truth-seeker, and for about the millionth time, she earned my complete respect. Dad saw it too, and rewarded her with honesty. "It's at Uncle Reggie's," he admitted.

She chewed on her marker for a few seconds and then went back to her coloring. After a few minutes passed, I really wondered if she was going to let the evening, week, month, year—forever—pass without saying another word on the subject. Finished with her picture, she closed her book and sighed contentedly. "Well," she said, as if there had been no gap in the conversation, "what's it doing *there?*"

Dad looked at her blankly for a moment. Then, a smile. Followed by a chuckle, then genuine laughter, which, frankly, amazed us all. He looked at his daughter with enchantment in his eyes. She returned his smile, warmly. "I'm just glad you're home Daddy," she said, making her way over to his chair and giving him a big hug. I was across the room, so I'm not sure, but I think my father's eyes were glistening.

I went outside later that night for a final cigarette before bed. The night had turned the air drastically colder than it was earlier. As I stood on the porch in my thickest sweater, I noticed a couple snowflakes hit the handrail. In a few short minutes, big cotton-ball-sized flakes were falling languorously to the ground. As I watched the first snowfall of the year, I couldn't help thinking *Isn't that just like you Aubrey. You took rainfall and made it into snow.* I went back inside, fully expecting to be greeted in the morning by twenty feet of accumulation, more or less.

———

What's most annoying is that every time The Devil sees her, she has a great excuse. He doesn't mean that sarcastically. There's always a fabulous excuse, one that makes complete sense and makes him feel foolish for being mad in the first place. Forces beyond her control have conspired to thwart whatever plans they had made. He's not used to dealing with people who have to routinely deal with forces beyond their control. The Devil is used to being in total control of his actions, or at least fighting to maintain some overwhelming degree of control. He can see how someone would give up if constantly thwarted, though. Just throw their hands up and say Whatever. That's where he feels he's at with them. Whatever. It's beyond his control. And the important thing is for him to stop blaming her for everything. He blames her for everything, and he's really trying not to. He is not happy blaming her for everything. He's happiest blaming someone else. Why does he have to blame anyone though? He doesn't know. Maybe he believes in that as well, that it is always someone's fault. Someone is always to blame for everything. He's not sure where this comes from. Maybe it's his own self-persecution complex, his tendency to blame himself for almost everything. It makes sense: if he is in complete control of his actions, as he tries to be, and something goes wrong, it is no one's fault but his own. He guesses that's why he hates outside forces so much: it's much harder to blame somebody. Maybe that's one of the advantages of believing in a higher power, because if you encounter a situation where you can't blame people, you have to chalk it up as an "act of god," and you certainly can't blame god for anything. And so you end up not blaming or resenting anyone, and you calm down, and things go much more smoothly.

She might cite the girls as the reason, as an excuse for not coming over. They're getting older, she wants to spend more time with them during their formative years. They are the most important things in her life and she does not want to neglect them, ever. It sounds like an unimpeachable explanation for her decreased visits, impossible to criticize. The Devil still thinks it's bullshit. The simple fact is that she came over when she wanted to, and when she wanted to, nothing could stop her. If she didn't want to come over, she didn't. It was always that simple. The Devil has no idea what makes her want to or not, but that's the way it works.

There is nothing she can say to convince him she loves him as intensely as she once did. There are plenty of things she can *do,* but he knows she'll never do them.

A part of The Devil really despises her. Never when she is in sight, full-bodied before him. Always when she is nowhere to be seen, her current bodily configuration unknown and cruelly imagined. He hates her at 3:32 in the morning, after tossing and turning for the last hour-and-a-half. He needs sleep, his mind races. He's not even sure how to put everything he's thinking into words. It kills him that she doesn't try anymore. She used to try, to make the effort. Now there's absolutely no effort on her part. All the things she used to do. All the notes she used to write him. The times she would come over and stay late into the night when there would be no way to explain it. He had no idea how she explained staying out so late, but she did it anyway. The way she'd make sure she saw him every day. The way she called, every morning. How she would hide in the bathroom with her cell at the end of the night, just so she could tell him "Good night, sweet dreams." How she would whisper into the home phone late at night, stashing it away in her pocket if someone came in unexpectedly. The time she came over drunk that one night, even after being pulled over. The Devil would kill the stalker in a second if he knew he would get away with it. In a *second.* If there was a button that would kill the stalker if pressed, The Devil would press it with absolutely no remorse. Think drone strikes are bad? The Devil would press that button repeatedly, just to make sure the stalker was dead. But even if The Devil had to slit the stalker's throat himself or stab him in the eye or insert a knife in his belly and forcibly rip out his intestines, The Devil would do it, if he knew he would get away with it. The Devil would be willing to murder the stalker in the most grisly way imaginable, as long as the stalker was dead in the end and The Devil would get away with it for all time.

It's much easier for one person to basically ruin your life

than it is for someone to make it worth living. As often as someone in your life dies and makes your life "worse" (which usually just means you feel awful for an indeterminate amount of time afterward, so it's somewhat arguable how "worse" your life is, though feeling bad all the time definitely inarguably makes your life worse), someone in your life dies and your life immediately improves instead. Maybe it doesn't happen as often, but it's just as likely to happen. The reason people are not as familiar with this phenomenon is that they are usually selective about who they let into their lives. People generally try to keep people who would make their lives worse out of their lives.

The Devil wonders if his best days are behind him. He used to anticipate Mondays so much . . . he lived for Mondays. He remembered the other Monday how much he loved Mondays. It made him want to die, realizing what a wasteland Mondays had become. The Devil would say to her, if he could: "We aren't making any new memories. It's like everything is in the past now, and all we have left are the old memories. My life seems essentially over."

The Devil has done everything right. He has not done one thing wrong. He has not made one misstep. He is faultless, in their relationship. He has played the role of perfect boyfriend impeccably. This forces her to do everything right, unfortunately. If she does just one little thing wrong, there will be an imbalance. So she can't do anything wrong, not even a little thing. The Devil almost feels bad for her. She can't do anything wrong. She has to do everything exactly right, because he has done everything right. So the second she doesn't call him when she should, or doesn't come in to see him, or goes off and does something with someone else and not him, it's over, she's failed completely and utterly and The Devil can sit back and truthfully say he has done nothing wrong, so he is the aggrieved party every time. The Devil will always be the one with grievances. She will never have any; it's not possible for her to have any because The Devil has never done anything wrong.

The Devil is all of a sudden mad at everything. She wonders what he's mad about. The answer is simple: Everything. Everything she can even think of as possibilities, he is mad about. Even things she thinks he doesn't know about. She knows all the things that would piss The Devil off if he knew them. Unfortunately for her, The Devil's been left alone with his thoughts long enough to think of *Everything*. And it all pisses him off. Truthfully, he is mad about the things he should've been mad about twelve years ago. There are years of accumulated things that should've made him mad, but never did, not really. He kept his anger bottled up, let it dissipate over time. But no more. He is going nuclear, and he will be explosively mad about Everything. Furious, about Everything. He will see red about Everything. No more bottling things up, no more stewing quietly. He is going to blow up about Everything. Everything is working against him, so he will be mad about Everything. Every goddamn little thing. And The Devil will be in the right. It will not surprise anyone who knows the whole story. Most people would've been a lot madder much earlier. It's The Devil's turn. His anger will burn the world, and The Devil won't care. He is in the right. The Devil is justified. The Devil thinks about how she intentionally and without warning stayed away from him two summers back. Just stopped coming in to see him. Just cut off all contact with him. And he just took it. He forgave her for that. He forgave her for all the shit he's had to put up with. All the times she just decided not to see him, not to come over, not to call. He forgave her. She did things she needed to be forgiven for and he did, he forgave her. That whole year, when she just decided she would stop seeing him, to see what that would be like, or whatever bullshit excuse she had. How she came over before Christmas after staying away from him for months. All teary and apologetic. And he forgave her instead of breaking up *right then.* He was not strong enough to break up with her right then. He was not strong enough during the four years after the eight good ones. But now he is strong enough. Now he is not worried about never seeing her again because he never sees her anyway. But most important, he has the strength of will. He has the confidence in himself. He knows what is most important in his life and it is not her.

The Devil told her that night that she would always be "the one" for him. It is true. She is his only shot at having anyone. He is so tired. The thought of doing for someone else even *half* of what he did for her fatigues him. He just does not have the *energy* to try again with someone else. She has drained him of everything he has, and there's nothing left to give anyone.

She's intentionally doing things to make The Devil mad. That's how he sees it. She's either intentionally doing these things or doesn't realize that what she's doing makes him see red. Either way, The Devil wants to tell her to go fuck herself. Because if she's doing it on purpose, then fuck her. And if she's totally oblivious to doing things that would hurt him, then fuck her for having zero consideration for him. Zero cognizance of how things would affect him. Zero awareness of his thoughts and feelings. Fuck her.

She would tell The Devil that she loves him. The Devil doesn't care anymore. He doesn't care about the words she's saying. She can tell him that she cares about him more than anything, that she loves him, is in love with him still, more deeply than she's ever been before. She loves him, she cares about him, she's in love with him. The Devil doesn't care. The Devil would tell her that he wished she loved him less and came over more. If it's true that she loves him more than ever, why did she come over more in the past when she supposedly loved him less? It doesn't make any sense. Come over and make the effort, The Devil would tell her. There are obstacles now, she might say. Bullshit, he would reply. She came over and said to hell with the consequences in the past. Now The Devil is not worth the trouble, or effort, or possible consequences. This is the only way to look at what's happened, The

Devil thinks. At a certain point, it doesn't matter what someone says or what they think. The Devil would ask someone: Imagine Miranda Kerr came over every day and fucked your brains out, and was enthusiastic and pleasant about it, and she left every day soon thereafter, and before she left she made it clear that she "didn't love" you, but she came back the next day and the day after that and every day for the rest of your sexually active life. Now imagine a life probably very similar to the one you're living now, one in which Miranda Kerr doesn't come over at all, and you don't see her for years, decades even, and before long you're on your deathbed and Miranda Kerr comes to see you then and she says she's been in love with you all her life, that you are the most important person in her life, that this love she feels for you is transcendent and has changed her life in so many wonderful ways and every minute of every day she feels this overwhelming love for you, and she tells you all this right before you die. The Devil asks you: Which is the better life? The Devil posits that an approximation of love can be just as good and sometimes better than real love. So, the Devil thinks, what good is it that he is the recipient of her true love, if that is even in fact what is happening? The other that gets her fake love is living a better life.

She is treating *him* better than she treats The Devil. She must be. If she were treating *him* the same way she treats The Devil, *he* would leave her immediately. The Devil is ready to abandon her himself, and he is the one she is supposedly in love with. The Devil has been treated like shit.

When will they be together? When she's 55, 60, 65? When she's 65 will she finally have things in order enough for them to be together? If that's the case, The Devil feels like he has lost already. They'd be together just in time for their bodies to start breaking down and falling apart, if they hadn't already. Someone else would've already stolen all her good years. He will have missed out on all her good years. The Devil will have lost, and he would truly view his life as one big fat waste of time.

He has wasted so much time, literally wasted it waiting

around for her to show up. Days, weeks, months he will never get back. There is no question he has wasted the last four years of his life, and there's a strong case to be made that he's wasted the last twelve years. While she was off living her life—a life that no longer included him to a large extent—he was stuck waiting around, wasting time.

So she called The Devil less and less and one day he realized she had stopped calling. A few Christmases ago, she didn't call him once the whole time he was at his parents' place, which was about a week. It was unusual but he reassured himself that it didn't mean anything. She was a lot busier than he was, always had been. But it was the new norm. She never called during Christmas again.

Her not calling and not showing up at his work progressed into not coming over. This happened so gradually that it took him a while to realize what was happening. At the beginning, she would come over three or four times a week, and visits at unscheduled times were not uncommon. She would pop in for ten minutes in the evening sometimes, on her way home from work. Sometimes in the morning, on her way to work. On weekends she could always find a few minutes to stop in. Things like that. But those surprise visits stopped at some point, maybe four or five years in. Then they stuck to a fairly regimented schedule.

Mondays were always free. They both made a point to be available to each other on Mondays. Monday was their day. Then the mornings of the rest of the weekdays were available, out of which she would take the opportunity to come over maybe two or three of those four available slots a week. It was not too unusual for her to come all four days. It was a fine arrangement for The Devil, to be honest. Sure he would've liked to see her more but between seeing her at work and constantly talking on the phone, he always felt as though they shared each other's lives to a significant degree. For The Devil especially, who was entering into it from basically nothing and with hardly any prior experience, it felt like he was getting to spend an exorbitant amount of time with her.

He finally snapped to what was happening when she didn't call, come into his work, or come over to his place for fourteen straight days. Then, a short time later, it happened again for ten straight days. He knew things had changed because she would've never done that when things were going well. She would've never done that in the first eight years. If she did that during those first eight years, it would've been a clear indication that something was wrong. Now she says it means nothing. It would've meant something before.

A part of him will never forgive her for 2015.

People can get inured to anything. The Devil feels strongly about this. All people, every single person, can get used to any situation, both good and bad. And it's always distasteful how people with tons of success can eventually reach a point where they think, "Well, isn't this how it's *always* been?" Unfortunately, it's an inevitable part of human nature. You can't constantly be grateful or appreciative every single second of your life when things are going well. Conversely, you can't feel sad or depressed all the time, either. Both lead to paralysis or oblivion or both, and then human nature doesn't apply to you because you're no longer a person.

Here's the truth as honestly as The Devil is capable of expressing it: He never took her for granted. He was never awash in a sense of complacency, nor did he let expectation become his default state of being. He always said to her she could end it any time she wanted with no explanation, and she always took it as a joke, but he was 90% serious. He knew how lucky he was, and he never lost sight of that, or if he did, he caught himself immediately and got his mind right, like a driver on a long stretch of highway getting distracted by his thoughts for the briefest of moments.

When you have this mentality, the hurt you feel because of someone's absence isn't due to thwarted expectations. It isn't because you counted on that person to be there and they didn't show up and that stings you. The pain isn't as acute as that. The pain is more constant and dull, deep within yourself, when the bad thing you always expected to happen actually does happen. You find yourself suddenly in the place you always imagined you'd end up, a place that logically you'd be sure to end up, but actually being there confirms all your worst suspicions and fears about yourself and other people and the world. And it hurts you.

It's the pain of being right—a way deeper, more wrenching pain than the pain of being wrong.

When their relationship was new, The Devil was mad a lot. He doesn't want to pretend he wasn't. Just because he wasn't complacent, just because he had these inevitabilities in his mind, doesn't mean he didn't rail against it, against the various unfairnesses of it all, both perceived and real. Certain of his friends can attest to this too, his anger.

The Devil would get mad at her, in the beginning. As mad as he's ever been at anything. She learned that about him pretty quickly. Screaming, yelling, tantrums. It was ugly and did not paint him in a good light.

And yet, he never did or said anything that made her have enough and just end it. She was preternaturally understanding about every outburst. She rarely snapped back at him. In fact, he can't remember when she ever did. She had the patience of a saint. (She had a way of embodying clichés and making them mean something, maybe for the first time ever.) She would quietly let him rant and rave, and then she would defuse the situation by either leaving him alone for a while or calmly pointing out the other side of the issue, which was invariably the better side to be on. He was always making it hard for himself, picking the more difficult, more hurtful way of look- ing at things. Quick to accuse and indict, The Devil found himself having to defend positions that were staked on nothing more than pride and willfulness. It amounted to a lot of yelling about things which nobody had control over. It was stupid.

He took issue with things he wishes he didn't. Her foibles, mostly. Those little forgivable things that were inextricable parts of the person she was. She was always late. She was forgetful sometimes (not about anything important, though). She was easily distracted. Little peccadillos, venial sins. Nothing to get worked up over. But he did. He wouldn't, if he had to do it over. It wouldn't change anything, but, still, he wouldn't.

She had a calming influence on him as time passed. He doesn't think he had a single blow-up the last five or six years. It was a combination of self-realization and being put through the fire—nothing fazed him after a while. He didn't get rip-roaring mad like he did at the beginning. There were even things he *should* have gotten mad about but didn't.

When someone tells you they're sorry, there's always something for them to be apologetic about, whether you know exactly what it is or not.

The Devil did get mad, just not in her presence. A lot of punching pillows at two in the morning. A lot of rehearsed vituperation directed toward the walls. A lot of seething, scowling, grinding of teeth, clenched fists. But for all she knows he didn't do any of it, so it's as if he never did.

The Devil wonders about his anger, and anger in general. After you go through something where the natural reaction is to get mad—"natural" meaning that people wouldn't hold it against you if you got mad, like if you lost someone or your house burnt down or you broke up with someone or whatever—you tend to wonder whether all your subsequent anger is rooted in that thing. This is especially true if you're trying to bury your anger deep inside and not let it show or if you're trying to sublimate it into something useful. It can be a decision to get angry sometimes, and you can just as easily decide to get angry about something as you can not to get angry about that thing.

But even if you decide not to get angry about something, you eventually do get angry about something else. It's inevitable. Something will piss you off eventually and make you have a traditional outburst. You will yell at someone or something eventually. The Devil doesn't really yell at people, never has. He tends to yell more at inanimate objects. Water's a big one, a constant thorn in his side. He seems to spill it on the floor more often than one would assume it should happen. Also it seems to hit him in the face more often than it should. The Devil will pour some water into a sink, for example, and half the time it splashes in exactly the right way and goes into his eye. It's ridiculous, really. It happens on a fairly regular basis. And every single time he thinks *What are the odds??* It must be incredibly unlikely, and yet it continues to happen, over and over again. Although, maybe the odds aren't as bad as he thinks they are. Maybe he just thinks it shouldn't be happening because he doesn't understand the physics behind it and if he did, he wouldn't be so surprised. Maybe there's a formula governing water splashing up into your eyeball that The Devil is not aware of and could never understand, so he is doomed to be perpetually mad about something that is just a function of the physical world we inhabit.

Take computers. The Devil gets mad at computers and electronics a lot. When it takes forever for his browser to open or when he can't seem to press some tiny thing on a tablet with his fingers. There's also some issue with his television, where he has to tilt the remote a certain way before hitting the power button or it won't register that he hit the button and it won't turn on. He thinks it has something to do with how the light transmitted to the TV from the remote is being emitted from the bottom of the remote. At least, that's what seems to be happening.

When The Devil presses the power button and the TV doesn't turn on and he notices it after walking out of the room to get himself a drink or something and comes back into the room fully expecting the TV to be on and it isn't, he will more often than not swear at the TV. Half the time he'll adopt a really sarcastic tone and say something like, "How about doing what I tell you this time?" Sometimes, to "prove his point" to the TV, he'll press the power button a million times, just to make sure.

He remembers a little while ago he was using my tablet and for the life of him he couldn't press the little 'X' to close a window. He kept narrowly missing it, apparently, because the window wouldn't close, but according to his perceptions, he was hitting it exactly right, right where the lines crossed on the 'X.' And he got irrationally mad for a second. His jaw clenched and his look was a murderous one, which was amusing to us because there he was getting super pissed at an inanimate object. And he pressed all around the 'X' in a ridiculous fashion, saying stuff like "Good enough for you? Is it good enough yet? How about now?" until it closed. And he actually had to settle down a little afterward. He was breathing hard and everything. And then it made him wonder: Did he just get more mad than he usually would've because their troubles were on his mind? Getting mad at objects was not uncommon for him. But did he get *extra* mad at it, because of what was going on? He wasn't sure then and is still not sure now.

She no longer calls or comes over. She has abandoned The Devil. She has abandoned him. She has abandoned him. He has been abandoned. She doesn't call anymore. She doesn't come over. She has abandoned him. He has been abandoned by her. He has been abandoned. He has been abandoned. She has abandoned him. She has abandoned him. She has abandoned him.

He's taken to checking her facebook without her knowledge. She gave him her password a while ago. She thinks he's forgotten it. He has not. He made a point to remember it.

It's a pretty distinctive password. It's vulgar, way more vulgar than someone who just casually knew her would assume she would make her password. It would make jaws drop. He logs on late at night, when all her friends would presumably be asleep. This is so no one would try to chat with her, or mention to her later that they saw her on facebook. He is erring on the side of caution, perhaps needlessly, because while these are possibilities, he really doesn't think anyone would.

She's not on facebook a lot at all. Her updates are a ghost town, a few scattered posts and likes over years and years. But it's still useful. The Devil can kind of triangulate her day-to-day life through the posts of her friends. For instance, he knows she went to a concert a couple weeks ago because of some pictures posted on her best friend's wall.

He knew about this concert; she told him she was going a couple months ago. But the details about it remain unknown to him. Did she do anything before the concert? After? Did she stay in Boston for the night? (Doubtful.) Did she have fun? Exactly how much did she drink exactly? If this had happened five years ago, he would've gotten the full rundown the very next morning. Plus calls during the concert, when a song came on that reminded her of them. This is how these things went, in the first half of their relationship. He might've even seen her that night. Her friend knows about them . . . she could've stopped over on her way home if she wanted to. That could've happened in what feels now like the distant past. It was not unusual for her to stop over very late at night and it would always be such a happy surprise. He hasn't seen her at night for a very long time.

Also the Fourth just happened. That used to be almost a de facto date night for them. While the others went to see the fireworks, she would bring over the scared and shivering, and together they would comfort them in his bed, blasting music to drown out the sounds of fireworks outside. He didn't even get a phone call this year. She must have been home, alone with them, and still she didn't even call.

He almost wants to leave her a note tucked in her facebook somewhere. Something to remind her he's still here. There are multiple problems with this: He doesn't know what the note would say, and he has so little understanding of facebook that he wouldn't know where a safe place to leave the note would be. Plus she never checks her facebook.

It can be painful for The Devil to check her facebook. There are pitfalls, holes to fall into that just make him despair and keep him up late into the night. Messages with her ex-boyfriends, for example. Stupid reconnections with past ex's, which seems to be one of the main underlying points of facebook. It makes The Devil want to destroy the site, permanently erase every last bit of code of that stupid goddamn site.

One time he checked her facebook and there was an earlier chat session still open. She was chatting with an ex, going back and forth, bantering. The ex said something like he was going out to Vegas for the weekend, so why didn't she join him? She agreed, jokingly. The ex asked, jokingly, if they should get one room or two. She, jokingly, said one. The Devil's insides turned to ice after reading that. It made him realize something: Nobody is above flirting. It's something everyone will do in any given situation. It's just something everyone does, and expecting someone not to do it is naive. Even she was not above it. Even her. Despite all her principles and solid sense of what is right and just and despite all her reassurances to The Devil that he was the only one she would ever want, still she flirts because it's basically harmless because nobody is there to witness it.

Also heart-breaking was seeing that she had a free weekend a couple weeks ago. The girls were taken by their "aunt" somewhere fun for two or three days. The Devil saw the pictures, he read the posts. Did he see her that weekend? No. Did he get a call that weekend? No. Ignorance has saved him on many occasions from feelings of betrayal and hurt. So basically she had a free weekend with *him* for company. The supremely stupid thing is The Devil still gets all worked up about the typical thing. Even after everything they've been through, even after all the shared experiences that have elevated their relationship so far beyond merely the physical, he still sees red when he thinks she might be sleeping with someone else. He can't even think straight when he considers the possibility. It's very ridiculous when one considers all the rest he puts up with. Why does that matter so much? He has no idea why, all he knows is that it does. It matters more than anything else matters. And it kills him, every time. The Devil thinks and he thinks and he can't stop thinking about it and it drives him crazy with rage.

The simple truth is that he has been on the verge of going crazy ever since they met. Fear, anger, despair, depression, abject misery . . . all of these things are roiling inside him at all times. But they can be kept at bay, they *were* kept at bay all those years. He doesn't think she ever fully understood the value of those phone calls, or the five minutes he got to see her at work, or—most heavenly—when she came over. Any of these things could sustain him for days. It kept all his demons from rising to the surface. It prevented him from drowning in his toxic thoughts. She doesn't realize how depressed he is now, after years of talking to her every morning, of seeing her pretty much every day, and now there's almost nothing. Does she realize how much his life sucks now? It does, it completely sucks. He is sad now, all the time. All . . . the . . . time.

And maybe she just needed to fuck The Devil more, so The Devil could continue to believe that she wasn't fucking *him*.

The Devil wrote selected lyrics around the rim of the mix CD with a sharpie, spiraling the words toward the hole in the center. These are the words he wrote:

TRUE LOVE WAITS IN HAUNTED OUTTAKES BUT IN ANOTHER LIFE WE'D KEEP ALL OUR PROMISES BE US AGAINST THE WORLD YOU DON'T LOOK DIFFERENT BUT YOU HAVE CHANGED DEEP WITHIN MY SOUL I FEEL NOTHING'S LIKE IT USED TO BE THIS IS LOOKING LIKE A CONTEST OF WHO CAN ACT LIKE THEY CARE LESS MAYBE YOU'LL GO MAYBE YOU'LL STAY I KNOW

I'M GOING TO MISS YOU EITHER WAY LOVING YOU IS
LIKE A BATTLE AND WE BOTH END UP WITH SCARS
BECAUSE YOU LET OUR LOVE JUST FALL APART YOU
NO LONGER HAVE MY HEART I'M TIRED OF FIGHTING
FOR A LOST CAUSE IF I COULD BE WHO YOU WANTED
ALL THE TIME I'D LIKE TO BE MY OLD SELF AGAIN BUT
I'M STILL TRYING TO FIND IT MOST OF THE TIME I
CAN'T EVEN BE SURE IF SHE WAS EVER WITH ME OR IF I
WAS EVER WITH HER ONE WORD WE NEVER COULD
LEARN GOODBYE I CAN'T EVEN RECOGNIZE YOU I
THINK YOU'RE CRAZY MAYBE I WILL SEE YOU IN THE
NEXT LIFE

ANGEL

Angel—

Sometimes I'm overwhelmed, thinking of all the things I want to thank you for—there are so many things! Your generosity, your caring, your love . . . it all means so much to me. I guess specifically, this week, I want to thank you for all the unbelievably nice things you've said about my writings. Your encouragement has worked wonders for me, culminating in the package I sent out earlier this week—something I never could've done without your help! I love you for so many things . . . I love you for enabling me to realize whatever potential I may have. I'm not sure if what I write deserves that much praise, but hearing it from you makes me indescribably happy . . . I feel like I need no further validation than your kind words. Thank you! I hope to share all my future successes with you, since I suspect you will be a huge reason for them. In fact, I want to share everything with you . . . I love you so much! I love you, I love you, I love you!

D. (xoxoxoxo)

Aug. 20th

HAPPY BIRTHDAY HAPPY BIRTHDAY HAPPY BIRTHDAY HAPPY BIRTHDAY

Hey you!—ok—the TRUTH. I've just spent 15 min. & 6 pages of paper from this book trying to put down a few "perfect" Hallmark lines about having a great birthday—but nothing sounded right and the spelling was—you know—a mess, as always (not that this won't be)—and I also thought you and I both know they don't employ me—so I'll just talk this one out. I would want a card to say I hope your day—this day & every day—go perfect. You'd get published, a raise, respect, and seen for the witty, sweet, funny, gentle, and wonderful person you are. God, please don't check my spelling—I have no dictionary near and it's making me very nervous!!! I would say I hope you have the smile I love on your face several times in one hour, the sparkle in your eyes several times in one minute. Your laugh—the one when you think something is very funny—hourly at least. Um . . . would have to say I love you. Thank you for <u>always</u> being there—for being so patient and waiting. Listening to me go on & on about a room, paint, even other things and never telling me to stop—though feel free once & a while!! Thank you for always wanting me to be happy, cared for and content. I wish all of these things for you. I hope you have a great day, every day of your life. No one has ever been so much of a support to me—I don't know how I don't drive you crazy. I go on & on all the time. Thank you for being there. I hope I can do a little for you what you do for me—you have no idea how happy I am to have you and your friendship, your everything. I love all of our times together, wish they were longer.

<u>Happy Birthday</u>

Love Angel (xo)

—ok—that wasn't all—I love the faces you make when we're together—I love your sweat on me, your skin on me, your hands. I love being close—just wanted to add that.

Love Me

Angel—

I'm sitting here wanting to write something to you, and I've been staring at this blank page for 10 minutes, going back and forth between not knowing where to start and wanting to tell you so much at once. I want to tell you direct things, without the flowery artifice that my mind tends to drift to when putting words down on paper. I'm going to try, here goes. . . .

Do you know you mean the world to me? If you do, then you know more than I do, sometimes. I don't ever take you for granted, I think. My heart never fails to race when I hear your signature buzzer at my door, my insides always go crazy the second I see you. But I sometimes get complacent with regards to you being my girl and in those moments are susceptible to these feelings of "Oh, it's always been this way, how else could it be?" I don't think these thoughts are rooted in arrogance or carelessness; instead it is born of a deep sense of comfort and ease that can only come after many years of joy and happiness.

But I never indulge these feelings very long because I inevitably snap out of it and remember: I am the luckiest guy in the world because I have you in my life in the way that I do, as a friend, a partner, a lover. One might think this would be a constant source of joy for me, and for the most part it is, but it also makes me anxious. Because I truly do believe it, that I'm truly blessed, which makes me think: "How did I get so lucky?" You are a dream come true for me, which on the one hand makes me so happy, but on the other hand worries me because what if I wake up? A part of me refuses to look too closely at it, to question it at all because I fear that if I do, I'll realize it doesn't make any sense and it'll disappear in a puff of smoke. So those thoughts of "Oh yeah, sure, she's my girlfriend, of course" are really just a defense mechanism: if I just pretend this is normal, it will be totally normal.

But this is not normal. This is not a typical boyfriend/ girlfriend relationship. This is something way more than that. I've found the love of my life, the person I can't imagine life without. How many people in relationships can honestly say that? This is the thing I keep going back to: You are all I need in this life. With you, I literally need nothing else. If I only had you in my life and nothing else, if my life was nothing but seeing you, talking with you, laughing with you, loving you . . . then I would be the happiest I could ever be. I don't need anything else but you.

I won't ever assume you feel the exact way about me. Even if you do, I don't ever want to assume that I alone am sufficient for you. I want to do things for you, I want to be better than I really am for you. You deserve the world, and I admit that I am oftentimes frustrated by my inability to give it to you. I try to do it in little small bursts, but please know that if I could I would buy you Katy tickets every day, the backstage ones where you definitely get to meet her. I'd buy every estate sale in New England so you could put it in your booth. I'd take you on a vacation to a tropical island every month. All that and more.

It seems clear that I'll always fall woefully short of giving you all that you deserve. For that, I am sorry. My eternal love might be a small offering in comparison, but it is the one thing I know I can give you. I love you, Angel. I love you so much. Thank you for letting me love you, and know that I'll keep trying to give you the world.

Always yours,

D.

Top reasons I love you—not in any order—

1—The way you look at me—with your eyes telling me you love me & I'm all you see. I love that look—and I know it's all mine!

2—I love your passion. I love that you love PTA, DFW, HT, DM, RP, and the other many names I'm forgetting and have yet to learn.

3—I love that you are always there for me. Listening to me babble about something I'm excited about, to something that makes me so mad I could scream.

4—I love the way you hold me, touch me, kiss me. I feel so wanted and loved. There is always meaning, not ever empty gestures.

5—I love how sweet & thoughtful you are. I know you would always put my feelings first. (Not that I want you to!)

There are way too many things . . . your scruffy face, so sexy . . . your dots I can connect and make a kite . . . that crazy sexy bit of hair low on your tummy, the way your hands are always a part of the action, on my face, head, body—so perfect, the way you light up when you see me—it's so nice! The way we can lock eyes and wish we were alone, the way you call me Angel, I know I'm not, but it's so sweet, the way you try to hide messes, movies, video games—I don't care!! I love your voice and listening to you talk on the phone with your friends—and I LOVE kissing you when you're on the phone trying to maintain a conversation. . . . I love that you get obsessed with your passions. I love that you have a word list and still want to know more. I love that you take weeks to decide on a new cell phone. I love that you're intelligent and can write—don't be checking my grammar and/or spelling!! I love that you are so sweet and gentle with me. I love that if I needed you, you would be there. I love, love, love our time alone in your room—doing anything—eating, talking, reading, watching TV, getting ready for work. . . . I love all of the times we've made love with our hearts and minds so in it. You are so wonderful—and I love that!!!

Angel—

I'll always remember Friday, July 8, as a horrible day. I didn't get to see you, I didn't get to talk to you, you felt awful all day . . . just an all-around rotten day. Your phone cut out before I could say Good Night . . . it makes me feel literally sick. I didn't get to say it enough all day—I Love You. I Love You. I Love You. I missed you all day . . . it felt like an empty day, a non-day. I'll take yesterday, tomorrow . . . anything but today. I Love You. I just can't say it enough . . . I'll spend the rest of my life saying it and it still won't add up to how I truly feel—I Love You <u>so much.</u> You know, you're so amazing that I know that I'm really not worthy of loving you . . . that no matter what I do, it wouldn't be enough for what you're worth, for what you are. Anybody who thinks they've given you enough is a fool, because you deserve nothing less than THE WORLD. But, with that said, I know nothing would make me happier than trying to give you the world, trying to make you happy, loving you <u>every</u> <u>single</u> <u>day</u> for as many days that I have left. I Love You. I Love You. <u>I Love You</u>. You save robins from getting eaten by cats, you save caterpillars from frying in the sun. You make sure a little boy gets another ice cream cone and you selflessly think of lonely people around Christmas-time. You single-handedly make the world a better place to live in. I Love You for that and more. How could anyone be complacent with you? How could anyone take you for granted? You're one-in-6 billion, a rose among weeds, the brightest star in the sky. Do you know how much you deserve? Could I ever say it enough times? I Love You, I Love You, I Love You, I Love You, I Love You, I Love You, I Love You, I Love You, I Love You, I Love You, I Love You, I Love You, I Love You, I Love You . . . with my last thought every night and first thought every morning, I LOVE YOU.

D.

p.s. - I Love You.

D.—

I can't believe I missed you! I was going to run in and give you the biggest kiss. I can't wait to be in your arms tomorrow. I love you!!

So instead of your lips on mine, your hand behind my head, you inside me—you're asking "cream & sugar?"! NOT FAIR!! I want to feel your skin!!

Your room is cozy though—better than nothing. I still need to go shopping. I have to go home w/ something.

I hope I can get here tomorrow—much earlier!

What's one of your favorite songs on our ipod? I've been listening and for me it would be a tough call. I guess it would change w/ your mood anyway, right? I wish the sun was out. I'm grumpy today. I need some bright rays . . . or you . . . guess I can't have either!

The movie was pretty cute. Amy was good, but not a lot of focus on her character. Owen was funny—smaller role, but very cute. I think you would like it. Oh . . . that reminds me. Sarah Marshall was on TV the other night and I'm sorry to say but I thought it was funny (yes corny), and cute. I wished I hated it to agree, but I kept thinking I can't believe he didn't get a kick out of this. Honey, you need to lighten up and not be so concerned with the quality of acting and just go with the flow!

And didn't you think the rocker boyfriend singing to Sarah about being inside her was sooo tender & sweet? (I am kidding, but I thought it was funny, in a disturbing kind of way!)

I wish we were kissing. I wish I had my mouth wrapped around you. You're so soft & smooth, it's nice. I miss you. I want to be close!

You didn't shut your closet door. Was that an oversight or did you figure I could open it if I wanted to? Well I'm not interested what's in there anymore—the big mystery is gone. Clothes, movies, CDs, x-mas, junk. I have all that at my own house!

This morning Bee was so sweet. She held my face w/ her paws and was full of kisses! Later in the day she was a royal pain in the ass. How can that be? Well you know—you've lived the experience—sweet dog-crazy dog!!

Well baby, I guess I should get to the store. Sorry this is so messy, I'm laying on my side in bed—and I don't feel like proofreading—so I hope it makes semi-sense!

My appt. is at 10:00, but I was ready to come to your house today at 8:20 AM, I'll do the same tomorrow because I <u>need</u> to see you!! I love you sweet guy!!

<u>Miss you</u>!!

Always,
Angel xo

PS!!! (Also forgive my awful spelling)

First of all, I want to thank you. Thank you for loving me, of course, but, more importantly, thank you for letting me love *you*. You're the first person I've ever wanted to love that has allowed me to do so. It is no small thing, so thank you.

I think in some way all I've ever wanted is to find someone I want to do things for and be there for in every way I can, and for that person to not only appreciate what I do for them, but also appreciate the fact that it was *I* who was doing those things. For example, you not only love the iced coffee I bring you, you love that I'm the one who got it for you. And that makes me feel so good, that I've found someone I can do things for who actually thinks what I'm doing is nice. I guess this might just be the definition of love, *true* love, not some unrequited pining after someone or something like that. True love might have less to do with what you are willing to do for another person and more to do with that person's willingness to receive what you have to give.

So you might be wondering why I didn't write a traditional short story about you, as I had for the other real-life referents in this collection. I want to explain that there are a couple reasons for this. One is I don't think I'm a good enough writer to accurately capture who you are on the page. I feel like any words I use would fall ridiculously short of who you really are. Words like "gorgeous" and "beautiful" and "generous" and "giving"—while completely valid descriptions of you—don't even begin to describe half of who you are. You're the most amazing woman I've ever met, and even that sounds not so much like a cliché but an understatement. I just wouldn't know how to capture you with words, at least not without taking 10,000 pages to do it. I mean I could try listing all the specific things I love about you in the hope it would all add up to something that conveyed just a tenth of who you are and what you mean to me. I'd mention things like your nice, flowing handwriting, and your toes, how I love that the second one is longer than your big toe, and the sound of your voice, how it's still the most melodious I've ever heard and how I could listen to it all day long—and some days I think I have!—and your incredible empathy, how you care for every living thing on the planet. I love how you smell and taste when you're ovulating (I'm sorry, I do). I love how every time you say "Guess what?" it's with such unalloyed wonder that it just instantly makes me happy every time I hear you say it. I love how you sing when you think no one is listening. I love how your kisses make me dizzy, still. All these idiosyncratic details in addition to your more obvious qualities, such as your jaw-dropping beauty that set the standard for attractiveness as soon as I saw you, and your unparalleled generosity that redefines what it means to be a compassionate human being, and your warm, uncynical nature that makes being around you my favorite place to be. I could go on and on and on. Ultimately though, what I feel about you can be summed up by some lyrics by our favorite songwriter Bob Dylan (I know I know, bear with me a second) that go: "All my powers of expression and thoughts so sublime could never do you justice in reason or rhyme." That's exactly how I feel about you. I am in awe of you as your boyfriend and you thoroughly humble me as a writer. And that's all there is to it.

Incidentally, it's fun to think of the memories I *would* fictionalize if I had to. There are so many things to choose from, from the tiniest moments to the unforgettable days. All the initial encounters, you asking me what I was reading and me sheepishly holding up a copy American Cinematographer with Harry Potter on the cover; the time you just happened to be pulling in to my work when I was locking up and you drove me home and you were a little tipsy on zinfandel and you reached out and briefly held my hand for the first time; our first kiss when you told me not to move and I followed that command exactly, until I didn't; our first Valentine's Day and the story of the wine glasses; April 20, 2005, of course. Even more memories as our relationship matured. The sleepovers, the time you were waiting for me when I came back from my parents' and you couldn't wait for me to hear Alicia Keys's new album and we listened to it in the dark in each other's arms. The joy of hearing your voice first thing in the morning and last thing at night. "Good morning, sweetie." "Good night, sweet dreams, I love you." And yes, the first time you came, and then the time you came twice in the span of ten minutes, and the year my birthday fell on a Friday and you made a point to see me even more than usual because you wanted that whole weekend to be special and we ended up having sex five times and it really was the best weekend of my life. So many unforgettable moments. . . . If I promise not to pass out, can we make some more?

Back to why I can't write a nice traditional short story about you. The second reason is because I seem to require something to be done and over with for me to consider writing about it, and then only after many years have passed. I need all the elements in the real-life event I'm drawing from to stop and sit still so I can dispassionately analyze them, and only then can I begin the process of fictionalizing it. The thing I learned about relationships is that they aren't something that you achieve and then have a big celebration about and then move on with your life. This was somewhat of a revelation to me because after numerous attempts over the years to "win" someone—combined with a lot of waiting around for the right person to come along—to finally find you in the end felt like the culmination of an epic journey and a major accomplishment. (And I still, to this day, feel like I won some sort of impossible lottery, and I continue to feel like the luckiest man who has ever lived.) But then the sun rose the next day and I found myself still in this thing called a relationship and I discovered that it's constantly moving forward, getting more intimate, more interesting, more comfortable. Its contour changes as it absorbs all our emotions, and we've gone through the entire spectrum during the course of being together, from happiness to sadness, from tenderness to anger, from passion to tranquility. Every day it shifts, hopefully evolving, sometimes regressing, but always in motion, and there's the sense that if it ever stopped moving that that was how we'd know it was over. Now, at this point, our relationship is a durable thing and the changes it undergoes these days are incremental instead of drastic. But my point is that every time I think I've got a handle on it, it changes. And that may sound bad, but really most of the changes are for the better, and they leave me with a much deeper appreciation of you and what we share together. Of course, it also means that for the purposes of my fiction, it's essentially useless; I'd have to write a novel a day in order to keep up with it. And in the end, instead of just writing stories about loving you, I'd rather just love you for real instead.

It occurred to me recently that a good way—perhaps the only way—to get to the heart of who a person is is to know two things about them. One: what they gave most of their time and energy to. And two: what they believed in. For me, the answer to both of these questions is you. You are the only thing I've given my all to. I've thought about you more than I've ever thought about anything; I've done more for you than I've done for anybody, including myself. I've used all my resources, all my ability, all my ingenuity in loving you. I've given everything I have to you, to us. I've always given you one hundred percent. And this isn't true of anything else in my life. Nothing—no person or task or endeavor—has ever gotten my best effort. Just you. The next closest thing I've given my total attention to is probably this book, and the thousands of hours I've spent toiling away on it is a mere fraction of the time and energy I've spent on you. That's a simple fact and one I'm totally fine with.

You've given me a concrete place on which to focus my lifelong fascination with romantic love, a fascination to which this book is a testament. When we fell in love with each other, I found someone with whom I could realize all my ideals and hopes and dreams, making them a reality for the first time. I was a disconnected mess of speculative notions and scattered thoughts before you met me, a non-entity living in my own theoretical universe. You brought me into the real world and made me a whole person.

As for what I believe in, it should come as no surprise that it's also you. I believe in you as a person as well as an instrument of inspiration and hope, and you make me believe that there will be a future I want to live in. You are the closest thing to divine grace I've ever seen on this earth. That is why, before I even knew it, the word "Angel" had escaped from my lips one day when I was addressing you, and the label seemed to me the most appropriate name for the heavenly creature in front of me, and that's how I've thought about you ever since.

If I needed any confirmation that my faith has not been misplaced, I got it during my recent medical troubles. As I've told you, when I looked into that series of bright lights, the only thing I thought of, the only thing that brought me any comfort at all, was you. And it made me realize that no matter what "success" or "achievement" I attain in life, they will pale in comparison with the overwhelming sense of fulfillment I get from being in the spotlight of your love. I see now that, in the end, you're only comforted by what you believe in. And I've arrived at the inescapable conclusion that it is only when these two things are the same—when you give your all to what you truly believe in—that you are truly blessed in this life.

I know this is a weird kind of tribute, and if this piece of writing doesn't live up to being my ultimate, end-all statement on us, that's ok. As I said before, a relationship is an ongoing thing, and I have the rest of our lives to try to get these words perfect.

As for whether it's even "worth it" to think about these things at such length, well, that's another matter entirely. Just like my conditions for fictionalizing a past event, I feel like one has to wait for something to end before judgments can be passed on it. And for something as far-reaching as what we have together, I'm going to have to wait for everything to stop before I evaluate how significant love is in the grand scheme of things. I will need *everything* to end and just be *still* before I do that. I'll need us to grow old together, and then die together. Everyone we know needs to grow old and die. Dozens, if not hundreds, of future generations need to be born, grow old, and die. Peak oil needs to happen, drastically changing everyone's lives for the worst. Bitter and violent wars need to break out over control of the planet's ever diminishing resources. All human life needs to be wiped out by nuclear war or ice age or an extinction-level asteroid. The sun needs to flare up, smothering the earth with lethal amounts of solar radiation. All plant and animal life needs to die. The oceans need to completely dry up. Every surface on the planet needs to literally melt away and become nothing more than pools of lava. All remaining single-celled organisms need to be eliminated. The sun needs to become a red giant and expand and swallow up the earth, leaving no trace that the planet ever existed. Stars and whole galaxies need to start colliding. The universe needs to begin the long process of cooling down. Stars need to stop being formed as all available hydrogen, helium, carbon, and oxygen dissipates. All the remaining stars need to dim and burn out. All the planets need to become unmoored from their suns and drift aimlessly through space. Galaxies need to become nothing more than supermassive black holes. All the protons need to decay. Entropy needs to continue increasing. All physical objects need to be reduced to subatomic particles. Even the black holes need to decay and dissipate. Thermodynamic free energy needs to be reduced to nothing. The universe needs to literally stop because there's no more energy for anything anywhere to even *move*. The universe needs to essentially die.

And it's only then that we can even begin to think about whether what we did with our lives, what we chose to think about and give our time and effort to, what we believed in, *truly* believed in, whether any of it was worth it.

We just have to get there.

Made in the USA
Middletown, DE
23 May 2023

30818739R00179